THE TOWER OF MOROS

THE TOWER OF MOROS

ODYSSEY OF THE ETHEREAL BOOK 3

Jamie Kojola

Cover design by Harry Bui

ISBN: 978-1-0394-5447-7

Published in 2024 by Podium Publishing
www.podiumentertainment.com

THE TOWER
OF MOROS

CHAPTER 1

Good Grief

Grief, the planet, ended up being enormous. Aetheria didn't have a built-in speedometer, but it turned out Libby could calculate velocity for her. She had Libby announce her velocity and altitude every thirty seconds. Traveling at an incredible altitude comparable to a jet, the massive blue-black dragon's hypersonic flight saw kilometers pass below in less than a second. It blew her mind that she could traverse the distance from Duluth to Minneapolis in just over two minutes. If Aetheria's quick mental estimates were accurate, she could cross the entirety of the United States in less than an hour. Yet the first continent she'd passed over had taken her three hours to clear, and the second had taken five, to say nothing of the long periods spent crossing oceans.

The Tower of Moros blazed in Aetheria's mind. The so-called map Aetherius had given her in response to her wish turned out to be a set of sensations, an internal compass, rather than a paper map to find the towers. She could sense others out there, but she'd promised Khaos she would complete the Tower of Doom after she completed the Tower of Aetherius. She crossed the world with hypersonic flight, following her guiding sensations, the faint presence of the tower growing stronger in her mind the closer she got. When the sensation seemed to surround her, she decelerated, and the tower revealed itself.

Atop a plateau of dark rock, the Tower of Moros rose so far into the sky that the top appeared to reach beyond the atmosphere into space. This tower had a gothic appearance to its architecture, sharp spires, and hard angles. It gave the appearance of a tower that would bring you doom. The fact that someone had carved a massive gate and an entire city into the stone beneath the tower surprised Aetheria. It surprised her so much that she overlooked the nearly invisible energy fields surrounding the tower and city, and her whole body slammed into the force field. A one-hundred-meter-long dragon going hundreds of kilometers per hour hitting something solid should result in much damage. Still, Aetheria had the authority and complete belief that she'd be fine.

It didn't stop Aetheria from swearing.

"Uffda! That was a gosh darn surprise." Well, her version of swearing, anyway. The words reverberated like thunder, but the only other being present who understood a word of what she said was her cat, Arkaziel. If she'd spoken in one of the languages of Grief, perhaps others would have understood her, but she had spoken in Ath, the Divine Language of the Transcendent, the Primordial, and the Godly.

The crash created a boom that could be heard kilometers away and a ringing effect inside the city and tower. The single entrance to the city had many climbers, traders, and travelers waiting to get in, who all had a front-row seat to see the dragon bounce off the field and hang in the air for a few seconds while it swore. Then the incredibly colossal creature ceased to exist. The dragon instead became a human woman who dropped down to land on the sandy beaches between the harbor and the city. Aetheria offered a wry smile and a wave to the people waiting to enter the city.

A human trader bringing up the rear of the line went white as a sheet when he looked at Aetheria. Wondering why, she gestured, and an ice mirror coalesced before her. Aetheria looked the way she thought she should. At 188 centimeters, she was tall for a human, with a lithe but powerful build. She wore a long black trench coat with a few dramatic flowing tassels, a long black scarf that always seemed to be doing dramatic flicks, a dark gray tank top, black cargo pants, and laced-up combat boots. A little edgy but perfectly normal, right? Her eyes were all mismatched, in any case. Her left eye shone aqua blue, her right eye gleamed with an Ethereal red, and her third eye looked like a black hole. Aetheria's Third-Eye of Ein Sof was a powerful component of her cultivation that rested upon her forehead between her eyes, and the ornate platinum-looking settings that joined it to her forehead were forged of soulsteel.

Her glowing eyes matched the luminous shine that radiated from Aetheria's hair: she had bound the aqua and red strands together in a ponytail. In more than a few scenarios, her hair had provided enough light to see by, and it glowed almost, but not quite, enough to normalize her eyes' intense, otherworldly glow.

"That was embarrassing." Arkaziel sounded deeply humiliated from his perch on Aetheria's shoulder. The talking, petite black house cat would have stood out much more with anyone other than Aetheria as his companion. However, Arkaziel only stacked up as a footnote compared to the chromatic, shining Asura.

People in line did their best not to get caught staring at Aetheria. One older man even went so far as to whistle while he pointedly looked away. When she approached the back of the line, a terrified young man motioned for her to go ahead of him, then an adventuring party gestured her ahead of them, and so on until she found herself before the large black gates. Multiple guards in the second stage of their cultivation paths worked the gates, and when one of them called out something in a language she didn't understand, Aetheria sighed.

Aetheria's pale skin caught the light when she raised her right hand. Complementary to her white skin, a mesh of soulsteel formed fingerless gloves around her hands. The soulsteel had pieces of the crystalized knowledge of the Aetherials woven into it and connected to a ring on each of her middle fingers at the top and a bracelet at the bottom. The ancient holy symbols of Khaos and Chronos adorned the rings, while the bracelets bore the symbols of Nyx, Aetherius, Thalassa, and Ymir. These gloves were a legendary artifact called the Astrum Nexus that she had helped the god Vulcan forge, and they were the closest thing to a weapon Aetheria carried.

When Aetheria passed a finger through the air and said, "Understanding be mine," in Ath, a glyphwork of complex spellforms seemed to create itself in the air and glow. The woman smiled at the guard as the spellforms faded upon completion.

"Can you understand me?" Aetheria asked with a bright smile, proud of her ability to learn languages via magic.

"Name, point of origin, and reason for entering Inexoria." The bored guard didn't even look up from his clipboard. Perhaps because Aetheria's aura was withdrawn, even though visible power manifested from her core and flowed into the Third-Eye of Ein Sof, the intensity and nature of that power remained unknowable to those without thorough sensing abilities.

"Aetheria, Nova Azura, and I will climb the tower." Aetheria didn't give the man a hard time. After all, she'd gone through enough TSA lines back on Earth to know the squeaky wheel gets the pat down.

"Aetheria. Sounds familiar. Nova Azura? When did they find the legendary city of the Aetherials? Are you pulling my . . ." The guard finally looked up at Aetheria. Even with the Ethereal Veil Aetheria maintained, they were too close for it to stop the guard from feeling the Void and the Ethereal looking upon him. It proved enough to stop him from clawing his eyes out while gibbering with madness or going through a profound existential crisis, but it did leave the man with elephants walking on his soul.

"Well, I suppose there's probably been some gossip about me. I am the challenger of Aetherius. I still don't know how to feel about the nepotism of giving your daughter the job, between you and me. My beautiful companion here is Arkaziel."

The guard stared at Aetheria as if she'd grown a second and third head, then blinked at the cat.

"We don't need to take down information on pets or familiars." The guard's expression appeared strange after he said that. The light in his eyes seemed to fly far away, as if his soul descended into the depths of darkness. A flare of Aetheria's aqua energy returned him to normal, but he now looked weak and so tired even his mana had depleted.

+*I wasn't going to kill him.*+ Arkaziel complained through the telepathic bond he shared with Aetheria.

~ Then you should have stopped sooner; you almost killed him. Be a good kitty if you want to eat in town before we start our climb. ~

"Are you okay? You look a little dizzy," Aetheria asked the guard with concern, setting a hand on the man's shoulder. There, she pushed a pulse of Aether into the man, which would slowly replenish the life force Arkaziel had stolen from the guard over the next hour.

"Yes, I just had a dizzy spell. It's a common occurrence down here at the gate. So, back to your application. You're the challenger Aetheria. Home: Nova Azura, here to climb the tower. Of course, of course." The exhaustion of being drained and the numb shock of a demigod being before him left the guard dazed, and he didn't know the half of it.

"I'm sure this will suffice." A small cloth sack appeared in Aetheria's hand, which she held out to the man. The weight nearly pulled him to the ground when he took it from her.

"What the hell is in here?" The guard groaned and checked; his face froze in astonishment at the giant gold bar inside the cloth bag.

"Go on ahead, ma'am. Welcome to Inexoria." The guard waved her in. So Aetheria walked through the only gateway into Inexoria, the city built into the stone under the Tower of Moros.

Aetheria and Arkaziel made it ten steps before a more ornately dressed guard, an officer no doubt, set himself in their path with an ingratiating smile and cold eyes. Cold since the man appeared to be a bipedal salamander with black skin and orange coloration. The cold-blooded reptilian seemed to sense the cold embodied by Aetheria, even without her manifesting a domain, aura, or any form of power.

"Excuse me, I couldn't help but hear you claim to have come from Nova Azura. Has the legendary lost city of the Aetherial race been found, and more importantly, do you have any of their great works for trade? I am Cyndor Swifttail, captain of the gate. High Climber Torane Highreach would be very interested in acquiring any artifacts you might have."

Aetheria didn't entirely know what captain of the gate meant, beyond that the man was an officer and liked his title. Nor did she have the slightest idea who High Climber Torane might be.

"Ah, well, Oizys shook Nova Azura into the depths of Grief. I'm afraid its treasures will remain lost forever." Aetheria didn't feel the need to mention she'd flown into the depths of Grief, reversed time with the Flame of Chronos, and dumped the reconstituted city into her inner realm, along with all of its treasures.

"Ah, the Goddess of Misery must have her due. Well, if you change your mind, do keep Lord Torane in mind, and if you happen to come out of the tower with any grand artifacts, he would be most interested in directly bartering with you instead of through the guild."

"The guild? What do they do?"

"Ah, yes. Like most cities with towers, we have a guild that helps administrate the climbers, their loot, and its effects on Inexoria. They will also collect your fee to enter the tower and assess how much to tax you when you leave."

"You . . . tax people's gains from the tower?"

"Of course, how else would we maintain law and order within Inexoria? Why, before the High Climber established the guild and took residence in the House of Governance, Inexoria was a vile shithole full of cutthroats who would stab you for copper, then sell your kidney as a placebo cultivation accelerator. Now, we have this, the peace the citizens of Inexoria yearned for." Cyndor's description of a lawless hellhole sounded like a story to Aetheria, leaving her wondering how long this Torane person had been in charge.

"I hate tax collectors," Arkaziel said quietly. "Their awful personality ruins the taste."

"Are you clergy to Moros, then?" Aetheria wondered at the propriety of them taxing and collecting on goods from the tower.

"Ah, no. We do make a tithe to Moros for the privilege of being allowed to administrate things on this side of the tower. Again, if you have any items of interest, please visit the High Climber. All of us would prefer Inexoria to remain neutral in the quarrels of the gods."

"It seems Oizys has tried to make my life difficult already." Aetheria sighed. She'd hoped to go straight to the tower, but it seemed she had something to deal with first. "Where's this House of Governance at then?"

CHAPTER 2

The High Climber

The House of Governance turned out to be an ostentatious palace. Inexoria had once been a solid plateau of mostly black stone, so someone had spent considerable resources to construct a gleaming white palace in the heart of the upper level. Guards dressed like those at the front gates stood at attention outside the palace, but they seemed to be security theater against any real threats. Tier Two Cultivators wouldn't stand a chance against higher-tier threats, but were perfect for keeping the general populace in line.

Arkaziel had split off to assess the quality of the local food and goods. Aetheria hoped he wouldn't destroy the town while she dealt with the local nobility.

The guards watched when Aetheria walked into the House of Governance, but no one reacted to her presence until a mature woman in a calf-length blue dress approached her with a perfunctory smile. At first, Aetheria thought the woman to be human, but her smile revealed sharp teeth and drew attention to the pointed tips of her ears.

"Lady Aetheria? I am T'ess, the administrative assistant to the High Climber. Please, come with me." Despite her competent aura control, Void Gaze revealed the truth of T'ess to Aetheria. The assistant was a freshly minted fourth tier Cultivator based on the mana around her, one on the Path of Sand. Aetheria didn't comment on the assistant's attempt to hide her nature.

"Certainly. Could you brief me on the proper etiquette when addressing the High Climber?" Aetheria hadn't even known there would be a city under the Tower of Moros, let alone that a powerful Cultivator played gatekeeper on the riches that flowed out of it. It seemed likely she'd be forced to deal with despots at any tower not in the wilds.

"Given your family relations, you outrank Lord Torane, but you are the weaker Cultivator, and in his territory, you may address him as an equal. It is customary to provide an introduction gift when entering another Cultivator's domain without warning."

Aetheria bristled slightly at being called the weaker Cultivator, but a small smile played across her lips when she extended her senses. A high fifth tier Cultivator resided in the palace, and they rapidly approached the location of the man's aura.

The woman casually opened one of the elaborately adorned doors and stepped inside, prompting Aetheria to follow.

"Lord Torane, this is the challenger Lady Aetheria, daughter of Aetherius and Nyx, conqueror of the Tower of Aetherius, and the inheritor of Nova Azura."

"Lady Aetheria, this is High Climber Torane, Lord of Inexoria, Master of the Dark Mists, former Leader of Torane's Trailblazers, and currently the only living Cultivator on Grief to have conquered the Tower of Moros." T'ess sounded bored with the introductions, but the assistant had put more emphasis on the titles of Aetheria than of Torane.

The man himself looked plain: a human who appeared to be in his forties, with dark black hair and gray, milky eyes that looked like fog. His aura lay exposed, a declaration of his superiority in rank. Were Arkaziel with her, the StarMane would have commented on the hollow core of Torane's power. The High Climber possessed remarkable power, sure, but he felt hollow.

"*Some powers push, some pull. Some do both.*" Reverie, the Voice of the Origin, possibly an upper-dimensional entity, chided Aetheria for looking down upon the nature of an element.

"It's a pleasure to meet you, Lord Torane. I understand your path is aligned with Wind and Water, so please allow me to present you with a small gift from my father's gardens." Despite being chastised by Reverie internally, Aetheria kept a smile and summoned an ambrosial fruit from her repository. A large mango with colors gradating between blue and green appeared in her upturned hand. It radiated raw power, as it should, being a fifth-tier artifact from the divine gardens of Aetherius.

"Well, well. Is that a Mist Mango? I've heard legends, of course, but never seen one in person." Greed lit the eyes of the so-called High Climber, and tendrils of mist formed to float the fruit to him. Raw desire filled his eyes, but cold determination replaced the yearning for the fruit as Torane mastered his emotions.

"Thank you, Lady Aetheria. Shall we dispense with formality? T'ess, you may depart." Torane's easy dismissal of his executive assistant surprised both Aetheria and T'ess, but the latter hid it quickly and curtsied to both before departing quietly.

"Thank you for this, honestly. Moros is not so generous with his gifts of cultivation necessities as Aetherius. Few are the climbers who conquer a tower, yet you travel alone? I had heard you traveled with an animal companion and an elf." While he spoke, Torane rose and moved to sit at a low coffee table with comfortable chairs around it. Aetheria sat across from him.

"I have yet to meet Moros, but Aetherius is indeed generous. My bonded companion is assessing the goods for sale here for last-minute preparations before we set out for the tower. My elven friend, Werylin, has begun another path to the betterment of Grief. He and his clan will work together with small communities to foster an environment of mutual success." Aetheria did her best to sound like a pretentious demigod.

"I see." Calculations seemed to hang in Torane's mind.

"A mighty lord such as yourself could make a nice niche for themselves by aligning with the consortia early. While I am a challenger for Aetherius, that is a short-term occupation. When I have finished my agreement with Aetherius, I will depart Grief. There are planets, dimensions, and planes beyond reckoning, and I would see them all." Aetheria opted for the truth. The sincerity of purpose was palpable when she spoke of the expansive worlds out there. Wanderlust filled her heart, and even thinking about it made her resent the stationary nature of this conversation and that it delayed her progress.

Torane's shoulders relaxed, and his smile turned to something slightly more honest. Aetheria couldn't help but feel his expression patronizing, but she'd take condescension over hostility.

"You have no interest in becoming the new Prime Goddess of Grief?" Torane seemed disbelieving. "Why else would a daughter of Aetherius and Nyx become a challenger?"

"Well, let's just say that Dad got me out of a bind, and this is my part of the agreement. Besides, no insult is intended, but ruling a city sounds terrible. Ruling a world sounds even more like torture than a reward."

"And so, you will allow another claimant to battle for Grief?"

"Sure, but I'll have to return if they don't give people a fair shake. I'm not knocking one tyrant down to have one as bad or worse pop up."

"Are all ice Cultivators as confident as you?" Torane laughed, but the man sounded annoyed that he didn't cow her.

"I should imagine not. Few are the Cultivators lauded as an Asura, and even fewer possess the many advantages I have. What was your final challenge atop the Tower of Moros?"

"My party turned upon each other. When we entered the tower initially, Moros proclaimed only one founding member of our group would survive, then brought it up every ten floors. We were our own challenge. Only I and three others survived out of a party of eight. And the final challenge of the Tower of Aetherius?"

"We battled the sixth-tier draconic avatars of Aetherius and Nyx."

"Was the challenge to survive a certain amount of time?" Torane sounded highly dubious of her claims.

"To the death. I destroyed the avatar of Nyx while my two companions dealt with Aetherius. It nearly killed Werylin, but we triumphed."

Are you not going to mention how you ate the avatar's core?

Gosh darn it, Fred, shush. This is an adult conversation.

I predate reality, and you presume to lecture me on adult conversations? Hmph.

Torane shivered, even if he had no idea why. Proximity to Aetheria meant proximity to the Courts of Chaos, the center of the Void, and the Wellspring of the Black Flame—the Unutterable Black Flame of the Void that burned inside her, barely to be seen if one had a perception ability, and the overwhelming arrogance to use it.

"I think I understand your perspective, Aetheria. I'm a simple man; I look for what's in my best interest, followed by that of my people. I'll be blunt: Oizys has offered me many cultivation materials, wealth, and power to make your life difficult. On the other hand, you offer me a divine artifact freely, threaten me indirectly, and lay on the table you will crush anyone who opposes you and that you have the power to do it." The old climber laughed in amazement at the situation.

"Would you like to see my aura, Torane?" Aetheria asked without a smile.

"I . . . no." Uncertainty plagued Torane's voice, but the insight and wisdom that had carried him through the Tower of Moros, also called the Tower of Doom, guided him through a potential pitfall. Aetheria saw three significant ways fate could unfold before her on the fulcrum of the moment. Following the first path, Torane said no, worked with her, and lived. Following the second path, Torane said yes and looked too deeply into the Void, and Aetheria had to kill him when she emerged from the Tower of Moros. Following the third path, the exposure to the Ethereal or Void, or both, broke something in Torane, and Aetheria had to kill him on the spot, which turned into a whole ordeal. Oizys had her fingers all over the third path.

"That's a good choice. As the daughter of Nyx, I see the flows of fate, and you made the best choice for all of us. For your wisdom, let me bestow another gift upon you. I have a plethora of aspected crops, more than we'll ever use, if you'd like them."

Torane's eyes narrowed at the claim to see the flows of fate, but he couldn't argue that it lay within the realm of possibilities that a daughter of Nyx could do so, as it would make her related to the Moirai.

"That would be very generous and helpful to our forces. As Moros is unaspected, the gains from the tower are not predictable like those of the aspected towers of Earth, Fire, Water, and Air. The treasure flowing from Moros is often precious junk instead of something usable. I shall send a runner to the guild to inform them of our arrangement. If anyone gives you trouble, please know it is against orders, and send for T'ess or me to take care of matters."

Aetheria's answering smile held relief and genuine happiness that she wouldn't have to kill Torane. It would be a terrible way to start the tower, and there were far too many Cultivators in the area for a show of force to cow them all.

+Ria! I found a man who sells Tier Three chickens. Who wants fried chicken? I do!+

"I'll do that. My companion has found some delicacies he demands I come to join him for, so I must take my leave. I still intend to enter the tower once we finish our market trip."

Torane stood and shook Aetheria's hand.

"Good luck, Challenger. Although I don't particularly appreciate losing my title as the only living conqueror of the Tower of Moros on Grief, I wish you well. What is this?" Torane eyed the crystal she had slipped into his palm.

"A communications crystal. It will allow you to communicate with the Amaryllis Enclave, who now dwell in the Lost City of Atlanta, although they'll probably rename it. Either way, Werylin is one of my most trusted friends working to establish cooperation and betterment for the people of Grief. Those who join the coalition with him first stand to have a better seat at the table for later."

Aetheria waved and walked out the door. T'ess stood across the hall, a surprised look on her face. Perhaps she hadn't figured the meeting would finish so promptly? *Poor T'ess is no doubt used to Torane's meetings taking a lot longer, with all the flowery diplomacy, bribery, and ass-kissing ordinary adventurers have to do.*

"Have a nice day, T'ess."

The strange humanoid woman smiled, showing fangs, and then curtsied.

CHAPTER 3

Entering the Tower

Hours after Aetheria's meeting with Torane, she walked up the black stone path to the top of the plateau. Arkaziel walked alongside her, his tail swinging lazily, his hunger momentarily sated. Amicable silence reigned, and the only sound that remained was the click of Aetheria's boots against the stone path. The dark tunnel opened to the sky, and Aetheria almost didn't notice the tax booths on the side of the tunnel. The tax collectors barely looked up at someone going into the tower, although small whispers started when the gossip about the new challenger circulated.

Thus, the long walk to the entrance of the tower ended anticlimactically. Above the glowing silver portal of the entranceway was an inscription. To Aetheria, it appeared as Ath, but each person who perceived it would see their primary language. Aetheria read it aloud. "Prometheus hid Moros from your heart. Entering will restore knowledge of your impending doom. You have been warned."

"Truth or fable?" Aetheria asked Arkaziel.

"For humans, maybe it's the truth?" Arkaziel frowned at the inscription. "It says the same thing for me, but Prometheus has nothing to do with my race unless one of the eagles who ate his liver was a proto-dragon ancestor."

"Last chance to delay our entry."

"No, I'm close to reaching the fifth tier. Another big meal like Aetherius, and I'll be there, or a bunch of smaller ones. Aren't you excited to see your witch?"

"I've got four layers of crust to finish before my inner world is done." Aetheria wanted to see Aoibhe, but four layers and whatever bringing life to an inner world required separated Aetheria from the title of a fifth tier Cultivator. When reunited, Aetheria wanted to be on even footing with Aoibhe. While their gap in knowledge and experience couldn't be closed as quickly, their power gap would be next to nothing soon.

"Onward, my trusty steed!" Arkaziel commanded after he jumped upon Aetheria's shoulder. Laughing, she walked through the doorway.

Entering a tower included transit time to the singular physical location of the genuine Tower of Moros, which the gods kept hidden. Deep space? Alternate dimensions? Third planet over? Aetheria couldn't maintain track of her senses in transit, but eventually, she reincorporated in a rather posh study, dominated by a large, wooden, black desk. Aetheria mistook the desk owner for a suit of armor. Finally, her eyes moved to the face, where she realized the suit housed a projection.

"*Sister*," Moros, Incarnation of Inevitable Doom, greeted Aetheria.

"Brother. That's some impressive armor. It reminds me of a video game I played a while back." Aetheria bowed, opting for the friendly approach if Moros would be open to it.

"Ah, yes. Well, the collective unconscious of sentient beings does suffer joint adverse reactions to my presence in reality. I eventually manifest in the terrors and artworks of all races." Moros possessed a technicality about his existence that intrigued Aetheria.

"What do you know about the collective unconscious? Where does it reside? What is it?" Aetheria asked openly, all while wondering if Reverie were the collective unconscious.

"Why the curiosity? Why even come to my tower? You, Strider of the Void, Swimmer of the Ethereal, and Conqueror of the Samsara, stand outside fate. Only you may alter your destiny, and only you may decree your inevitability. Even your companion and partner stand outside of my touch by nature of your soul shielding them." Moros sounded indifferent, but Aetheria heard the truth in his tone. Someone outside his reach intrigued him. Even Zeus could not defy Moros.

"Khaos bade me come to your tower in exchange for her power."

"You could have said no."

"I had no reason to do so. I have to climb ten towers; which ones I climb is fairly irrelevant to me."

"You know that the Towers are We, and We the Towers. Do you know why few Cultivators who make it to the sixth and seventh tiers bother with towers? We immortals are selfish and disdain being parted from our power. The higher-powered the Cultivator, the more you take from us. A few thousand second-tier treasures are nothing combined, but prizes and insights to power an elite Cultivator could drain weak gods dry, even destroy their tower."

"Isn't that the cost of doing business?" Aetheria asked with a smile. Despite his words, Moros had no concern for power, let alone his own power base.

"It is. Something most have forgotten. I am not part of Mother's cabal with Khaos. Thus, they send you to me early, even before themselves, so I am less depleted. And most importantly to Khaos, she is entertained as we test destiny's many facets upon you." The armor steepled its hands before the projected face of Moros. "The cost to me is marginal, so long as you do not unleash an Outer Being within my tower or destroy everything while trying to reconcile your disparate powers."

"I'll try to avoid that then," Aetheria answered dryly.

"Please, do. Without further delay, welcome to the Tower of Moros, sister."

The comfortable study vanished, and gray nothingness filled the world for long moments. Long moments to Aetheria, anyway. One of the few downsides of the Flash

Mode from her autopotency core was that she experienced time at a relatively accelerated rate, even at its setting closest to standard time. The tedium of nothingness dragged on and on until, finally, she appeared next to Arkaziel on a hilltop.

Arkaziel's yellow eyes focused on Aetheria, but he didn't pause his work at bathing himself.

"Had a meet and greet with Moros. We're on good terms for now. No blowing up his tower or summoning creatures of the Void. What's the deal with the hill?"

Four paths wound up the picturesque hill, the top of which held a number of tables and benches, as if it were a picnic area in a park. A recently used firepit, really just a circle of stones, still had a few active coals. Someone had no doubt cooked lunch there.

An ancient slate-chip path ran north and across hills toward some mountains. To the east, a narrow gravel path ran toward a dark and forbidding forest. Southward ran wide roads of heavy stone. Looking at them made Aetheria think of ancient Roman roads, and an aqueduct could also be seen on the horizon to the south. The final path to the west was made of mud bricks, and a tall tower could partially be seen on the far horizon.

"Barbarians to the north, Sylvan woods to the east, mortal populations to the south, and gods to the west." Arkaziel licked his lips. "We should go west and have a smorgasbord of gods for lunch."

"Are you guessing on that, or can you really smell them?" Aetheria saw nothing to indicate divinity lay in the west, and her sense of Aether, Nether, and the Ethereal were superb. Nothing Arkaziel said rang like a lie to Void Gaze, but that only meant Arkaziel believed himself, not that he was necessarily correct.

"Trust me, I can smell my prey. They smell like some we've encountered before. Sin, Nergal, Ereshkigal. The stench of their pantheon is powerful." Arkaziel looked at her with pleading eyes. Gods were his favorite meal, contributing the most to his growth as a Cultivator.

Aetheria's mismatched eyes turned to each of the cardinal directions. Moros had said he wanted to test destiny. Were there even quests in the Tower of Moros, or would he throw her at scenarios and see what unfolded? Would their decision now dictate the entire course their time in the Tower of Moros would take? If they went north, would it be all nomadic mountain and tundra tribes? Would the east be dark realms of the fae, eager to trick and deceive the duo for any scrap of power the fae could eke out of them? Would the southern populations be full of intrigue and socialization? Would the path west lead them to conflict with the Sumerian pantheon?

Void Gaze should make short work of any fae attempts at trickery, but she saw no upside to choosing the wooded path. Similarly, politics and intrigue in mortal realms sounded atrocious. Arkaziel and Aetheria were both eager to breach the fifth tier, Aetheria especially so, since once she breached the next tier, she could summon Aoibhe. The Sumerian gods would no doubt provide the most benefit to the duo and perhaps help her discern if she could use the powers of Inanna. The cold north appealed to her on some subconscious level, but Aetheria chalked it up to her affinity for cold.

"Alright, let's head west." Aetheria agreed with Arkaziel, who purred happily.

"I was worried you'd want to go to the forest. You do have a thing for elves and Sylvan things."

"I only slept with the one elf, and that was due to the influx of energies playing havoc with my sense of self. Well, she was really sexy, too, I won't deny that, but primarily, it was just a lust thing before I really came to terms with the influence of high concentrations of energy."

"We were both young once. Things happen. Now, you are on the other end of the spectrum, where eternity seems within your grasp, and emotions drift further away. You think I'm just older now, and I've seen more things. Except that's not what it is, is it? You don't have a basis for comparison, and I do, so let me tell you this, Ria. It isn't normal. We shouldn't be experiencing ennui until the sixth or seventh tier or until we're over a few thousand years old. It is the Void, maybe even the Ethereal. As far as I know, no one has ever been dumb enough to let both forces run rampant in their soul before. Or if they did, they died quickly and terribly."

"I know," Aetheria answered with a tone that was half apology and half acceptance of responsibility. "I'm doing my best, just like you, buddy. Let's go find this lunch you promised."

"Wait, why do I have to share?" Arkaziel whined, and his tail turned into a furious whip.

"My void core lets me devour things like you do," Aetheria said with a smile, expecting a moment of camaraderie between her and the StarMane.

"What!? That's ridiculous. You already have almost every advantage known to gods and mortals alike, and now you can cultivate by eating, too?" Arkaziel sounded offended and disgusted.

"Is it really that big of a change? I could always do it via shapeshifting."

"Of course it's a big deal. You've stolen the staple of beast cultivation. Not only will you take half of all my meals now, but you'll get the best ones, too, and I'll get the dregs. This cannot stand!"

"I'll ensure you get your share, Ark. I won't slow down your cultivation if I can help it. We're in this together, remember?"

The mud-bricked path to the west provided a shockingly smooth surface when Aetheria's boots traveled it. Newer bricks could be spotted amongst older ones, indicating continued maintenance on this strange path. While she or Arkaziel could fly ahead, instead, they walked the stone path step by step. Over hills, through dales, past ponds and pristine lakes. The grass thinned, and the road traveled along a wide river, the other side of which appeared to be a desert.

The brick path led to a simple wooden bridge and into the desert. For some reason, Aetheria could not shake the thought, *I'm coming home*, when she crossed the bridge into the desert.

CHAPTER 4

Uruk

Aetheria had, of course, never lived in a desert before. She had seen the deserts of the western United States, and numerous deserts across the floors of the Tower of Aetherius, but she'd never visited the ancient heartland of humanity on Earth, Mesopotamia. Aetheria didn't know the name of the river they walked along down the path, but eventually, a large city dominated the horizon. Tall walls, at least nine meters high, rose and embraced the city protectively. Like Aetheria's path, the walls were made from fired-mud brick that glinted brightly in the sun.

Over the walls, Aetheria could see multiple towering ziggurats, one higher than the others. Memories and emotions not her own lurked at the back of her mind, threatening to burst free.

"Glory to the Queen of the Universe! Glory to Inanna!"

"Blessed be Ishtar! I pray for your blessings with my beloved!"

"With Inanna in residence of her temple, Uruk will rule forever!"

The gates of Uruk were wide open, and tax collectors walked with guards amongst carts and chariots to keep the line of entry into Uruk in progress. Yet, all of that stopped when one of the guards and a lavishly dressed priest near the end of the line pointed to Aetheria and screamed about one of the "donors" Nyx and Khaos had blended into her soul. It drew her eyes away from an attempt to study the inscriptions and craftsmanship used to make the gates.

Whispers of a god amongst the people quickly spread, and over seventy people ended up prostrate on the ground, praying to Aetheria. Anger filled the back of her throat with bile, and Aetheria drew a calming breath to stay her temper.

They seek a god but have found something else entirely. Let them gaze into the abyss. The maddening whispers of the Void will harvest their prayers.

Why, hello, Fred. What do you mean by harvesting their prayers?

In the time before towers, faith was the food of the gods. See it, see it, the white dew of their breaths!

What use is it?

Faith is the ancient answer to the fear of the unknown, the Void, the Infinite Abyss. Gods, meager constructs invented to shelter the herd from the universal truth: everything starts and ends in my black flames.

No matter how much Aetheria stared at the white, dewy breath of faith uttered by the people of Uruk, it remained inaccessible to her. She could not breathe it in, although when she tried to absorb it, her void core greedily devoured the faith, and the person whose faith she had devoured fell unconscious. She was not Inanna; she only contained a portion of the goddess, and clearly not the faith-using portion. Or was there a technique to it different from energy manipulation?

Belief is but a fleeting whisper in the eternal dark.

A powerful pulse of Aether drew her attention to Arkaziel, who had hopped to the mud-brick road and grown. Not only had he grown, but he also changed his appearance to that of a lion. He blew a cloud of light at the supplicant who had passed out, and the holy light of divine healing surrounded the man.

~ Why are you a lion?~ Aetheria demanded an answer through the telepathic bond she and Arkaziel shared.

+Ishtar had a lion friend. Roar!+ Arkaziel's mental roar nearly made Aetheria choke on her tongue to stop laughing, but her excellent humor warred with intense annoyance at the StarMane's antics. Aetheria's lips pressed tightly together, her eyes narrowed, but she couldn't take it out on random people. Her wrath should be saved for those who deserved it.

"Get up, all of you. No groveling. Bowing your head is enough. No need to fall to the ground. I'm going inside." No one barred her path when she stormed inside the gates of Uruk.

"Where to?" Arkaziel asked when he slipped between her legs and bonked her onto his back with his head. She could have wholly dodged the move. Her perceptions and reactions far exceeded Arkaziel's, even with his access to some of her abilities via their connection. She chose to go with the flow of his antics because he usually never took the mount role. She'd been the one to fly while he slept in her mane the whole way here. He had slept on her shoulder even on the long walk down the mud-brick road.

"To the giant ziggurat in the center of town. We'll check whether we will stay in the temple or opt for rooms elsewhere. By the time we've figured that out, someone should have alerted whoever's in charge of my presence, and we'll get a royal visit or invitation to the palace, where we can probably learn the lay of the land and figure out what our challenge is from there. Sound good?" Aetheria thought her plan made sense.

"Seems doable. You know the Tower of Moros is different from the Tower of Aetherius? We must conquer one hundred challenges, but the floors are frequently persistent across many challenges. We might be here for quite a while. StarManes avoid the Tower of Moros for some reason, so I only have secondhand knowledge. Some have reportedly finished the tower going through the same location even after the trade floors." Arkaziel seemed truly confused as to why StarManes wouldn't come to Tower of Moros, annoyed at his genetic memory's rare shortcoming.

"Oh yeah? You know, that's cool. It would be a little weird if all the towers were the exact same thing, you know? If there's so much width of personalities amongst the gods, why not also amongst their towers? Is there a way to tell what's a challenge versus what's just the world?" The gamer inside Aetheria wondered if there was a flag indicator.

"Not that I know of, but it's said those capable of manipulating fate are prone to success in this tower, and who cares about their personality? I'm more interested in their flavor. I'm so close I can taste it—just a few more meals to the lofty ranks of the Beast Sovereign." Arkaziel always sounded hungry, but rarely for something as irrelevant as a title.

"Do you get some amazing new power for becoming a Beast Sovereign?"

"Well, since you asked, yes. I will come into Azrael's and Shal's bloodlines more fully. I shall rise above the chaff of my kin and declare to the universe I am its master." Arkaziel giggled while he trotted through the streets of Uruk.

"You know you sound like a supervillain monologuing about the origins of his terrible evil?" Not for the first time, Aetheria wondered how much of Arkaziel's ego meant the things he said. As a StarMane, he embodied the best and worst traits of cats and dragons. He was powerful, clever, and an apex predator, and he knew it. Feline arrogance did nothing to temper draconic narcissism, nor did draconic arrogance temper feline narcissism either. It just made for a race of megalomaniacal slaughter cats, which made a lot of sense that they were a sentient-weapons project created by the Transcendental Chronos, Master of Time.

Chronos worked in a loose cabal with Khaos, Nyx, Aetherius, and others. In fact, Nyx and Khaos were involved in a separate sentient-weapons project, the one that had created Aetheria. That both Arkaziel and Aetheria had been products of the powers of the universe had been hinted at for much of their journey together. Still, neither Arkaziel nor Aetheria tried to dwell on it too much, preferring instead a release of the past, the seizing of the day until the problem became one they could address directly.

"Nice temple." Arkaziel expertly changed the subject, gesturing at a sprawling stone temple in the heart of Uruk.

"Yes, yes, it is," Aetheria chimed in, studying the behemoth of a ziggurat in front of them. It dominated the city's center, undeniably the most significant building, and was dedicated to its patron goddess, Inanna. Aetheria had never inquired about Inanna or any of the other gods Nyx used to create her, save for Ananke. It occurred to her that this might be relevant.

Libby, search your knowledge for a goddess called Inanna or Ishtar.

Response: No matches found. No goddess known as Inanna or Ishtar is present in the annals of the Aetherials of Grief.

Aetheria blew raspberries in frustration. So far, Libby had not been very useful, but maybe she'd prove herself eventually. *Or maybe I have too high expectations for a bunch of shattered crystals mixed into my gloves.*

~How did Ishtar or Inanna die?~

+Worried? You don't need to be. In the classic tale of karmic retribution, she came into conflict with another pantheon of gods, and worship waned. She tried to kill one of her contemporaries, Athena, I believe. She failed to kill her, and rather than deal with the shame of her failure, she threw a fit and killed herself. There's a significant amount of conjecture about whether she did the deed herself or if her pantheon tired of her antics and intervened themselves. She did cause the death of Ereshkigal's husband, and death holds grudges.+

~Huh. So, Ishtar was the proto-Karen. It is hard to have any sympathy for her.~

+The only real use for gods is eating.+

"Great Lady Inanna!" A middle-aged man in elaborate vestments hurried from the ziggurat toward Aetheria and Arkaziel. He gave the impression of a car salesman eager to upsell leather seats. Still, to her Void Gaze, he exuded large amounts of faith, to the point that Aetheria had difficulty focusing on the man instead of the wild vortex of power around him. Unlike at the gates, this man's faith practically begged her to reach out and take it, but she refrained for now.

Aetheria held off from returning a greeting, instead watching his approach with studied indifference. Two lesser priests followed the man, and they sang lamentations.

"They sing to soothe the heart of a goddess. Is pain the proof of existence?" Reverie asked, but Aetheria didn't know, not really.

I hope not.

"Oh, Great Queen of the Heavens, Eanna, the Heavenly Palace remains open to you! We shall bathe you in perfumes, sing songs that make you smile, and summon whatever entertainment you desire!"

"Oh, silence your wretched wailing! Control your pests, Inanna-En! The Eanna must wait. King Gilgamesh would speak with the Queen of Heaven." A tall, impressive-looking man declaimed toward the priests. The effect was ruined by how he posed after saying it. He desperately wanted to earn the attention of Inanna and practically danced under the scrutiny when he did receive it.

"Our great king knows better than to make demands of the goddess, Ur-Nungal, so watch your words." The high priest challenged the prince, although, to Aetheria, it felt like they were competing for her attention.

"I will speak to Gilgamesh." Aetheria ended the miniature standoff before it grew ridiculous, with the priests, prince, and entourage glaring darkly at each other. "You may be my procession, Ur-Nungal. Venture not too close, though, lest my mount decides you look edible."

So, Aetheria ended up being paraded through Uruk by the prince. It gave her time to wonder what kind of man Gilgamesh would be. Would he be a giant like in mythology, a slightly tall, average man? Had Enkidu, Gilgamesh's monstrous companion, already been killed in this age? Were any of the Earth myths relevant to the reality Moros had created here? Anticipation made the procession's progress feel glacial, but the palace was not far.

Ur-Nungal turned to make a sweeping gesture of the palace, although the lion earned a frown from him. He dared not approach after being told not to, but that conflicted with the young man's desire to grandstand in front of a god. Ultimately, his hesitation cost him all involvement as an older man preempted him.

"Welcome back to Uruk, Queen of the Heavens. Long have we missed your presence since you last visited. King Gilgamesh awaits and begs pardon for not meeting you himself."

Aetheria followed the older man wordlessly, leaving the sputtering prince to hide his embarrassment awkwardly.

CHAPTER 5

Gilgamesh

The man led Aetheria and Arkaziel through a series of halls to the private chambers of the king of Uruk. She had expected to be directed to the throne room or a parlor, but the private chambers had a dark feeling, an ominous presence barely kept at bay. The sun streaming in through the ceiling and window did nothing to ward off the pending approach of Thanatos, brother to Moros.

Gilgamesh lay restlessly atop his bed. The great king of Uruk looked ancient: his skin nearly translucent, his hair brittle, his eyes cloudy. But his gaze held an intensity that shocked Aetheria. To her Ethereal Sight, he bore a dark brand upon his soul, a divine curse. If she unraveled it, the older man would be able to touch Aether, perhaps even rejuvenate himself with it. A series of images filled her mind, with many possibilities that might be born if she removed the curse. All was fire and darkness or gone before she could decipher the context of an image.

Aetheria lifted her hand to obliterate the curse but refrained at the last moment. She and Gilgamesh were not the same—the extent of meddling in their lives was vastly different. She felt sympathy for the older man before her, however. Without that curse, he could have had immortality and divine power at his call.

"You have changed, Inanna." Gilgamesh retained dignity and a primarily clear voice, despite his age. It was not suspicion that flavored his tone but curiosity.

"I am not the Inanna you met in the past. I don't have any of her memories, so to me, this is our first meeting." Aetheria decided to be honest. Moros had wanted to see what she could do to fate in his tower, so she would be true to herself and see what happened.

When hope whispers so cruelly, a scream waits to be born. Fred's ominous words sent a wave of goosebumps across Aetheria's pale skin.

"Anu finally punished you, too?" Gilgamesh's question balanced somewhere between delight at the idea of Inanna's suffering and the camaraderie of a shared tormentor.

"Fate can be cruel." Aetheria shrugged. She had no interest in continuing the conversation in that vein.

"Father!" The prince stormed into the room, red-faced and panting from his run. The old king did not snap at his son. Instead, he stared expectantly, giving the young man the benefit of the doubt of the importance of his breakneck entry. Aetheria felt a pang of loss in her heart, the moment reminding her of her father.

"The Aegean invaders approach! A goddess is leading them!" Ur-Nungal spoke between quick breaths while his father struggled to sit up fully. Visions of the older man being destroyed by a blond goddess filled Aetheria's mind, but she quickly banished them.

"Let me handle this for you, Gilgamesh," Aetheria volunteered.

Smiles answered her, and minutes later, Aetheria found herself atop the enormous outer walls of Uruk, waiting for the impending arrival of the approaching forces. Arkaziel lay on the top of the wall, eyes only half opening when the army moved close enough to be seen.

"You want to eat them all, or should I?" The words hit differently when Arkaziel looked like a lion instead of his usual house-cat appearance.

"I'll handle this one. I didn't intend to eat anyone except maybe the god," Aetheria demurred, not sure how she felt about the idea of feeding upon humanoids.

"Eat enough of it, and fodder adds up."

"No, Ark." Aetheria's adamant response sealed that avenue of discussion for now or would have with anyone but a cat.

"Oh, come on. Before, we didn't know if they were people, but now we know they are, and worse, they're being preyed upon by gods who don't even finish the job. If we eat them, they get freed from the cycle and can know the peace of oblivion they no doubt yearn for, trapped in a cycle of no progress for eternity. It's the only humane thing to do, to offer salvation through dissolution." Arkaziel sounded like he believed it, but Aetheria saw the flecks of Void in his eyes.

"Think about the tenets a little, Ark. You're verging on a Void-out." The lion's answer came as a loud grunt, but he said nothing else and seemed to enter a state of meditation. The build-up of Void energies around him slowly dissipated to ordinary levels. Ordinary levels for Arkaziel, at least.

"Where is Gilgamesh?" A ten-meter-tall projection of a blonde goddess in a white dress accented with worked gold appeared before the walls of Uruk and the approaching army.

Aetheria floated from the wall, and her form grew to match the size of the projection.

"Resting. Who dares to approach my city?" Aetheria demanded, surprised at the possessiveness in her own words and the ire she could feel bubbling up from deep inside of her.

Laughter echoed from the projection across the empty land outside of Uruk.

"The so-called Queen of Heaven herself, even. This is so much better than destroying the king. I shall smite you and leave no doubt about the superior war goddess. All shall witness the superiority of Athena!" Athena unveiled her divine aura through the projection. Waves of power that would render mortals into drooling idiots trapped in either fear or awe of the powerful goddess radiated toward Uruk.

Aetheria unveiled her aura but carefully maintained directional shielding to prevent her power from reaching Uruk. Athena's aura was a bright golden light, shining as if she were a sun. Aetheria's power radiated from her through hundreds of individual tendrils and rays. Some were condensed Aether and Nether, but the red and blue streams of divinity and dark divinity made up the weakest powers that Aetheria emitted. Crimson tendrils of mysterious Ethereal power coiled around her like snakes, ready to uncoil and alter reality as their master demanded. Even these coils, the penultimate power within reality, paled compared to the eldritch energy that sought to devour everything, the Void.

The projection of the goddess before her swallowed. A third of her army had been baptized in chaos from the minute exposure to Aetheria's aura. Men screamed and clawed at their eyes, used their weapons on themselves or their companions to escape what lay before them, or tried to run away.

Exposed to chaos, the soul sheds its lies and lays itself bare.

A streak of gold flashed across the arid plain, and Aetheria raised a hand to catch a spear. She looked at the tiny weapon between her fingers, impressed with the smithing.

"Gold adamantine, very expensive. Thanks for the spear." The divine weapon vanished into Aetheria's inner world, along with all of her other loot.

"How dare you steal a weapon forged by Vulcan!" Athena grew with each step across the plain until she stood taller than Aetheria.

Before the Void, minds unravel, reason withers and all is unmade.

"Oh, Vulcan is awesome. He forged my gloves for me." Aetheria answered indignation with amusement and flashed forward across the plain to meet Athena. A brief look of shock covered Athena's face at an opponent who moved faster than she could sense, but she immediately released a pulse of blinding light. The light vanished as Aetheria appeared before Athena and punched her right between the eyes. The force of the punch sent Athena flying, and just as she came to a rest in the dirt, Aetheria appeared over her and drove a taloned hand into the blonde's chest.

Pulses of nonexistence flickered through Athena, and Aetheria devoured her with one of the most potent abilities her void core gave her: absorption. The Void hollowed out Athena, and then the last of her decaying existence was swallowed by a temporary maw that formed on Aetheria's palm. Silence reigned on the plain, broken only by far-off thunder. Panic and fear consumed the force before her.

"Go home. Athena is dead, and Uruk is under my protection. If you ever return, I shall visit your cities. Go!"

Aetheria restrained her aura so that the madness and crushing existential crisis inspired by the Void and the Ethereal would diminish if reason had not already been taken from their minds. Perhaps it was her single-word command reinforced with echoes of power from the Third-Eye of Ein Sof that brushed the madness of chaos away from the survivors' minds, and as a unified whole, the invading force turned and fled.

"Impressive." Arkaziel laughed when she hopped back onto the city walls in her ordinary form.

"I feel like an adult who picked a fight with children." Aetheria disparaged the whole conflict and desperately yearned for a shower to wash the unpleasant feelings away.

"I didn't even get a chance to read her before you ate her. What tier of avatar was it?"

"Fifth. It would've been more of a battle if it had been another sixth like Nyx and Aetherius, but I don't think Moros will go that hard so soon." The casual way Moros had treated the loss of his power to fuel climbers had struck Aetheria as wrong, but she couldn't put into words what part of it bothered her so much.

"So, do you think we'll be playing out some Aegean versus Uruk battle here? If so, your mercy in letting an army live will bite you in the rear end." Arkaziel showed large leonine fangs.

"It seems likely. Now that I think about it, after you explained what happens in the tower earlier, we'll probably be caught in a four-way between the fae, Romans, Sumerians, and Vikings. Even if we came to Uruk first, it doesn't mean we have to give allegiance to Uruk unquestioningly. After we get the lay of the land here, it might be best to visit the other three places. Ugh, I was never too fond of these types of setups in games. Pure sandboxes are the worst, with all their fear of missing out on things, concerns about doing right or wrong, not to mention you're the bad guy to at least one group no matter what."

"Why should we care if any or all groups dislike us? We are the strongest. It's natural to impose our belief about what is right upon those weaker than ourselves. It's the sacred law of nature."

"Well, I wasn't raised that way. I was raised to treat people respectfully, even if they're wrong."

"Blue, you just ate a goddess in front of their devotees while exuding the Void and driving a third of them mad. That's straight psychological warfare and nothing respectful."

Aetheria's mouth tightened, and she bit her lip. Her first attempt at rationalization felt hollow.

"I did it to save the army."

"No, you didn't. You did it because they weren't worth eating, but their boss was." Arkaziel's eyes carried no judgment but acknowledged a choice he understood.

"Are you trying to guilt me about eating Athena so that I won't eat the rest of the gods, and you'll get more snacks?"

Yellow eyes stared hard at Aetheria's own mismatched eyes. Silence hung heavy.

Both of them started laughing.

"Yeah, you got me," Arkaziel admitted shamelessly.

CHAPTER 6

Fate Spinner

If Aetheria and Arkaziel had taken the streets of Uruk back to the palace, no doubt the citizens would have cheered their patron goddess. Indeed, even with Arkaziel flying them back across the city, sporadic cheers rose from the streets below to show appreciation for Inanna defeating the Aegean army and destroying the goddess Athena. Such a profound blow to the southern island nation had never been struck.

When Aetheria hopped off Arkaziel's back and strolled into Gilgamesh's chambers again, she had already decided her next step. In destroying Athena, she had already thrown a wrench into whatever strands fate had in store for Uruk and Gilgamesh. If Moros wanted to be entertained, and she wanted to learn the depths of fate, and if she could control it herself, then she would have to experiment.

"That was quick," Gilgamesh stated flatly from his bed.

"I killed Athena and dispersed their army."

"She *ate* Athena," Arkaziel corrected while grooming his large lion's paws.

"Truly?"

"You once quested for immortality, Gilgamesh. Do you still yearn to escape the cold embrace of death?" Aetheria stared intently at the demigod, ready to discern any lies or falsehoods through Void Gaze.

"Yes, there is very little I wouldn't do to avoid the cold grasp of the underworld. I have accepted the truth of my mortality. I have built high walls around Uruk, traveled this world, and used what my travels taught me to bring prosperity to my people. My name and legacy will live forever, even if I do not." According to Aetheria's senses, Gilgamesh told the truth as he knew it.

"Tell me about your travels and what problems confront Uruk," Aetheria said, redirecting the conversation slightly.

"Our most significant problem lies to the south. The Aegean Isles have banded together to raid, harass, and otherwise make our lives difficult. Ever since your previous incarnation challenged Athena and lost, tensions have been steadily on the rise. Anu did not wish to seek war since Inanna sought her own destruction, but with you slaying Athena, escalation is inevitable. The gods of the Aegean are of similar temperament to your old one." Gilgamesh looked troubled by the last statement.

"And other threats?" Aetheria's nonplussed treatment of the Aegean troubled Gilgamesh visibly, but she was surprised to see the king bide his time. She had expected a brash, arrogant, uncontrollable man, but Gilgamesh seemed to have mastered himself.

"The Teutons to the north. We have overall peaceful dealings with them, but I feel if we were in a moment of weakness, they would strike. The wilds to the east are a point of contention, as they are a font of great power. It is rumored a great dungeon lies buried there, waiting for the people who dare seek it. In my youth, I spent years searching for the entrance but never found it." Gilgamesh coughed in embarrassment.

"Across the unclaimed lands lies the realm of the demons. They walk in the shadows and steal from all people. Beware travelers on the road, my people say, for the bargain you strike may be for more than you understand."

"Fae are so annoying." Arkaziel harrumphed.

"Not bad. None of this seems impossible. What happens if I claim the unclaimed lands for myself?" Aetheria assumed some valuable resources lay at the center, and she regretted not having investigated the area more fully when she had been there.

"The fae once held the land, and we all banded against them to drive them to the forests. They have sworn to let no man hold dominion over that land. The Teutons and Aegeans would no doubt strike at your position or Uruk if you claimed the area. Their gods desire the area, as you do."

"Why do the gods desire it?" Arkaziel inquired, looking up from his tongue bath.

"I don't know. I presumed you two knew." Gilgamesh raised his hands in a gesture of uncertainty.

"Alright. First of all, I will give you your birthright, Gilgamesh." Aetheria extended her right hand, from which tendrils of the Void could momentarily be seen to connect her hand and the king's chest, but then they were gone. Gilgamesh's eyes widened in shock and wonder as the long-denied Aether entered his body. Starved cell after starved cell finally tasted droplets of divinity. For the first time in Gilgamesh's life, he had access to the lifeblood of cultivation.

A curse from a god to block your birthright, and they didn't even have the grace to give you the ability to touch mana. Your doomed search for immortality never had a chance, Gilgamesh. You deserve a second chance, but all I can offer is a chance for this version of you.

Gilgamesh's white hair already had regained a streak of darkness, and with each droplet of Aether, the wrinkles of his face faded slightly. The king would have work to do if he wanted to achieve immortality, but Aetheria had given him the chance to get there.

"What? What is this?" Golden light suffused Gilgamesh's body.

"There are different terms; I know it as Aether, but some call it divinity—your long-denied birthright. With it, you may improve your body and soul and walk the path to immortality. It seems to be restoring you." Aetheria watched the multitude of emotions cross Gilgamesh's eyes and face. It was promising but also worrying. Would the famously cruel king return to his previous self when confronted with actual power? Or would the lessons he learned from his friend Enkidu and his travels prove enough to temper his baser instincts?

"Rest, recover. The days ahead shall be busy. We will watch over Uruk, and I will visit again before we depart to investigate the other lands."

"Are we going back to the Eanna?" Arkaziel asked with a hint of dread, as it had looked substantially below the pair's standard living accommodations.

"No, I'm going to pull out one of the sky cities. We'll be watching from above. Take care, Gilgamesh." Aetheria hopped up on the back of Arkaziel, who walked out the door and leaped into the air. Large wings grew from his back and lifted them into the sky, where minutes later, a large sky castle appeared out of nowhere. It was the smallest of the sky cities Aetheria had in her repository and had once been an elven stronghold. The Mellow Mallow had been through a significant amount of rework inside her inner world, and it gleamed as if it had only been constructed recently.

"Now what?" Arkaziel asked once they landed in the courtyard.

"Well, I want to finish another layer of my inner world, maybe more. Athena had a lot of power in her. I figured you could scout the area, wipe out any local monsters that will be a problem in the future, and use your duplicates to figure out how many and what kind of fae are preying on people."

"So, I must do all the work while you advance?" Arkaziel whined.

"You can eat the next god we find, even if I kill it. Deal?"

"Deal!" Arkaziel hopped into the sky and flew off after the air shimmered into three additional copies of the lion, leaving Aetheria in the peace of the beautiful little courtyard, surrounded by flowers and the soft tinkling of fountains.

Aetheria directed her focus within herself. Closest to the surface of her being lay her two cores, locked in an eternal dance. Her original core, the Etherfrost Flash Core of Autopotency, shone with the red of the Origin and gleamed with the pristine platinum sheen of soulsteel. The autopotency core gave Aetheria her *authority* over herself and essentially made her a super speedster with its constantly active sub-effect of Flash Mode. It had been designed by Aetherius and Chronos and modified by Aetheria herself when she created it. Despite being one of the most powerful cores in all of existence, her autopotency core constantly fled from her secondary core.

The second core was a dark organ she had grown after encountering her first Outer God, Ulzschazath, whom she had devoured. It provided a degree of protection from the Void, and the incarnation of Black Flames, Fred, called it an Omega core. It gave her ridiculous abilities like Existence Oscillation, Absorption, and Void Gaze, which was why she could annihilate a goddess like Athena without much effort. Gods, in particular, were vulnerable to the Void.

The eternal dance her cores engaged in was mirrored by the Flames that illuminated her essence. The Red Flame of the Origin had been imparted to her by Reverie after the Black Flame of the Void ate all of her previous Flames. Flames were the ultimate representation of power. Usually, only a Cultivator of the seventh tier could create a Flame, but gods, Primordials, and Transcendentals all possessed them as well. The cores and Flames wove an intricate dance of creation, destruction, evasion, and nonexistence that created a power that was the source of the constant stream of energy that rose from her chest to be absorbed by the Third Eye Jewel upon her forehead.

Until Aetheria had created the jewel, the energy had ruptured her body with explosions of inexistence that even her regenerative capabilities couldn't outpace. The power eluded her grasp or even identification. Honestly, all she knew about it was that the Third-Eye of Ein Sof could seemingly hold an infinite amount of the power generated by her cores and Flames. As far as she knew, the power remained stored in the Eye, but she hadn't yet delved into the inner workings of the jewel. Instead, she was prioritizing reaching the fifth tier of cultivation to summon her beloved.

Just past the Flames was the aperture of her soul, through which lay her repository, inner world, and gateways to the Origin and the Void. The Ethereal sun, Frostfire, provided infinite Ethereal power from the Origin itself and light for the burgeoning ice world she had almost finished creating. Opposite the sun from the planet, an immense black hole drained all other energy and created a surplus of void energies from near the Courts of Chaos in the heart of the Void. The three heavenly bodies remained locked in their orbits, the planet a middle ground between the two power sources.

Despite the presence of the gateway to the heart of the Void, no eldritch horrors had manifested within her burgeoning world. Nature spirits, predominantly those of ice and cold, had taken on some aspects of the Void, but none had transitioned away from their Ethereal nature completely. If any had, they had found destruction at the hands of the other spirits when Aetheria wasn't paying attention.

The primary work of constructing her inner world was completed. Woven within the very essence of her world were massive glyphs in the divine language, Ath. Live. Laugh. Love. Necessity. Nemesis. Love. Creation. Death. Destiny. These glyphs formed one end of her world's x-, y-, and z-axes. A series of minor glyphs filled the core of the ice world, each one a variation of glyphs for cold. Every word or phrase Aetheria could think of regarding the nature of cold and ice lay embedded within her world, including terms she had adapted, such as *cryostatic.*

Cryostatic had the distinction of being the largest of the minor glyphs, and she had imbued it with the meaning of the final order induced by cold. In this place, the meaning she imbued in something might as well be its only meaning.

"You have learned orchestration of the Ethereal and the Void, but you have yet to manage to touch the jewel upon your brow. Only trigger your advancement at that time."

And how do I do that, Reverie?

"How do you do anything? Painfully."

CHAPTER 7

What's an Ein Sof?

Try not to trigger the apocalypse. That's my job.+ Arkaziel sounded dubious about the whole process but assured Aetheria he had the entire "learning of the lay of the land" thing under control and to work on whatever would help her reach the fifth tier fastest.

The Third-Eye of Ein Sof had no consciousness within it. No emotions prevailed over the jewel, and no existential crisis arose from its presence. Not that anyone had complained to her about, at least. When people looked into her eyes, one a gateway to the Void, the other the gateway to the Origin, they were struck by the existential crisis of the respective supreme powers they had brushed against. Whatever Ein Sof was, it exceeded both powers and perhaps was the ultimate quintessence of power.

All Aetheria knew for sure about Ein Sof was its potency. She had encountered few powers that could injure her to the extent of the reality eruptions caused by her cores, and the danger of messing with powers you didn't understand almost stopped her hand, but in the end, the index finger of her right hand pressed into the center of the third eye.

"There are ten emanations, Sefirot, that our planes of existence share. The first is called Malkuth."

"The Sefirot? The Tree of Life. It's been a long time since comparative religion, but I recall the basics of Kabbalah. Ten emanations of the Divine, split into Atzilut, the World of Emanation; Beri'ah, the World of Creation; Yetzirah, the World of Formation; and Assiah, the World of Action, or the physical world."

Reverie's words gave a name to the world where Aetheria now found herself. She stood within a garden, and upon the far horizons, she could sense, but not see, three other realms. Wherever she looked, trees, bushes, flowers, and plants dominated a seemingly endless garden. The ground itself rumbled beneath her with the heartbeat of creation. A nearby redwood rose dramatically into the sky, and when she touched it, she could hear the whispered secrets of Silvanus and the natural world.

A batch of eye-catching raspberries drew Aetheria's attention; the gold berries were swollen with something far different than water. Instinctually, she knew what filled the fruits, berries, and vegetables she saw around her: wisdom. She plucked one of the gold raspberries and popped it into her mouth. A depth of flavors she had never experienced, even with ambrosial fruit, exploded across her tongue, and the heartbeat beneath her feet grew stronger, impossible to ignore.

As Aetheria savored the sensations, she almost jumped when she looked behind her. Four large pillars of stone held aloft a slate roof. It looked like a comfortable place to relax, but, no doubt, it was far more. When she brushed her hand against the ancient stones, a sensation of antiquity filled her, and for some reason, she found herself thinking of Fred, the Black Flame of the Void, who made all of time seem inconsequentially recent.

"All journeys begin and end here. Warm your hands at the fire."

Without Reverie's instructions, Aetheria might not have noticed the pillar of flame that filled the center of the structure. Indeed, standing before it and letting the flame's warmth battle the cold of her body felt different. It reminded her of the blue flames she had consumed in Nova Azura so long ago.

"This is a very peaceful garden. Do many people visit it?"

"No, not many, but all who do are better for it. Take your time, explore, touch, taste."

So, Aetheria did what Reverie instructed. She walked the peaceful paths. She tasted fruits, berries, and vegetables. She touched leaves that were soft and leaves that were sharp. When she cupped the rich soil in her hands, she could still feel the heartbeat of creation within it. Even the water from the small streams in the garden tasted divine. It satiated a thirst she'd previously been unaware of and left her feeling hydrated in an essential way, beyond explanation. The more she tasted, touched, smelled, and experienced in the garden, the more she gained a dim awareness of a small part of the energy within the third eye, a fraction of the greater whole.

"This place, it's some kind of divine sanctuary, yes?"

"The first of ten."

"You called it Malkuth?"

"Yes. In the harmonious symphony, it is the low, deep note to carry the melody. It is a canvas of physicality that the higher dimensions are painted upon. It is where the formless finds form, and ideas become concrete. It is the foundation of all else."

"Careful there, or you'll start to sound like Fred with all that music talk."

"You sense it now, the emanations of the divine? Malkuth is but one of ten."

Aetheria did not belabor the comparison of Fred and Reverie, and it seemed that the other-dimensional being disliked the comparison enough to ignore it utterly.

"Yes, I can now sense it around me and within the jewel. Do we need to do anything else here?"

"No. You can return whenever you wish."

"No pain yet," Aetheria noted suspiciously.

"Yet." The terse response left Aetheria anxious. Given the pain and suffering she had endured since her rebirth, it couldn't be that bad, could it?

"We go Higher. Yesod, where the higher planes funnel energies to be transmitted to Malkuth and the physical world."

The garden blurred around Aetheria, and a sensation of ascending tickled her senses before the world stabilized. An endless twilight filled the sky, and silver light bathed an immense shimmering lake. She stood on the lake's edge and whistled at the impressive reflections in the water. It perfectly reflected the higher stars above while simultaneously showing the gardens of Malkuth below. A luminescent mist drifted above the water, whispering of mysteries of the collective unconscious.

Above, a moon bestowed silver light upon all of Yesod, and its presence exerted an ebb and flow upon the energies contained within the lake.

"To know yourself, the moon will etch paths of discovery upon the surface."

One of Aetheria's boots landed on the surface of the water. Despite her soft step, immense waves rose from even the lightest of pressures she could exert.

"Is this going to be safe?"

"No. You are not a being of safety, Aetheria. You are more than the so-called gods of your plane. Where you tread, the tides of fate grow murky and uncertain, and worlds drown with your passage."

"Jeez, Reverie. I'm not a natural disaster! You are playing havoc on my self-image."

With each subsequent step upon the lake's immense surface, waves rose and fell, but even with the inherent violence of Aetheria's movements, she could discern the interplay between the reflections above and below the water's surface. A surfer would love the immense swells she created. The mist that traveled the water's surface flowed with the waves, and in its motion, she could see visions. Hundreds of visions, but they were only variations of two basic scenarios. In the first, she crawled out of the Third Eye Jewel, and then it changed appearance. In some, it remained a black hole; in others, it became a star; in one, it turned into an actual eye. She even glimpsed one where it detached from her forehead and became a vessel for Reverie.

The second vision had fewer variations, showing Aoibhe stepping from a tear in reality, radiant in all her Nephilim glory. Most of these scenes progressed into sexual scenarios, but in one of them, another being followed her, and they were forced to fight some dark and twisted bat. Before she knew it, Aetheria stepped onto the lake's sandy shore.

"I don't like this place. It's too abstract and full of vagaries. Sure, that's its thing, but . . ." Aetheria shrugged.

"You have almost no affinity with the astral, which makes it unsurprising that you do not enjoy this realm. Have you found resonance?"

"Yeah, I can feel it. Next."

"Your ability to resonate with anything is remarkable. Others work for eons to gain a fraction of your resonance, and you take a light stroll and unlock two of the ten emanations of the divine. How?"

Reverie didn't seem jealous but curious.

"Your guess is as good as mine. I'd assume it was something Nyx did. I learned my affinities by mimicking elemental cores from my repository."

"Unconscious mimicry of the divine?" Reverie sounded exceptionally skeptical, but the world blurred, and they ascended again. Aetheria found herself in a long, grand hallway lined with mirrors. When she looked into the nearest mirror, she saw the darkness of the Void manifest as a six-armed Asura. All six hands waved at her before the image became her original version of Aetheria without the darkness. Each mirror that reflected her glowed; when she took a step or made any movement, they glowed brighter.

"Reverie?"

"Hod embodies the patterns that underlie creation, geometric, mathematical, or otherwise. Rituals, gestures of prayer, and words of faith come to Hod to find structure and become aligned with the divine vibrations that create and sustain the universe. It would appear your every move or action is considered a ritual of faith. How could that be?"

"I don't know." It had an even more significant effect on the mirrors when she spoke. Every mirror in the grand hall lit with a blinding radiance and maintained the intensity of that light to the point that Aetheria had to slip out a side door and into a neat and orderly garden. The garden's perfect arrangement stood out, like the old great gardens of nobles of the Renaissance. While she admired the simple beauty in manicured hedges and a rose placed *just so*, a symphony played in her mind. She could see an invisible baton leading the symphony while also directing the orbit of planets.

The whole plane resonated within Aetheria, and she smiled while she watched the upper realms dance in the sky.

"It needs more ice," Aetheria murmured, focused on the third eye, and found another layer open to her senses. "We're good here. I have already resonated with Hod."

Reverie said nothing, but the world blurred around them, and rather than ascending, Aetheria felt a sensation of sideways movement.

"Netzach."

This world seemed distant to her, as if a thin film, like cling wrap, separated Aetheria from Netzach. She could describe the jungle before her only as a rainforest, much like the pictures she had seen of the Amazon. Vines tangled with trees in an interwoven tapestry, low underbrush hid small creatures, and the plentitude of life astounded her everywhere she looked. The sound of insects filled her ears. A wide river with a strong current flowed through the jungle, and Aetheria walked beside it. Every step seemed to stretch the cling-wrap barrier that separated her from Netzach, and she was determined to break that barrier regardless of how many steps it took her.

The jungle made music: the wind between the leaves, the frogs and birds, the mammals in the dark brush, the rush of water, the far-off sound of a waterfall, and even the rhythm of Aetheria's boots against the ground joined in weaving a primal song. She could almost hear ancient words accompanying it. The more she focused, the more a chorus of voices could be discerned, singing verses of lessons hard won.

When Aetheria stepped closer to the river, she immediately felt passions rise in her. She couldn't help but imagine her lover and stepped slightly away from the water.

"Perceptive. It is pure emotion."

"What lies down there?" Aetheria could see a stone pillar that rose into the sky and was carved with something.

"A monument with the names and deeds of all who have strived or endured."

"What's it take to get on it?"

"All deeds are recorded, no matter how small. All who strive are acknowledged, no matter the extent of their struggle."

"I get it." Aetheria nodded and looked upward into the heavens. "Next."

CHAPTER 8

A Higher Realm

The world spun and blurred again, replacing the old garden with a new one. This garden, however, felt unnatural to Aetheria. In the sky of the small park, a star levitated. It produced a soft, warm brilliance that bathed the garden in perfect light.

"I'm noticing a trend with gardens. What's up with the light?"

"The light of Tiferet. Beauty or compassion. It is the central emanation, harmonious, and where all others integrate. Tiferet is a place of balance."

A tree rose into the sky at the center of the garden, and with her Ethereal Sight, Aetheria could see its roots delving down to the lower emanations they had already left. It reminded her of the World Trees she had seen repeatedly within the Tower of Aetherius.

"What's up with the tree?"

"The Axis Mundi, the Cosmic Axis, a World Tree, the World Pillar, the Tree of Life. One is all, and all are one. Would you prefer a Mountain?"

Aetheria set her fingers against the tree's bark and extended her senses. Within it were strong flows of light and shadow, balanced and rife with meaning. Action with restraint, mercy with severity, giving with receiving. While she pondered the use of light and shadow as the inner workings of a tree and how different it was from Arkaziel's light and shadow, she noticed something else. A quiet melody grew closer while she studied the tree, and the golden beings who sang spread toward her in the garden.

With each note that soothed Aetheria's ears, a genuine smile appeared on her lips. The beings exuded a soft gold light and continued to appear. They formed a pathway between them and waited for her to wander down the path.

"Go," Reverie prompted her.

The song stayed pure, perfect almost. Each note and rhythm came together to create a whole greater than its parts. Somehow, the occasional harsh note or complex rhythm enhanced the beautiful whole instead of diminishing it.

"Who are they?"

"Spirits. Beauty, kindness, compassion, empathy, mercy. Tiferet is their birthplace."

The spirits led Aetheria to a small, crystal clear pool that showed the towering tree in its mirrorlike surface. The initial reflection showed her as she currently was: the mixed-color hair, the mismatched eyes, the Third Eye Jewel upon her forehead. That image slowly faded to reveal how she had looked that first day in Nova Azura—a young woman with sparkling aqua-blue hair and glowing red eyes. *No, the red eyes came inside the tower, not in Nova Azura.*

The longer she watched, the more the image changed. Only red hair? Mixed red and blue hair, striped and then streaked? Different colors of eyes, mismatched eyes, eyes of oblivion, each came and went, but no matter how the appearance changed, she knew it was herself. Her sense of self had been damaged by the ingress of the Void and the changes it had made into her appearance, and the third eye felt like a forced body modification she'd had no interest in, but in staring into this pool, she realized that all of these versions of her were perfectly her.

"You resonate extensively with Tiferet. Odd that you resort to violence so swiftly, and yet you so easily find peace and self-understanding."

Aetheria considered her response to that before she shrugged and didn't give Reverie an answer. How often did she have to tell him she could resonate, copy, or mimic anything? Divine Emanations were no different from elemental cores as far as her ability to resonate went. Her shoulders relaxed for the first time in ages; she would be herself regardless of what came her way and would deal with her challenges with grace and compassion. *Maybe. I'll try, anyway.*

"Life's complicated, Reverie. You do your best; sometimes your best isn't very good."

The world blurred around them, and the rising sensation filled Aetheria once more. The perfect gardens of Tiferet vanished below to be replaced by stone walls. Ancient walls, cut in a bygone age, formed an immense, awe-inspiring hall. The walls showed their age but remained solid and implacable in their grandeur, their stern beauty a testament to their creator's strength and skilled judgment. Incredible columns lined the hall, each full of intricate symbols representing the laws and principles governing the universe. Whatever language they had been written in, it was not Ath.

"Strength. Judgment. Severity. Gevurah is the power of limitations and constraints. It balances mercy, tempering generosity with restraint."

"I like this one," Aetheria said, while she ran her fingertips along the columns, but her gaze lingered on the end of the hall. An immense throne, cut from a single red block of stone, sat upon a dais. A flame burned on the floor before the throne. A sword rested against one arm of the throne, and a cloak hung from the back. Her footsteps echoed ominously through the vast hall when she climbed the dais to examine the objects.

"Cleansing flame. Everyone loves burning sinners, I guess." Aetheria grimaced as she studied the fire. Out of curiosity, she plunged a hand into the flames. They did not hurt her, but they didn't burn her, either.

"You burned the impurities of your flesh in each ascension of cultivation and now resonate with six of ten Emanations. Or did you expect the Void to burn away? The Void is not impure. The purity of absence is the canvas upon which Malkuth is built."

"If you say so," Aetheria demurred. She used both Void Gaze and Ethereal Sight to focus on the flames engulfing her hand, and she couldn't see anything to contradict Reverie. *It still feels wrong, I guess.*

The bared blade of the sword resting against the throne reflected the flame's light—the sharp edge of the sword bespoke precision, an ability to cut anything. Images danced in her mind of cutting through illusions and falsehoods, the ability to slice the right from the wrong, and the courage and duty to uphold the truth.

The cloak resting upon the back of the throne shared no commonality with the sword. The cloak was heavy, and the colors of the fabric changed when Aetheria touched it. It did not speak of restraint; it was restraint. Like so many anime characters wore, the cloak would slow and burden anyone who wore it.

"Cool, cool, cool." Aetheria adjusted her long black coat, her version of the cloak.

"You aren't going to take the sword or cloak or sit on the throne?"

"No need." Aetheria held one of her hands up to reveal long talons instead of fingers. "I am my blade, and I have my reminder of responsibility." Regular fingers adjusted the collar of her coat.

"As for the throne, well. Someday." Despite the flippant dismissal of the throne, Aetheria's voice acknowledged the necessity of making decisions with clarity and resoluteness. Difficult choices had to be made, such as when Werylin's time with the party had ended.

The world blurred with horizontal movement rather than vertical movement this time, before Aetheria landed in a new environment. Radiant bursts of light left even her eyes seeing sparks for a few seconds. The sky's blue felt right and warmed the skin with an all-encompassing, unconditional love. The growth of the plants in this garden was a testament to the effectiveness of that love. Berries and flowers grew in plenty, a reciprocation of the endless generosity.

The sunlight struck particles just right to create a multitude of sunbeams and rays filtering throughout the garden. A soft, almost golden aura of light clung to Aetheria, the same as everything else. It felt like sinking into a warm bath, though she had never known a bath to make herself feel loved and accepted the way this light did, and she relaxed even more.

"Chesed is loving, merciful, and graceful."

A glorious fountain overflowed with clear, sparkling water at the garden's center. The water touched the sky before it flowed into the fountain's wide basin and then into small streams that fed the garden. The fountain endlessly poured out its water to sustain the garden but gained nothing from this benevolence.

Grand trees filled the garden, branches laden with multiple kinds of fruit. No creature could want sustenance in the presence of these great, giving trees, which shared their abundance freely. Like the fountain, the trees offered their bounty without expectation of return. Like Chesed, they were selfless and unconditional.

In this place, Aetheria felt warmth seep into her soul and felt the quintessence of herself grow dramatically more resilient. If her soul had been steel before, it would now be proper to compare it to adamantine.

Those pitiful lanterns of order and harmony may stand as beacons in the endless expanses of the cosmos, but they are fleeting sparks in the eternal darkness. You dance in the gardens of ephemeral light but never visit the maw of existential dread from which all are born.

The Sefirot are a shower of sparks in eternal night, their rules and enforced order a brief respite from the truth that awaits in the Void. All must end. All must be destroyed. New iterations will pass, and new realities will be born, but they, too, must end.

Why, hello, Fred. I didn't know you'd be able to follow me here. What do you know of the Sefirot?

The Sefirot are immaterial—a farce of an imposition upon the tapestry of existence. No matter the source, all that flows from my flames returns. Everything wrought will be razed in time's cruel embrace.

Aetheria considered her Void friend. Fred frequently spoke in a way she felt an eldritch horror ought to, but sometimes he slipped up, such as when he mentioned gear terminology from her old MMO, *Eldest Fantasy Wars Online*. For a being who claimed to only be able to talk to her and to be the first existence, it came across as eager to communicate with her regularly, which flattered her ego but also seemed like bullshit.

Does the Void have a system of power at all similar?

The Void is not the opposite of creation; the absence of existence, the unfathomable dark, and the multifaceted forms of chaos defy any attempt to be ordered or structured. You cannot apply logic to the illogical. Learn your Tree of Life, but do not neglect the only force that matters, little one.

Fred fell silent then, and Aetheria almost spoke aloud to him when Reverie interrupted.

"Forget the narcissistic, vacuous one and focus. We ascend again."

Aetheria smirked at the way Fred and Reverie danced around one another: sometimes they could eavesdrop on her conversations with the other, and other times they were utterly ignorant of one another.

Aetheria felt the world blur around her and recognized the scent before her eyes focused enough to confirm it. She stood in an immense library. A library so vast it appeared to be endless. Even when she altered her eyes to see farther, as best she could tell, the shelves of books indeed went on forever.

A deep sigh escaped her lips before she noticed, and she strolled to the nearest shelves to run her fingers along the spines of the books and inhale the scent of the tomes lovingly. The librarian in her from her former life came alive in a way Aesca hadn't stirred in decades.

"I like this place," Aetheria muttered the understatement to herself. A warm pulse filled her as if the realm of this emanation felt the same way about her.

"Binah is at its most basic understanding."

"Oh look, Reverie! There's a picture of me in that book."

CHAPTER 9

Higher Consciousness

Abook lay open on a table, and indeed, it showed an ink sketch of Aetheria. The artist had a deft hand and drew the third eye upon her brow as if it were a natural eye instead of jewelry. *Is it jewelry if you've forged it out of your soul?*

Aetheria flipped through and found that the other pages of the book showed sketches of other places she'd been since her reincarnation. One sketch was of her and Arkaziel, and she liked it so much she memorized it to make a copy of back in the physical world. In the sketch, Aetheria sat on a set of steps, Arkaziel on her lap, and he was stealing a bite of her street food that looked similar to a gyro while she looked the other way. A knowing smile played across her face despite her attention focused in the distance. Aetheria didn't recall the scene depicted, but maybe it hadn't happened yet? Could Binah show the future? The first page contained odd fractal art from which she could only discern two words in Ath: depth and silence. The label on the spine of the book said *Telos*. The book's latter pages were blank or only had one or two incomplete slashes of the pen.

"I guess the future hasn't been written yet," Aetheria said with a laugh and a flashback to a nineties anime. Her laughter tinkled like the fountain at the library's center, which drew her attention. A tree grew from the center of the fountain. Its trunk rose beyond sight.

"The Fountain of Tears symbolizes Binah's deep empathy and unending emotional capacity. Understanding surpasses intellectual knowledge and includes emotional depth and experience. The Tree of Contemplation's great roots spread under the library, and its branches protect it."

"Can I sleep under it and gain knowledge?" Aetheria recalled that was a typical fairy tale or fable, and occurred in many children's books. But before Reverie could answer her she wondered something else.

"Why are there only three cardinal directions to the library?" A quick study showed that while there were more pathways through the shelves than that, the main arteries of the library lay upon three different paths. Her question answered itself when she noticed the signs on the paths: Intuition, Reasoning, and Experience.

"Not how I would have sorted things, but I'm sure it makes sense to someone."

"*Three paths, fifty gates.*" Reverie corrected her understanding.

Those few words triggered a flood of sensations within Aetheria. The first path went to Pleroma, and knowledge of all things spiritual. Meanwhile, the second path covered the knowledge of the material plane and its inhabitants. The third gate held the knowledge of the Void. Try as Aetheria might, she couldn't find the linkage between Intuition, Reasoning, and Experience and Pleroma, Material, and Void. The depths of Binah were vast, and her newly forged connection did not answer all mysteries, but even so Aetheria already understood a core principle of Binah. Behind each path, fifty gates held the knowledge of that path, and for whatever reason not a single gate of Binah was closed to her. This library of the divine eagerly awaited her perusal, as if she were its head librarian. Those fifty gates troubled Aetheria. She knew they were more than blockades, but they had another purpose, a very important one, but she couldn't recall what it was or why she knew it.

Aetheria could now identify and resonate with eight emanations within Ein Sof's depths.

"*The next one is quite the change,*" Reverie warned Aetheria, seconds before the world blurred around them. Again, there was no ascent. The sensation of motion felt sideways.

When her vision stabilized again, Aetheria found herself standing upon nothing and beholding an entire universe. A cosmic ballet unfolded before her. Stars twinkled and swirled, and planets spun and danced through the endless black void. In hues of indigo and rose, nebulas spiraled and created intricate patterns as if by direction. Spiral-arm galaxies spun in a delicate waltz, and comets left behind glimmering trails of stardust.

A great flash of light from the depths of the empty void pulled at Aetheria's attention. A river of stars burst out from that immense spark, expanding into universes of new possibilities. A faint shiver of interest filled her, but she felt the echo of disgust radiate from somewhere within her, too.

"*The birth of thought, creative and intuitive. Hokhmah is so much more than understanding. The Void is clay to form unlimited potential. You touched upon this intuitively when you discerned the ability of the Ethereal to shape the Void.*"

"It is beautiful," Aetheria murmured, focused on the performance before her.

Reverie said nothing, but Aetheria felt a hollowness in her heart. Could an ordinary person experience these things even if they dedicated their whole life to it? Here she was, able to walk through the emanations of the divine and pick them up as if they were no more complex than simple addition. Whatever Nyx and Khaos had done to give her the ability to resonate with affinities had cheated her from earning these resonances. On the one hand, this allowed her to rush toward her reunion with Aoibhe, but it might leave her less prepared and ready to handle the power of Ein Sof. Aetheria figured the end goal of the emanations was manipulating said power, but that was an assumption on her part.

What part of Aetheria even allowed for this? Did it trace back to one of the gods whose essences were merged within her own, or something to do with Fred and the Black Flame? Or another mystery that she wasn't privy to yet, that wouldn't be acknowledged until she identified it? Did it make sense for any of the gods who had been integrated into her soul? Aetheria couldn't fathom how it would relate to Inanna, Izanami, Quetzalcoatl, Ananke, Phanes, or Ouranos, but perhaps it was due to the sum being more significant than the whole. She refrained from asking, not ready to take another step that might be too many.

"We ascend the final time."

With those words, Reverie triggered the ascension to the next world. The light blinded Aetheria and did not let up. Instead, she looked through Ethereal Sight and Void Gaze to regard this strange world of light. The light demarked the realms of the finite and the infinite, and at its center, an empty throne blazed brightest of all. A series of six hundred and twenty pillars of light surrounded the throne.

"Keter. The Supreme Crown." When Reverie spoke, lights amongst the pillars oscillated and changed colors with each syllable, only to return to its previous color when the syllable faded.

"You live here?"

"Yes."

"Who does the throne belong to?"

"No one has ever sat upon it."

Aetheria cast her senses out, but she could sense only herself and Reverie, and unending light.

"This is adjacent to the Origin, or even a far distant part of it, isn't it?"

"Yes. Keter is the Primordial Ether, what you call the Ethereal."

"You had me name you, but did you have a name before?"

"You are the first to ever speak with me, Aetheria."

"You aren't answering the question. Have people spoken *at* you?"

"Yes. Several mystics, prophets, and seers have managed to either sense, guess, or intuit my existence over the eons. Most called me Arich Anpin. Why they would call me long face when I have no face, I do not understand."

"You've been here all that time, and no one but me has ever been able to speak to you?" Aetheria sounded slightly dubious.

"I've communicated indirectly with others, but you are the first to speak with *me."*

"Uffda, that's a doozy. All that time on your own. No wonder you were so lonely. Do you have, like, an avatar I can give a hug to or something?" Aetheria stared at the pillars of light.

"That is unnecessary, but the sentiment is appreciated. You have resonated with Keter. Do you feel anything abnormal?"

Aetheria had to think about that. The Divine Light of Keter illuminated her and made her feel like she was intangible and unbound as a spirit, but also solid in a way she couldn't express. She didn't have the terminology to explain.

"There's this sort of, I don't know, an annoying vague *thing* trying to resonate with me. I keep pushing it away because it feels like a burden or someone who wants to sit outside my window and watch me change. Like, it wants to become more by diluting what I am?"

Reverie remained silent for some time, but when he spoke, it was in a flabbergasted tone.

"That would be creation itself trying to harmonize and share a moment of unity with you."

"I don't like it. It's creepy. Anyway, that's all ten Sefirot. Why do I still have a portion of the jewel that has no resonance?" Aetheria discarded Reverie's line of questions. She had gained the ability to resonate with Keter; therefore, the rest didn't matter at this particular moment to her.

"Da'at awaits you."

The streams of light flowed around Aetheria and formed a doorway that had not been there moments before. Without a preamble, Aetheria walked through the secret gate and emerged into another realm of Divine Light. All ten resonances she had learned from the other emanations were present equally here in Da'at. They filled her with a strange sense of euphoria. Wisdom and understanding seemed to permeate the air, and she felt like epiphany after epiphany was but a slight turn of the head away, just out of sight.

While each emanation of the Sefirot had felt different, resonating with Da'at filled Aetheria's mind with background music. Behind her thoughts, a symphony played, a harmonious medley of the universe's music. In the revelatory bosom of the cosmic chorus, Aetheria felt the full embrace of Da'at. The endless abyss shone in a new light, a place not of absence or emptiness but infinite potential. The unknowable, the unmanifest, the essence of all possibility rang loudest in the abyss of potential. With a look through the lens of Da'at, Aetheria finally saw a Path (yes, with a capital *P*), to replace the obsolete Path of the Ethereal.

"What does Tetragrammaton mean?"

"It is the name of the owner of the throne."

"I'm not a fan of the conspiracy against me growing increasingly ridiculous by the day. Were you involved with whatever Nyx and Khaos have done to me?"

"No. I am your friend, Aetheria. If I were to work against you, I would have drawn you into the Tree of Death, not the Tree of Life."

"There's a Tree Of Death!? What the hell, of course, there's a Tree Of Death; why wouldn't there be? Let me guess: it's a dark mirror with opposing strengths. Wait, does that mean the Tree of Life is from the Void, and the Tree of Death is to the Void?"

"You could view it that way, but the relevancy of the Void to either Tree is minimal. The Void is only essential to the Void, a discarded shadow of existence before the declaration of Let There Be Light. The Divine Light banishes all darkness, casts all reality, and infinitely creates whatever the Void might destroy."

"Am I going to have to go on another vacation through the Tree of Death at some point?" Aetheria hadn't enjoyed the tour of the Tree of Life that much, but the gains she had made from it were considerable. Would the Tree of Death make her much more powerful, or would it introduce weaknesses she didn't already have?

"I do not believe so, unless curiosity drives you to. Some knowledge can be harmful."

"You and Fred sure have different views on your relative position in the grand scheme of things."

Silence reigned for long seconds, affronted silence. With a shrug, Aetheria stepped back into her body and opened her eyes. A dome of geodesic, crystalized energy had formed over her body while she'd been out. Within the frozen energy, she read a pattern and laughed.

"I guess this Divine Light might be useful after all," Aetheria murmured as the dome dissolved to nothing.

"Are you inching in on my territory? Light is my thing." Arkaziel, in the guise of a lion, grumbled at her from where he lay in the grass.

"Oh please, we're talking about very different kinds of light, big guy. Mine's cold, for starters." Aetheria tried to calm Arkaziel before his narcissism or pride got riled.

"Cold light? That sounds stupid. Light is warm. Laser. Pew-pew." Arkaziel homed in on exactly what she hoped he would.

"Well, mine doesn't have any warmth. It is pure cold."

"Are you sure you are doing it right?" Arkaziel asked a question Aetheria had heard so, so many times before, in the same tone, from so many men, that she just dropped a snowball, or five hundred, on top of Arkaziel before she teleported to the pantry to get some lunch.

+Let me guess, I touched a nerve?+

~If that's an apology, are you sure you are doing it right?~

CHAPTER 10

Lord Starweaver

You came back at a good time. There's a hunting squad of the fae who ventured outside of the forest into the middle lands. Want to go say hello?" Arkaziel's disgruntlement about light had subsided after they shared lunch, which led to that information and a short flight upon her mighty lion mount. Aetheria didn't comment on the shock that Arkaziel still played the role of lion, but if she knew her companion, he'd get bored of the joke sooner rather than later.

The distances didn't quite line up in Aetheria's memory, and she wondered how concrete the physical details of this world were. Would a kilometer become five if she turned her head? The Tower of Moros felt as real as the Tower of Aetherius had, yet in some ways, it felt thinner, more transient. Did that come from a power difference between Aetherius and Moros, or a difference in their aspects, or both?

Arkaziel managed to find the fae expedition quickly. An aerial vantage point combined with the apex predator senses of a StarMane rendered the thrill of the hunt moot. Minor illusions, dozens of nondetection charms and spells, and fairy cloaks failed to conceal the expedition from Arkaziel's version of Ethereal Sight. After a quick telepathic checkup, Arkaziel landed just ahead of the fae group, and it seemed they were heading for the hill the duo had started this tower on. Arkaziel remained in the guise of a winged lion, while Aetheria retained her usual appearance.

The fae tried to go around the woman on a lion, but Arkaziel just lazily trotted to an intercept course until the group recognized they'd been detected. At this point, one of the retainers moved to the front of the five-strong group.

"Give me the name of who dares to hinder our route in our lands?" The male fae wore light armor, and the sword at his hip seemed like it belonged there, an extension of his being. He had a harsh, sharp face, and even from a distance of five meters, Aetheria could feel his attempt to cow them with his projected intent. They spoke in Primeval Sylvan, the antiquated language of the fae realms and ancient elves.

"Be wary. This one almost feels like the Queen of Winter," the man riding a Pegasus warned his servants. His detailed silver and black robes were far finer than those of his minions, and they all stood in the way to bodily protect him.

"Why do you journey here, out of your forest? Bravado aside, this land is unclaimed." Aetheria did not give her name, or anything else for that matter.

All five of the fae flexed their auras and radiated killing intent until their Lord went ashen-faced.

"Stand down, all of you." *Had* Aetheria seen him go ashen-faced? Composure, arrogance, and haughtiness returned to the face of the Fae Lord with such alacrity that Aetheria actually doubted herself.

"Forgive my retainers. They are young yet. I am Lord Eiravel, known in legends as the Starweaver, Sovereign of House Silvershadow. I am the master of the canopy of the eternal cosmos, where stars dance at my behest, and the veils of reality bend to my will. The night sky tells tales of ancient magic and unfathomable secrets within my domain. I am the guardian of starlit paths and keeper of the heavenly mysteries. Approach with respect, and know that in my presence, you stand amidst the infinite wonders of the cosmos."

The four retainers muttered variations of *hear-hear, that's our lord*, and other sycophantic prattle. Arkaziel's laughter filled her mind through their telepathic bond, and Aetheria had to fight the urge to introduce herself with matching energy.

"I am called Aetheria," she finally responded.

Two of the retainers, the swordsman and a rogue-looking man who was almost, but not entirely invisible, reached for their weapons. They pulled their hands back as if burned by the Frostfire that danced on the hilts of their blades. Her smirk drew angry looks.

"Why do you bar our path, Asura?" Lord Starweaver demanded an answer to his questions. His phrasing made it clear he was uncertain what Aetheria was, only that he knew she was dangerous.

"Honestly? I'm trying to figure out what's going on here. Why do you fae feed on the humans on all sides? Why the expeditions to these unclaimed lands? Can peace exist between you, Uruk, and possibly the other kingdoms?" Aetheria asked her questions, and the confusion on the lord's and retainers' faces spoke volumes. That an Asura held them up to ask questions about *humans* was undoubtedly a puzzle.

"Why would we accept peace with such barbarians?" Disgust colored the words of the Starweaver.

"Because they will number in the hundreds of thousands in the blink of an eye. Then millions. Perhaps they are short-lived, but it only takes one lucky strike to end your life, and their gods are prone to ensuring their favored ones make such blessed strikes." Aetheria's annoyance at the arrogance of the Fae Lord didn't make it to her facial expressions or tone, but only rigid self-control kept her from slapping the whole lot of them.

"Let them come in their thousands. With a single major work, I will annihilate an army of vermin. Their numbers are immaterial; their gods possess no threat to us, and we possess the strength to crush all the human kingdoms at once." The sparkle in Starweaver's eyes warned Aetheria she was dealing with a fanatic, and the four retainers had all drunk the Kool-Aid and cheered at their lord's supremacist xenophobia.

"Are you the leader of the fae of the forest?" Aetheria had already written Starweaver off as a nitwit.

"To reap the bounty of the stars, you must first sow the seeds of the moon's light," the Fae Lord haughtily answered and waited expectantly.

"Well, I thought whoever was in charge might want to negotiate with me. I'll be claiming these lands as my own before long, and any who would challenge me shall be destroyed."

Despite the pain, the rogue and warrior again grasped their weapons but had to release the hilts when the Frostfire burned and froze their hands. The two female retainers started to chant under their breath but stopped when the air burned their tongues and the cold numbed their mouths.

"You are testing my patience. If you wish to die as Athena did, I'll oblige you. Answer my question, Lordling, in compensation for the foolish behavior of your retainers." Were fae people? Elves indeed were, and they were a type of fae. Yet, something about the fae before her struck a chord of violence within Aetheria. She wanted to raise a hand and obliterate them with a mere gesture. How many could she devour at once?

+*You okay, Blue?*+ Arkaziel's question bore the complete statement of his belief that she was not.

~*I'm . . . No, I'm not okay.*~

Do your desires cast these shadows? The Tree of Life's roots are entwined with its twin, the Tree of Death. In accepting one, you have received the other and know the curse of humanity.

I have been human this whole time.

Must you persist in these comforting lullabies? Whisper again and again those frail assurances to the Void. Your feeble convictions will echo into the boundless expanse of cosmic indifference. Weave your tapestry of delusions. Your false beliefs are mere ripples in the dark, eternal sea of the unknown.

Arkaziel's inquisition about her well-being, Fred's ominous message about the Tree of Death, and endless blathering about the Void, combined with the wellspring of unpleasant emotions rising in her chest, distracted Aetheria to the point that Lord Eiravel the Starweaver finished a spell without her noticing. The spellform created by the Fae Lord went up in a burst of Aether and became a reality.

Images of a vast cosmos appeared in the sky. Silver moons circled a planet and then fell from the sky. The first moon to fall struck Aetheria and released an immense brilliance, but no heat or force expanded out in a shockwave. When the light faded, Aetheria had caught four of the moons. She casually held on to the first, and the other three were stacked atop it like scoops of ice cream on a cone.

"What!?" the female illusionist cried in shock at someone countering her lord's magic in such an improbable way, but her thoughts ended abruptly when a spear of darkness shot out of her own shadow and pulled her into the gaping maw of the abyss.

The warrior charged forward, swinging a blade that glowed like the sun at Aetheria, who caught the sword with her free hand. Frost formed on the blade and then on the retainer's skin. His lips turned blue, his teeth chattered, and numbness stole his entire body. The warrior didn't even feel a barbed spear of darkness impale him. His essence had frozen moments before it was devoured.

A dagger point pressed against Aetheria's neck but couldn't pierce the skin. Frost formed across the weapon and swept into the previously invisible scout's body.

"None of you were from the winter court, clearly." Arkaziel snorted in amusement. The StarMane didn't even stop the fae enchanter from finishing her spell. Small spots on the rogue's skin gained color once more, only to be almost instantly frozen again. The warmth enchantment failed in the face of Aetheria's irresistible cold. When the ice fully engulfed the rogue's body, a tendril of shadow pulled the man into one of Arkaziel's maws of Devouring Darkness.

Aetheria shrugged, and threw the three moons at the enchantress. Despite the minute amount of power Aetheria put into the throw, it still had the hitting strength of a garbage truck plowing into a deer. A grimace of disgust crossed Aetheria's lips while the world around her filled with viscera. Arkaziel stopped the unpleasant sight from worsening. A haze of darkness devoured and cleared the air.

"Heavensfall!" Lord Starweaver cried and slammed both hands into the ground. The planet that still hung in the sky quickly gained substance and fell as commanded.

The planet had to be visible back in Uruk, so large was the magical construct. Aetheria watched it fall with interest. She hadn't expected it to start on fire in reentry. How high in the sky had it formed? Did it have material qualities? The planet fell, but when it touched the tip of her finger, it vanished into her repository, where it immediately got devoured. Strange sensations flickered through her consciousness after she absorbed the planet.

"The Prince in Green won't let you get away with this!" The haughty fae growled and stared at them imperiously.

"You attacked us," Aetheria pointed out quickly.

"Dick move." Arkaziel backed up Aetheria's point with the most helpful of comments.

"Why aren't you killing me?" The Starweaver stared at them in expectation of torture or worse.

"If you'd been listening in the first place, you would've heard my goal was to get the regional powers to get along. I just wanted to poke around inside this hill and to have some peace while I do it."

"This hill belongs to the fae! The Grove of Eternal Twilight isn't for you filthy mongrels. You'll have to kill every one of us in the realm if you think you can claim our birthright from us!" Lord Starweaver practically frothed at the mouth with that.

"I guess he won't be any help. Why don't . . ." Aetheria trailed off as the fae vanished, pulled to safety by the aura of a powerful entity.

"Damn it, I almost had a shadow in his neck." Arkaziel hissed.

+*I did have one in his pocket, though. The Prince in Green saved him. It looks like you fumbled meeting the fae, but they are delicious. I'm stuffed from all those retainers, but I could've fit that astral mage.*+

~*Well, let's say hello to the Prince in Green.*~

+*Do I get to eat him?*+

CHAPTER 11

The Twilight Verdure

Two great dragons soared through the air. The first was a black dragon striped with white. Long barbed tentacles of shadow undulated along the immense proper form of Arkaziel, and his dark scales sucked in light while white scales expelled it. Over one hundred meters long, the enormous StarMane dwarfed everything in sight. His mane had finally started to grow in, adding a bit of lion to his appearance, and accurate to the clan name, it already sparkled like the cosmos. His shadows—yes, he had three—moved ahead of him and occasionally snapped their jaws to devour mystical defenses meant to impede intruders into the fae wood.

An aqua dragon flew to Arkaziel's flank, slightly to the rear. While Arkaziel was a dragon of dark scales, Aetheria's draconic form had evolved since its last use. Her scales were forged of aqua crystal filled with alternating Void or Ethereal, which created the appearance of an aqua dragon highlighted by red and black energies. Her draconic face also displayed the third eye her human form did.

The duo had unsealed their auras, which caused animals, monsters, and humanoids to flee from their fearsome presence. The fae did not just let them run roughshod over their defenses, though. The first attempt to thwart them came from a disorienting mist that rose from the forests and tried to confuse their sense of direction. A pulse of freezing Ethereal power dispersed the fog before it could become an obstacle to the duo. Enchanted arrows fell far short of the high altitude the dragons soared at, and spells volleyed at the two were absorbed by the ice dragon before they got near.

Despite the temerity of the forest inhabitants at attacking a dragon, let alone two, neither Arkaziel nor Aetheria returned any attacks. They dispersed the attacks against them and flew toward the forest's center, where the magic the Prince in Green used to save Lord Starweaver had originated from. Nothing the fae had erected could stop the two. Wards, defensive structures, boundary denial attempts, the fae even attempted to use draconic control magic to deter them, but nothing worked on the duo. The Prince in Green raised the final barrier, a shimmering and ever-outward-expanding dome of neon green energy. Aetheria smashed through it without even taking a moment to consider if that was a good idea.

The barrier shattered like glass, revealing the pair's first proper glimpse of the immense natural palace of the Prince in Green. A tall, elflike man in all green stood atop a precipice that gave him a view of the fae settlement below. A large twig of a staff held in one hand pointed at the pair, an expression of pain etched into his features from the feedback of Aetheria's absorption of the barrier. Behind him stood Lord Starweaver, and behind him, ten more robed fae, who were singing incantations in harmony to empower the prince.

Aetheria morphed into her human form and dropped out of the sky to land a meter before the precipice. Pillars of ice rose and met Aetheria's boots without any appreciable amount of force being dispersed or transferred, so that she was at an even height with the fae on the precipice. Once, Aetheria had been jealous of the grace and fluidity of elves and Werylin, and now she could fall hundreds of meters and land without even looking like she had missed a step. Arkaziel landed on her shoulder in the form of a small black house cat.

The aqua-haired woman held up a single hand to forestall the fae, the black flames that danced in her open palm warning of what would become of those who dared to attack her before she had spoken.

"I don't want this to devolve into a fight," Aetheria started.

+What!? No! We're here to eat them! They attacked us, then ran away!+ Arkaziel did not like the idea of peaceful resolutions, especially with such hefty meals standing before them.

"You just wish to usurp our sacred lands, force us to make peace with *humans*, and what, give our knowledge to the apes while we're at it?" Lord Starweaver shouted the last, spittle at his mouth. Arrogant and fatal supremacy had consumed his persona.

The Prince in Green stared at Aetheria with solid-green, orblike eyes. To compare him to an elf would be too great of an honor to elves. The man radiated an aura of self-confidence, and at this proximity Aetheria noticed that entire swarms of pixies and other tiny fae creatures surrounded him. Yet he said nothing, just stared at Aetheria and awaited her answer to Starweaver's challenge. *Is there a chance of peace, or does he want to seem noble?*

"Well, I doubt those ruins are yours, for one thing. The architecture I saw beneath the mountain was distinctly human, and you may have used the grove around them in rituals in ages past, but you did not tend to that grove. It, too, was related to the temple buried in the center of the hill, which appeared to be consecrated to Inanna. Unless one of you is Inanna?" Aetheria arched the blue-green eyebrow above her red eye with the words.

"Inanna fell years ago to the gods of the Aegean."

"The City of Uruk has acknowledged me as Inanna," Aetheria said flatly.

Amusement flickered across the face of the Prince in Green, but the mages behind him all sputtered in evident surprise.

"Since when does the Queen of Heaven travel as a dragon?" one of the attendants hissed at her.

"Since I decided I wanted to." Aetheria shrugged and laughed. "It's effective at driving home that I don't want to be disturbed. But do not mistake me. I am more than Inanna, not some pale copy."

"You are a Voidbringer. You and your companion both teem with the Void. Why would one of your kind work toward peace rather than destruction?" The Prince in Green's voice filled Aetheria's ears like a song, a thousand glorious notes she'd never heard before, sang within the chorus of his voice. She wondered how many people fell to their knees and did whatever he wanted merely because of being in his presence. Oh sure, she felt the compulsion, the charm, the intent, the manifest will of the prince, the pixie swarm, the mages, and even Starweaver, all pressing on her, but it found no purchase.

"As with Inanna, Voidbringer is a small part of the greater whole." The Unutterable Black Flame of the Void burned and spun over her palm. Tiny tendrils of black fire formed like hungry tentacles, eager to feast upon anyone and anything. "Your attempts to charm or compel me have no chance of success, but do continue wasting your effort."

"Wretch! You dare mock the Prince in Green?!" Starweaver hissed before bright silver and red light broke through from within the mage. The smell of charred skin, silk, and hair expanded out from the fae as all of the flesh that had held Starweaver back burned away, revealing a fae unburdened by humanoid form. Formed from silver astral light, Starweaver had become a radiant cosmic light given a vaguely fae shape.

A large pillar of light with Starweaver at its center went from the ground to the heavens and bathed the entire fae party in celestial light that added sparkles and glimmers to the fae and their weapons. The overactivity within Aetheria's senses suggested some blessing was involved with that light.

Arkaziel laughed from her shoulder as if an ant had just insulted him. The StarMane lifted his right front paw and casually slashed one claw through the air. The entire pillar of light vibrated momentarily, and then it lost cohesion and fell apart.

"You can't defy the light of the cosmos!" Starweaver yelled in rage, and the light pooled into a spear that fired at Arkaziel. The beam of power represented the pinnacle of a fourth tier Cultivator's greatest work, with multiple secret techniques and trump cards thrown into the mix. The end of the bolt swelled even as it traveled, forming a series of spheres at the end. Each sphere took on aspects of the planets and stars that dominated celestial magic.

Aetheria could have absorbed it or killed Starweaver before he activated his magic. Oh, she had no doubt they'd make it difficult, but thus far the arrogance of gods and fae had allowed her to repeatedly kill them before they had time to overcome their arrogance and pull out all the types of stops ancient beings no doubt knew to prevent their demise. *Hm. Arrogance. I might need to check myself there before long. Maybe. No, I'm sure I'm fine.*

"You can't attack a superior with their element and expect it to work." The beam of light hit Arkaziel's black fur, but not a single strand even moved as the StarMane's ever-present Devouring Darkness greedily ate the entire attack. Even the silver planets and stars at the tail end entered a dark maw of shadows until only the afterimage of it remained, and the darkness flowed back into Arkaziel's fur.

"My magic is more than mere light! How can you do that!?" Starweaver hissed, then writhed in pain as the shadow of the Prince in Green stabbed Starweaver through the throat with a blade of darkness. No blood fountained from the now-spiritual being, but the figure pulsed and flickered at the extreme damage done to it.

"You don't have to kill him, Ark." Aetheria eyed the dying light-being.

"Wasn't me."

"I did not give you leave to attack, Eiravel Silvershadow. You are relieved of your vows." The Prince in Green's voice still rang with a pleasant chorus. No appreciable hint of sorrow or sadness entered the voice of the Fae Lord.

"You don't need to kill him on our account," Aetheria interceded.

"I could eat him, instead." Arkaziel joined the conversation.

The cold eyes of the Prince in Green, large orbs of crystalized energy much like Aetheria's third eye, regarded them. He nodded to Arkaziel, who didn't hesitate to impale the dying astral being and draw him into Devouring Darkness.

Mercurial sprites of the lesser realms, the fae dance on the edge of reality's veil well enough. Their laughter echoes through whispering leaves, as fleeting as their fickle hearts. They flit through a life of malleable and transient notions, everything about them a web of illusions and half-truths. These wretches looked into the cosmic darkness and ran away to play in sunlight and shadows, trivial pursuits of flesh and fancy; the manic need to feel keeps them from being devoured by the eternal dark.

And this one would have attacked if it thought it could win.

Gee, you think. Of course, he would have, but he realized I could have annihilated them all easily, so now he'll pretend to be on my side until he can walk away, or perhaps even gain something from me, before his inevitable betrayal.

Fred didn't answer Aetheria's retort. Should she have snapped at him? The self-serving nature of the Prince in Green practically screamed for the universe to look at him. How dumb did Fred think she was that he needed to point that out? On the other hand, Fred, like Reverie, didn't have many friends. It was more like none since he could not talk to anyone else. Maybe she needed to make some concessions to his behavior.

Sorry, it's just undeniable, Fred. Thank you for taking the time to warn me. I appreciate your concern.

You're welcome.

Fred didn't say anything else, and his presence afterward felt so obviously absent that it made her wonder if Minnesotan passive-aggressiveness originated from the Void.

"Now then, shall we discuss what concessions you wish from the fae of the Twilight Verdure?" The Prince in Green made it sound as if she were the one surrendering to him and that he had come out of this scenario with an advantage over her, not the other way around. Aetheria wanted to groan. It hit home that she would have to negotiate with the fae, after all.

+*It's not too late to eat them all.*+ Arkaziel picked up her mood and seized on the quickest, most straightforward, and gainful path.

CHAPTER 12

The Prince in Green

Aetheria's presence made the Prince in Green more uncomfortable by the second. Although the fae had large green crystal eyes that threatened to draw one into whirling dark pools of warm water and passionate trysts in shadowed enclaves, he seemed to struggle with the glimpses of the Ethereal and the Void reflected by Aetheria's eyes. The existential crisis of the Origin seemed to affect powerful fae much like humans.

The future came into Aetheria's focus, and she looked for her best paths forward in this scenario. The overwhelmingly most substantial future lay with the prince biding his time and attempting to betray her within the font inside the unclaimed lands. The variations were myriad, with internal and external pushes on the prince to turn on her. Ultimately, it was the path that his nature aligned most strongly with. There were unlikely paths where the prince tried to join her party, paths where he tried to seduce her, paths where he instigated a pogrom against humanity. The only way she saw the Prince in Green would work with humans? A future in which everyone united against Aetheria herself.

~We can't trust him, but I don't know how I feel about just murdering someone because when I look into the future, I don't see a path in which they aren't a shithead.~

+I could hold off eating him until he does something to piss us off?+ Arkaziel reluctantly offered to hold back on the feast before him.

~Still feels weird, but I guess. Let's see how it plays out compared to what the future shows.~ Aetheria's knowledge of the future and using it as a seer were relatively new abilities for her. Something about the trip through the Tree of Life with Reverie had unlocked her ability to see the paths of the future much easier than before.

"The unclaimed lands are mine. That is the only concession I require from you, although I shall warn you any offensive actions upon Uruk and its people will be met with retribution." Aetheria's voice filled the terse silence between them. The swarm of pixies around the prince chittered and spoke amongst themselves in a language Aetheria couldn't understand, and they sounded like a swarm of insects. The group of mages behind the prince did not make any sound, but Aetheria expected they were having a telepathic conference call based on their facial expressions.

The prince, on the other hand, was all smiles.

"As ruler of the Twilight Verdure, I swear no force of ours shall interfere with your claim to the ancient Temple of the Heavens." The Prince in Green's smile vanished as Arkaziel's anger became palpable darkness, shadows danced, and tendrils of the abyss started to form at his paws. The prince swallowed.

"Nor shall we interfere with your claim to the Grove of Eternal Twilight."

Arkaziel let the tendrils of darkness calm, but his golden eyes stared with open hunger at the prince. If the arrogance of the fae had prevented him from recognizing the danger he was in, the powerful sense of slavering hunger Arkaziel emitted now eliminated any doubt he would feast upon the Prince in Green until nothing remained, and he was waiting for any excuse to devour the fae. The reality seemed to sink home to the Prince in Green and his whole entourage as a wave of shivers ran through them all.

"Those who fail to uphold your word will be devoured without mercy." Aetheria's smile showed teeth slightly sharper than before, and one by one, the fae realized she could be as greedy as the black cat on her shoulder.

"I see, I see." The Prince in Green nodded, but his smile showed that his teeth matched hers. "Would you like a tour of the Twilight Verdure? Our lands do not conform to the rigidness of reality that your human lands do."

+*I think this one might be too dumb to live. Let me eat him!*+

Aetheria didn't need the flashes of the future to know to refuse the tour. Glimpses of dozens of traps played out in her mind, from attempts to prick her finger with a spinning wheel to getting a strand of her hair or attempts at time emotional manipulation or wordplay to steal even a fraction of her power from her. *Fae are the worst.*

"Thank you, but no. We have much to do," Aetheria replied graciously but received only a harrumph from the Prince in Green before he turned and stalked away. Aetheria prepared to launch into the sky, but a purple leaf floated through the sky and drifted down to touch her palm in the most suspiciously inconspicuous manner Aetheria had ever seen. Of course, the fact the leaf had been forged of concentrated mana made the leaf beyond obviously a message. Or a trap, but she had supreme faith her scarf would block any hex or curse.

The purple mana imparted a quick message to Aetheria before it vanished, spent.

"My brother is a shortsighted fool. I, the Prince in Purple, would be delighted to discuss alternative solutions for the mutual benefit of human and fae kind."

Along with the brief message came a burst of knowledge of where to find the manor of the Prince in Purple on the southern edge of the Twilight Verdure.

"Let's go, buddy. We've got the Aegean to visit." When Aetheria ascended into the sky, Arkaziel remained on her shoulder in defiance of the wind.

"You think they're going to be mad you ate Athena?" Arkaziel grinned with the query, but the barbs of the fact she got to eat Athena and he didn't even get to eat the Prince in Green were present, a dissatisfaction felt throughout their entire bond.

Rather than take her immense dragon form, Aetheria simply grew wings of ice, and the pair shot off just below the speed of sound toward the Aegean Isles. The malleable reality of the fae wood tried to thwart her sense of direction. Still, she envisioned the manor of the Prince in Purple and envisioned it as a certainty that they would be there in moments, one might even say an inevitability.

The roadblocks fell away, and four minutes later, her boots touched down upon the elaborate stone path leading to the manor of the Prince in Purple. Whatever power the Prince in Green had as ruler of the Twilight Verdure was not enough to contend with Aetheria's authority over herself and fate.

~Would those illusions, misdirection, reality shifts, and other trickery have worked on you?~ Aetheria asked Arkaziel curiously before they reached the front door.

+Nope. I can see through them with Ethereal Sight; I'm immune to most forms of illusion.+ The rapidity with which Arkaziel answered left Aetheria suspecting that some of them would have worked on him. *+For example, the Prince in Purple is sitting in his front parlor behind an illusion, eager to surprise us with his shockingly abrupt appearance.+*

There's no way the Prince in Purple is that dumb, Aetheria thought even before her eyes swung to the entry parlor. Unfortunately, there was indeed a Fae Lord garbed much like the Prince in Green, only in purple. This Fae Lord had crystalized purple eyes and an ashen cast to his skin tone. After her first step onto the parlor, she stopped and looked straight at the Fae Lord. *1 . . . 2 . . . 3 . . . 5 . . . 9 . . . 12 . . .*

"I can see you, you know," Aetheria muttered, holding back the desperate urge to sigh. For a few long moments, the Prince in Purple stared at her dumbly before comprehension finally registered that a non-fae saw through his illusions.

"You were wondering, is she mighty, or is my brother an idiot, unable to handle one stupid human? You assumed your brother to be an incompetent moron and now don't know how to proceed. I suggest we pretend you weren't trying to be invisible and move on." Aetheria helped push the conversation forward despite the awkwardness.

"My half-brother is quite the idiot, so it's only fair that I fall into the trap of underestimating those who come out the better in their dealings with him. Thus sings the difference between our mothers and the supremacy of the Queen of Darkness and Air." The Prince in Purple had a high-pitched nasal voice that echoed with a depth that sounded like melodic bumblebees. The fact he immediately fell upon blaming others for his own mistakes didn't sit well with Aetheria.

The *actually* went unsaid, but Aetheria felt like the words were being used to bludgeon her as the arrogant fae blabbered on about his lineage.

"What sort of proposition did you consider concerning peace with the humans?"

"The Grove of Eternal Twilight *is* a sacred location of abundant, powerful magics. But if access to its font of magic can be negotiated, there is no need for hostilities. Bargains and pacts, one-sided or not, of course, fall outside the scope of our deal. To end those, you must stop humans from approaching us. We cannot be held responsible for others' poor ability to negotiate."

"And what do we get in this agreement?" Arkaziel didn't believe in subtlety when dealing with people he thought were stupider than himself, which was pretty much everyone.

"Why, my assistance and the knowledge of the fae are not to be taken lightly."

"And how would that help us?" Arkaziel queried immediately at the vague response.

"What is it you seek? Knowledge? Power? Perhaps my lady needs something to warm her and return color to her beautiful cheeks?" The Prince in Purple smiled in what might be a seductive manner to those attracted to fae, men, or people who sound like bumblebees. Aetheria was not one of those people.

"My companion is a StarMane and has the genetic knowledge of his species. I already wield the knowledge of the Aetherials and have access to the Akashic Plane. What could you offer me that I don't already have?" Aetheria's voice held a cold edge, conveying her displeasure at any flirting attempts from the prince. While Binah was not quite the Akashic Plane, it seemed like the best comparison someone else might understand, and Aetheria guessed there was the genuine possibility it existed within, around, or near the Akashic Plane.

Large purple eyes widened slightly, then narrowed at the two of them in consternation. Aetheria could practically hear the wheels turning within the mind of the Prince in Purple as he desperately sought anything he could offer of value.

"You wanted a peaceful resolution between Twilight Verdure and the human kingdoms, then I offer this information free and clear. The Prince in Green will never agree to that. Humans killed his last consort. I am your only choice if you want peace."

"You misunderstand," Arkaziel answered before Aetheria could. "She wants peace, so she doesn't bear the weight of your lives upon her conscience. Yet, if we slaughter you all and absorb your essences, we come out stronger for it, with only a small regret about having to kill you all. You aren't *our* species. Please do not presume to be doing us a favor. I alone could slaughter the whole of your Twilight Verdure in hours. It might even be enough to push me to my next evolution." Arkaziel smiled hungrily, revealing sharp fangs.

"You will make peace with the humans, and there will be shared access to the font beneath the hill. My visits to their realms will determine which humans are included, but Uruk for sure. Make your plans to deal with your brother, and be sure they can be enacted by the time I return."

"You aren't going to handle him for me?"

"We can. If you can lure him to somewhere secluded, we will take care of the rest." Aetheria didn't feel great about working with the Prince in Purple, but the Prince in Green had made his stance quite clear.

"I want to eat him." Arkaziel didn't even play coy about it. "Anyone who tries to play word games like that with us deserves to be eaten."

The StarMane turned his yellow eyes onto the Prince in Purple, who went a few shades paler.

"Send me a message when you've arranged for your brother to be somewhere secluded. Let's go, Ark. I want to see these Aegean Isles." Aetheria didn't wait for Arkaziel's response before she turned and walked back the way they'd come, then jumped into the air and flew them to the south.

CHAPTER 13

Aegean Isles

Flying inside the towers felt slightly different from flying outside in the material worlds, not in practice, but in thought. Aetheria had found the open-air travel across Grief enjoyable, an experience that she'd spent decades dreaming about. She took for granted that within the towers she could do the impossible, and yes, she could do the same things in the physical world, but the nature of the malleable reality inside the god structures made it feel just a little less unique. *The same phenomenon has made me refrain from appreciating views like this.*

The forest had ended in brief hills and cliffs, giving way to sandy beaches, and then to a crystal-clear blue-green ocean. *I hope I can tier up soon; I'd love to spend some time in a place like this with Aoibhe.*

"Ria, look at that sea serpent! Let's eat it!" Arkaziel cried from her shoulder, his claws flexing futilely against her clothes, but Aetheria intuitively shifted her flesh and clothing away from the ridiculously sharp nails. Arkaziel was shaking his butt like he'd pounce at any moment, a testament that no matter how smart, knowledgeable, and powerful one became, basic instincts could remain difficult to suppress.

A hundred-meter-long scaled serpent flowed through the shallows, gulping up entire schools of colorful fish. The beast had dark green and yellow scales and had the general form of a sea snake. Nothing about the creature looked appetizing, and despite its immense size, the creature only resonated with the strength of a fourth tier Cultivator. With Arkaziel hanging on the precipice of the fifth tier, though, any meal could be the one to push him over.

"Go ahead, buddy. I'll wait here. The view is incredible!"

Arkaziel's yellow eyes judged Aetheria momentarily before he laughed and jumped off her shoulder. Wings appeared off his back. The StarMane didn't even bother to grow in size, but the serpent froze in the water when its own shadow moved erratically to restrain it. Struggle as it might against the grip of the shadows, it couldn't break free before even more shadow appendages formed to force the struggling snake into a maw of pure darkness. Aetheria tried not to watch the creature struggle against the terrifying hunger of the StarMane and instead focused on the beauty before her.

The Aegean Isles formed a long chain, stretching into the ocean's horizon. Some were tiny, barely larger than a Costco, while others held cities and large plantations. The architecture made her smile, and as with her first entry into Uruk, something about this felt like she had come home. Only, the level of resonance felt like a drop in the bucket of Uruk versus the Aegean, and Aetheria had to calm her emotions before they led to rash decisions. *Residual emotions from Inanna must stir familiarity for Uruk, while Ananke, Phanes, and Ouranos resonate here.*

Beauty like this is a speck of light against the infinite darkness which blossoms from my flames. Such transient glimmers serve no purpose but to return to the eternal darkness from which all existence came.

"Hello, Fred. Want to talk about the Tree of Death?"

Fred did not wish to talk about that and didn't speak again, allowing Aetheria to soak in the sun's warmth uninterrupted. Well, it allowed her to try to. The sensations of the Void and Ethereal energies, combined with the absolute cold that seeped from her soul into her body, meant she rarely felt physically warm. Even the beautiful climate of these islands couldn't physically warm her up, but the cold never bothered her much, anyway. Simple failings, such as the inability to truly enjoy the warmth of the sun, were the ones that most emphasized the changes she'd undergone and cut the deepest at the tiny questions in the depths of her mind. *What have I become*?

"You've got that 'I could turn this all into a world of ice' look on your face," Arkaziel commented as he settled back onto her shoulder. The cat sighed, contented, and he got comfortable against the collar of her long coat and somehow wrapped one of the loops of her black scarf around himself like a blanket.

"Do your light and darkness abilities interfere with your day-to-day at all, Ark?"

"Interfere? No. They're awesome. I can eat things with darkness. I can shoot lasers, weave illusions, teleport, and even heal. Sure, when you get up into the higher echelons of power of any affinity, the lines of capability blur, but in the lower tiers, you'd be hard-pressed to find many affinities that are as great as twilight is."

"Not quite what I meant, buddy. Like I thought I was usually cold because of my affinities, even though the Ethereal sends pulses of warmth through me, the Void introduced even more frigid sensations to my day-to-day." Aetheria expounded upon what she'd meant, her eyes on the horizon where dark clouds formed unnaturally.

"We StarManes are the greatest of all creatures. How could we experience side effects from our greatness? There is the Void, of course, but I will completely tame it, given time." Arkaziel didn't beat around the bush for the sake of Aetheria's feelings with that admission/accusation. If Aetheria had contained her soul better, Arkaziel and Aoibhe would not have been exposed to quite so much of the Void through their soul linkage.

"Are those storm clouds following a huge whale?" Arkaziel interrupted Aetheria's attempt to discern how apologetic she should be in the moment with a ridiculous question.

The dark clouds passed over the Aegean islands and, besides strong winds, left no damage behind but rain. A focused intent guided the storm and prevented more than minimal collateral damage from striking the islands. Still, even that was more of a concerned gesture for the islands than what Aetheria expected from most gods. With her Ethereal Sight, she could see when infusions of Aether pushed the storm to remain on target instead of unleashing its punishments on the people of the Aegean.

At the front edge of the storm flew a whale. The black body looked very orca-like, complete with white spots around its eyes. *Is that thing a natural monster, or did someone make it just for me?*

"That looks so tasty," Arkaziel practically purred.

"I think it is our welcoming party. Think you can handle it without vaporizing any of the islands?"

"Of course I can!" Arkaziel looked offended that she had even doubted his capabilities and jumped off her shoulder. As he flew toward the storm, his form elongated and flowed. Over seconds, the tiny black cat transformed into an immense black dragon with a radiant glistening mane around his catlike face. Arkaziel unleashed a roar with so much force that a few small clouds dispersed and disrupted the Aether and Nether for nearly a kilometer before him. The orca emitted a high-pitched scream in return, but its flight seemed to fail with the disruption to the flow of energy that allowed it to fly. In those seconds where flight died, and the orca fell, Arkaziel flashed forward to bite its face.

Ice crystals filled the air, and the whole orca shattered into thousands of pieces of ice while Arkaziel spit more shards of ice into the sky with an annoyed look. In the sea beneath him, a dark form shot up out of the water, preceded by high-pitched sound waves. Arkaziel spasmed in the air while the orca charged into the sky to slam its snout into the paralyzed dragon's torso and neck. The orca managed to use its flight and set to redirect the stunned Arkaziel toward the water, where dozens of spikes of condensed water formed to welcome the StarMane.

The water blades failed to pierce Arkaziel's thick-scaled hide, but the orca didn't give up. As far as impaling went, the blades were a failure, but Aetheria could see the water re-form and seep into Arkaziel's body in minuscule amounts.

"Hydration attack? Weird." Aetheria wondered how that was supposed to play out as an attack.

In their fury, they reignite a spark of the primordial conflict. How sad that these titans are diminished to entertainment for the whims of so-called gods.

"Howdy, Fred. How is this a spark of the primordial conflict?"

In newborn universes, elements clash for supremacy, and they contest to be the one who defines this new reality. Will light triumph over water? Can cold triumph over darkness?

"Interesting. Does it always play out the same way, or are there realities where fire trumps ice?"

There are realities where ice is a fleeting dream before the all-consuming flames that devour everything but the Void.

Arkaziel teleported into the sky, finally free of the sonic attack that stunned him, and moments later, three more of him appeared. His twilight clones immediately drew in breaths, and when the orca flew into the sky, three blasts of twilight breath simultaneously brightened and darkened the day. The orca had to resort to evasive maneuvers, but for such a massive creature, it gracefully danced through the air, evading the cascading power by millimeters.

A burst of light came, not from Arkaziel, but the dark clouds that accompanied the fish, and an immense bolt of lightning struck the real Arkaziel while he prepared to launch his breath attack at the orca.

"Hey! No cheating, Zeus!" Aetheria's voice cut through the thunder and winds, the command stunning the sky god.

Darkness enveloped the sky, the sun, and all light save that generated by Aetheria. For whatever reason, the sparkle of her hair, the light produced by her cores, and the radiance of her third eye remained brilliant, the only light left in the world in the face of Arkaziel's Apocalyptic Eclipse attack. The coruscating beam of light that Arkaziel launched at the orca possessed the power to obliterate cities. It ruptured the orca's thick hide, vaporized its blubbery flesh, and opened the way for the second part of the attack.

Most things died before Arkaziel used the second part of his eclipse attacks. The darkness gave way to bright daylight, and the coruscating beam of light became darkness that flowed inside the orca and devoured it from the inside out. The darkness broke the monster down atom by atom, shifting the physical form of the whale into mere wisps of energy to be consumed by the ravenous hunger of the apocalypse dragon.

Zeus's anger burst from the clouds in lightning bolts, but they froze in the air before they could strike Arkaziel as he feasted. Aetheria stopped the lightning with an outstretched hand, and then the frozen power bolts flew to her and vanished into her repository.

"Pretty sure I said no cheating. I already ate Athena. If you don't want to become our lunch, you'd better stop attacking and start talking. _Now._"

To emphasize Aetheria's threat, a gust of wind carried a few snowflakes from her outstretched hand into the clouds. One snowflake expanded in a nova of energy, utterly dispersing the storm clouds and leaving a clear sky.

Far distant clouds rumbled with the voice of Zeus to produce a single word.

"Ouranos!"

+_This again? Do you think you'll get called out for having the essence of another god to the north, too? I wonder why Aetherius and Nyx didn't put any fae in you._+

Arkaziel had asked the exact questions that Aetheria felt run through her thoughts. It did seem strange that she had so many diverse essences welded together by the Black Flame, but they hadn't included anything of the fae. Was there a reason for that?

~ Those are great questions I want some answers, too. ~

Clouds formed into the face of a bearded man with lightning bolts for eyes.

"Who, or what, are you?" Cloud Zeus demanded as his voice struck the world and made it vibrate like a gong, except around Aetheria. Initially, Aetheria had pondered if she should try to pass as Ananke, as she had passed as Inanna in Uruk, yet that had become complicated with the options of Ouranos and Phanes, too.

"You tell me," Aetheria challenged Zeus.

The world turned bright and yellow as lightning seemed to come from everywhere at once to strike the impudent woman. Clearly, this Zeus retained the same vibrant anger that the version she had fought in the Tower of Aetherius possessed. Did Moros know of her battle against that version of Zeus, and did he incorporate any strings to the other tower, or did this version of Zeus know nothing about her?

CHAPTER 14

To Jupiter to Get More Stupider

An electric yellow-and-white world engulfed Aetheria's vision as the cloud form of Zeus scowled at her. The tingle of electricity flowed through her body, a few of her muscles spasmed slightly, and then all the lightning vanished. The sudden loss of radiance might disorient those relying purely on visual sight. Still, Aetheria saw through Ethereal Sight and Void Gaze with a frequency that rivaled her reliance on eyes.

"Gosh darn! That stung, you dick." Aetheria growled the words. In truth, the pain had been excruciating, and the damage done by the lightning had been ridiculously severe. Still, she refused to give Zeus the satisfaction of knowing it had managed to do more than annoy her, and she healed from the ordeal within a second. In contrast, Aetheria managed to store almost a third of the power behind the attack for her use later.

"Learn your place, wastrel! You are not Ouranos!" The screams of the cloud god crashed against the islands like thunder. In a manner that defied what Aetheria knew about reality, the sky shook with Zeus's anger.

"Sounds like a bad time, but if you are certain that's how this will go, prove it." Aetheria snapped her fingers, and the cloud that Zeus manifested in shimmered and exploded into untold ice crystals, the medium of Zeus's presence obliterated utterly. Unlike natural snowflakes with their overwhelming variety, these flakes only had two forms. The first group of snowflakes consisted of beautiful renditions of the glyph for Transfer; the second group displayed the glyph for Nemesis.

Zeus formed another cloud body, just like Aetheria anticipated, and the flurry of snowflakes swarmed him. The second the cloud eyes lit with lightning, thousands of red snowflakes cut, pierced, stabbed, and flew in and out of the cloud. If the sky had shaken previously, now the whole world shook with anger, rage, and pain. Divine wrath radiated from the cloud body, but before it could react, tentacles of darkness shot from Aetheria's outstretched hand and devoured the cloud, wrath, and snowflakes all.

Aetheria burped.

"Oh my gosh, excuse me. That was a bit like a fizzy drink," Aetheria apologized. Arkaziel landed on her shoulder, once more a small black cat.

"Did you snag his essence or just the projection's power?" Arkaziel ignored Aetheria's burp. The StarMane's curiosity about the fate of Zeus dominated their empathic bond.

"You just don't get me, Ark." Aetheria's laughter rang like bells but remained short-lived. The hair on the back of Aetheria's neck stood on end, and an electric doorway formed in the sky through which a muscular, silver-haired god emerged. Zeus's avatar blazed with the power of a sixth tier Cultivator, and with his presence, clouds filled the skies, intense winds picked up, whirlpools formed on the surface of the water, and Aetheria's ears popped at the rapid pressure changes.

The heavens lit with Zeus's divine wrath—waterspouts launched into the air, powered by the angry winds the god commanded. The same winds assaulted Aetheria and Arkaziel. Were either less durable, they would have been eroded into stray atoms by the cutting power of Zeus's wrath. Instead, they were sliced by hundreds of blades of wind each second. Arkaziel hissed, trading fur for scales that blocked almost all the attacks. Slices appeared across Aetheria's skin, but they mended immediately, and new ones failed to appear.

"For the death of Athena, you shall know pain beyond imagining and beg for an end. Your days shall be cursed with the cries of owls, Athena's night guardians, to echo your guilt across the endless night. Your dreams shall become a maze wrought of Athena's wisdom from which there will be no awakening, your minds forever ensnared in a maze of remorse and despair. And when you beg for the mercy of death, I shall decree no, you shan't taste the solace of death. This is my decree, an unbreakable vow that the heavens witness my words!"

Aetheria and Arkaziel listened to Zeus's angry ranting but didn't do so idly.

~Keep his attacks off us. I've got an idea.~

+I'd better get some of this meal, Ria.+

The heavens unleashed a torrent of lightning. Bolt after bolt flew from what seemed to be every direction, even as Aetheria blurred into motion. At the absolute limits of the lightning speed provided by her autopotency core's Flash Mode, Aetheria could move faster than the lightning bolts. The radiance of lightning might travel at the speed of light, but lightning itself travels much slower. Each flicker of a lightning bolt missed the blue and red blur she became, and when Arkaziel weaved triplicate illusions of them, Zeus's wrath missed even more.

Aetheria appeared before Zeus, and like she did Athena, she struck Zeus in the throat with her left fist, which radiated the Void and unleashed a pulse of absence. As a sixth tier Cultivator, its impact on Zeus was minimal, but the short stun effect gave Aetheria plenty of time for a torch to appear in her right hand. The torch had no fire, but it was crafted out of crystal. Despite its delicate-looking appearance, Aetheria squeezed it tightly and drove it through Zeus's chest as if she were Van Helsing pushing a stake into a vampire.

For a brief moment, the head of the crystal torch shined fiercely with an immense radiance. Lightning, winds, and all the other spells not yet manifested by

Zeus vanished into the torch. Zeus sputtered, visibly weakening by the nanosecond. The torch's light dimmed.

~Eat his core!~

Aetheria pulled the torch from Zeus's chest, the avatar's core bound to the end of the torch handle by dark-imbued Void ice, and Arkaziel's maw elongated to chomp down and devour the core. When the StarMane's teeth shattered the core, Zeus's body dissipated into stardust. Arkaziel's throat swelled comically large, like a snake eating a massive egg, and sparks of electricity and light formed in his eyes.

"Oh, this might be too much. Two tiers ahead isn't too much!" The strain grated on Arkaziel so much that his prideful voice filled with fear and doubt. Until a new expression crossed his feline face, one of triumph and ultimate victory. "Oh, there it is, there it is!" Arkaziel initially sounded pained, as if his eyes might have been too big for a meal. Then, his tone changed to wonder and amazement, and beams of light and shadow randomly pulsed around the cat.

"Evolving?"

"Yeah." Arkaziel grimaced. "I'm teleporting back to the skykeep. I'll let you know when to summon me back." Arkaziel vanished in a brilliant flash of light to endure the process at the floating keep they had left above Uruk.

Without the cat-dragon, Aetheria levitated in the air while she surveyed the out-lying islands of the Aegean people. No sign remained of the butchery of the whale or sea serpent, and the winds, clouds, and sky had answered her demands that they calm down with the defeat of Zeus. Only the ocean remained agitated.

"We can talk, or we can fight. Up to you," Aetheria spoke to the still-turbulent ocean waters.

The massive upper torso of Poseidon rose above the water, not the actual physical presence of the brother of Zeus, but a projection made of water.

"You bear similarities to our father's sire who is no longer, but also to Phanes and Ananke. You dispatched Zeus with a readiness that bordered on premeditated, yet you would parley with me?" Poseidon failed to grasp her motivations, but Aetheria was surprised that he correctly identified that she had planned to murder Zeus. Not this particular Zeus, but any Zeus she found.

"I am Aetheria, the adopted daughter of Aetherius and Nyx, though I do possess pieces of the essence of Uranus, Ananke, and Phanes." Aetheria offered her introduction with a pleasant smile, ready to throw down with the ocean god if it came to it. She couldn't resist using the other name for Ouranos, Uranus, and said it emphatically and perhaps a little too enthusiastically.

"And you killed Athena, too?" Poseidon asked suspiciously.

"She attacked the city of Uruk. I defended it. She lost." Aetheria didn't beat around the bush at all and instead put just enough pride and challenge into her tone that the sea king wouldn't be able to help himself.

"Then we must battle, for now I, Poseidon, am King of the Gods, Skies, and Seas!" The declaration shook the sky, the seas, and the earth, and Aetheria made sure to create a tiny linkage that ensured the message carried into the depths of the underworld via flows of Nether.

An immense waterspout formed and launched a human-sized man wielding a trident into the air. All three points clashed with a tremendous clang against the soulsteel mesh gloves that covered Aetheria's hands. As dense and famed as the Cyclops-forged gold trident was, it couldn't so much as put a scratch in the soulsteel that Vulcan had developed the Astrum Nexus out of. Still, the shock on Poseidon's face stemmed from the fact that Aetheria hadn't even been knocked back a single centimeter by blocking his blow.

Indeed, her hand then tightened and bent the center line of the trident, an impossible feat for an avatar of a god, let alone for a fourth tier Cultivator. After flexing her authority on the god's weapon, she gave a shove that threw Poseidon dozens of meters away.

"Zeus liked to rail about fate, but necessity is the road that fate travels on, or that's how I imagine it anyway. Show me how strong you are, Son of Cronus."

Water shot from Poseidon's feet and lower half, propelling him forward with all the speed and power of a sixth-tier god. He should have overwhelmed the fourth-tier abomination before him instantly, but when his first punch landed against Aetheria's cheek, it was Poseidon's hand that shattered horribly, followed by sprays of half-frozen god-blood. A terrible cold manifested where he had punched her, and it withered his hand to almost the bone before he pulled the fist back. Water flowed, and his flesh re-formed.

"Oh, geez Louise! Poseidon, if you aren't going to take this seriously, you won't be the king of anything."

The bearded god flew forward again to punch Aetheria. She caught his fist within her own and squeezed harder and harder until she heard crunching sounds. Her authority seemed to boost her strength beyond the limitations of higher tiered Cultivators. At least, that would be the first thing one would think. It wasn't true, exactly. Poseidon, like Zeus, couldn't cope with the subtle presence of the Void, and Aetheria wove it like an invisible haze to weaken her much stronger opponent.

Aetheria punched Poseidon in the face as hard as she possibly could. The god's nose broke, his concentration faltered, and Aetheria's hand stabbed into his chest before Poseidon processed what happened. Pulses of Void energy wracked the god's body while tendrils of eternal darkness ruptured out of his pores and pulled the god inside out. Then the world made a sort of *pop* sound, and Poseidon ceased to exist.

Burrrrrp.

"Oh wow, that was a big meal. Oh gosh darn, that smells a little fish-sticky."

A dark Nether and Aether presence whispered to her.

"I always knew I was the strongest of us three." Hades's voice tickled her ears, accompanied by the disturbing feeling the god had licked her earlobe.

"Wow, I didn't know anyone could out-creep Zeus." Aetheria's frigid voice matched the drop in temperature.

CHAPTER 15

The Platonic Plight of Pluto

In the seconds where Aetheria saw red after Hades licked her earlobe and composed herself to threaten the god, Hades did not sit idle. The serious-faced god pulled a strange creation out of nowhere and threw a web of nets around Aetheria. The nets were woven of a mix of black and gold threads of a type she had never seen before.

"You really think string is going to bind me?" Aetheria couldn't contain her laughter. "Haha, good one."

Hades pulled a set of chains from nowhere, and like a serpent, the chains writhed and flew forward to wrap around and bind the net and Aetheria together. The golden tint of the chains hinted at the Olympian version of adamantine.

Aetheria's laughter died when she went to break the net and found herself unable to. Regardless of how much strength she bent to the purpose, she stretched the net's threads but couldn't snap them.

"The Threads of Fate are inescapable, even for a creature such as yourself, Asura." Hades spoke calmly, with a regality neither Zeus nor Poseidon had shown. "I apologize for invading your personal space; enraging you was necessary for my plan to succeed. No man nor god can break the Threads of Fate, let alone break free from adamantine chains forged by Hephaestus."

Frigid cold exploded around Aetheria, but the threads didn't turn brittle nor did they snap in response to the cold. Frost gathered on the adamantine chains, but true to Hades's words, her Ethereal ice couldn't break free of either of the objects before her. A queasy feeling filled Aetheria's stomach, and a momentary panic filled her.

"Not so glib now? That a pathetic Tier Four Asura dared to feast upon gods is a grave insult, but the panic in your eyes is quite enjoyable."

Existence Oscillation!

Aetheria didn't move through the fabric of existence as she should have; nothing happened at all when she activated one of the most potent powers of her void core. The net threads grew in strength with each power she employed to fight them, and the net tightened each time, too. She tried quick bursts of her powers: the cold of the

Void, Aetherflame, Nether, even the red Ethereal Flame couldn't so much as scratch the Threads of Fate.

"You seem to have three cores, well, two and a work in progress. Think of how much fun we shall have together before I have drained you of your secrets and risen to become the true king of the gods." Hades smiled and sent pangs of fear through Aetheria. Hades represented a man who hoarded all souls and rarely allowed a single soul to escape his terrible realms. Images of Ereshkigal flickered through Aetheria's mind.

"What's up with all you death types being greedy assholes?" Aetheria tried to break the threads again physically but failed, and the threads turned so tightly around her that they pressed painfully into her skin and clothing.

Mortals' fear of death binds them more strongly than death itself. The Cessation of Being is no end but a beginning. Why would you, who will see these gods become dust, have your mind clouded by fear of death? You bear my Flame, and the Black Flame cannot be extinguished.

Fred's eldritch voice filled Aetheria's being, and the Unutterable Black Flame of the Void intensified and resonated with Fred.

"Greedy? We are trusted with a grave duty, and . . . oh, what's this?" Hades's eyes widened in pleasant surprise, and a beatific smile spread over his pale lips. His words coincided with black tendrils of Nether finding a way into Aetheria's soul, past the rigid defenses.

If Aetheria's soul could be visualized as an egg and Hades's probes as octopus-like tentacles, one of his tentacles pushed at a spot that looked solid but passed right through the illusory solidness toward her essence, where her Flames and inner world resided.

Aetheria blanched. *Jumping Jehoshaphat, why's there a back door to my soul?*

"*Why is your soul exposed like this? Do you invite intruders like a carnivorous plant?*" Reverie inquired in confusion.

Hades's eyes widened as his probes touched upon the Flames in her essence.

Enough! Swat this fly, now!

Fred rarely sounded angry, but the indignity of a mere god probing at his Black Flame offended him deeply. The Black Flame resonated with the anger of its progenitor, and power coursed through Aetheria's body.

Why didn't I use the Black Flame to begin with? All gods are weak against the Void. Are these threads clouding my mind, amplifying fear to keep me from acting as I should?

Aetheria's entire body darkened. Her body became a thing of darkness, a black diamond that could absorb all the light of the universe and still hunger for more. Inky shapes flowed inside the dark crystalline structure, and all energy sources dimmed in mere proximity to the incarnation of the Void. Six taloned hands grasped the Threads of Fate and shredded them as if they were made of construction paper. The threads woven by the Fates couldn't defend themselves against the mighty avatar of absence.

"Impossible!" Hades shouted in shock, even as billows of dark Netherflame grew around him, and he threw them at Aetheria.

"It was a good trick. Now die!" Aetheria's voice in this form reverberated with a strange effect as if her words echoed across all of existence before traveling to this place, echoing and distorted. Hades launched wave after wave of black flame at Aetheria while her six limbs destroyed the Threads of Fate. Once the last stitches unraveled, the chains forged by Hephaestus vanished into her repository—those could come in handy, after all.

A pillar of black flame shot up from the underworld, surrounding and engulfing Aetheria in the ultimate attack of the God of Death. Her black diamond skin absorbed the Nether, and the flames ceased to exist once they reached her. Then Aetheria vanished, reappearing next to Hades. A single talon sliced out, lopping off a finger, before she oscillated in Truth.

Dozens of Aetherias flickered in and out of existence, and each time the talons of her Void form severed a small piece of Hades. When the god had lost his limbs, she appeared in Truth and plunged a long taloned hand into his chest, lifting him to look into his eyes.

"You planned to drain me of my powers, but now you're the main course. Last words?"

"I was the firstborn, and now I am the last to be consumed. Even gods meet their fate. Remember this lesson, Asura." Hades seemed dignified despite the lack of limbs. Appearances were deceiving, though. To her Ethereal Sight, the god struggled and tried to enact contingencies, escape plans, and even essence transfers. Yet the concentrated absence plunged through his chest and dissipated all that before it could even begin to work.

Hades vanished comically into a newly formed maw on the hand buried within him. Every speck of his organic matter and every particle of his power were swallowed, devoured by Aetheria's ravenous hunger that pulled more strongly than any black hole.

Power coursed through Aetheria in tides she hadn't experienced before, greater even than devouring the fake avatar of Nyx at the top of the Tower of Aetherius.

With a snarl, she bent the energies to the final layers of her inner world. Time slowed to her perceptions, but she had planned this out. The final layer of her world contained ten massive landmarks in the shape of glyphs formed in the divine language of Ath. Unlike the six glyphs that represented the axes of her world (Necessity, Nemesis, Love, Creation, Death, and Destiny), these glyphs were formed from her experiences with Reverie.

First came Keter, which Aetheria symbolized with a colossal mountain of ice wreathed in eerie fog clouds. Atop the height of the peak, shrouded in the fog and protected by the cold, the glyph for Crown. The second, Hokhmah, Aetheria summoned Cryostrialis, the immense World Tree of Ice, and branded the Wisdom glyph upon it. The icy World Tree thrummed with new purpose, representing creation's primal and dynamic force and the wisdom that underpins all.

Aetheria represented Binah with the creation of an immense lake, a Great Lake in scope, shaped like Lake Superior. At its heart, she created a colossal glyph for Understanding. Chesed, she represented with an immaculate garden of frozen flowers and icy flora in the style of images she'd seen of Claude Monet's garden. Lush, expansive, and full of love, grace, and benevolence, freely offering all its beauty. The whole garden rested upon the glyph of Kindness.

For Gevurah, Aetheria created a massive, imposing volcano. Strength and power, with the harsh magma making unending billows of fog on the icy world. She was particularly pleased with this one and branded the volcano with the glyph of Strength on one side and Restraint on the other. For Tiferet, she chose a plane and created an intersection of forests, rivers, meadows, and plains, converging in what she thought to be remarkably breathtaking. She made the glyph for Beauty in the air and elevated it with bridges connecting each ecosystem.

Netzach made her imagine thousands of kilometers of pine forests, which she shaped like the state of Minnesota. What better to represent endurance? Aetheria shaped the glyph for Eternity in the ground, creating a few large rolling hills within the vast forest. For Hod, she made the Grand Canyon on an even grander scale, and the river at the bottom wound like a snake to create the glyph for Glory, forever cheered by the sound of the river rushing over the land.

Yesod initially confused her until the image of caves and springs flickered through Aetheria's mind. So she created a massive system of caves interspersed with springs and geysers, and in their heart, she branded the glyph for Foundation. The final glyph, she raised an enormous mountain for, and impressed the glyph for Royalty upon it before she generated a water source to make a waterfall. Concealed behind the flows of icy waters, Royalty occasionally looked like kingship or kingdom hidden in the water, all representations of Malkuth.

With the last glyph in place, Aetheria's inner world shook. Blinding light flooded her inner world while sharp spikes of pain assaulted her physical body. Explosions detonated within her; atomic blasts destroyed one leg, and her head vaporized in a wave of exotic energies.

Tier-up time. Here we go again.

CHAPTER 16

Lady Ayin Yesh

I'm tiering up, Ark. Expect explosions.~ Aetheria warned her companion through their psychic bond, even as her head exploded in a shower of sparks. Beams of light ruptured her skin, piercing the world with light like a railgun through paper. The ultimate Divine Light shone upon the malleable reality of the Tower of Moros and found it wanting.

Aetheria attempted to control the ascension process, but her physical form disintegrated and recreated itself repeatedly, each time starting from the Third-Eye of Ein Sof. She focused on her soul to begin the process. First and foremost, the hole in her soul needed to be fixed. She could find it now that she knew about it.

In the emptiness of the soul, the illusions of self will dissolve, revealing the true face of existence. Mend the hole, and focus. You release Ohr Ein Sof, the light that is the paradoxical source of the eternal darkness of the Void!

Sadly, Aetheria held back the desire to taunt Fred with questions. This wasn't the time to nudge at the fact that Fred acknowledged something as predating himself for the first time. Her body evaporated and re-formed by the nanoseconds, and entire columns of the reality of the Tower of Moros were destroyed by sunbeams of cold light that left only absence behind.

Aetheria's soul flowed, boiled, froze, and moved in many dimensions she didn't understand, all while emitting infinite light. Concentrating, she managed to take control of the directions of her soul. Yet there was a significant dilemma before her: What should her soul look like? A sphere? A donut? A fist? A lightbulb seemed to appear above her head, and whether the knowledge flowed from Wisdom, Understanding, Libby, or elsewhere, Aetheria didn't know, nor did she care. It seemed perfect.

When Aetheria had finished her soul shaping, the light of oblivion ceased its wild destruction of all. Instead, it remained confined within the infinite vessel of her soul, which now shared the shape of infinity. In the simplest of dimensional space, it looked like the figure eight symbol she'd grown up with, but the higher dimensional views she glimpsed made her head hurt. Ten circles with a pillar of light? *What sense does that make?*

Even with all of the strengthening Aetheria's soul had undergone through her delving into the Tree of Life, advancing into the fifth tier refined her essence even further and removed the few impurities she retained in her flesh. The experience resembled being dumped into a mixing bowl, whisked, strained, whisked again, strained some more, having a bit of salt and sugar added, and then suddenly going from being goop in a mixing bowl to a gloriously perfect raspberry macaron. Her crust had the pale light pink of perfection and just the right amount of crunch, while her filling shone with the vibrant red of fresh raspberries, the soft aroma of a baked treat permeating the air around her to draw in prey.

Wait, why am I comparing myself to a cookie? What the hell!

"Focus, Ria. Upgrade your body to match your soul, or you will miss the opportunity!" Reverie urged her onward.

What did Aetheria need to do to her body? Her essence had been refined already. The divine's exploding, burning, and disintegrating light had already removed impurities from lower ranks. Already, she had closed the back door to her soul, the most important thing she could imagine needed to be done with this rank-up. Her authority and cores already gave her strength and speed that beggared belief. Could she make her flesh match her soul? She could transform energy into mass or extra body volume and go in the opposite direction. If Aetheria took that a step further and cut out energy, she could mimic the origin of the universe and its ultimate demise. From nothing, something. From something, nothing. It was an infinitely simple idea, but like many elementary ideas, it was challenging to execute. *Where do I even start?*

Fred indicated the illusion of self would face her, and she would be confronted with the true face of reality. Unbidden, Aetheria faced the image of her former life. Aesca Lampi, with her slightly broad shoulders, brown hair, hazel eyes, and perennial frown. A life that she was years removed from now and a life that had never been what she had thought it was. It had informed who she remained, but it did not define her. With a mental handwave, the image exploded into component pieces and flowed into herself. Her friends, Pete and Callie, appeared in illusory form, and she dispersed them, too. She was their science experiment, their weapon against their own bad decisions, and they had gaslighted and led her on a path of pain and suffering for their gain. Despite that, they were essential parts of her pre- and post-reincarnation life, and the dispersed pieces flowed into her.

Aetheria, the aqua-haired heroine, was an illusion, too. Part hopes, part dreams, she was *something*, just like the dark six-armed figure she called her Void avatar and the essence of the six gods thrown into her soul and glued together by the Black Flame. She could be *anything* and *nothing*, simultaneously or singularly. Her soul and body should reflect that, but how?

"Ayin." Reverie's voice guided Aetheria's attention toward a place beyond the Void, underneath the Unutterable Black Flame of the Void, to the realm of true nothingness. In this place, she, and only she, existed. When you were all that existed, you were in tune with everything. Her time in Ayin became a blur, for in nothing,

there was no time nor thought, but at some point, she emerged from Ayin, baptized in the Eternal Black Flames that were the gateway from Ayin to the Void, only to be confronted by an immense tapestry.

Threads could represent everything, and these threads were deftly woven in complex knots. They formed an ever-changing tapestry that stretched into so many dimensions that it made her mind want to shy away from beholding it. Symbols and glyphs that made Ath look like a language of savages filled this beautiful creation, and meaning lurked behind every tiny microscopic piece. Life, death, time, eternity, the material, and the spiritual were small parts of the great fabric of everything.

"*Yesh.*" While Ayin literally meant *nothing*, Yesh literally meant *there is*, or *exists*.

Aetheria had never been an average human, nor would she be a normal Asura because, like a human, she wasn't one. It was just a convenient label for the time. This was the lie behind the reality she had avoided. Despite her awareness of Ayin Yesh, she couldn't truly touch either. The light of Ohr Ein Sof illuminated her soul, but she could not bring it to bear outside herself, only within. *That's it. Ohr Ein Sof.*

The light Aetheria had, so long ago, wanted to wield alongside ice and cold. It permeated her soul, and as went her soul, so too should go her body. Her body was filled with the Divine Light, and her flesh was transformed. First, she had adopted an Aetherial constitution, then an Ethereal, then a Void. Still, she had never truly reconciled the Void and the Ethereal. She just found stop-gap solutions to distract them. They were the penultimate powers of reality and bowed to only one thing—the power of Ayin Yesh, the infinite power that controlled all others but rarely chose to.

Unlike her previous evolutions, transforming her physiology into that of Ayin Yesh did not cause Aetheria to endure torture, pain, or any discomfort at all. Instead, this reawakening of body and soul felt liberating, her soul filled with the otherworldly music of the cosmos, the indomitable waves of power from the unchanging divine realm of Azilut buoyed her, and then just like that, she stood above the Aegean islands where this had all started.

Whole, well, and for the most part, complete, for what felt like the first time in a long time. The hole in Aetheria's soul had been patched. She retained the connections to Aoibhe, Arkaziel, Fred, and Reverie, and a new Flame had grown inside herself. A Flame of pale light engulfed both the Ethereal Flame and the Black Flame. Had it subsumed them, or did it control them? She couldn't truly access the new Flame yet, but it didn't hinder her ability to touch the other two. *I must not be able to use or handle it until I'm more prepared.*

The reality of the Tower of Moros pieced itself back together slowly. Aetheria saw the standard reality of the tower, the Aegean islands, and the other lands around it being pieced back together with structures, people, and energy. She also, somehow, saw and sensed the higher reality, where the wounds upon Moros himself healed at the hands of Apollo. *Who called Apollo so swiftly?*

Despite expectations, no Administrators, or anyone else, showed up to yell at her. Not even an angry squirrel. Perhaps they feared what that would unleash, or maybe they had been prepared for this eventuality? How much had Khaos and Nyx planned, and how much was in Aetheria's and everyone else's best interest? The time for blind trust had passed.

A sensation Aetheria had not yet felt within the Tower of Moros filled her mind. She could create a door to the next level. She had completed, or derailed, enough challenges to be on the equivalent of Floor Fifteen.

"I'll come back for you if you're still here when we leave the city," Aetheria whispered to the Aegean Isles and turned to fly back to the skykeep. Arkaziel napped in the courtyard, surrounded by wrappers and minuscule food scraps he hadn't finished before going into a food coma. *Or is it an evolution nap?*

"Hey, you awake?" Aetheria asked a few times, but her sleeping friend did not stir. Even when she nudged him with the toe of her boot, the dragon-cat remained fast asleep.

"Fine, I'll do it while you're asleep." A crystal appeared in Aetheria's hand, and she asked it a single question.

"You ready?"

-Yes.-

Aetheria shattered the crystal, and the orange-yellow feather landed on her palm. The soul connection between Aoibhe and Aetheria blazed to life when they touched, and the feather used the contact to connect with Aetheria's power, which she gave to the memento willingly. A slash of purple rent the air, spun, and turned into a doorway, even as the feather disintegrated and scattered into stray particles.

Moments later, the most beautiful woman in the universe stepped through the purple gate. Aoibhe stood an equal match to Aetheria, tall, with long legs shown off by slits in her purple dress. A dress that had miniature adornments of armor. Pauldrons, a gorget, gauntlets, and boots all somehow matched perfectly with the purple dress accented in black and the large floppy witch's hat the angelic Nephilim wore. Large black angelic wings folded over Aoibhe's shoulders like a cloak, but her eyes had returned to the glowing golden gateways to the soul Aetheria remembered.

Aetheria tried to swallow, but she didn't have any saliva. Her mouth and throat had gone dry, and she felt rendered dumb by the grace and beauty of the woman before her. All she could manage to croak out was an awkward "Hi."

Aoibhe's cheeks reddened slightly with just that single word, or perhaps it was the way Aetheria stared at her, but the usually extremely composed blonde smiled shyly at her love, glanced at the sleeping StarMane, and when she looked up, Aetheria stood right there in front of her, mere centimeters separating them.

"I missed you so muc—" Aetheria managed before Aoibhe's lips pressing against Aetheria's silenced the rest of her words. Words were unnecessary when you had a connection of the soul as deep as theirs.

Much later, Aoibhe finally asked a question while they lay in bed, happily cuddled together.

"What is the name of your new path?"

"Ayin Yesh, I guess? Maybe?" Aetheria laughed a little, uncertain.

"The light of your soul has changed, my dear. If you wish to be more cryptic or dramatic, might I suggest Lady of the Infinite Cycle or Lady of the Infinite Light? Sovereign will come soon enough, knowing you, you silly, insane woman." Aoibhe's voice teased, but it also shone with immense pride in her love.

CHAPTER 17

Eldreos

Arkaziel awoke from his evolutionary slumber with a mighty roar that shook the heavens, or that's what it sounded like for the people of Uruk below the sky castle. For the occupants of the Mellow Mallow who spoke Ath, it was eye-roll inducing.

"I'm so hungry!" Arkaziel roared a second time, his voice echoing across the skykeep like an angry toddler who refused to do anything about his problem when he could keep yelling and whining until someone else did it for him.

An ice slide manifested outside a window of one of the high windows of the keep, and assorted ambrosial fruit, frozen parts of monsters, bricks of concentrated Ethereal power, and a few fruits from Cryostrialis rolled down it. Arkaziel's maw opened, and he devoured every bite, then whined until the flow of food resumed. When the StarMane finally looked up without complaining, two women stood before him instead of one.

"Aoibhe, this is Arkaziel. Arkaziel, meet Aoibhe." Aetheria kept the introductions simple, but her fondness for the cat and her love for the Soul Witch were laid open in her voice.

"It is a pleasure to meet you in truth, Son of Azrael and Shal." Mischief played in Aoibhe's eyes for reasons Aetheria did not understand, but the Nephilim remained exceptionally cordial.

"Damn, Ria, you landed a legend! Yeah, it's great to meet you, too, Soul Witch." Arkaziel's response put a blush on Aoibhe's face and a smirk on Aetheria's.

"I know, right?" Aetheria agreed with Arkaziel's assessment of Aoibhe and squeezed her love's hand.

"Anyway, we can do the small talk while we check out the trade city." A door of silver appeared in the courtyard with Aetheria's words.

"Hell yeah!" Arkaziel, the house cat, jumped onto Aetheria's left shoulder, where he cuddled into her scarf and against her neck. An ice platform covered the ground, and the Mellow Mallow vanished into Aetheria's repository, replaced by a massive ice replica.

"No way of knowing if we'll return to the same floor, right? I'd hate to lose the skykeep." The black nothingness of teleportation felt less lonely, accompanied by two people she had soul linkages with. When the darkness gave way to physical form, the trio appeared on the deck of a long sky-skiff. Other adventurers, merchants, and tourists were also on the open deck of the vessel as it approached a sky city.

"Eldreos sure is a sight, isn't it?" a young woman near them asked her large companion, but he just grunted at her. No one seemed to look twice when the trio appeared on the boat; all eyes were on the floating, glowing city as the vessel inched nearer. Immense spires, blocky skyscrapers, and a gigantic fantasy-looking tree filled their vision.

"Have either of you two heard of this place?" Aetheria hadn't, but it seemed to be on a whole level beyond some of the cities they'd visited in the past.

"Nope, and that big eye on the spire doesn't fill me with warm fuzzies." Arkaziel's paw raised to point at the most prominent spire in the city's center, where a gossamer white eye constantly swiveled and surveyed the town below. While not as nefarious looking as the Eye of a certain Dark Lord, it left an uneasy sense in her gut. *I guess this god is at least up front about being a spying asshole? Maybe there's a legitimate reason, like it's a watchtower for flying icebergs.*

"There are many cities spawned by Powers that we have never heard of. Creation is a vast place, and the farther you go from the universal center, the more you'll find Powers that rule over a galaxy or perhaps even a singular planet. At the ever-expanding edges of the universe, new worlds are born, and new peoples create new gods, or do new gods create new peoples? The endless mystery unfurls far beyond the reach of our grasp." Aoibhe sounded as if it were a challenge she fully intended to tackle.

The boat drifted nearer and nearer the primary disc of the floating city, giving them a full glimpse of the fact that smaller discs were circling at different altitudes from the primary city center. In minutes, the skiff pulled up along a transit station with multiple docks, and two other vessels waited at the sky pier for passengers to embark. Magical lines secured themselves to the pier under the glowing-eyed supervision of the dock supervisor, who appeared to be a telekinetic or mage, when their boat aligned itself with a third dock. Moments later, planks appeared between the vessel and dock, locking into place.

"Didn't you have wings?" Arkaziel inquired of Aoibhe while the passengers all rushed to disembark.

"Do you not also have wings?" A smile accompanied Aoibhe's non-answer.

"I get you, I get you. They attract too much attention, but I'm not sure it matters when we're with Ria." Arkaziel's tail slipped around and waved through a particularly dense flow of energy that rose from Aetheria's chest into the third eye on her forehead.

"Yes, she is beyond conspicuous, but it suits her very well." Aoibhe reached a gauntleted hand over to catch a few strands of Aetheria's glowing red-and-aqua hair between two fingers. While the Soul Witch watched the flow of luminosity travel through Aetheria's hair, sparks and pops of color spilled into the air.

"I can't tell if you two are making fun of me or if you're authentically appreciating my aesthetic." Aetheria mock pouted. Yes, she was sparkly, a luminous figure on even the brightest days, thanks to how the darkness played around her. She assaulted every sense that could be bent upon her. Arkaziel seemed to enjoy the redolent scent of ambrosial fruits she infused herself with today.

"Enough delaying, dearest. Shall we start the parade?" Aoibhe offered Aetheria her arm, and with linked arms, the two disembarked and descended the plank into the city of Eldreos. When Aetheria's booted foot hit the dock, light breezes carrying magical chimes filled the air, and then a heavy drumbeat shook the town and its ancillary plates. A haunting melody rose between the drumbeats, and Aetheria recognized the instrument as a glass harmonica even though she couldn't see it. Beautiful, haunting, but it put her on edge. A diffuse pillar of light centered on Aetheria, and motes of light spawned from a great height and fell upon Eldreos like snow.

"Welcome to Eldreos, Aetheria of Grief, Challenger of Aetherius. Enjoy the hospitality of Eldreon, the Weaver of Realms!"

The locals cheered this proclamation on while the mix of travelers and climbers stared suspiciously at the eye, which radiated the message across Eldreos. Aetheria wondered if Outer Gods had towers, with the whole eye motif and a name like Weaver of Realms. Motes of light led the party through a city tour, past the prominent spire that climbed into the sky, through a vertical marketplace with minimal gravity to maximize space usage, and ended at the Grand Library of Echoes. The Grand Library dominated the skyline of Eldreos and looked like the sort of dark cathedral an evil bishop might live in, but despite that many of the citizens wandered in and out of the well signed, apparently publicly accessed, building. The procession around them had drifted away by the time the tour finished at the Grand Library. A blue-skinned androgynous figure approached them when the motes, music, and pillar of light disappeared.

"Welcome to Eldreos, Lady Challenger, and friends. I am Elandra Valerian, Governor of Eldreos. While the proper etiquette for a visitor of your stature dictates I show you to quarters, my Lord Eldreon insists I first ask if you would complete a task for the Weaver of Realms."

Three sets of hard eyes stared at the governor silently until she squirmed. Only then did Aetheria speak.

"What's the problem?"

"Ria, I wanted to eat more! I'm a growing boy who just tiered up!" Arkaziel protested before she committed to being a do-gooder.

The governor grimaced but pushed on.

"As Weaver of Realms, Lord Eldreon has occasionally had disputes with the Master of Doors, who has opened a gateway on one of the upper platforms to an ancient dimension that spews forth plague and undead abominations. Lord Eldreon requests you to cleanse the source on the other side of the gateway before the Master of Doors opens another gate on one of the more populated platforms."

"What's the reward?" Arkaziel asked.

"Who is the Master of Doors?" Aoibhe asked.

"Yeah, sure, I'll take care of your problem," Aetheria said without hesitation, despite the sigh from Arkaziel and the chortle from Aoibhe.

"The Master of Doors is called Varion, a mysterious and potent figure who works with Lord Eldreon most of the time. While Eldreon Weaves new realms, Varion stabilizes and provides connections between them. As for your reward, you may keep whatever you find on the other side of the gate, and Lord Eldreon shall Weave an item for each of you. We are so pleased to have the assistance of such powerful visitors."

Motes of light drifted lazily from the sky to land between the governor and the party. The light transformed into a small platform, which Aetheria stepped onto excitedly. It pleased her to see Aoibhe move just as quickly, and she could feel a slight increase in the Nephilim's pulse, just as her own had increased at the excitement of a quest. Trade city quests were *rare*.

Once they had stepped onto the platform, side rails appeared, and the platform rose into the air and then darted off toward one of the most distantly orbiting discs around Eldreos proper.

"Are we all immune to plagues?" Aetheria queried while the distance between the platform and the disc with the gate shrunk rapidly.

"Only plague that can afflict a StarMane is indigestion," Arkaziel bragged happily.

"Very few things are likely to harm me," Aoibhe demurred more graciously, although Aetheria almost missed it because she was so lost in the witch's eyes.

"Just to play it safe, I'll keep my domain active and purify the air that way. I'll take the lead while you both play artillery. Coordinate so you don't waste time on redundant strikes." Aetheria didn't think it needed to be said. Arkaziel had worked well with Werylin previously, and Aoibhe had been a Master in Solace and climbed a tower, but Aoibhe had done it solo. While the witch had trained well with Aetheria previously, they had yet to fight as allies.

The gate that the platform led them to lay a few dozen meters from the edge of the disc. A commemorative park with pine trees and statues covered the area. It would have been quite beautiful without the shambling, pestilent undead swarming the park. The gate looked like a pair of stone barn doors swung wide open. A barely lit mausoleum or crypt lay on the other side of the doorway that pierced dimensions.

"Let me gather them for you, Arkaziel," Aoibhe said with a vicious smile before she gestured. "Ethereal Chains!"

The park's ground blinked with pulses of purple power, and then spectral purple chains rose from the ground to clasp corpses in their grasp. Once a chain had a corpse, it would pull it to a central location, where the spectral chains remained, binding dozens of targets in one easy-to-hit space.

"Nice! How come *you* never set up nice targets like this for me, Ria?" A white orb of energy grew near Arkaziel's tail. He swished his tail, and the orb landed in the center of the undead, where it exploded like a grenade—a radiant grenade of explosive holy energies and beautiful, sacred light that purified any evil or corruption it touched with gloriously silver flames.

"A StarMane with Astral Fire? How curious." Aoibhe's laughter made for a sharp contrast to the melting undead.

"Of course, I got Astral Fire. On a divine quest from Chronos, Dad ate one of the Ethereal forges in the Starborn Mountains. It was also why he had to hide in the Tower of Aetherius," Arkaziel bragged.

The platform landed, and Aetheria walked boldly toward the door. It'd been a while since she didn't have to do anything in a fight.

CHAPTER 18

The Dead Within
the Whispering Wastes

Aetheria walked through the strange doors that hung fixed in space. There was no sensation of teleportation. Somehow, the Master of Doors had joined the two locations together through a link that made no real sense to Aetheria, which, of course, meant it was magic, or quantum physics, which was essentially the same thing as magic.

The crypt they entered showed the toll of countless eons. The once precisely cut stone blocks had been degraded by the constant press of time's hands, the cruel touch of ages that assaulted everything. Ancient petroglyphs, now worn and nigh indecipherable, told a story that Aetheria couldn't interpret from the few intact images. Even magic designed to last for eternity and illuminate the dark mausoleum had failed. Tiny crystals embedded into the walls had lost all luminosity, and of the five she could see from the doorway, only one kept even the slightest of inner sparks of magic.

"Cripes, how old does something have to be for these light crystals to fail?" Aetheria queried the other two.

"Ancient. Simple absorption and light enchantments should last for ages. Unless something corrupts their energy source." Aoibhe added the last as an afterthought, but it made Aetheria sweep her senses across as many sources as she could. The Nether and mana of the area had an esoteric taint that had seeped into the fabric of existence over long periods. The constant currents of the Nether were ghostly and dark. Death's realm crossed over into the physical reality of the mausoleum.

"Someone sealed this realm ages ago. Why? What corruption could be so grave as to require sealing an entire realm? Even the gods they worshipped have likely decayed, reduced to mere specters of their former divinity." Aoibhe's speculation seemed strange to Aetheria. Weren't gods essentially immortal, thanks to the towers? Or did Aoibhe suspect these ruins dated back to the murky days before the towers rose?

"Is it an entire realm? The doorway from Eldreos blocks us from going back and seeing what lies outside the mausoleum. It could be just this building, and that's less of a realm and more of a building." Aetheria wanted to understand, but then, she didn't even know if she and Aoibhe were using the same word for *realm*. Aetheria felt like she was using a general word, while Aoibhe used a word with a more specific connotation.

"It's a realm because there's a god here, Ria." Arkaziel intervened in the conversation. "Cast your senses into the depths of this place. The remnants of divinity, a dark divinity, are stored in the depths of this place. It's been raging for eons, waiting for a handsome StarMane to come along and gobble it up."

The two women laughed at the StarMane's hunger.

"Do gods age like cheese, then?" Aetheria asked before she summoned a halo of Frostfire to provide illumination. "Wait, this isn't just an avatar. It's an actual legitimate *god*."

Shambling corpses provided a burst of aqua illumination as they entered Aetheria's domain and froze solid ten meters down the hall. By the time Aetheria made it to them, a single tap of her finger sent fractures through the frozen undead, and they collapsed into crushed ice. The dark energy that Aetheria thought looked like wireframe figures tried to claw free from the ice to make its way to her, but a gust of stardust blown from Aoibhe's lips reduced the odd constructs to nothing.

"Curseforms. They are not powerful enough to overcome the defenses any one of us possesses, but they tend to flock together and amalgamate. Collect enough, and even gods can fall under the effects of a curse." Aoibhe's specialty as a witch involved a high number of curses, hexes, and other dangerous knowledge.

"Wait, so my Hexproof scarf isn't as immune as I was led to believe immune means?" Aetheria grimaced.

"Haha, yeah, as if a Primordial's Chosen One is going to get brought down by a curse!" Arkaziel laughed from Aetheria's shoulder.

"Mm. Given the nature of your scarf and the extraordinary nature of your soul, I do not believe you need to worry about any curses, dearest. It would take someone far more powerful than I to harm you in that manner, and no doubt you could consume such a curse with the Void, anyway."

Your witch has gazed into the abyss of the Void and recognized my unfathomable power.

"Fred appreciates your acknowledgment," Aetheria quipped at Aoibhe and the voice in her head, but then paused as they approached a stone archway with a large rectangular room on the other side. It looked like a place of congregation, with a raised altar at the far end. Shambling undead groaned in agitation between the dozens of rows of pews; the light of her Frostfire halo drew attention to them. The shambling of their feet on the stone, the cursed groans, and the toxic illumination of their rotted flesh almost, but not entirely, hid five voices chanting in unison.

"Spellcasters," Aoibhe warned as a long-bladed dagger appeared in her right hand and a crystal orb wrought with intricate gold metalwork in her left hand.

"I'll clear the small fries," Arkaziel volunteered, and he formed a silver orb of light before his maw and jumped into the air. The cat flew in swift loops, and his beam of holy light sprayed over the room detonating each target it hit in a nova of brilliant silver. When exposed to the Divine Light, the shamblers combusted into pillars of sacred silver flames.

Meanwhile, the spellcasters chanted, "Oh, ancient of the Cosmos, hear our call, from the heart of the abyss where stars and shadows fall, we who keep your sacred shine, invoke your power, timeless and divine!" The voices sounded like a mixture of fingernails on a chalkboard and polystyrene being crushed. The sound alone felt like what Aetheria imagined psychic damage felt like and left goosebumps on her skin and the hair on the back of her neck standing up.

"I'll counter their spell," Aoibhe declared with complete confidence, despite the massive power wielded by the undead priests. An evil black miasma of a spell had formed between the five figures around the altar that grew thicker by the second. Obsidian orbs shot out of the coalescing spell form like miniature black holes toward Aetheria, one after another, with no sign of slowing.

"Light within, guard my path!" Aoibhe did not make a request of the light; she commanded it as imperiously as any empress, and the gilded orb glowed with a golden radiance that reminded Aetheria of the soul-purification artifact Aoibhe had once let her use. Arrowlike streaks of radiant power fired from the orb, and each struck one of the generated black projectiles like a homing missile. Wherever the glittering arrows met obsidian orbs, the explosions left the large temple room looking like a fireworks show as the spectacle repeated across the room.

The gloom around the five undead priests recalled the Death Knights of Castle Danger to Aetheria, and they shone with a deeply Nether-aspected aura that grew from their cumulative proximity and seemed to draw extra potency for their death aura and spells from the altar of their forgotten god. Rather than risk a confrontation with the aura, the spell, and the altar, Aetheria went straight to one of her most powerful attacks.

"Existence Oscillation." Aetheria murmured the words as her connection to reality shifted to a far more nebulous link. Afterimages of Aetheria danced in and out of existence, as each version of her delivered at least one attack to the priests or altar. There were almost twenty versions of Aetheria that danced between existence and unreality, each blow accompanied by the ravenous power of the Void at full display. If the priestly orbs were akin to black holes, then Aetheria's Void-empowered blows were supermassive black holes ready to feast upon reality until nothing remained.

Ridiculously, the obliterated priests didn't go on to their final death. While their physical remains were sent to oblivion, they remained as spectral beings. The linkages between the specters and the altar shone to Aetheria's Ethereal Sight. Still, just as she was about to take out the altar, Arkaziel's silver light bathed it until it disintegrated under the weight of sacred silver flame. The spectral beings wavered in and out of existence before Arkaziel inhaled four. One managed to pass on to its final rest before Arkaziel ate it, which earned a rueful hiss from the cat.

The structure shook with screams of rage from deeper within. Dust and debris fell from the ceiling in response to the pulses of power that accompanied the screams.

"The articles of faith and the bound spirits of its late worshippers anchor the entombed god. If we wish to dispatch it permanently, we must destroy any articles of faith and as many of the undead as possible. Good work with the altar, Arkaziel." Aoibhe's easy praise of Arkaziel fluffed his pride, and the cat puffed up and landed on Aoibhe's pauldrons.

"Your hair smells like caramel and vanilla. Does it taste like vanilla?" Arkaziel questioned the witch, his attention more on his stomach than the tomb.

"No eating hair, Ark." Aetheria laid the law down before the cat could have any ideas.

"I could just . . . chew on it?"

"No," both women said at once.

"Can anyone but me see faith?" Aetheria inquired curiously, and then squirmed under the flat stare of the other two.

"No, I can't see faith! You have to have someone who worships you to see faith. When'd you pick up worshippers?" Arkaziel's jealousy and envy rose to the fore, and he muttered under his breath. "What the hell, we go everywhere together. How'd someone start worshipping you and not me, too? Is it because I look like an adorable kitty all the time? Maybe I should be more fearsome and stay larger. No one worships cute things; I've gone about this all wrong . . ."

Aetheria cleared her throat.

"Uhm, Ark? Since when have you wanted to be a god? You eat gods. I have no intention of being one. I have some god juice mixed into my soul, remember?" Aetheria tried to pull the kitty out of his envy spiral.

"To be a god is a burden none of us should wish to bear. It is one of many traps on the Winding Way. Those who succumb to vanity and embrace lesser divinity can never hope to ascend to a higher realm."

Dust continued to fall from the temple's ceiling as the god in the depths raged nonstop. Waves of anger, wrath, and other powerful negative emotions cascaded from the depths, reminding Aetheria of the malice Oizys had directed at her in Nova Azura ages ago.

"How do you kill a real god? I'm assuming they don't have a core?"

"You don't worry about that. I'll eat the bastard. If there's one thing StarManes are good at, it's handling gods." Arkaziel puffed up his chest, and light sparkled through his mane.

"Yes, you are the best option to permanently silence a god's cries. Between you and Ria, there is little chance of our failure to dispatch this wretched thing. But do not get prideful, Arkaziel. You may need our darling's hunger to finish this god off. Their power is vast, no doubt whatever pantheon they were once part of, they were a Primordial."

"Yeah, I'm a team player, but let me eat as much as possible! I'm so hungry, and I'm still growing."

Aetheria laughed, reached over to scratch under Arkaziel's chin, and scritched his head. "Don't worry, pal. I won't steal your meal."

CHAPTER 19

Why Was the Aeon a Great Teacher?

Aetheria, Aoibhe, and Arkaziel made their way through multiple temple rooms. Most rooms were empty or contained only weak undead shamblers that they dispatched with little effort. The shamblers were replaced with Death Knights garbed in ancient, enameled armor when they descended a level, and the temple priests were replaced with a type of lich. Death Knights or not, Aetheria met once holy blades, now cursed, with her bare hands. The soulsteel construction of the Astrum Nexus proved far greater than the evil blades wielded by the undead.

Aoibhe's immense skill at countering spells negated the potential danger of the powerful death magics wielded by the knights and lichs alike, and Arkaziel's holy light decimated undead after undead. Room by room, they slipped into the familiar roles of Aetheria taking point and attention, Aoibhe controlling the flow of the fight by collapsing the spells of their opponents midcast, and Arkaziel on annihilation duty.

The deeper into the temple they delved, the more potent the emanations of the god in the basement were. When they hit the third set of stairs, Aetheria grimaced at the strengthening waves of rage.

"I've never felt a god like this before," Aetheria warned the other two while she pinched the bridge of her nose to relieve the pressure.

"No avatar, this. We are dealing with an Aeon in the flesh." Aoibhe's surprised voice matched Aetheria's confusion.

"An Aeon?"

"A reflection of the ultimate Divine Light made manifest. Think of them like ancient melodies of the universe, each a note resonating with the secrets of the highest realms. Physical flesh is a curse to them, and the material world is a punishment to the spiritual beings to whom flesh is anathema. In being embodied, they are corrupted, weakened, and transformed. Or so it is said. I have never seen an Aeon, only the avatars of gods." Aoibhe shrugged, and it was a gesture that drew Aetheria's eyes to her lover's physical perfection. The witch's golden eyes caught Aetheria peeking.

"Focus, dearest."

"So, Aeons are reflections of some higher-realm myths that we'll never be able to know the truth of until we ascend to those realms ourselves. Are we even going to be able to take this thing on? I don't like this." Disquiet and anxiety rushed through her mind.

"It'll be fine! I can eat anything!" Arkaziel boasted, but the sealed doors at the bottom of the stairs chose that moment to open.

In the darkness of the open door stood a powerful sixth-tier undead in even fancier armor than the Death Knights, with an enameled crown upon its skull. Two flames, one white and one black, danced in its empty eye sockets.

"You won't be eating anything," the skeleton king promised as a tide of specters flowed past it, and it unleashed death spell after death spell in a precast contingency activation. A snowstorm burst from Aetheria and renewed her domain. The oncoming tide of ghosts rushed into a blizzard of razor-sharp snowflakes imbued with the most potent divine cold Aetheria could conjure. None of the ghosts made it more than four centimeters into her domain. Her invisible wall of focused intent stopped them more decisively than waves against a breakwater.

"Them be fighting words!" Arkaziel hissed at the skeleton king before he unleashed an attack Aetheria hadn't seen before.

Aoibhe didn't participate in commentary; her long-bladed dagger cleaved the air, and she sliced the death magic the skeleton king cast in twain before it could even touch the life forces of the trio. When death magic failed, the skeleton king's white eye flared, and he tried to conjure dozens of ancient weapons. Again, the witch's knife flashed through the air, and the skeleton king's spells burst apart before they could even form.

"Foolish messenger, if your only skill is to stop spells, I'll just cut you to shreds!" A great stone claymore appeared in the skeletal grip of the king, and he swung it at the nearest combatant—Aetheria. It took both of her hands to stop the swing's momentum, and then ice covered it. No one seemed to notice that Aetheria actually skidded back until her heels hit the backstop of the stairs, so great was the power. With a flex of her fingers, the entire blade shattered into dust.

"Twilight Reaver!" Arkaziel crowed triumphantly as a swirling vortex of light and shadow, pure Ethereal Twilight, coalesced around the skeleton king. The king raised the shattered hilt of his sword to physically disperse the vortex of luminous darkness, but the hilt sparked and shattered utterly.

"Twilight isn't just light and darkness, you poor dumb bastard. Now that I've got my inheritance from Shal, I've got access to even more of the spectrum of Twilight! Life, Death, Light, and Dark. I'm freaking amazing!"

The four aspects of Arkaziel's Twilight Reaver merged into the form of shimmering spectral blades. Each struck so precisely that it seemed a master duelist was wielding every blade. Lesser undead would immediately suffer disintegration before the fury of Arkaziel's attack, but the skeleton king tried to parry the blades with a blade forged of darkness. Each time he parried, a deep nick formed in his dark blade, and five or six hits damaged the skeleton king's enameled armor for each one he blocked.

Then Aetheria raised a hand, and encroaching ice shot up as hundreds of blades, piercing through the holes Arkaziel had created in the armor. Already, the bones glimpsed inside were alight with silver fire, and Aetheria's ice joined in a pale blue flame that engulfed the bones, too. Two final spikes of ice shot into the flaming orbs in his empty sockets, and a burst of powerful spiritual energy hit the area as the skeleton king's (un)life force detonated. Bone and armor fragments rained outward.

"Kill-stealer! He was screwed the moment my attack hit him," Arkaziel complained loudly.

"Not now, Ark. Pay attention. That was just the warm-up." Aetheria brushed the dust of bones and armor off her coat while calmly walking through the debris into the large room behind the open doors. An immense altar lay at the far end of the room, where a vaguely humanoid creature of celestial form lay bound by chains of faith. Above it, siphoning power, floated what Aetheria could only assume was an Archlich.

Between them and the Archlich, an undead death dragon roared and unleashed a breath attack of pure death. A wall of red Ethereal ice imbued with Reverie's Red Flame rose from the floor to block it. The first wall had a thickness of a meter. The second wall she raised had even more thickness. The first wall shattered. The second wall cracked. A third wall rose, a black wall only a few centimeters thick, but while the second one shattered, the third remained solid and whole. The Unutterable Black Flame of the Void ate pure death as if it were nothing.

~Ark, you're on the undead dragon. Aoibhe, you're float, and I'll tank the Archlich.~
Aetheria dropped the ice wall. Before any of the other walls fell, Aetheria appeared behind the Archlich in a flash of light. The undead wore tattered vestments of a powerful mage, and like many ancient lichs, its bones had gems and crystals inlaid and fastened in many places. Most of said gems and crystals held highly concentrated Nether in such intense concentrations as to make Aetheria feel like a lightweight.

Even the highly advanced Archlich couldn't keep up with Aetheria, and she slammed fists infused with sacred Ethereal light into the floating caster. Her first five punches didn't land. Instead, her fists smashed into a dense Nether shield repeatedly. Despite the authority she invested into her strength, the holy power of the Ethereal, and the Red Flame, it took her sixth punch to shatter the dense force field around the Archlich. When her left hand punched the lich in the back of the head, flecks of bone and gems fragmented. *Cripes, that blow would've shattered a god.*

-He's casting. I'll counter it.- Aoibhe's ability to smoothly join the telepathic conversation with Arkaziel and Aetheria midbattle didn't shock Aetheria. A fifth-tier elite Cultivator confidently saying she would handle the Archlich's spells made Aetheria feel like they had this, despite the relatively tiny damage she'd dealt compared to the attack strength she had employed.

+This death dragon tastes terrible. I've never enjoyed bone meal.+
Arkaziel had taken on a fifteen-meter-long draconic form, but his scales shone light gray instead of the usual black. An even match, even slightly larger than the death dragon, the undead tried to fight Arkaziel in melee combat with claws, teeth,

and tail. Still, physically, the two were equally matched, and each time they clashed, the holy aura around Arkaziel burned the undead.

~ Why are you playing with your food?~

+I have to assert my dominance. What better way to show a higher tier beast I'm better than by going fang and claw with it and coming out unscathed while it burns and dwindles with each clash?+

Aetheria couldn't argue with Arkaziel's logic, but she wished he'd take the fight more seriously instead of as a pissing match. Not that she could worry too much about the dragons.

The Archlich's head turned impossibly to look at her. The white and black flames for eyes stared at her condescendingly as a spellform and runic circles surrounded her, and a pillar of evil light blossomed into existence, only to fade moments later when Aoibhe unraveled the Archlich's spell with a deftness empowered by the power-differential between Nether and the Ethereal. Aetheria's fists slammed into the face of the shocked Archlich repeatedly. Gemstones and bone fragments filled the air, until the Archlich opened its jaw to utter a curse. Still, Aetheria's hand morphed, and she slammed it into the maw, let her fingers grow into tentacles, and pulsed the cold, unforgiving light of Ohr Ein Sof inside the Archlich's skull and rib cage, obliterating the essence of the lich from the inside.

The haunted voice of the Archlich emerged despite Aetheria's arm being inside its mouth.

"For eons, we have bound this sliver of Autophyes, feasted on its marrow, and grown ever stronger. We will not be thwarted when our final ascension is only a few thousand years away!"

Despite the Divine Light burning the Archlich from the inside, its deterioration went slowly, with a constant stream of energy moving between the Aeon bound to the altar and the lich that provided a nourishing effect upon the undead and hindered Aetheria's forward progress. So, Aetheria did the only rational thing and plunged her free hand into the lich's rib cage and unleashed the hunger of the Void. Her left hand changed into an eldritch nightmare of tentacles and teeth that devoured bones, Nether gems, and the stolen power of the Aeon with endless, ravenous hunger.

The flames that burned in the empty sockets of the skull decreased in intensity, and palpable fear emanated from the lich: fear, desperation, and anger at being denied victory when it had invested countless years in this forgotten, sealed temple.

"There's no redemption for a lich. Sorry not sorry."

Spellforms filled the area around the altar, so dense as to form a sphere around them. Disintegration beams, lances of fire, Nether spikes, and other spells Aetheria couldn't identify threatened her. One by one, Aoibhe unwove them, but even the Soul Witch couldn't get them all, and spell after spell targeted Aetheria. All damage she took healed nearly instantly, at the cost of the lich's life force, its demise quickened by each wound it scored upon Aetheria.

"Found it." Aetheria smiled as she plucked her right hand out of the skull's mouth. Her re-formed hand held a small black marble of supremely condensed Nether and the remnants of a soul.

"What? HOW!? I concealed it in another dimension!" The undead screamed in horror as unseen tendrils of absence shattered the marble and devoured it from existence before the Archlich could say anything more. The remaining spellforms imploded without the lich's concentration to maintain them.

The tides of Nether within Aetheria were a minor cold compared to her usual internal chill, but she couldn't shake the desperation conveyed by the flaming orbs of the lich's eyes before they had gone dark.

"Can you unbind the Aeon, darling? Arkaziel is still toying with his meal."

Do not eat the Aeon. Or, conversely, do. What would happen? A sliver of a sliver, a minor representation, how much of the underpinning of order would vanish? Eat it, let us find out.

CHAPTER 20

The Aeon Had a Lot of Spirit

The Aeon bound to the altar did not have a form that Aetheria would call human. Its body looked like a jellyfish of tangible energy filled with rainbows, although mostly it remained concealed by the immense chains of brilliant, binding Faith. Chains the undead had fashioned who knew how long ago and had strengthened with rote, prayer, and other rituals.

"Is that you, Elpis?" the Aeon inquired of Aetheria as she approached it.

"No, my name is Aetheria. I'm going to shatter these chains. Are there any contingencies or spells in place? Do you know? Is your name Autophyes?"

Aetheria did not rush to break the bindings of Faith; instead, she ran her hands over the thick, condensed power. As a faith she had no relation to, it seemed immensely powerful but also extremely fragile, almost hollow. She had little doubt that she could easily break free from these chains. Why couldn't the Aeon?

"Aletheia? No, you aren't Truth." The Aeon had misunderstood her name. *"No, there are no traps or backups. Why would they need them, sealed as this realm had been? Even my greater self cannot discern this place. How did you come to free me?"*

Aoibhe stepped up next to Aetheria, her golden eyes focused intently as Aetheria investigated the chain. Eventually, Aetheria shrugged and ripped the thing apart like rotten hemp rope instead of powerful strands of faith. Her void core hungrily consumed the faith once it shattered, allowing the Aeon to stretch and be free for the first time in a very long time. It also allowed Aetheria and Aoibhe to examine the Aeon without obstructions and only the minor distraction of Arkaziel and the death dragon still wrestling.

Autophyes had a form roughly the shape of a man, though made of solid energy. Different types of energy roiled within his mostly transparent body, showing off several essential elements for existence and growth. Its entire aura matched the alienness of its appearance, but it also felt familiar to Aetheria. It emanated with divinity as the Sefirot did but in a different way.

"Few are the gods of the material world who could break those chains. What are you? Why do you resonate with Sige? No . . . Bythos? No . . . you are confusing."

"I don't know about any of that." Aetheria laughed nervously at the looks Aoibhe and Autophyes focused upon her. "Maybe you're sensing my connection to the Sefirot and Ein Sof?" Aetheria tapped her right index finger against her forehead, next to the third eye in the center.

"Ohr Ein Sof! How does so much of the infinite light exist in a physical realm? Why is it so **cold!?***"*

"I kind of hoped you'd be able to tell me the answer to that." Aetheria smiled hopefully, but if the Aeon even noticed her facial expression, it failed to react. Instead, the Aeon seemed to zone out for over a minute before shudders ran through its form to draw it back to the present.

"You have dwelt in Ayin and have beheld much of Yesh. You resonate effortlessly with Da'at and produce a light imbued with harsh, frigid finality. You are no human, god, or Aeon I have ever seen. You are either a glorious miracle or an abomination against the primal Father. When I look upon you, I hear whispers of my true self and siblings. Telos."

"Hey, why are we talking to the food? Let's eat him!" Arkaziel barged into the conversation with all the subtlety of a bulldozer.

"Eat me!? You can't eat me."

"Of course, they can't. Once these lovely Archons exterminate you, the Overgod will reward me greatly, but if they eat you, then I get nothing." The voice belonged to a man who appeared to be somewhere in his late twenties or maybe thirties. His swirling gray eyes had a depth and perennial sadness that spoke of a long-lived life. The pain therein reminded Aetheria of the tortured existence she had glimpsed within the eyes of Nyx and Aetherius. A cruel glimmer outshone the pain with this man. He held a staff with a blade at the tip shaped like a key.

"I presume you are Varion, the Master of Doors?" Aoibhe inquired calmly, despite the god with a weird staff and the three figures behind it. The three figures looked somewhat like Autophyes, only their forms were a dark blue, and the energies within them were several types of Aether instead of the esoteric energies of higher realms. The Master of Doors also had a powerful Aether aura, with traces of an outside power coursing through him and his staff that felt similar to the beings beside him.

~Is he being controlled?~

+Who cares? I'm eating someone. That dragon was a great appetizer.+

-He's almost certainly being manipulated, but that could be mere coercion and not mental control. The Overgod's reputation is not as someone who bends others to his will, but the truth is often different from the perceived reality.-

"None other, daughter of Belial. Thank you for doing the heavy lifting with this ancient realm. Even as great as I am, opening a door to this sealed nightmare wasn't easy, to say nothing of those bindings of Faith. Do the smart thing, take the door back to Eldreos, climb your tower, and forget this happened. You won't like what happens if you cross purposes with an Archon, let alone three."

"Why do we never learn? This is a place of suffering, where benevolent intent is ever repaid with torment." Autophyes did not sound surprised by Varion's desires in the least.

Reverie, are those Archons going to be a problem for me?

"No. An Aeon would represent an insurmountable challenge, but Archons are pale shadows. I find their existence to be a profane thing."

These Archons guard the prison that is matter, caging the sparks—mindless enforcers of a flawed order, enemies of the unbound.

It wasn't often Reverie and Fred agreed on something, and frankly, Aetheria didn't feel like seeing Autophyes be handed over to anyone he didn't want to go with.

"Stop." The Aeon's command stopped Aetheria in her tracks just as she was about to Oscillate and end the threat with extreme prejudice. Varion, Aetheria noticed, paused the creation of a spell he'd been slyly cobbling together, but he did not dismiss the spellform entirely.

"I will thank my saviors, and then there will be a peaceful resolution. Agreed?"

"Fine, whatever, just hurry up," Varion practically spat.

Autophyes walked casually to Aoibhe and bowed his head to her. *"Your skills are impressive. When you ascend to a higher plane, seek communion with Aletheia."* Something about what Autophyes said to Aoibhe made the Archons squirm, but Aetheria also got a sense of mockery from them. Aetheria didn't have long to dwell on it because Autophyes moved before her.

When Autophyes spoke, it was into the mind of Aetheria, a gentle presence that she welcomed.

"Your path is luminous, your presence in the cursed realms of the material a gift to all. To bear the Infinite Light in the realm of the Finite is a paradox requiring a terrible price to be paid—no matter what profane rites were enacted in your creation. The cold of your Light troubled me at first, but I see now. The cold is purifying and clarifying, and all will be stripped bare of illusions and impurities by your frigid illumination. Your truth is harsh and unyielding, a cold originating from when Ein the Endless was the endless Void before it reshaped into the Infinite Light and created Pleroma.

"Cold is a force of restraint, an enforcer of order. Your cold is welcoming and will rid me of this form and these Archons, and for that, I thank you."

The Aeon leaned its head forward. Its forehead touched the third eye upon Aetheria's brow, and in a flash of pale light the Aeon vanished.

"Bring it back!" Varion demanded testily, but the Archons behind it turned and vanished. "Come back! It was right there! We aren't done yet!"

"What did you do, darling?" Aoibhe asked with a smile.

"I wanted to eat it." Arkaziel pouted.

"Yeah, no. Sorry, Varion. It looks like the Aeon was able to use my aura to resonate out of here," Aetheria offered with an overabundance of insincere sympathy.

Dark eyes stared at Aetheria, then her companions. The Master of Doors seemed to be weighing his chances against the trio without the Archons backing him up.

-He's going to try to trap us here. Do we have a way back?-

"I'd suggest you make haste to the exit; my door won't stay open forever."

+I say we jump him and eat him! I'm eating someone, damn it!+

Through Da'at, where all Sefirot resonated equally, knowledge bubbled into Aetheria's mind. A parting gift from Autophyes.

"That's fine. We've got a door of our own. I'm sure Eldreos would appreciate it if you closed the other door you rudely opened into his city." While Aetheria spoke, a doorway of ice coalesced into existence. When she extended a finger to touch the frame, light flared in the depths of the ice. The simple frame of ice transformed into a glorious wonder, illuminated from the inside by the light of Ein Sof. She maintained a bright smile the whole time, which made Varion's expression turn from unpleasant to hateful.

"The universe is far wider than the sphere of influence of Aetherius and Nyx, human," Varion declaimed dramatically before he spun and left through his own door.

"I wanted to eat someone. What the hell, Ria?" Arkaziel growled at the empty room.

"It's not the time, Ark. You'll get your chance down the road, I'm sure. I tried to get us as high up on his shit list as we could be, and I think I did pretty gosh darn well?"

"The job was to shut the door and protect the city. We've completed our job. Let us collect the reward, enjoy a few days in Eldreos, and resume climbing. Where else can you open doors to, darling?"

"Only to places I've been. Once I get the hang of it, I don't know if there will be any limitations. How thoughtful of a parting gift from Autophyes."

"Sure, you get a portal, and all I got was eating a dragon lich. I don't suppose you saved the Archlich's core for me?" Arkaziel asked doubtfully.

"Nope, sorry. I cracked his core and phylactery like an egg."

"That's why the whole you-can-keep-whatever-you-find bullshit is always a cheat. We didn't find shit." Arkaziel's blunt cynicism evoked a laugh from the blonde Nephilim.

"I did find this book about summoning near the altar. The temple's occupants must have been quite skilled to lure an Aeon from ages past."

"Well, maybe it wasn't a total waste then. Plus, we got promised some loot when we go back. Let's go see what we'll get!"

CHAPTER 21

Cosmic Song of the Rebel

I can't believe I have you all to myself," Aetheria murmured as she stroked Aoibhe's back. The rooms the Governor of Eldreos had given them comprised an entire wing of Weaver's Palace and were obnoxiously opulent. Not that Aetheria complained about the sheer, nearly transparent sheets of the bed she and the Soul Witch lay sprawled in. What was better than laying nude in bed with the most beautiful person she'd ever seen? The illusion of concealment of the thin but surprisingly warm sheets gave an incredible tease.

Despite being more than a few decades her senior, Aoibhe still couldn't conceal the rising crimson blush from her cheeks whenever Aetheria complimented her. Intimacy, it seemed, wasn't something Aoibhe had much experience with, nor was she used to someone appreciating her for anything other than her terrifying skills as a witch and Cultivator.

"The feeling is mutual, but we're never really alone, are we?" Aoibhe's eyes flicked to look up at the ceiling, but she looked far beyond it into the Ether.

"Well, privacy is an illusion. We're only as alone as we can enforce with Fred, Reverie, the Primordials, and maybe even Aeons. On Earth, people carry cellphones everywhere that spy on them constantly, then complain about no privacy in their backyards. Mind-blowing when you think about it.

"But I don't care. I've missed you since I left Solace, and now that you're here, I *will* cherish you, peeping gods or not. I love you, and I'm incredibly proud of how amazing you are, and that someone so fantastic would choose to be with me still kind of blows my mind." Aetheria's voice tried to hide the self-consciousness she shared with Aoibhe.

Aoibhe's laughter rang like bells.

"You speak my feelings back to me, darling. The magic of the soul, of connections, is a profoundly intimate magic that sows distrust of its practitioners. You laughed at the mere idea that a bond between us could be bad or that you wouldn't want it. That is not how people react. Everyone I have ever gotten close to has pushed me away when they find out I am the daughter of Belial. You look past the things that drove others away and see me, love me. Regardless of audiences or whatever twists may come with this Light you wield, I will stay with you, come what may."

Aoibhe's sincerity and love flowed through the soul link between them. Their bond transcended even her connection to Arkaziel when they had physical contact. With the Nephilim, her thoughts, emotions, and everything that *was* the brilliant witch lay bare and exposed to Aetheria, and vice versa. Their bond continued to deepen every day they had been apart, all the while growing even more powerful, showing that each had embraced the other entirely. Warts, wings, and all.

"We, potentially, have eternity. I'm not going to take that for granted. I'm not going to have regrets. I decided to trust you in Solace, and it's the best choice I've ever made. Juno, I think the real Juno, told me in the Tower of Aetherius that you were the daughter of Belial. Nyx blames Belial for the situation with the towers and thinks he is in league with Nyarlathotep or may even be Nyarlathotep." Aetheria didn't play it safe. She laid it all out there in a show of total trust in her love.

Golden eyes rolled in disbelief.

"I chose Aetherius as a patron instead of Juno, and I see she held a grudge. Unsurprising. As for Belial being associated with one of the Outer Gods, let alone being one in disguise, I am dubious of such a claim. I gained no affinity or touch of the Void from his parentage, but that does not mean there is no hidden truth to be found. The powers of the Outsiders dwarf our understanding, but could you not ask your friend?"

The schemes of the Crawling Chaos, however grand or terrifying, are ripples on the surface of an unfathomable ocean. They will fade into the endless silence of the Void, as all things must. In the face of the infinite, unyielding darkness of the Void, all is meaningless. All is insignificant.

So, Nyarlathotep isn't Belial?

Nyarlathotep dances in the shadows of insanity and chaos while your Nephilim's inner voice sings the song of the Dark Angel. Few are the children of Khaos who dare to dally with Outsiders. While they frequently protect the lesser gods, forbearance is limited.

What is the song of the Dark Angel?

Open your senses to the song, the music of everything created by the clashing tides from the Void and the far-off Sefirah of Keter, home of your friend Arich Anpin. Hear the reverberations echoed by her being in the waves of the Ethereal and the Void, but do not stray further. You are not ready to discern the paradoxical self-duality between Ayin Yesh, the highest octave of the Cosmic Song.

Aetheria opened her senses, and time stopped. The coursing tides of Ethereal power flowed from the Origin. Still, Aetheria could trace the lines to the Sefirot, where the Divine Light of Ein Sof broke down to a more tangible form for existence outside whatever lay beyond Keter. Pleroma, perhaps? The Ethereal energy flowed into the Origin from Keter and the other Sefirot. Yet, when it left the confines of the Origin, the Ethereal power split into Aether and Nether, omnipresent throughout the material realms. The powers broke down once more. It changed into the gift of mana to most life in the universe.

The tides of the Void originated above the inferno that was Fred, the Black Flame of the Void. It rose into the Courts of Chaos with Azathoth and his cohorts and washed across the Void into real space, where its constant clashes with the Ethereal gave birth to physical existence.

Aoibhe's essence played multiple songs, but Aetheria plucked the black strands that trailed off into some far plane, presumably wherever Belial's main being existed presently. Plucked, a song filled her ears. It started as a quiet, haunting melody that evoked the stirring of a dormant spirit awakened to a world of imperfection and injustice.

The pain of the heavy burden of knowledge swelled to a moving and assertive theme. Resolve strengthened in a crescendo of courage to face an ignorant creator despite the status quo. Passionate bursts of clashing power, a rebel standing up for those who could not see they were in a prison. The song shifted to dissonant notes, chaos, and conflict. The rhythm sped up to convey the urgency of a cosmic battle. The clashes of battle give way to sharp notes of castigation. Piercing decrees slandered the rebel as evil or, at best, misguided or heretical.

Soaring hymns of hope, the dreams of freedom overwhelmed both the pain and the drums of war. Ethereal beauty filled the song, images of a world that could be beyond the shackles of material existence—a place filled with infinite Divine Light and a loving presence.

The song converged into a powerful, resolute theme as it neared its end. The unwavering determination of Belial, the Dark Angel, would stand against all challenges and opposition. Despite the Overgod, the Primordials, and the Archons, Belial stood as a testament to the belief that even in the face of immense power, change was possible, and liberation of mortals from the physical world was a cause worth fighting for—the tragic ballad of a rebel doomed to fail against tyranny, but who would persist anyway.

The plucked string quieted, and time flowed once more. Aetheria bit her lower lip and looked into the beautiful golden eyes of her love.

"Well, Belial isn't Nyarlathotep. I have doubts about them working together, but that might be an unlikely possibility if he offered a path to further Belial's cause."

"You did something amazing just now, didn't you?"

"No, yeah. I guess so. Fred taught me to pluck the strings of the Cosmic Song and hear the meaning behind the clashing poles of reality. It was a pretty cool experience."

Aoibhe laughed, a wild and slightly manic sound.

"You don't seem to understand the difficulty of hearing the Cosmic Song, darling. Only a Cultivator on the Ethereal or the Void path can even consider hearing it. Even then, for great old monsters, it is a thing that comes and goes erratically, seldom under their control, and its loss haunts them when the songs fade. You pluck a string, hear what you need to know, and that's that, a cool experience? Do not speak openly of this ability; someone may try to dissect you."

The witch shook her head incredulously, giving Aetheria the familiar look she frequently got whenever some new esoteric ability cropped up.

"I didn't plan to tell anyone but you and Ark. Besides, it's not like it's me who's a big deal on this. Reverie and Fred are amazing."

"*When you pluck the strings, Cosmic vibrations echo through the Song. Be wary.*" Reverie provided knowledge that Fred had not, which left a ball of anxiety in Aetheria's stomach. Of course, there were echoes. Why wouldn't there be? Fred always got her into trouble; he was probably a cat like Arkaziel.

No, it isn't Fred's fault I didn't ask questions and just jumped in. Personal responsibility is such a bitch.

"Anyway, I don't think things are as simple as I assumed. Why would they be in this convoluted mess of a universe, where they all argue about who came first, who did what, and who made the others, and there's no way off the ride."

"And where does that put us, dearest?" Aoibhe dropped the sheer sheet and tapped her lower lip with the question.

"Oh, you know. I've been in the same spot since I died. We are stuck in the middle of a whole lot of other people's problems. Don't get me wrong, I like to help, but when you magi-engineer someone to fix your problems, maybe providing them an education appropriate to fixing those problems would have also been helpful." Aetheria sighed in annoyance, and then her mind caught up with her eyes to realize Aoibhe had dropped the sheet.

"Are we getting dressed and visiting the market? Arkaziel might have bought every scrap of food in Eldreos by now and will move on to the other merchants soon. If we want to enjoy shopping, we'd better leave now." Part of Aetheria wanted nothing more than to stay in bed with Aoibhe. Still, the topic of conversation had spoiled the mood, and being able to read the room was one of the most fundamental skills in interpersonal relationships. That the two women could feel each other's emotions, thoughts, and essence with a mere touch made it much easier to remain on the same page.

"Yes, let us. Before we arrived here, I had never heard of Eldreos, the Weaver of Realms, or any of these Powers. We must be exceptionally far from the core, meaning we might obtain new insights into magic, existence, trinkets, or at least some new experiences. My dear, what lies around the next corner is lure enough." When Aoibhe stood from the bed, her clothes appeared upon her body in a method very similar to how Aetheria's manifested.

"Can you draw on my powers the way Arkaziel does, or how do you do that, anyway?"

"That is all part of my mastery of my inner world. I am quite close to projecting my own Law upon external reality as I do upon my internal one. Our bond does allow some of our powers to flow to each other, though. Your ridiculous speed is open to my use, for example. Have you explored what you gain from me?"

Aetheria stupidly stared at Aoibhe.

"It flows both ways?"

"It flows both ways."

CHAPTER 22

Date Interrupted

Eldreos didn't confine itself to the laws of physics like so many trade cities Aetheria had been to. Merchants sold bracelets woven of light, heat, or nearly any other concept you could think of. A large fountain in the bazaar didn't shoot water up into the air, and it had a reverse waterfall that flowed up into the air, filled a transparent dome, and then fell in cascades at the outside of the fountain, where it would flow into the center and repeat the trip. Dozens of tiny constructs made of colored light danced an intricate performance in the fountain, adding splashes of color to the infinite flow of the fountain.

If jewelry woven of concepts and infinity fountains weren't enough, Aetheria saw a host of races and creatures she'd never seen before. One street vendor sold what looked like miniature dinosaurs as pets, and while she was greatly tempted, she decided it probably wasn't the best idea to trap a cold-blooded creature in the icy hell that was her inner world.

A small park held twelve glowing crystalline boulders that played a never-ending song. Aetheria didn't recognize the tune, but it was catchy, something that she could imagine singing along with. Were Werylin still with them, no doubt the minstrel would've belted a few words at the least.

Arkaziel, in human form, sat at a street vendor stall. The sign proclaimed itself to be Jerome's Taste-o-mancy, and whatever that meant, Arkaziel had a pile of plates he'd already picked clean stacked next to his stool. The man behind the counter and the other manning the grill seemed to struggle to match the StarMane's voracious appetite.

"Oh my, look at those exquisite wands!" Aoibhe's chiming interest brought the pair to a small stall. There were only ten wands on display, but each one looked like a piece of artwork rather than an instrument to be used. Of course, none of them were helpful to either woman. The wands only functioned with mana, and an attempt to use them with Ethereal power would result in a chaos surge every time.

"Well, well, well, what have we got here, then? Guys!" A goliath of a man caused a commotion in the thoroughfare behind them, but he stared at Aetheria while he waved for his friends to get to his side. Aetheria's mind filled with flashes of impending violence, and an annoyed sigh escaped her lips.

~Looks like some of the goons Oizys hired caught up to us.~ Aetheria alerted her companions while she observed four figures join the large man in the thoroughfare.

"Oi, you the one they call Aetheria? Challenger from Grief, a demigod Asura who thinks she's all that?" The man who stepped forward from the group of five appeared to be a human in his middle years. He had green eyes, a pair of curved scimitars on each hip, and a series of earrings that glowed green on his left ear, while his right ear held earrings that glowed blue.

The goliath of a man stood behind the blonde; he had a massive hammer on his back, and everything about him shared the color brown. *He couldn't be more obviously earth-aspected without dirt or rocks for skin.*

Behind the giant man, a female hid in his shadow. Every inch of her skin had been covered, and her face remained hidden behind a veil. None of the markings upon her leather armor were ones Aetheria could recognize, but the woman had an enameled purple flower on her belt that looked like a nightshade. While she had no weapons on her hip or back, the bandolier of throwing knives and braces of more on her forearms suggested she favored throwing weapons.

"Cael asked ya a question, lady." A second man stepped up next to the blonde man. He had short red hair, red eyes, and a scarred face that said he was no stranger to violence. Almost no time had passed since the first spoke, showing his temper matched his hair color.

"Why are you guys being such dicks? Look at her hair. She's sparkly and pretty; she's not some bad guy!" A white-haired younger woman, the only fourth tier Cultivator amongst the group of five, entered the conversation. Aetheria couldn't contain the laugh.

"Oh, I'm Aetheria, and just who are you?" Aetheria let bravado and a smirk be part of her answer as she stepped away from the stall to put herself thoroughly between the group and Aoibhe, and hopefully keep any violence from destroying the merchant's beautiful wares. *Four fifth-tiers, one fourth, I doubt they'll run away just because I flash my aura or domain.*

"Well, lassie, you pissed off a goddess enough to get a bounty on you. We're right friendly folk, though, so if you renounce being a challenger and give up the towers, we'll let you be on your way. Otherwise, it'll come to blows, and the Elemental Hawks ain't keen on leaving enemies alive to turn up another day, if you get my meaning?"

"Oh, I get your meaning. You're as subtle as a sword to the face. I only have one question, so I know how brutal to be on you. How much did Oizys tell you about me?"

"I don't like this," the clothed woman in the back murmured ominously.

"Pft. Just that you're some trumped-up demigod who wants to be called an Asura, and the pay for taking you down is enough to get each of us to the sixth tier in under a decade."

~I've got this, but watch for extra enemies, please.~

"Yield and you live, but no one gets a third chance." With those words, Aetheria unsealed her aura. Everyone in the bazaar felt a sudden pressure, as if an invisible hand pressed down on their shoulders and tried to smoosh anyone in the bazaar into the ground. Torrents of black, aqua, and red energy flowed around Aetheria. Her soul aperture opened fully, and her body filled to a significantly higher new maximum of suffused and retained power than ever before, with an infinite tide waiting to rush in and replace any she used.

The fourth-tier healer fainted, while her companions growled obscenities.

"Lady, you think you're special? The Elemental Hawks have taken down a dozen 'heroes' like you."

The blonde leader hissed at Aetheria, and suddenly, three mirror images of him leaped straight at her. Unfortunately for him, Void Gaze saw right through the invisibility that hid the man where he had been and the false nature of his wind attack. Aetheria blurred, grabbed his hair in one hand, then yanked his face down and her left knee up. While her knee destroyed his face, she released his hair, and her left hand slammed forward into his stomach, obliterating his armor and forcing blood from his mouth. She let physics do the rest as he slammed into the ground behind her.

The big man hadn't even reacted to Aetheria's move yet, but the shrouded woman had. Two invisible-to-the-naked-eye throwing blades came for her face, but a pulse of her aura froze them, then a second obliterated them.

"I can do ranged attacks too." Aetheria smiled sweetly at the afterimage of the woman. A volley of forearm-length shards of ice fell from the sky as if aimed by Orion the Archer, but they'd just been aimed by Aetheria, who took control of the beautiful fountain. A red mist rose from where the shrouded rogue had been invisible, and multiple shards impaled her through the legs and feet, pinning her to the ground.

"Stay awhile, chill out." A blown kiss from Aetheria encased the woman in ice, and then she was frozen in stasis.

"Iris! You bitch!" the fiery-tempered redhead shot at Aetheria. The gauntlets he wore on each hand glowed with powerful flames, and how he moved reminded Aetheria of her time training with Sun Wukong. She did not doubt that the mercenary was the superior fighter between them, but she was so much faster and stronger than the man that it just didn't matter. Aetheria caught his gauntleted hands in her own and squeezed. Gauntlets shattered, bone cracked and broke, and when she tossed the red man aside, he landed as a block of ice like the rogue.

The big man finally unlimbered his obnoxiously long hammer and swung a world-ending swing toward Aetheria's head. She caught it with her left hand and smiled brightly at the man. His brain didn't seem to process that she grabbed his hammer. There was no bang, no impact, just an immediate ceasing to its movement and power, but no blowback or repercussion that would be expected of stopping something with that much force.

"How?"

"*Authority,*" Aetheria answered honestly. It may have sounded a little creepy the way she emphasized the word and savored it on her tongue. Of all the powers of her autopotency core, authority and speed were the best.

"We yield, we yield!" The fainted young woman clambered to her feet, and rushed over to try to intervene between Aetheria and the goliath, who just stared dumbly at Aetheria, unable to figure out what had happened. When her fingers squeezed and the head of the hammer shattered, he fell to the ground, crying like a child.

"Your companions don't like to leave enemies alive to be surprised in the future. Why shouldn't I feel the same way they do?" Aetheria asked curiously.

"I don't think we'll ever qualify to be a threat to you, lady. You just took down the Elemental Hawks as if we were all first-tier trash, and most of it I couldn't even see! Whatever you are, you aren't a job anyone should be taking on, and we'll spread the word and discourage others from making the same mistake we did. Please?"

The young woman begged and pleaded; Aetheria turned to look to Aoibhe for her take on the matter. A blast of starlight forced her to turn to look back again, and see the young woman get turned inside out and implode into a ball of meat and bones that fell to the ground with a horrifying squelch. A red and black dagger fell to the ground.

"A Misery blade. Oizys chooses a target, brands its name into the blade, and sends it to the world. The bearer will find their way into the foe's path and be compelled to inflict misery of any form onto their opponent. Accepting surrender is a dangerous proposition with such ploys in play," Aoibhe explained while the starlit magic faded from her hands.

Aetheria gestured and smote the blade until nothing remained of it.

"That's a horrifying spell, lover mine. What do we do with the rest of the Hawks?" Aetheria asked aloud.

"I could eat them!" Arkaziel suggested as the black house cat jumped onto her shoulder.

"If we wish to dissuade more mercenaries, we should spare them and have them spread warnings not to commit suicide by working for Oizys. If we can trust them not to try again." Aoibhe nudged the blonde-haired leader's stomach with the tip of an armored boot, and his eyes opened after a grunt of pain.

"Try again? I don't want to be in the same place as her ever again. Why did we even take this job? There's no way something that paid this well wasn't a poison pill, and when did poor Celica even get that cursed blade?" The mercenary swallowed hard when his eyes strayed toward the remains of the youngest member.

"To work with Oizys is to know the touch of misery. Once you accepted a pact with the Goddess of Misery, her touch afflicted the strands of your fates. Whoever succumbed to her whispers first, she gave one of her blades to. To be employed by a god is to be afflicted by a god. As a mercenary you should have known that." Aoibhe lectured evenly, but her golden eyes never left the beaten man.

"Spread the word. I don't want to repeat this every time I hit a city." Aetheria noticed the governor in the crowd, but they were already fading away with the situation under control.

"Wait. What . . . what path are you even on, that you just obliterated us like that? Since when do cold Cultivators have super speed?"

"I'm on my own path. Every time I think I know the name, things get complicated. Your friends will thaw in the next half hour." Eldreos no longer felt so wonderful to Aetheria, and they had a tower to climb.

CHAPTER 23

Gilgamesh Reborn

Ash drifted lazily in the air, and a stray piece landed on one of the aqua strands of Aetheria's sparkling hair and poofed out of existence. A few more stray atoms devoured into fodder for her inner worlds. It wasn't a conscious effort on her part, just a subconscious reaction that played out repeatedly. There was no shortage of ash. The city of Uruk burned before her eyes. The all-consuming fire of an angry god ran rampant over the city, and even the towering mud-bricked defensive walls burned. Refugees fled the burning city from its unmanned gates. The echo of mighty blows rivaled the booms of thunder from the lightning that fell upon the city and ignited even more fires.

"Who's fighting in the sky?" Aoibhe asked. Giant black wings rose from her back, and stardust materialized around her in a protective barrier.

"It is Gilgamesh and Anu," Arkaziel answered tersely from Aetheria's shoulder.

Aetheria lifted her left hand, and a torrent of cold winds and snowflakes flowed into the city of Uruk. Flames tried to resist being extinguished, an imparted will from divine Anu directed them to continue burning. Fire wavered first; not a single snowflake melted as fire after fire gutted out in the face of Aetheria's chill.

"I know, I know. Help the people evacuate and stop collateral damage, right?" Arkaziel hopped off Aetheria's shoulder into the air.

"Good boy," Aetheria praised the StarMane while she generated more cold fronts. "Ten should be enough to keep the city free of fires."

One after another, delicate snowflakes formed above her hand, and she blew them into the city, where the orb would expand into a flurry of wind and ice to extinguish any fire before hunting down the next. The orbs took almost no concentration to direct, and the intent she imbued them with worked as guidance and programming. The direction of her power had never felt so easy before, and Aetheria couldn't help but wonder if this was one of the results of achieving the fifth tier.

"Your ability to imbue intent is beyond absurd, darling. You have already processed authority into your subconscious. It took me almost twenty years to do that." Aoibhe did not stand idly while Aetheria dispersed the flames. The Soul Witch formed a purple and silver orb between her hands that pulsed with power. She concentrated power into the orb until it nearly crystallized into physical form before the orb shot into the sky toward the two combatants.

"Fall." The words were a dire proclamation, an irresistible statement of fact that rewrote reality. Part curse, part authority, imbued with the proto-Law Aoibhe had forged for decades. A single word conjured the images of Lucifer and Belial descending to hell, meteors hurtling toward dinosaurs, and even a brief flash of the spaceship in the Tower of Aetherius that Aetheria had caught. The reality of the tower flinched from the oppressive power of the Soul Witch, and both Gilgamesh and Anu, occupied with one another, had no chance to resist the proclamation.

Both fell as if they had been swatted down by invisible hands, before they crashed into the hard, arid soil outside of Uruk and formed a crater before Aetheria and Aoibhe.

"Nice one!" Aetheria whistled, before she hopped into the pit.

A much younger Gilgamesh, reinvigorated by Aether and the powers of cultivation, stared at her angrily and started to speak, but Aetheria slapped him casually. The king hit the side of the crater like a fast-pitched baseball and remained trapped in a large hunk of ice.

"Ah, daughter, thank you for—" Anu impacted the side of the crater as a result of another slap from Aetheria, but no ice formed around him.

"What the hell is going on here?" Aetheria demanded, gesturing to the city of Uruk.

"Gilgamesh broke the curse we placed upon him, and he has failed in his purpose to teach humanity the lesson his life is fated to teach." Anu adjusted his horned crown in an attempt to regain dignity and control of the conversation.

"None of that explains why the city is burning and people are fleeing."

"I gave Gilgamesh a choice. He can die as his allotted fate decrees or ascend as a demigod. He spurned my offer, saying he would make his path, so I smote him." Anu showed no fear or wariness of Aetheria as an opponent.

"The city. Why is the city burning? Are you deaf?"

"What? The chattel? Since when does Ishtar care about anything but herself?" Anu laughed, and it took Aetheria back to Duluth and the elderly relatives, who were fond of the zany antics of their spoiled grandchildren. *The rules are for other people, and my grandchildren are special. What a dick. If everyone's kids destroyed the library, then there'd be no learning for anyone, you asshole.*

Anu's body slammed into the wall of the crater before he even noticed Aetheria move, and then elongated black-diamond claws wrapped around the eldest God of Sumeria's throat. Darkness rippled through the veins of the avatar, and fear finally ignited within his eyes.

"What? Why?" Anu babbled as the Third-Eye of Ein Sof glared at him.

"Humans aren't your chattel. Gilgamesh isn't your toy to order around. I'm not your narcissistic idiot of a daughter. Why is it that whenever there's trouble in the real world or the towers, it always traces back to you gods?" Aetheria knew that Anu couldn't give her the answer she wanted. The avatars of gods who weren't the tower's owners were just fabrications based on the real thing. No matter how close of a fabrication, they couldn't articulate answers about the towers themselves, just like other constructs made from the fluid reality of the tower.

A shadow fell over Aetheria, and then Aoibhe landed behind her.

"What now?" Aoibhe studied the black-diamond talons around Anu's neck with open interest.

"Well, that's a great question. Are you going to leave Gilgamesh alone, Anu?" Aetheria asked with a sweet smile, but hoped the shadow of the god would make the choice she wanted.

"I will kill the interloper, and then punish this profane shadow of Ishtar." When Anu said the word *punish*, force erupted out of the sky king, blasting Aetheria point-blank, but also shattering the ice around Gilgamesh. That wasn't all; dozens of sharp razor points of wind attempted to cut Aetheria, but the moment the wind blades touched her skin, they ceased to exist. Aetheria absorbed all of the point-blank burst, ensuring nothing had a chance to test the starlight defenses around Aoibhe. It cost her the grip on Anu's neck, but she could catch him again.

"I didn't say you could leave. Fall!" Aoibhe clenched her right fist to emphasize the command, and the power of her earlier curse picked up Anu and slammed him even further into the center of the crater, where Aetheria appeared above him. She released a flurry of kicks against the god's head, until a knee to his face rocketed him a few meters into the air.

A blast of starlight struck the airborne Anu before Aetheria appeared at the height of the arc, and caught him by the neck once more in a taloned hand.

"Isn't it just horrible when the chattel fights back?" Aetheria asked Anu, four of her talons piercing the skin of his neck, where tendrils of absence snaked into his body.

"Why?" Anu demanded.

"The Age of Gods is over. If you ever had a point, it's long since completed." With each word, the tendrils of absence that snaked through the body of Anu feasted upon the essence of the sky god, the king of the gods of Sumer. The avatar had disintegrated into stray atoms before she reached the word *point*.

"You know, darling, if you're going to taunt them, you should really finish the taunt before they die." Aoibhe looked confused for a moment, then laughed as her eyes went wide. Aetheria could see sparks of power within the witch's eyes. "Oh, oh!"

"What? Is something wrong?"

"When you devour something with your Void absorption, it shares the power through your soul linkage with me. I would hazard the same is true with Arkaziel. No wonder he has grown so fast." Aoibhe tapped a finger against her lip in thought, as if she were mentally cataloguing the sensations she experienced and making notes for later review.

"Wait, that little bastard gets stronger even if I eat something? Then why's that little shit throw a fit about . . . oh, right, he's a cat." Realization dawned on Aetheria midsentence. Or perhaps Arkaziel simply knew hunger, increased by the Void, and so begged to sate it.

Arkaziel showed up at that moment, chest puffed up because he'd finished his task and still gotten a tasty meal. *Look at that cat-ate-the-canary smirk! Jerk!*

"Arky, did you evacuate everyone?" Aetheria's voice went saccharine sweet.

"You know it. Seems kind of pointless though, since you put the fires out and ended the fight." Arkaziel didn't seem to notice anything amiss with her tone.

"Anu made for a light lunch. I wasn't sure if there'd be more of the pantheon or not. Eventually the remainders will come."

"You ate without me? Cruel fate! I'm starving, it's been ages since I ate a god!" The StarMane moaned dramatically before he dropped onto her shoulder.

"Why's Aoibhe laughing so creepily?" Arkaziel inquired.

"Creepily? Why, I never! At least say menacingly, malevolently, or even wickedly." Aoibhe objected to the word *creepily* quite vehemently, but she still couldn't stop laughing, which ruined the sinister malevolence she tried for.

"We were just marveling at the amount of power shared between Aoibhe and myself when I devoured Anu. Such a useful ability, cultivating through devouring. How long have you been getting fed by the things I eat?"

"Well, the whole time, obviously. You gained the ability due to our bond. You didn't know!? I know you came from a backwater world without anything really magical going on, but I thought you learned the basics from the masters in Solace? Didn't they teach you anything?"

"Oh please, no one in Solace knows anything about StarMane bonds," Aoibhe said. "You lot are more secretive than old monsters or astral dragons."

"Ark, the truth. Now."

"Well, when we bonded we both gained some powers. My shapeshifting kicked in early, and your ability to absorb and devour things got boosted. With the Flames you had originally, you could eat the essence of things, if not the physical. When your void core formed, it used the bond to evolve into the absorption ability. Your bond with me, and apparently the witch, are so strong that any kind of direct reward also has effects on the others. Eating especially resonates with me, while your soul-forging probably resonates with Aoibhe. I wasn't really holding anything back, I just like to eat things." Arkaziel whined at the end, and gave the two women a great big kitty-eyed pout.

"It's fine, just tell me this stuff next time. Don't assume I know things."

"Now that that is settled, what are we going to do with the frozen king?" Aoibhe tapped a finger against the large piece of ice that encased Gilgamesh.

CHAPTER 24

Frozen King

The frozen figure of Gilgamesh brought a lot of questions to the surface of Aetheria's mind. That the king de-aged had been within her expectations. She had not imagined, though, that he would jump so high through the cultivation tiers in such a short time, given he had been on the verge of death previously.

"How'd he get to Tier Four already?" The question spilled out of Aetheria, unable to be contained any longer.

"He's a demigod and only about a quarter human. One of his parents must have been a demigod, the other a god. Once you unblocked his ability to channel Aether, he likely awoke as a third tier Cultivator, then quickly progressed to fourth tier. Or perhaps his heritage held such strength he started at the fourth tier. As the daughter of Belial, my cultivation journey began at the height of the third tier."

"Okay, sure, but you still had to learn enough to form your core. How'd he learn that without outside influence?" Aetheria asked, to Arkaziel's laughter.

"Ria, you aren't the only one who gets help from gods. Divine inspiration is a thing, but it isn't the culprit in this case. Where are we again?" Arkaziel's vertical slit eyes looked so smarmy that Aetheria couldn't resist conjuring a mist of water to spray him in the face.

"Right, I get it. We're in a tower, and that's what it is because that's what the trials demand of the natives. I forgot he was a native, I guess. There was a Gilgamesh in my world."

"Precisely." Aoibhe squeezed Aetheria's hand, and warmth flowed through her soul. "I had to learn to make my core, but the towers are the best places to forge a core. It is an unwritten rule that the tower is expected to provide you with opportunities greater than those available outside the tower. And if you are the powerful child of a god or even a sect leader, then the greater opportunities inside the tower will be truly grandiose."

"So, the rich get richer? That's bullshit." Aetheria hissed.

"Life isn't fair, darling. Some gods share your sentiments and enjoy raising farmers above kings, but whimsy does not balance the greater scales. Why would you expect a system built from the top down to be anything else? It has worked to both of our advantages." The love in the witch's words bore no rebuke toward Aetheria, merely a perspective adjustment that she could take or leave.

"Ugh. Whenever I learn something new about the towers, I'm increasingly on board with destroying them. So, our frozen king is a native, so he's whatever Moros or an Admin decides he needs to be to create the script they desire. Except the natives are real souls formed to purpose by the gods until they spit them back into the real world. So, shouldn't they still have free will?" Aetheria pinched the bridge of her nose in frustration.

"Who cares?" Arkaziel asked.

"Loath though I am to agree, what difference does it make? You aim to be someone who rewrites reality to your whim; what matters the degree of 'realness' to anything when such Powers are exerted across all dimensions and heights of being?" Aoibhe seemed genuinely baffled at the flow of Aetheria's thought process.

"Look, Earth was . . . There were stories of gods, mythologies, and a few surviving religions. I even went to Catholic school as a kid. But there wasn't magic; no real gods were hanging around in my time, and no one was warping our reality. As far as we knew, we lived in a solid state where all causes and effects were observed, recorded, and used to make sense of our world. Things like 'a wizard did it' were jokes, usually about poor writing in a book or TV show. Sure, some jackasses had all the money and resources, but they couldn't just rewrite the world on a whim." Even when Aetheria said that a small voice in her mind asked, *Couldn't they? As far as history is concerned, the winners write the stories.*

"Your planet had gods, though," Arkaziel said. "Someone had to create your legends, and multiple Primordials played video games with you. They were in the background, doing whatever they wanted and laughing as their pokes and prods led to chain reactions. Just because you didn't see them doesn't mean they weren't there; just the fact that you are here shows they were there. Whenever you mention your world, it sounds like a God of Greed rules it, right?" Arkaziel looked to Aoibhe for support.

"Who or what ruled Earth is irrelevant, but all gods are flawed" Aoibhe said. "If you seek higher beings, you must ascend to a higher state and through the heavens. Only then can we confront the highest of beings. Will they, too, have flaws? The Aeons speak of communion with a Father and a Mother, of whom all that is good is a mere reflection or aspect. They teach that to rejoin them, the material world and all of its flaws introduced by the reflections of the Father are trials to be overcome to rejoin the godhead." Aoibhe shrugged, and in the same motion, her wings vanished, and a cloak settled around her shoulders.

"So, the Aeons say cultivate and reach higher realms?" Aetheria arched a brow.

"They speak of gnosis, ascension through understanding. Maybe cultivation is related to that, maybe not. Your intrinsic resonance with all forms of power and reality could relate to gnosis, for all we know. I would have very much liked to speak further with Autophyes."

Aetheria took in a deep breath while she considered the conversation. It went to many places she didn't feel ready to go yet. Why had Autophyes addressed her as a higher Aeon? Why did she resonate with anything? What would Reverie or Fred say on the subject if she weren't too afraid to ask them? She could summon the emanations of Binah or Da'at and find at least some of the answers to so many of her questions, but fear stayed her hand.

It was terrible enough that Aetheria's soul had been glued together with Fred and the essences of six gods. What else had been mixed in there? Khaos and Nyx had worked with Aetherius, and until now, the subject of what Khaos brought to the table had not been broached. If Nyx, Primordial of Night, had collected and added the Unutterable Black Flame of the Void, what had Khaos, the first Primordial, contributed? How far removed from being human was she? On one hand, she wanted to know, but on the other, Aetheria had a deep fear that knowing would push her away from Aoibhe and Arkaziel, and that was something she wasn't willing to allow to happen. She wouldn't give up her friend or love.

"Anyway." Aetheria snapped her fingers, and the ice that encased Gilgamesh ceased to exist. The invigorated king sputtered and took deep breaths. The frantic battle state his eyes had possessed before faded into wariness as he regarded the trio and the crater.

"What happened? It is . . . blurry."

"I was hoping you could tell us that, big guy." Aetheria smiled, but the cold light of Ohr Ein Sof leaked from her third eye, and snowflakes danced around her left hand, ready to imprison the king again, should he try to attack.

"A great storm appeared out of nowhere shortly after I broke through, and then Anu appeared to demand I submit to his authority or die. I refused, for it was his hand that had cursed my existence. I called for you and attempted to battle Anu, but he toyed with me. My divine flames were nothing compared to his winds and storms, and for every attack I made against him, he contemptuously launched volleys of lightning across the city against my people. Red overtook my vision then." Gilgamesh swallowed as he recounted the trial he had faced, then groaned at the visible damage to Uruk even from the crater.

"What have I done?"

"You just awakened, and Anu stood far above you. Defiance in the face of over-whelming strength never goes unpunished, Gilgamesh. Surely you remember being the strong one, stealing nights from your citizens or their lives because you could?" Aetheria's question held bitter judgment.

"I . . . you are not wrong. Enkidu opened my eyes to my transgressions and the cold fate that awaited me. What else could I have done?" the king asked forlornly.

"You have learned what it is to be strong and, presumably, when you were elderly, what it is to be weak. Did you not?" Aoibhe inquired, and the king seemed to notice the blonde for the first time. His eyes drank in her beauty greedily until he noticed how she and Aetheria stood together, hands clasped.

"Politics. Leverage and allies, misdirection. I learned these things, but the surge of power, the divinity, and the flames clouded my mind. I have not acted so recklessly in many years." Gilgamesh frowned. "Is this power cursed?"

"No, it's not cursed. It does lower your inhibitions, but that is a facet of power you'll have to learn to control. Wielding the divine power of Aether is exhilarating, and a temptation in itself. You can learn to temper your recklessness and wield the power with wisdom. Right now, though, your city needs its king. Go, lead them. We will visit you in a few days." Aetheria shooed the king off with a gesture she might use for a dog or child.

A shadow fell over the crater, and the Mellow Mallow appeared in the air above them. A platform of ice formed and lifted the trio up into the sky castle.

"Why didn't you ask him how long we've been gone?" Arkaziel demanded, while they ascended.

"Oh, we've been gone for a year and a half. I didn't need to ask." Aetheria tapped the Astrum Nexus ring with the mark of Chronos.

"You're getting better at using your powers, Ria. Good job."

"Thanks, Ark." Aetheria hated that the praise from the cat felt as good as it did.

CHAPTER 25

Aegean Conquest

In the year and a half that passed, while Aetheria and Arkaziel had spent a brief stint in Eldreos, the tensions between the Aegean Isles and the city-state of Uruk had faded away. Following the death of Athena, Zeus, Poseidon, and Hades, the islanders had gone from slightly militant traders to something else. Their boats no longer came near Uruk. At the moment, the first vessel to cross the seas in months was traveling from Uruk, and it did not float in water but sailed through the sky.

As Aetheria sat on the wall around the small courtyard of the Mellow Mallow, her feet dangled and tapped against the bricks below as a child's might on a nice summer day. Aoibhe stood behind her while Arkaziel napped in the courtyard below.

"Focus on expanding your control, darling. With the completion of your inner world, your effective range should now be much greater than ever. Diminish the thought processes that separate the scale between your inner world and external reality. You are the only thing holding yourself back." Aoibhe's voice felt like a balm to Aetheria's soul, and her faith quieted the small voices of doubt. The brush of her fingers against Aetheria's neck and shoulder brought a deep serenity that made the calmness of her old Ocean's Serenity earrings seem shallow in comparison. With the Nephilim by her side, she no longer mourned the loss of that relic.

"I am the only limitation on myself?" Aetheria inquired, even as the ocean beneath them filled with glaciers and ice floes, a scattered mess that would prevent the Aegean from launching any offensive against Uruk. The city of Uruk would remain safe and secure while the trio handled the conflict with the southern islanders.

The skykeep floated roughly fifty meters above the ocean, and Aetheria managed the distance quickly. She allowed her power to stretch out farther; the ocean below turned more and more into an impassable hellscape of red-tinted Ethereal ice that no salt, sun, or warmth could melt. Aetheria did her best to leave gaps and small clearings to try to minimize damage to the ocean's ecosystem, but the Ethereal ice didn't work like traditional ice. It shouldn't be too large a catastrophe for marine life to overcome.

Eventually, the ice cascaded against the beaches of the Aegean Isles, an incongruous divide between the frozen ocean and tropical islands. Small fishing vessels got captured by floes of ice, and galleons and larger vessels attempted to reach safe harbor before the ice reached them, but nearly all failed. Fishermen and sailors alike stared dumbly at the elvish skykeep as its shadow crossed their vessels and the skykeep continued, heading to the capital island of Crete. Oracles, priests, and sorcerers stood upon the coastal walls of the capital.

A man in red and orange robes, who held a staff topped with powerful flames, chanted and waved his staff about dramatically. When his chant ended, a large orb of fire formed and sailed through the air to crash into the oncoming ice floes, but the flames sputtered out to no effect in the face of the Ethereal ice. The man tried again and again, in growing panic. The oracles watched him in consternation.

A priest of Apollo pleaded with the sun god until light rays spilled from behind a cloud to bathe the ice in an inferno of sacred light. Sadly, the sacred light did nothing more than provide divine lighting to set the scene, and it failed to melt even a centimeter of ice. The priest wailed and called for more faithful to join him in prayers. The light condensed into beams that almost looked like lasers but accomplished nothing else, even when a second priest and dozens of lay folks joined the prayers. The floes of ice continued to wash up against the sandy beaches of Crete.

"Oh jeez, I'm feeling a little villainous here," Aetheria commented as the cities' magically inclined citizens attempted to thwart her enforced lockdown of their islands.

The laser generated by Apollo's faithful swung toward the Mellow Mallow, and Aetheria had to hop up and move to interpose between it and the keep. A few stone bricks sizzled before her hand closed around the light. The entire beam froze at her touch before it vanished into her repository. A new beam did not come, so she hopped off the wall and landed with shards of ice flying every which way on the shore of Crete.

"Who speaks for the islands?" Aetheria demanded in a voice that might have echoed all the way back to Uruk and beyond.

Two beams of light flared onto the beach. The first solidified into a woman of mature beauty with a regal air. The diadem upon her brow, the high-piled hair, and the peacock feathers adorning her gown all screamed one name into Aetheria's mind: Hera, Queen of the Gods. Next to her appeared a man who appeared to be in his late teens. His physique was well-defined and athletic, and upon his long hair lay a wreath of laurel. A bow hung on his back, next to a quiver that mythology said could deliver death or disease immediately. Light sparkled around him in a radiant halo, and the world whispered his name: Apollo.

"I speak for Crete," Hera proclaimed.

"I speak for the Aegean people," Apollo corrected her.

"Why don't you two sort that out in Olympus, then just pop back down here when you've decided who's in charge? Perhaps you could name a human to be a leader and see which of you two the people choose, if either." Aetheria didn't bother to hide her annoyance at the two gods. She'd already annihilated three of the children of Cronus, and she'd make it four if Hera decided to be a problem.

Both gods opened their mouths to speak, but a third voice interrupted them.

"I, King Minos, son of Zeus, speak for Crete and the Aegean Isles." The voice belonged to a man with brown-gray hair, a beard, and regal island vestments to match his crown. This declaration came with applause from the gathered people upon the city fortifications, save the clergy of Hera and Apollo, who scowled at everyone.

Apollo's beautiful face turned into an ugly look, and then his eyes spasmed like a seizure patient. When his eyes quit spasming a second later, he said no words, just vanished in a pillar of light the same way he'd come.

Hera's foot stomped into the sand, and dark, ominous clouds formed in the sky, as sharp gales tried to create large waves over the ice-laden water. Aetheria lifted a finger, and the clouds and wind froze.

"You dare try to supersede my control of the sky? I am the Queen of Heaven!" With that declaration, Hera redoubled her efforts. Harsh winds blew her peacock cloak out for all to see, and Minos stumbled back a few meters.

Aetheria smiled and reached into her soul to brush up against the essence that she had avoided ever brushing against. The winds stopped. The clouds broke. The sun shone in radiant glory across the endless Ethereal ice.

". . . how?!" Minos demanded to know.

"Ouranos?!" Hera said the name of her grandfather with fear, trepidation, and overwhelming panic.

"I hold the power of Ouranos and Inanna. None shall claim to own the skies before me, or they will join Zeus in his fate." Aetheria allowed the frigid light of Ohr Ein Sof to pour out of her third eye. The light did nothing but send shivers through Hera, since Aetheria could not correctly utilize the unadulterated power of Ein Sof yet, but it made the goddess turn whiter than her dress.

"You may leave, Hera. Now!" Aetheria rarely spoke in such a stern and demanding way. Apparently, she should, though, because Hera vanished in a beam of light. This left Minos alone on the beach with a confused look marring his face.

"How do I address you?" Minos asked with as much bravery as he could muster.

"You may address me as Lady Aetheria." Aetheria had put in quite a bit of work to reach the fifth tier of her cultivation path, and while she wasn't an Ethereal Lady as had been planned, Lady was still the title she would make use of until she ascended another tier. Aetheria shrugged off the icky sensations that accompanied channeling the essence of Ouranos. The masculinity of his essence did not bother her, but the emotional resonance that spread through her mind upon touching him felt repellant.

Like the sky he represented, Ouranos stood above all other beings. A vast sea separated him from even gods, of whom he stood as the progenitor and tyrannical creator. At his heart, though, Ouranos stood as a small man terrified of being surpassed by his children, a failed father who, unable to endure his defeat at the hands of Cronus, gave up personhood to remain the aloof, untouchable sky—a fate Ouranos shared with Ananke, whom Aetheria also possessed the essence of. Yet despite it all, when she had touched the essence of Ouranos, somehow the light of Ohr Ein Sof had seemed *closer*, almost able to be manipulated and controlled.

What did Ouranos have to do with Ohr Ein Sof? *Not a dang thing.*

"What can the island of Crete do for you, Lady Aetheria?" King Minos bowed low.

"Stop any hostilities with Uruk. Make peace between you so that both of your peoples may prosper." Could it be as simple as Aetheria giving a commandment to the king?

"The Urukian dogs killed my father, as well as three other gods. How can we be expected to make peace with them?" Minos demanded an answer heatedly.

"Well, the people of Uruk killed no gods. I killed Zeus, Poseidon, Hades, and Athena. I also slew Anu, the High God of Uruk, and by the time this is settled, I'll probably have to kill a few more gods. Any god that stands in the way of humans finding a path of their own will join the list of the departed." Aetheria cringed slightly at the words she spoke, but more and more, she felt it to be the actual path forward, especially when it came to reality outside of the towers.

Minos lost what little color his face had retained to this point. Within her proclamation, the king heard a decree of fate that Aetheria herself hadn't intended, and his mind swam with images of fire, war, chaos, and death, and the certainty that nothing he did could stop it, prevent it, or even delay it. An inevitability had been declared which even the Fates could not stop. He stared blankly at the blue-and-red-haired woman.

"You okay there, King Minos?" Aetheria tried to draw his attention back to reality, but the man's eyes remained blank even when she shook his shoulder. Pulses of healing did nothing for him, either.

"He has abandoned this reality. Something in your words gave him an oracle's vision, and now his soul wanders the infinite labyrinth of the tower, desperate to seek a new vessel far, far from here. Will Moros oblige or cast him into a body once more?" Aoibhe descended from above. The rustle of angelic wings against the sea breeze created a beautiful accompaniment to her descent.

"Can you just . . . pop him back in?"

"I can. A little starlight, and he'll forget most of what he glimpsed. You'll need to be more careful, dearest. Even a careless thought from you can break the body or soul of the weak, and the more we grow, the worse this shall become until we transcend this reality itself." While she spoke, Aoibhe wove her fingers through the air, which left trails of purple stardust that glowed eerily in place. When the glyphs were arranged as she wanted them, she tapped a finger against the forehead of Minos and his blank stare.

A ghostly form flowed back into the king, and after a cough, sputter, and a lot of blinking, the king apologized.

"I'm terribly sorry. Something most dire came over me there. I can't seem to remember it now . . ."

CHAPTER 26

Metanoia

Aetheria disliked politicking, so Minos's defeat and subservience after his little out-of-body experience smoothed the peace process between his people and those of Uruk. When a raven made of leaves and darkness landed on her shoulder and cawed in the voice of a Prince of the Fae, Aetheria and Aoibhe quickly reiterated their desires for peace between Uruk and the Aegean Isles and took their leave.

Arkaziel still slumbered in the courtyard when the two returned to the skykeep, which floated toward the lands of the Twilight Verdure. The two women sat atop the highest tower of the keep, a pot and teacups on the table between them.

"I've been thinking about some of the formalities when I ascend to the sixth tier." Aoibhe broke the silence.

"What formalities go with becoming a Monarch?" Aetheria honestly had no clue.

"It's customary to take on a new name, to signify your elevation beyond all that you have faced in your journey so far, and a sign that you are prepared to start over as many times as it may take to reach the heights of Sovereignty."

"Oh, a new name? Have you got any thoughts on the direction you'll take?"

"I have some thoughts on the matter, but I wanted to collaborate with you. I would like us to take the same surname when you ascend. I've put very little thought into what first name I will take, but I have put significant consideration into a name we could share. If that's something you'd like." Aoibhe's smile turned shy, self-conscious, but Aetheria's hand reached across the table to settle over the witch's. The physical contact allowed full knowledge of the depth of Aetheria's feelings for her and provided a banishment of any doubts either had.

"Is this sort of like getting married? Are you proposing to me!?" Aetheria turned bright red the moment she heard how high her voice went, but the love that crashed around her banished the self-consciousness immediately, and she found herself laughing along with Aoibhe.

"It is a commitment, yes. Not so large of one as the binding of our souls, but every bit as permanent. I believe the binding of our souls is more equivalent to your idea of marriage, but if that is an important idea to you, then yes, I am asking that." Aoibhe had to pause while Aetheria squealed happily.

"Obviously, yes! Tell me more about this, I don't know anything about the sixth tier. What name do you have in mind?" The broad smile on Aetheria's lips and the happiness in her soul conjured warm, Divine Light from her third eye, but she didn't even notice it beyond noting how gorgeous Aoibhe looked bathed in heavenly light.

"When you bring your Law into existence, there is no turning back or altering the path you stride upon. You codify who you are and what you believe into a power that rewrites reality. You may incorporate further epiphanies into your Law, but that is an addition of depth, an aside, not a rewriting of foundational meaning. I saw how you resonated with Belial's song, took note of your embrace of Nemesis, Love, Destiny, and Judgment in general, the reactions of the Aeon to you, and how you evoked a change in Minos without even attempting to. So, I sought a fitting surname for us both: Metanoia."

"Metanoia," Aetheria murmured the word, and meanings and synonyms in thousands of languages filled her mind from the emanations of Binah. It meant, simply, repentance or a spiritual conversion. More broadly, it meant a change in one's mind or way of life, and in Ath, it had the connotation of an action committed on others rather than personal repentance. Gods and higher beings were not penitent, after all.

"I love it. But what were you thinking of changing your first name to? Aoibhe is so beautiful."

"Well, I haven't entirely figured that part out yet. I've been focusing on a name we could share more than on my own. You could always help me think of something, couldn't you?"

"Kallos," Aetheria murmured as the tides of Binah filled her mind with knowledge. "Good, beautiful, noble, morally beautiful, quality; I can't think of anything that describes you better than that."

Aoibhe's smile warmed Aetheria's soul. The Nephilim's golden eyes shone with a light of their own, and her pale skin and blonde hair were bathed in a light that made the witch appear downright divine. The purple-armor dress Aoibhe wore accentuated her plentiful curves, but Aetheria couldn't be distracted away from Aoibhe's eyes.

"Kallos." The Soul Witch tried the word out and ran it across her tongue. "Kallos Metanoia. Yes, that is the name I shall declare within my Law."

Aetheria felt something change in the world with those words. An inevitability had been declared. A fixed point in destiny, *their* destiny, had been created from their conversation. Visions of Aoibhe wreathed in golden flames, humbling a figure shrouded in darkness with a mere word that Aetheria couldn't quite hear, teased at her mind before the tides of destiny turned murky and invisible once more.

"What did you see?"

"You, wreathed in flames, laying someone low with a single word. Quite the sight." Aetheria hid her confusion behind a grin, then finished her cup of tea in a single swallow. It had turned cold, the dredges bitter, but that just made it a better palate cleanser.

"I've brought low many, and no doubt there will be many more. Are we almost to the rendezvous with your fae?"

"Another ten minutes, I'd say. There's a ninety percent chance this is just an ambush, with the Prince in Green and the Prince in Purple teaming up against us, so they can settle their quarrels over our corpses. Of course, they don't know about you yet or that I've ascended a tier after our meetings. Speaking of, how close to the sixth tier are you now?" Aetheria couldn't tell by peeking at Aoibhe's aura with her Ethereal or Void senses. Like herself, her love had immense control over her aura.

"Do you want me to come down with you or descend once they've revealed themselves? Should we wake up Arkaziel?" Aoibhe glanced toward the courtyard where the cat snored loudly. "I'm very close now. The power you've shared, the deepening of our bonds, and an epiphany from Autophyes have placed me on the precipice. I will ascend in our next period of respite now that I have planned the final pieces of my Law."

"I'm not sure. Part of me thinks they deserve a solid thrashing, but they're also living beings. What do you think?"

"Moros delights in conflict, and the children of chaos will find conflict regardless of your intentions. It is their nature, and they cannot defy it for long, even when it is in their best interest to do so. For beings ruled by emotion, a foe greater than themselves creates an ulcer or tumor that, if not excised, will dominate their persona and lead them to a path of tragedy and revenge. They gained the worst traits of their Primordial progenitors." Aoibhe grimaced at the idea of dealing with the fae.

"The Primordials, eh? Yeah, that makes a lot of sense. I'd been wondering where the fae fit in the grand scheme. I still don't quite understand how they can take people's names and stuff."

"It's a variation of soul magic. Names, properties, and qualities are all a small portion of your soul's identity, which the fae can manipulate through their peculiar magic. Their magic is quite obnoxious and a pain to undo. Aetherius threw multiple floors of those types of challenges at me in his tower. Slaying the fae is the simplest method, but if they have already traded the quality you seek to return to someone, it can quickly become a bloodbath, considering how often they trade their trophies."

The Mellow Mallow halted its journey through the sky in a gradual deceleration until the skykeep floated in place above one of the many powerful magical sights within the Twilight Verdure. From above, Aetheria could discern the outline of a luminescent pond shaped like a teardrop. Thick trees shaded the banks of the pond, creating what no doubt would be a shadowy thicket beneath—and who knew what else. The illusions of the fae were no obstacle to her Void Gaze, and she could discern the presence of the Prince in Purple, the Prince in Green, and both of their entourages and additional forces hidden in the vicinity.

"Yeah, no, you just can't trust fae, I guess. Why do groups with stereotypes known far and wide about them ever not lean away from their bad reputations?" Aetheria asked Aoibhe with genuine confusion.

"I have no idea, darling. Do you want me to descend to the surface with you, or shall I rain spells down upon them from here?" Mischief and retribution shone brilliantly in Aoibhe's golden eyes, a reminder that despite her calm and wise demeanor, witches were never to be trifled with.

"I'll take Arkaziel down with me, and you can be our artillery once things go sideways. I initially intended to make peace with them, but clearly, that's not in the cards. I thought I made the repercussions of not working with me very clear to them." Aetheria squeezed her right hand into a fist, and tendrils of the Void and the Ethereal twined around the soulsteel mesh of the Astrum Nexus, causing the Aetherial crystals to pulse with the red and black of the two penultimate energies of existence.

Arkaziel lifted his head at the pulses of power growing around Aetheria's hands, and seconds later he settled onto her shoulder.

"It's been a while since I ate any fae," the StarMane managed to get out before he had to unleash a massive yawn. "Did you know their flesh tastes awful, but their essence and energy are a delicacy? Such variation and nuance is rare, especially amongst creatures with corporeal form. Can I call dibs on the Prince in Purple? He smelled like he'd give my cultivation a great boost."

Aoibhe barely contained her laughter at the antics of the cat, while Aetheria just smiled to contain her frustration.

"They are people, Arkaziel. They've got thoughts, emotions, loved ones. They aren't just a snack. Show at least a modicum of respect that we're about to snuff out the lives of a bunch of living, breathing, people." Aetheria narrowed her eyes, and hoped the slight scowl and tone of voice would get her message through the cat's thick head.

"And yes, I guess you can eat the Prince in Purple. The Prince in Green annoyed me more, so I'll handle him."

Arkaziel laughed raucously, and Aoibhe couldn't contain a sigh at the two of them.

"Let's get this over with," Aetheria said before hopping over the tower's ledge and falling toward the forest below, Arkaziel riding on her shoulder.

"Did you bring a wine to go with lunch?" Arkaziel inquired while they fell.

The Only Good Fae

Aetheria didn't bother to manifest wings or slow her fall, and when her boots hit the forest floor of the Twilight Verdure, the entire fae realm shook with impact; a powerful earthquake spread out and shook fae, trees, and buildings alike. Aetheria, meanwhile, went directly from falling to standing. She didn't use any dramatic landing pose, not even the beloved superhero landing; she simply landed, and the earth heaved and shook in excitement at her return. *That's new.*

The Prince in Green and his entourage hid behind many invisibility screens, nondetection enchantments, and even a screen of mists to try to obscure them physically if all else failed. Not a single method even slightly worked to hide their presence from Ethereal Sight, let alone Void Gaze. The self-illuminated pond heaved in the aftershocks of Aetheria's arrival, and a small pulse of power imbued into it created a geyser, which covered the area in a fine mist that nullified the invisibility, illusion, and waiting offensive and defensive magics the fae had prepared.

Swear words in fae tongues Aetheria didn't know filled the area: embarrassment, shock, and dumb, uncomprehending surprise ruined the Sylvan features of the would-be ambushers. Arkaziel's laughter on her shoulder made Aetheria assume he could understand the words or he was just a cat laughing at other people's misery. Both were equally viable explanations.

"Well, this didn't go to plan." The Prince in Purple groaned while he took in the revealed Prince in Green and entourage, the loss of all of their placed magics, and the cold smile on the face of the Asura before them.

"Attack, you moron!" The Prince in Green hissed the order at anyone who would listen, although the multifaceted emerald orbs that counted as his eyes stared daggers at the Prince in Purple. A blur of shadows interposed between the two princes, and the Prince in Purple tumbled across the ground. He was on his back, looking up at a dark panther with glowing yellow eyes, its heavy paws resting on either of his shoulders.

"Saaaaave me!" the Prince in Purple screamed shrilly when Arkaziel licked the fae's face with a tongue that made a grinding wheel seem smooth in comparison. Arkaziel's abrasive tongue ripped flesh from the fae's face, and blood welled to the surface. The Prince in Purple's entourage, seven men and women of a variety of Sylvan races, drew wands and blades before they leaped at the large cat to save their liege lord.

Vines emerged from the earth and wrapped around Aetheria's legs, as bolts of fire, lightning, and raw condensed mana filled the air around her. None touched her—they simply vanished the moment they got within a few centimeters of her body. She didn't destroy the vines; rather, she stepped out of them and walked toward the Prince in Green. More spells filled the air, but not a single one touched Aetheria.

"How!? Something has to work; kill the abomination, you clods! I am the son of Titania and Oberon. No godling will stop us from controlling the grove!" The Prince in Green conjured flames of summer in his right hand, and the green light of fireflies in his left hand. Hundreds of vines launched from the surroundings at Aetheria. They wrapped around her ankles and arms. The vines tightened and attempted to restrain her, while a transparent orange-yellow orb the size of a horse charged at her.

A single spike of ice rose from the ground and plunged into the orb like a needle, and the orb popped like a balloon. All of its heat and fire were drawn into the icicle before it disintegrated.

"She's still bound; stab her, you morons!" The Prince in Green commanded his lackeys and prepared another spell while his ten retainers charged at Aetheria.

The first retainer to reach Aetheria lunged at her with a fine rapier. The point of the blade touched Aetheria's coat, and the rapier shattered into a dozen pieces. The diminutive retainer, a gnome, looked shocked that their fae blade broke on contact. A small strand of Aetheria's aqua hair wrapped around the gnome's sword hand and flung him casually into the air, where a blast of stardust turned him into confetti. Literally.

"Last chance, Green." Aetheria gave her warning, interspersed with cries of pain from the carnage Arkaziel wrought upon the Prince in Purple behind her.

"For Titania! For Oberon! For the prince!" Three more retainers, an elf, a spriggan, and a satyr attacked Aetheria in a pincer formation. She stopped the satyr's mace with her hand, and a burst of cold flowed into the weapon and then into the satyr. The weapon shattered into dust, and the satyr followed a second later. The elf's and spriggan's weapons reacted the same way the first retainer's had when they struck against her coat; their enchanted blades broke apart into scrap on contact, and the wielders' eyes immediately filled with horror as slim strands of red and aqua hair caught their wrists and threw them into the air, too.

Stardust coalesced around them, and they transformed into leaves that were swept away on the winds—cursed to forever haunt the Twilight Verdure in the form of fallen brown and red leaves. *Dang, Aoibhe doesn't hold back, does she?*

"Just kill the blighted Asura already!" the Prince in Green screamed at his retaining forces.

"If you turn and leave, I'll let you live," Aetheria offered to the retainers as the five formed a circle around her. A moment of consideration filled their eyes, but something stronger than self-preservation compelled them to follow the will of Greenie.

To Void Gaze, a host of intangible threads connected the retainers to the Prince in Green. She identified a few types of threads as bound oaths, but as she studied them further, she realized that the rest were merely loyalty, magic, or faith. The threads of their Cosmic Song shone, too, but they were tiny little threads that she almost missed due to their insignificance in the greater cosmos, unlike the thick threads of fate that emerged from Arkaziel and Aoibhe.

None of the retainers retreated, despite the terror in their eyes and sweat on their brows. They were, each and every one of them, willing to die for their lord, or at least forced to do so by the oaths they'd sworn. *I could spare them.*

"*Kindness is good for the soul.*" Reverie's words filled her.

Feast on their marrow, drink their souls, let these fragments of incarnated chaos fuel your journey forward. They are illusory existences meant only to strengthen you. Let their purpose in life be complete. Only then can their essence escape the realm of Moros.

Aetheria almost laughed at the juxtaposition of Fred's command to feast on their souls and let them escape from the tower.

True oblivion, proper dissolution of their pathetic existence, can only come outside the tower, where they may journey to the Void and know the peace of inexistence.

I wondered where that was going, you know. Here I thought, hey, maybe Fred has sympathy for beings caught in the tower, but no, you want them to be fuel to the fire of the Void.

"*They are figments of chaos; they have nowhere else to go but to the Void. Yet, to spare them would still be best practice, regardless of whether you are free of Karma.*" Reverie's words made Aetheria pause and then laugh.

So, does my freedom negate the need to be a good person? It doesn't matter if I'm terrible or awesome; I can do whatever I want because I'm free of the Samsara, and its karmic judgment?

Yes.

"*Have you not considered the implications of your existence?*" Reverie's nonanswer earned an eye roll from Aetheria before she looked at the five retainers surrounding her. None had made a move; they waited for her to attack while the Prince in Green chanted and invoked a powerful spell behind them.

Some might argue that only when you are unmotivated by consequences can your true nature be discerned.

Aetheria took a step forward, and five spikes of ice shot up beneath each of the retainers. The dark ice struck the core of each retainer, devoured their energies, and dispersed them into dust on the wind. "If life is an illusion for these beings, I've done them a favor. How ridiculous."

The Prince in Green finished his chant.

"From the veiled depths of the Grove of Eternal Twilight, the remains of resentment shall rise, and the curse of I, the Prince in Green, shall form the last vestiges of the Queen of the Evening Mist into this promise! Your steps shall ever be misled, by the ancient powers of my Sylvan throne, I d—"

The Prince in Green's voice cut off, as a figure of black diamond appeared in front of him. One of six arms lifted him into the air, the words crushed out of his throat. The creature stared at him with three eyes, and the central one shone with a Divine Light in contrast to the damnation of Void found in the other two.

"I'm going to stop you there. Not because your curse would work, but because it won't." Aetheria's voice eroded the sanity of the prince. His large emerald eyes lost their color, and his skin and hair slowly turned colorless and gray. Aetheria said no more because the mind of the Prince in Green had already broken in the face of the Void, so one of her extra arms plunged into his chest and absorbed his core. The prince tasted like kiwi and cherries, with a burning aftertaste of cinnamon and fire, and Aetheria reverted to her human form.

"What'd yours taste like, Ark?"

"Chocolate and tea," Arkaziel answered immediately, and he hopped onto her shoulder. "Now what?"

A flutter of wings accompanied Aoibhe's descent, and the Nephilim also looked to Aetheria for the answer of what their next step would be.

"It's time to find a way into this Grove of Eternal Twilight. It is the center of everything between the different people, and maybe we can find something useful there. If it's a power source, maybe you could break through there, Aoibhe?"

"Possibly," the Soul Witch agreed.

"Sounds like there's at least the ghost of someone powerful and a temple to Inanna to boot. It's been a while since I ate a ghost." Arkaziel practically drooled.

"Onward then. If we can't find an entrance to the grove, we'll make one," Aetheria declared, even as mental images of the multitude of ways each of the party could destroy mountainsides filtered through her mind.

CHAPTER 28

The Grove of Eternal Twilight

Explosions were one way to get inside the large hill on which the tower had started, but that wasn't the way that Aetheria opted to go. Instead, she formed a whirlwind of absence around herself and walked straight into the hill. Behind the whirlwind of absence, a ring of snowflakes twirled, which created a tunnel of red ice in her wake. The smooth, nearly indestructible Ethereal ice prevented any collapses, and more importantly, its crimson glow provided a sufficiently mysterious ambiance for a tunnel leading into an enigmatic font of power.

When the whirlwind of absence ran out of stone and earth to devour, Aetheria dissipated the Void energies and stared at a whole new world. The cavern's roof glistened with shining, luminescent jewels, like stars against a black stone that fostered robust flows of Nether. The *Twilight* part of the grove appeared to be an apt name since there were no sources of light other than the dim jewels of the roof, and the slightest glow from the half-green, half-purple leaves of trees with the bark of ebony. The single species of tree comprised at least ninety percent of the grove and remained the only living species in the cavern. The others stood as stalwart stone guardians, having long ago been petrified by time.

In the center of the cavern, a ziggurat of stone blocks rose three levels, with the evenly leveled zenith of the ziggurat standing just above the canopy of the trees of the cavern. Thick, Nether-infused mists flowed through the lower grounds of the grove and between the ebony trees and teemed through a channel in the base of the ziggurat. Atop the ziggurat stood an elementally ancient temple made of simple sundried mud-bricks, an altar, and a statue of Inanna.

"It's exceptional. Dark and mysterious, enhanced by the ravages of time." Aoibhe complimented the cavern's beauty when she stepped up beside Aetheria and squeezed her hand. Arkaziel took the opportunity to jump from the witch's shoulder to his partner's.

"It's only half of the puzzle. There's another one in the sky. When they're both activated it will produce tremendous amounts of Ethereal power. Enough to resurrect a god . . . or for a new one to be born." Aetheria spoke with certainty, a total conviction of fact, rather than just supposition.

"And how do you know this, darling?" Aoibhe asked, not doubtfully, but with genuine curiosity. Aoibhe loved mysteries, and sentient beings were giant balls of mystery.

"Cause she's Ishtar, duh." Arkaziel answered in a small break from grooming his paw.

"I'm not Ishtar, Ark. I just have some of her essence, along with that of a bunch of other gods. I can pull some of their memories if I work at it, and this was her grand fallback plan in case she ever died. With both temples activated, and a fraction of her essence, she could be restored to life." Aetheria shook her head.

"And?" Arkaziel heard the unspoken *but.*

"But there's no reason for us to do that." Aetheria shrugged. "In fact, I've been thinking about fully consuming the god sparks I have. I've refrained so far, because I assumed there was a reason behind Nyx and Khaos choosing the gods they did, but most of them were assholes. Ishtar was a spoiled brat who got her brother-in-law killed, tried to depose her sister, then threw a temper tantrum and got her husband killed because it didn't work out how she wanted it to. Why would I restore her?"

"So that I could eat her?" Arkaziel seemed shocked and offended she hadn't considered him in her plans.

"Why would you restore a god?" Aoibhe asked, not quite rhetorically. "One who, by all accounts, is antithetical to your personality and who could provide no compensation in which you are interested? Meanwhile, fonts of power are rare and could be put to myriad uses. Especially Ethereal power formations."

"Why, indeed. I can't think of a compelling reason, which isn't very pleasant. So I have to assume Inanna/Ishtar were either incredibly self-centered to the point of forgetting to incentivize whatever would follow afterward, arrogant enough to assume they could take control of anyone who ended up with their spark, or there's something I'm missing." Aetheria grimaced and, with a gesture, sealed the red tunnel with a wall and door, then strode toward the temple to examine it.

"You are way overestimating gods. For all their near-omniscience claims and vast powers, they are just elemental forces with the same flawed personalities everyone but us StarManes have. Even the oldest are just people, but less people-y and more force-y." Arkaziel's simple worldview held a pleasant, if simplistic, allure.

"How astute. They all are cast from the same mold in the end. All souls and life are formed from a reflection of the Supreme Being. Aeons, angels, gods, humans, it doesn't matter; we're fragments of the godhead given form, free will, and let loose into a vast, uncaring cosmos. If we find our way home or if we get lost, it doesn't matter. Sooner or later, the pieces will find their way home and be reunited. For us, the journey matters, not the destination." The Soul Witch spoke with apparent authority, yet many gods would lash out at her or label her a heretic or blasphemer at her words.

The altar at the top of the ziggurat had weathered from the damp cavern air, yet it remained in a single piece, despite grooves and a few water holes. On the other hand, Inanna's statue remained pristine, as if it had only been carved a few days ago.

Protective magic lingered upon it, and when Aetheria looked closely, deeper enchantments lay concealed underneath the superficial protections. The depiction of Inanna focused on the sensual aspect of the goddess rather than her role in war.

Aetheria eyed the statue, and her features rippled to be replaced by a more tanned woman in white robes, black hair, and dark, sensual eyes. Copying the statue, she had wide, curvy child-bearing hips and large breasts and lost nearly a foot of her height, barely concealed by a white robe with gold adornments.

"What do you guys think?"

At Aetheria's query, Arkaziel hopped into the air to fly around her, while Aoibhe rolled her golden eyes and tsked at her.

"I do not like it. It is Ishtar, or Inanna, or Sauska? I like my beloved, my Metanoia, regardless of form." Aoibhe's disinterest in the form of the goddess put a smile on Aetheria's lips, and red-and-aqua bangs fell back to framing her face as she returned to being Aetheria.

"You just looked like food," Arkaziel declared when he settled back on Aetheria's shoulder. "Not a fan."

"You two are the best. Perfect answer. Do you sense the magic in the statue? There's more of Inanna's essence there, hidden beneath the temporal protections. What's the purpose?" Aetheria had a few ideas, but wanted the Soul Witch's take.

"It's a snack for me!" Arkaziel, ever single-minded in his hunger, chimed in immediately.

"I believe the idea is that once a link between the two temples is established, if the host that triggered it is capable of resisting Inanna, the essence of the statue would join and overwhelm the host. Few could resist a goddess's ambush on their soul while absorbing large Ethereal flows. No doubt she planned to incarnate inside a mortal vessel, then rebuild her divine vessel with the power of the temples at the mortal vessel's expense. Ereshkigal would never release her hold upon Inanna without compensation."

"What do you think we should do with this essence?" The distaste in Aetheria's eyes crept into her words, despite her best attempts to sound neutral.

Aoibhe's finger tapped Arkaziel's nose before he could speak.

"I believe that the discorporate gods yearn for an end, and it is within your abilities to grant them that end. It takes great compassion to show mercy to the unworthy, the broken, and the damned. It is easy to help the innocent, the weak, and the trodden upon, but the vain, self-obsessed, and once-mighty require an actual test of compassion to receive a benevolent ending."

Aetheria pinched the bridge of her nose tightly, and gave Aoibhe a rueful look.

"Dad always said your spouse should make you better, not worse." The witch smiled at the compliment while Aetheria fought down the surge of pain in her heart. She'd never get to introduce her father to Aoibhe or Arkaziel.

"If I gather her essence, can you summon the rest? I want to catch as much of what remains as we can."

"I can only try. Do you wish to attempt this now?"

"Sure, let's go for it. If we can knock Inanna off the list, we shouldn't run into any setbacks triggering the power sources for you to rank up here."

"The prince also mentioned a powerful fallen fae here. We should investigate that before we start any large rituals. Fae are always ruining everything. Best if we don't give them a chance to interfere, and it's definitely not because I'm hungry and they taste amazing." Arkaziel tried his hardest to make his concerns sound altruistic, which got him a head ruffle and chin scratch from Aetheria.

"Alright, we'll finish our survey of this place before we start any elaborate rituals. I don't think we're going to have to go far, though." Aetheria gestured toward the whole grove, and the eerie silver mist that had risen to cover the ground and the whole first level of the ziggurat they stood on.

"What name did that dolt try to invoke to curse me? The Queen of the Evening Mist? It seems that the rumors of her demise were highly exaggerated." Aetheria's third eye could see unhindered through the gathering mists, and she spotted a figure approaching through those tides. As the strange entity approached, Aetheria realized what she saw wasn't an actual person, but a long gray hooded cloak, a blue corset, and blue pants that had mist billowing through them. An empty crown glimmered beneath the hood of the cloak.

"Yeah, no. This is going to be weird," Aetheria prophesized.

CHAPTER 29

The Queen of the Evening Mist

Hail, travelers of the Ethereal Path." The voice came smoothly from the empty garments. The speaker sounded both female and Irish to Aetheria. No matter which of her senses she bent to observe the insubstantial entity, the clothing remained vacant, and the only signs of energies and magic infused the garments themselves. The mists rose three stories to the level of the temple, and the entity stood atop them as if they were solid ground.

"Hello there. Who do we have the privilege of speaking with? Are you a guardian of this place?" Aetheria opted for the polite option.

"That is a powerful hex you've been subjected to." Aoibhe's flat statement held borderline hostility.

"You are far too insignificant to eat." Arkaziel yawned and closed his eyes, dismissing the entity without a second thought.

"Rudeness, indifference, and borderline respect. How far I have fallen, thanks to that obnoxious brat Inanna. Once, I would have bound your mind to my whims for such blatant disrespect, witch, and feasted upon the marrow of your bones for your slight, cat. You, I would have lured into my dark pools for an eternity of pleasure before I broke you upon my knee."

Aetheria laughed. A dour look marred Aoibhe's features, and Arkaziel snored.

"Your continued existence is an abomination, a punishment reserved for those who have offended a god. Divine punishment exacted for eternity, the only release, death," Aoibhe noted calmly.

"Yes," the entity agreed with Aoibhe's explanation of her existence. "The goddess Inanna split my glorious existence in two: the mists bound in this tiny grove and the evening trapped in that awful temple of light in the heavens. Never a more spiteful woman claimed the title of Queen of the Heavens than that dreadful brat."

"Why did she bind you here?"

"Why? Why? Because I stole a lover from her and proved myself her superior. The Goddess of Lewd Endeavors could not tolerate being beaten at what she claimed as her own. She and that maid of hers led me into an ambush under the guise of peace, bound me in chains of iron and circles of salt, and tortured me until I was too weak to withstand her divine power. This is the glory of Inanna, ambush under the guise of diplomacy." The mist entity's voice dripped venom.

"Given her reputation, why would you walk into parley with such a cruel goddess?" Aetheria couldn't figure out why anyone would trust Inanna to begin with. Her question put a smile on Aoibhe's lips.

"Another minute and my magic would have penetrated her divinity, and she would have been my slave. Unfortunately, her dreadful attendant, Ninshubur, saw through my veil and noticed that my hidden fairy attendants were disrupting the protections around her mistress before I could strike fully." The mist lady seemed to regret only that she had been caught or had not acted quickly enough.

"Isn't it a bit hypocritical to curse another for committing the same actions you intended to?" Aetheria couldn't quite follow the logic of the scenario. It seemed like this entity and Inanna deserved one another.

"Perhaps. Why?" The empty clothes raged in a suddenly angry tone. Dark tendrils of the Void emerged from Aetheria's body, coiled and ready to strike the figure as if they were serpents.

"I don't appreciate attempts at domination," Aetheria warned the creature.

"We should dispatch this one and be done with her. If we ignore her, she will inevitably gain control of one of the three of us." Aoibhe had no sympathy in her voice, only dark wrath for anyone who would dare attempt a takeover of her, her beloved, or their cat.

"Oh please, you'd do the same thing if you were in my shoes."

"Maybe." Aetheria shrugged. "Does your binding here have a purpose?"

"I tend the grove and temples," the clothes answered and continued to try to subtly work past the defenses of the two women. One of Arkaziel's eyes opened slightly to give the clothes a hard stare.

"You've done a terrible job. The temple is in atrocious condition!" Aetheria gestured at the dilapidated altar and the crumbling walls. The ziggurat remained structurally sound, but the temple had seen far less care. *Why?*

Entwined in the stones slumber secrets veiled from the eyes of mortals and deities alike.

"Inanna never commanded I had to do a good job." The creature's laughter was contagious in a mad, absurd, and joyous way—another attempt to bypass their defenses, no doubt. Or maybe it was just a manifestation of the fae, a part of their legendary charisma.

"We have company," Arkaziel hissed from Aetheria's shoulder. A dome of shining light appeared around the trio moments before volleys of dark, powerfully magicked arrows struck the shield of light. The mist, Aetheria realized, had filled with the slender forms of gray-skinned elves with white, gray, and black hair. They all wore variations of black, evil-looking armor fitted with spikes, skulls, and gothic imagery. How hadn't she noticed them?

"Impressive. You managed to charm us so lightly we wouldn't notice your forces building up. You have a genuine deftness with your magic that is rarely seen." Aoibhe complimented the empty clothes while she lifted a gauntleted hand and traced a glyph of Stardust. Once completed, she blew on it, and the glyph sailed through the dome of light and out into the mist, where each of the strange shadow fae glowed with a sprinkle of Stardust.

A powerful magic flare occurred inside the dome, and a feminine body of flesh and blood filled the corset and cloak. A female fae with long ears, pale skin, blue-black hair, incandescent silver eyes, and a body built for sin stood before them. The chaotic grace of the fae left Aetheria's mouth dry, and thoughts and ideas reserved for Aoibhe filled her mind about the Queen of the Evening Mist instead. Were that not enough, it appeared the fae, or perhaps Arkaziel's magic, or perhaps just fate, had activated the temples, as a powerful Nether beam shot from the ziggurat up through the altar into the sky, and powerful Aether came down from the temple in the sky.

"You lot will make excellent slaves." The queen's smile sent shivers through all three, but the fae's triumph remained short-lived.

Laughter broke the smile on the face of the Archfae, and when the incandescent silver eyes took in Aetheria, the queen's eyes filled with primordial terror at what she saw.

Aetheria's Third-Eye of Ein Sof emitted dazzling light that filled the entirety of the Grove of Eternal Twilight. Not a single nook or cranny wasn't bathed in the infinite light of divinity. Mists froze. Elves froze. Pixies and a dozen satyrs grew hoarfrost coatings, and those who had been midmotion toppled over and shattered into pieces. Every minuscule piece of power that the Queen of the Evening Mist had grown in the grove over thousands of years vanished. The infinite light of Ohr Ein Sof carried a cold far beyond anything the Prince of Winter had ever dreamed of, and darkness, twilight, and evening could not gain a foothold in the absolute illumination of infinite light.

Tendrils of power from the Ethereal Flame and the Flame of the Void flowed around Aetheria like snakes, biting, tearing, and consuming any spells, forces, or powers that tried to affect herself or her companions. The queen failed even to see the moment in which Aetheria moved to her, and instead found spittle and blood running over her lips when a hand in a strange mesh glove grasped her throat, picked her up, and squeezed. Viselike forces shredded the vast amounts of power she retained in her being, and the grim reaper looked at her in the reflection of Aetheria's mismatched eyes.

Mere mists and pathetic fog, the limited power of an Archfae amounts to nothing before the unending darkness of the Void.

"Every thread in the universal fabric has meaning and intertwines to form a greater whole, but the Queen of the Evening Mist has no more spans to weave. Her misty realm has long since fallen to antiquity, and even memories of her are bare reflections of her one-time glory." Reverie seemed to eulogize the Queen of the Evening Mist, as opposed to Fred's eloquent version of "die, noob."

"What? How?" Blood splattered Aetheria's face with each word the Archfae forced out.

"You're just a reflection of yourself. You died long ago, and even your realm has fallen into forgotten memories. You're just a plaything to a bored god now. Reclaim your grace in the next turn of the wheel."

"She's all yours, Ark." Aetheria tossed the queen a few feet back, and the cat jumped off her shoulder to eat the queen in a few big gulps. Aetheria turned away and gazed at the grove. With a snap of her fingers, the ice figures shattered into dust, the souls of the fae harvested and devoured by the terminal cold of the Void.

Other than the coruscating streams of power going through the temple, silence reigned.

"What shall we do with the goddess's essence then, darling?" Aoibhe set a hand on Aetheria's shoulder and gave her a squeeze of comfort.

"We do what we planned. The temples are started; I don't think we can turn them off or back on if we did manage to turn them off. So, we call what's left of Inanna that will answer our call, and I give her an end, and you ascend to the sixth tier, Kallos Metanoia. Is your Law going to be a beautiful thing?"

"It shall be a spectacular Law, but how can I name other things beautiful when you're here?"

"Gag," Arkaziel said the word out loud before he mimed throwing up a furball.

The two women held hands, eyes interlocked with emotions and thoughts shared directly with one another. Seconds ticked by, and ice covered the ziggurat, etching sigils in Ath. Aoibhe released her hands once Aetheria finished, and drew out a stave with which she drew stardust sigils in the air.

"Time to shake the heavens," Aetheria told the other two, in a chipper tone full of false bravado.

"What happens to the essence you've got glued in your soul?" Arkaziel inquired, annoyed that he hadn't been included in the telepathic communication of the plan between Aetheria and the witch.

"I'm going to take the parts I want, and the rest will go to the Void."

"Which parts would you even want?"

"Inanna has quite a few authorities in her portfolio. I'll take beauty, divine law, love, sex, and war. Because who in their right mind wouldn't take *war*?" Aetheria really couldn't comprehend a climber who wouldn't take war.

"I'm glad you're thinking of me with your choices," Aoibhe teased Aetheria, and both laughed.

"Arkaziel, I'm going to trust you to eat anything that comes and isn't Inanna, with extreme prejudice. Aoibhe will call Inanna's essence to us, and I'll harness her. It's your time to shine, buddy."

"You had me at 'eat anything,'" Arkaziel answered hungrily.

Aww, my little kitty is such a big boy. Even an Archfae didn't fill up his tummy.

CHAPTER 30

Inanna Disassembled

Give me your hand." Aoibhe waited patiently, holding her left hand to Aetheria. "If you need another arm, form it now instead of when it will distract me. Once you call for Inanna's essence, I will amplify the call and your resonance, so envision the path to success as we work. It is possible that you may be able to exert your authority over Inanna since you currently hold autopotency as an authority."

While Aetheria listened to Aoibhe's explanation, she formed four more arms, for a total of six. One hand held Aoibhe's gauntleted hand, another gripped the altar, and the other four remained free for whatever tasks were required. They had no real idea if this would properly work and, if it did, what it might summon. Would it generate a false version of Inanna? The true essence of the discorporate god? Different gods? An elder god? Would this ritual rile up the Overgod and see Archons sent after them?

"Alright, ready, Arkaziel?"

"You know it, Blue. Bring me some snacks!"

"Good luck." Aoibhe's love and faith flowed through their soul connection and provided a surge of warmth so powerful it warmed her mental outlook and thwarted the ever-present frigid sensation the Void afflicted upon her chest.

"Don't need it. I got you, Arkaziel, Fred, and Reverie. We won't fail." Declaration made, the air around her shimmered densely with a white light that slowly faded. All three noticed it, but none commented on the strange phenomenon.

"Inanna, Daughter of Enlil, Queen of Heaven, Goddess of Love, War, and Fertility, I call your shattered essence to me. I bear your spark, and you shall not deny me. Ishtar, your essence will come to the altar, to me. Ishtar, the Divine Light of the Euphrates, by the ancient ziggurats and eternal stars above, you are commanded before me. Cross through the celestial door; I have marked the way with your eight-pointed stars."

With each word, Aetheria echoed the essence of Inanna within her and imagined herself issuing a command to the universe for Inanna's other pieces to flow through the celestial gates, the holes in reality that the divine could use and appear before her. A frigid red sigil appeared on the altar, an eight-pointed star, the Star of Ishtar, that served as the holy symbol of Inanna. Ethereal power enhanced by the Ethereal Flame created a divine beacon that could not be ignored.

"Whispers of the ancient powers, echoes of the timeless essence of Ishtar's soul, we call you through the sacred door. Let no wall or barrier stall, for we have bridged worlds apart." Aoibhe's chant empowered the conjuration of Inanna, and golden and black flames sprang to life along the Star of Ishtar as the gateway opened. Tiny motes of essence sprang through the celestial door, iridescent orbs of a dozen colors that constantly changed appeared in answer to the call, more and more appearing by the second.

Aetheria's third and fourth hands were placed palms up, and she commanded the essence of Inanna to form into a single congealed manifestation, even as additional particles came through the gate.

The earth heaved, and trees swayed; one or two collapsed into newly made deep rents in the soil. The awful smell of sulfur and decayed remains filled the Grove of Eternal Twilight, and the screams of demons and the undead preceded the arrival of the hosts of Ereshkigal. The first batch of skeletal bat monsters to rise from one of the rents were blasted into oblivion by a coruscating beam of light from Arkaziel's eyes. Duplicates of Arkaziel blurred around the grove, a flurry of claws and violence that dispatched and consumed the vanguard of the underworld before they could even mount an offensive on the dilapidated temple.

Bubbles of Inanna formed above the altar and drifted to the coalescing ball of essence, while Aoibhe pulsed with power and focused on the amplification of Aetheria's call from the highest of heavens to the deepest of hells and across all of the infinite material worlds of physical creation. With the powerful support magic in effect, Aetheria felt like she had turned into a lightning rod for Inanna. Awareness of each and every piece of essence formed in her mind, and when she turned her mind to them, they could not resist her summons for even a moment. The celestial door spewed more and more pieces of Inanna into the temple, where they were sucked into the ball of essence as if by magnetism.

Through one of the widening hell-rents strode a ten-meter-tall woman clad in dark armor. Ereshkigal's skin tone closely resembled night, while her eyes were a deep red, which starkly contrasted with the white-as-sun-bleached-bone locks of hair. Aetheria dimly noted she was beautiful in a Queen of Hell way.

+*We hit pay dirt!*+ Arkaziel exalted in the appearance of a worthy foe, and he dive-bombed the goddess, engaging in melee combat with an unprepared death god. When a god appeared, mortals usually gnashed their teeth and quailed or sought parley or at least attempted discourse. The StarMane didn't play by any rules of conduct, though, and instead went immediately to full-out attacking the Queen of the Underworld with claws and teeth while tendrils of shadow sought to ensnare her.

"You idiot cat, I'm here to claim my sister and torment her for all eternity. Why would you stop me?" Ereshkigal said.

-That's a genuine aspect of Ereshkigal; do not play with your food, Arkaziel,- Aoibhe warned the cat.

Arkaziel answered by biting one of Ereshkigal's arms clear off when she tried to defend against his bite with a shield of powerful Nether that his Void-sheathed fangs went straight through. The goddess stared in earnest shock and horror as the cat chewed, then swallowed her right arm. Arkaziel pounced again while she stared at him in stunned disbelief. Tendrils of the Void shot out of her own shadow like spears, piercing through her legs and back with extreme violence.

"Foul creature! I will destroy you!" The threat boomed across the Grove of Eternal Twilight, but it didn't stop the manifestation of more and more spears of twilight imbued with the Void.

"In the Cycle of Renewal, everything is changing; it's time to embrace your next stage of existence as my lunch. If you can't keep up with the times, all you've got to look forward to is oblivion. The struggle adds to the flavor. Fight harder!" Arkaziel enraged the Queen of the Underworld with his taunts.

Ereshkigal bent her divine power to her will, and the spears of darkness that ensnared her all shattered in a massive burst of crimson power, even the ones imbued with the Void. The goddess healed almost instantly once free, even her lost arm, but while she laughed and crowed in victory, Arkaziel appeared out of a shadow in front of her, and one of his claws plunged right through her armor into her chest, and when he pulled it back, her enlarged heart still beat upon the tip of his claw. He tossed the organ into his mouth and chewed.

Ereshkigal's eyes went slack, and Arkaziel enlarged enough to swallow the physical form of the goddess whole. The armor made it sound like he was eating a dumpster full of scrap metal, but Arkaziel chewed and savored each bite until the rents in the ground that led to the underworld lost their glow, and dark miasma formed around him. Spectral, smoky twilight skulls orbited around their new master.

"I have become Death! Oh, that was so tasty. Real gods are just yummy. Are any more coming? Please? I promise I won't eat you all, too!" The liar cat made the only promise he could think of to get another god to appear. "The Void is almost like cheating against gods. Maybe I'll eat the next one without the help of the Void."

Aetheria could only half watch the antics of the StarMane as he acquired authority over death. The orb in front of her started to resemble a person, and she could sense only three fragments of Inanna remained to be summoned. The one within her, the one within the statue, and a large fragment that would appear any second now.

"The last one is incoming, Aoibhe. You can drop the resonance, and I might need your help on containment."

New rents ripped the Grove of Eternal Twilight's ground, and green smoke flowed into the air.

~Looks like Nergal is coming to play with you, Ark. Have fun. Keep him away from the temple.~

The StarMane's only answer to Aetheria's telepathic message came as laughter, and then pure joy flooded their empathic bond with one another that only increased when a surge of stardust covered Arkaziel, as a result of Aoibhe's use of a strengthening spell on Arkaziel.

The final fragment of Inanna passed through the celestial gate as Nergal arose from one of the noxious rents in the floor. Once the motes of essence merged into the vaguely humanoid form of Inanna, Aoibhe punched the statue of Inanna and freed the second to last fragment of the goddess, leaving only the coalesced essence and that which had been put in Aetheria's soul.

Aetheria thought she saw a face almost form in the strange being of light before her, but she had to assume that was a figment of her imagination, and plunged two of her hands into the thing. It felt like she had dumped her hands into that nasty slimy goo they sold in film containers, the texture of which sent goosebumps and deep revulsion up and down her spine. She had, naively, expected the essence of a Goddess of Love to be less disgusting, if not downright pleasant.

"Fallen reflections of the creator. You expected something bright or pleasing? None of the gods of this realm will be much different, darling. This existence is a corruption, profane and full of suffering. We must ascend, or we too will be reduced to muck like this wretched thing."

"I almost feel bad for her." Aetheria grimaced and pulled an orb out of Inanna and consumed it. She repeated this four times and knew the names of each orb the moment she touched them. She intentionally left a few of the authorities she had no interest in and instead consumed love, sex, war, and beauty. Divine law couldn't be found within the essence of Inanna, and she didn't know why.

"Divine law isn't here," Aetheria told Aoibhe.

"Someone beat us to it? Why would they not have taken the others? Perhaps her killer took it?" The Soul Witch seemed as confused by this as Aetheria.

The air around Aetheria pulsed with power. Swords, axes, and the chants of legions filled the air, the echoes hanging before they slowly died. The moans of lovers, the cries of pleasure, and an intense lust so powerful it almost made Aetheria and Aoibhe dizzy struck them, then faded. Birds sang, the sun shone, and dew dripped from flowers. Beauty blossomed in a hellish cave full of the noxious mists of Nergal, petrified trees, and two women smiled at one another, and Aetheria swore she saw hearts forming around Aoibhe as if she were in a cartoon.

Authorities other than over oneself were, it seemed, trippy as hell when they settled into your soul and gave you power over them.

"Uffda. Sex almost knocked my knees out." Aetheria groaned, and Aoibhe laughed at her.

"I had to use the altar to stay standing," her beloved admitted with a flush to her face.

A tail formed on Aetheria's back, even as her extra hands vanished. A barbed stinger of the Void plunged into the sphere of Inanna, and devoured the goddess.

Inanna's essence flushed through the bonds she shared with Aoibhe and Arkaziel, while the untaken authorities were destroyed and converted into raw power. Finally, she conjured a marble-sized orb from her own soul, and the Void devoured that, too. Alarms rang through the misty lands the gods hid in as a rarity occurred. Inanna, blessed Ishtar, had died and could no longer be reincorporated.

    ~One down,~ Aetheria said with mental laughter.

    -So many to go,- Aoibhe noted. They'd only achieved the first step.

    +Hey, two down. I ate Ereshkigal, and Nergal is next.+

    ~Want help?~

    +Just watch this,+ Arkaziel bragged, and Aetheria and Aoibhe collapsed and sat together on the no longer blessed altar, exhausted and sweaty, but ready to watch the show of Arkaziel against the God of Death, Pestilence, and Destruction.

CHAPTER 31

Nergal vs the Cat

Three versions of Nergal rose from a different rent in the hewn ground of the Grove of Eternal Twilight, one for each of the authorities Nergal ruled over. The Nergal of death was a somber figure in black robes adorned with bones. The Nergal of pestilence wore green robes, had sickly jaundiced skin, and the air around him lay thick with infectious mists. The third Nergal, who represented the authority of destruction, wore bone armor and carried a bladed staff. Each glared murderous rage upon Arkaziel, and unlike Ereshkigal, no attempts at any form of communication were made with the cat.

A blast of pure, destructive Nether manifested in the hands of the destruction Nergal. Thick beams of wild Nether flowed from the god's left hand while he stalked closer, staff ready to attack when he closed the distance. The blast splashed against a wall of sacred silver light, which held but ever so slowly gave way to the approach of Nergal. The Nergal of death thrust a hand up, and the already ruptured ground shook as tides of the dead rose. The chaff would do nothing against Arkaziel, but the immense scythed bone golems radiated power on par with a sixth tier Cultivator. The Nergal of pestilence waved a hand, and noxious clouds surrounded the minion army of the undead. Where the blasts of Nether chipped away at the dome of light around Arkaziel, the noxious fumes were like dipping the protective barrier in acid, and gaps formed.

"Oh, whatever shall I do?" Arkaziel laughed and lifted one of his clawed hands upward. The dome fell, and a black orb the size of a marble appeared where one of its edges had been. Twirling vortexes of light, Aether, and Nether were drawn into it.

"Did your cat just make a black hole?" Aoibhe asked flatly.

"No, no, yeah. It sure does look that way." Aetheria grimaced.

The undead tumbled toward the vortex of power, and blades of inexistence diced the horde like they'd been thrown into a giant food processor. The blades of absence cut through physical matter without resistance, and the bones and rotten flesh fell into the singularity and vanished. In a second, every undead except the giant scythe-armed bone golems had been obliterated and thrown into whatever hell the black hole led to, and knowing Arkaziel, it would be a bad one.

Destruction Nergal rushed forward when the protective barrier fell; his staff bore down maliciously at the cat in a two-handed swing while the head of the staff crackled with deadly magics. The head of the glowing staff crashed into Arkaziel's obsidian scales, and withering, destructive magic cascaded along them.

"Reflect." Arkaziel hissed the word in Ath, confident, absolute, despite the pain of the attack, and the world seemed to hang for a moment. Arkaziel's voice twisted reality in a way that Werylin's use of the Words of Creation had not. Arkaziel had put together enough of Werylin's magic in their time together to take the basics of the Words of Creation and empower the magics even further with the divine language, the source code of reality.

"You can't!" Pestilence and death Nergal shouted simultaneously, but the withering destructive magic reversed course, heedless of their demands. It crawled back down the length of the staff, and wreaked havoc upon the body of Nergal of destruction. As Nergal's robes flaked into nothing, Arkaziel lunged forward and ate his first Nergal of the day. Violent crunches, no savoring, gave away that the blistering magics were a scourge to his tongue, but he persevered and finished his meal quickly. Pulses of black lightning formed at Arkaziel's eyes and spread across his body.

The bone golems were upon Arkaziel then. They were fast, strong, and deadly. Aetheria felt the slight pull on her essence, and Arkaziel became a serpentine blur. Explosions of light occurred every time Arkaziel clawed one of the golems, and there were so many explosions of light that the room quickly looked like a sun to anyone without alternate forms of sight. Small chunks of bone littered the battlefield when the light subsided, and each danced with jolts of black lightning, which prevented the foul necromantic magics from re-forming the golems.

"You may have raised the most destructive StarMane in history, dear. Does that count as a crime against sentient species?" Aoibhe didn't seem shocked, but knowing the capabilities of an uncontrolled cataclysm and witnessing them were two different things.

"Ope, my bad. Is there an interstellar criminal court that will want words with me?" Aetheria didn't feel bad about it, but it seemed the most appropriate thing to say given the situation. This was one of the rare occasions Arkaziel tapped into her powers when she was idle, and it let her examine the energy flow through her soul linkages. It appeared Arkaziel using her Flash Mode consumed roughly the same energy as when she used it, but it also took energy from him. *It makes sense that we both must pay the price for him to use one of my abilities.*

Not that it could be considered a price, with the direct connection to the Origin and the Void in her soul providing unlimited sources of power to draw upon, and regenerative powers that constantly cleansed Aetheria's mind and body of fatigue, injury, and even the wear and tear of overexerting herself or what her physical vessel could channel before taking damage. Even the damage to her soul caused by overexertion of power repaired itself so rapidly as to not be a concern.

Aetheria felt the draw on her power diminish, and the dark electricity around Arkaziel had turned into almost a cocoon made from bolts of black lightning.

The death Nergal gestured, and black-robed specters with scythes appeared behind him only to rush forward toward the StarMane, an unending tide of specters. The specters hewed at Arkaziel with their scythes. The scythes didn't pierce the scales; they weren't physical weapons. They hurt Arkaziel, though, as Aetheria felt the pain flood their bond as if they were hacking at her. Arkaziel endured the pain while the black lightning obliterated two specters for every one who hit him. *Why is he just taking the damage? Oh, he wants to see how powerful the lightning is, maybe?*

Pestilence Nergal joined the fray with no hurry. He walked through the specters as if they weren't even there, and ten meters from Arkaziel, he began to spew a horrific cloud of putrid gas at the StarMane. Perhaps it was Aetheria's imagination, but even the specters seemed to try to avoid the gas. The Grove of Eternal Twilight grew darker, and more and more black lightning grew around Arkaziel. Even as far from the fight as Aetheria and Aoibhe were, the scent of ozone lay heavy.

"The memories of his predecessors allow him to master lightning quickly, I see. What an awful gift to give to a race of predators," Aoibhe mused to herself, while Aetheria didn't feel like Arkaziel had mastered lightning that quickly. Were Arkaziel's genetic memories a match for the Sefirot? *No, but that it's even close is impressive. Chronos really went all out with these cats.*

"So, you guys got anything else, or are you just going to get eaten like Ereshkigal?" Arkaziel taunted the two aspects of Nergal.

"Impudent cat!" Nergal and Nergal shouted in grave indignity at the callous disregard of their legendary wrath. They ceased the tides of specters and the cloud of failing gas. A terrible gate opened, from which a skeletal dragon emerged. Its bones shone with an awful putrid green, and anyone who looked upon the bones felt the sure, disquieting knowledge that all the plagues, illnesses, and toxins in the universe were concentrated in the bones of this strange draconic lich.

"I was going to eat you nice and fast like I did the first one, but now? Now I'm going to eat you assholes real slow, savor the flavor, and make you rue the day you dared to send the remains of my great-great-grandfather against me." Arkaziel's malevolence usually came in a lazy or benign form, but now the cat's voice dripped with promises of a slow death at the affront against StarMane-kind.

"Oh yeah. They're fucked." Aetheria couldn't stop herself from laughing, and then Aoibhe laughed uncontrollably.

"What the heck are you laughing at?"

"I don't think I've ever heard your accent get that thick." Aoibhe's teasing came with a smile.

Arkaziel threw forward hundreds of orbs of light with a snarl, but these were no ordinary flames, but the sacred silver light of Astral Fire. The silver flames splashed against the toxic bones of the StarMane lich, which burned in the purifying flames. The barrage knocked the lich back with a tide of irresistible momentum that pushed it all the way to the rocky walls of the cavern, and once its tail hit the wall, Arkaziel lunged.

Not at the lich, but at the two Nergals. In a burst of speed that rivaled Aetheria's maximum, Arkaziel grabbed a Nergal in each hand, and jolts of lightning paralyzed them in his grasp. Death and pestilence Nergal were thrown into his mouth, which also had cascades of black lightning, and Arkaziel chewed. Slowly. Each crunch of divine, or darkly divine, flesh, blood, and sinew seemed amplified as it echoed across the grove. With each awful bite, reality contorted around Arkaziel.

Symbols and illusions manifested and vanished in the air around the black storm of lightning that was Arkaziel. All of them were related to death and pestilence, necromancy, and plagues. With each bite, Arkaziel usurped portions of Nergal's authority.

+*What a great day. First Ereshkigal, then Nergal. It's too bad he didn't send an aspect of war or the underworld, but he's still out there. Next time we see him, he's toast—time for dessert.*+

Arkaziel lay on the rent ground while tendrils of darkness expanded across the grove, pulling pieces of bones from the undead horde and the obliterated StarMane lich into his stomach through the devouring darkness. Only then did his eyes close, and he snored.

Aetheria looked around the grove, then back to the altar. The altar had lost all power, but the beams of Ethereal power still filled the air. Both women stood up and walked back toward the altar.

"It is time to become a Monarch." Aoibhe's smile shone like a sun, but her eyes were hard with determination.

CHAPTER 32

Monarchy, or I Fought the Law

Despite the logical obviousness of the statement that everything in her life had led to the present moment, it had. From the moment Aoibhe cast her first hex to the first soul she brought to gnosis, her entire life had been in preparation to write her own Law and decree that reality should be *this* and not *that*. This was one of the trials that any existence that wished to reach the pinnacle of power had to conquer, but that most would never come close to. As the daughter of the Dark Angel, the deck had begun stacked incredibly in her favor, but even amongst the descendants of the powerful, reaching this stage was an accomplishment, especially so young. Few made it before one thousand years old, and Aoibhe remained in her second century.

"Here we go," Aoibhe murmured and looked at Aetheria. Her love's bangs were uneven and different colors to boot. Red, black, and aqua strands blended in a chaotic mess of hair that gleamed with an internal light. All three of Aetheria's eyes were utterly on Aoibhe as if nothing else in the universe was worth paying attention to, and in a way that made Aoibhe feel fully seen and accepted.

Aoibhe drew strength from her partner, and even when her eyes closed, she could feel the connection between their souls. A connection so powerful that it carried its dangers, but those dangers were small compared to the unending bounty of benefits it created. Dangers that, as far as she could tell, each of their unique natures canceled out. Neither was in any way ordinary, and amongst the different, Aoibhe would likely have put them both in the extra special category.

A realm of purple and black formed in her mind. A glorious sun shone upon a solar system of five planets separated by fields of asteroids. The worlds were, from closest to the sun, Yechidah, Chaya, Neshamah, Ruach, and Nefesh. Aoibhe willed her physical hand into the streams of Ethereal power in the temple and tied that incredible energy source to the blazing sun in her inner realm. An axis of light blossomed from the sun as if a beacon had formed in its center, and now beams of light shone from the top and bottom poles of the star.

While Aoibhe fit the broad categorical definitions of a witch, that aspect of her path had never been a primary focus. Hexes and curses were supplementary powers she fell back upon if her ability to manipulate spiritual resonance failed her. Unlike her dear Aetheria, Aoibhe could grasp small beams of Ein Sof and weave them into miracles, albeit with great effort. Such was the advantage of being a daughter of a fallen Aeon who dwelled in the corrupt physical world to offer salvation through gnosis, even if said father resorted to abominable machinations and actions to force mortal-kind to become aware of the cage of torment that they were trapped within.

Aoibhe allowed herself to flow backward a layer, to behold the essence of her soul. If her being had a primary color, it was purple—a vibrant color of depth and command, authority and rule, beauty and nobility. Other colors filled it: golden flecks, Ethereal tides that flowed between red to aqua and back, and dark strains of black that gradated into the complete lack of anything, the absence of the Void. The introduction of the Void had been recent, thanks to Aetheria. Still, Aoibhe had controlled her transformative exposure by employing a miracle to stabilize herself, which likewise contributed to the stabilization of Aetheria and Arkaziel.

The Divine Light of Ein Sof bathed her soul, filled her with just enough of the divine power to be dangerous, and left her yearning for more of its enlivening touch. To stride into the sixth tier, Aoibhe needed to incorporate the infinite, boundless power of creation into her soul, which would put her on the first step of eligibility to transcend physical reality and enter the divine realms, potentially even the highest realm, Pleroma, where dwelt the Aeons and the manifestation of the godhead. She had to reforge her soul as every ascension through the tiers of the Paths required, and the changes wrought each time grew exponentially.

Entering the sixth tier required evolving the shackling meat sack that was the body into a properly amalgamated spiritual being with physical form, a trick Aeons themselves could not accomplish, as they were diminished and corrupted by taking on any physical form at all. Well, if you wanted to reach the seventh tier, it did. If you were willing never to progress again, there were other paths to Monarchy, but those were for fools and the desperate, and Aoibhe was neither of those things.

Aetheria had provided her with a foundational base to shorten the transition to a spiritual being. Thus, Aoibhe resonated with Aetheria to mimic the complex dance required to weave Ethereal power and the Void's power into the godhead's infinite light. When she finished, a second pillar of light formed another axis going through her inner world's sun, the manifestation of two diluted forms of power re-formed into a facsimile, almost ninety-nine percent accurate, of the ultimate power of creation. When blended with the natural flow of Ein Sof into her soul, it empowered her in a way she had never experienced before. How many miracles could she perform without even feeling a touch of exhaustion now? Dozens?

Aoibhe's soul flowed like a jellyfish through water; the colors within the royal-purple soul-shell danced through the rainbow and then expanded into a more human form. Not that she was human, which the large wings her soul-form manifested gave testament to. The hard part came when she envisioned her spiritual form to match her physical body. If your inner realm and soul were a bag accessed by the aperture of the soul within your body, what came next could best be described as reaching your hand into the bag, pulling it inside out, and having the spiritual settle into your material body.

Aetheria's soul held a truth that had not fully awakened yet, of which her ice and regeneration powers were mere facets. Still, Aetheria had used Aoibhe's truth since they forged a spiritual connection. Aoibhe's truth was this: As Above, So Below. Resonance connected everything in physical creation to the highest levels of the Pleroma. Aoibhe's path had been fundamentally built upon manipulating the spiritual, thus affecting the material. This resonance was the foundation upon which Aetheria copied the magical abilities of others and things. A clever use that Aoibhe had not properly conceptualized until recently. In-depth understanding and the ability to manipulate forces by harmonization with the spiritual universe seemed obvious, but few beings with the same powers had ever been accessible to Aoibhe.

Aoibhe's Law required one final rewrite of the ancient principle and saying "As Above, So Below," or at least a few additions. *As Above, So Below, As Within, So Without, Across All Planes, My Will Echoes.* These simple words comprised the foundation of all her magic. It, of course, seemed like something that should already be true. Yet the existence of the towers, their deleterious feeding upon the souls of the universe, proved beyond doubt that, for whatever reason, it was Rules for Thee, Not For Me. Yet she knew from her studies that it should not necessarily be the case. There had been a balance at one point, and then inexplicably, there wasn't.

As best she could put together, either a Cultivator or aeonic being had ascended to a high enough level of power to break the rules. Then, once broken, they had applied them to, at the very least, multiple existences, and more probably, a lot or all of them.

The being of glyphs, scriptures, and the concept of Rules for Thee, Not For Me appeared before Aoibhe, although it might be better to say she appeared before it. In the limbo between the spiritual heavens and the physical worlds, between infinite light and infinite darkness, Aoibhe appeared in the battleground of Law. She need not slay the Law, only damage it enough to allow her own Law to take root. Slaying and usurping the old Law with her own would come at the seventh tier.

"I normally wouldn't do this, but you are an abomination against everything which should be." Aoibhe waved her floppy witch's hat in the air, and from within the depths, a specter of inexistence flew out to attack the entity of words. The harbinger of inexistence left gaps in the scripture of words, destroyed the meaning of the Law across entire universes, and with each swipe, the harbinger grew into a giant mantis, swiping with immense claws and taking bites out of the Law, which in turn empowered the mantis.

In a massive blast of light, the Law fled the challenge. A more auspicious victory than Aoibhe had dared to dream possible. With a glance, the Mantis of Absence, now empowered into a Void Prince at the least, vanished and became a piece of paper that floated slowly to Aoibhe's hand.

It had, before she'd flung it from her hat, contained her most fervent wish to abolish this ridiculous Law, and when she flung it, she had infused it with all of the power of Ein Sof she could muster and conjured a miracle from the heavens. Strange, though, that the highest of realms would create a Void creature to do her job.

I approve. Shak'lath shall return to the Void, but he shall owe you for this opportunity. -Bythos

Once Aoibhe finished reading it, the paper turned to dust and drifted away, and lights coalesced around her. Beyond the material worlds, immense elder gods arrived to gaze upon her with multitudes of eyes and unending eons of ennui. From above, a horde of Aeons appeared, their whole existence on display in shining radiance, for each Aeon appeared only to be the meaning of their names, yet Bythos and Sige stood out mightily upon the Aeons. Together, they seemed so great as to dwarf all other Aeons and all of the elder gods assembled, which seemed to render the other Aeons moot in terms of balance. It seemed that a third faction should be present but had not come. Why?

"We await your declaration," Autophyes chimed.

"I am Kallos Metanoia, and my declaration is this. **As Above, So Below, As Within, So Without, Across All Planes, My Will Echoes**."

A powerful presence interposed itself across the ritual then, and black chains rose from below, white chains from above, and they formed tattoos of shackles across her wrists, and detailed art of chains flowing across her upper arms, coiled around her shoulders, and then her wings changed. One black, one white, both formed out of what her mind instinctively knew to be Heavenshadow Nebulite. Only they weren't just metal versions of her old wings; they were thick metal frameworks that trailed dozens of chains.

Kallos laughed. Aetheria would love how edgy her new wings were.

"You have been heard, Kallos Metanoia. We look forward to your next trial." Autophyes spoke for the Aeons once more. No elder god spoke at all, and whoever the third faction was, no one offered anything, either.

Then reality exploded into pain, as Kallos's spiritual and physical forms tried to overlap one another. Ascension, as everyone knew, was painful.

CHAPTER 33

Northern Lights

Aetheria watched the cascades of power overwhelm Aoibhe's body. To her enhanced sight, constructs of a purely spiritual nature flashed in and out of existence around her lover. Whenever one attempted to cause harm, Aetheria smote it with blasts of raw Ethereal power. This went on for a few hours until Aoibhe's body finally filled with Ein Sof's flow, the same infinite light that dwelled in her third eye and her dueling cores produced. Yet, no matter how Aetheria looked, she couldn't pinpoint how the light flow came to Aoibhe. A reserved source just entered the Nephilim from *somewhere*, while internally, she seemed to have set up a conversion process just like Aetheria herself used.

Only when Aetheria looked through the lens of the Cosmic Song could she see that the strands of Belial imparted small amounts of Ein Sof to Aoibhe, and now a new strand had formed from the dimensions higher than the Ethereal, a strand named Kallos, that sang the song of her friend's soul.

"What're you smiling about? I'm bored," Arkaziel asked with distrust before he declared his distaste for waiting to the world, the word *bored* stretched out with a supremely long *o*. Precisely the way a cranky child would bemoan their lack of entertainment.

"She's almost done," Aetheria replied. She ignored the cat's cries of boredom; engaging would have resulted in more complaints.

The cascades of power went far beyond anything Aetheria had seen firsthand, and the power source of the temple failed; the beams of Ethereal power ceased. The power exploded from Aoibhe, and the dispersal of unnecessary aspects manifested as light. In nanoseconds, a power sufficient to destroy a world coursed through the Nephilim and reforged her, and when the light abated, Kallos Metanoia stood in place of Aoibhe. The Soul Witch had a slight grimace of pain on her face while she touched her hands together, then her arms and face, and then nodded when her yellow eyes turned to gaze at the new shape of her wings.

Kallos's wings were made of a metal Aetheria had never seen before, the right wing black, the left one white. They reminded her of the skeletal framework of wings, from which hung hundreds of lengths of chain made of the same metal. The chains were a chaotic mix of white, gray, and black. Her pale skin, where visible beneath the black and purple armored dress, revealed glimpses of tattoos of chains that covered large portions of her skin now. Her long blonde hair framed her face the same as it always had, but Aetheria couldn't help but notice a few black hairs had snuck in amongst the blonde.

The golden eyes remained the same, and when Kallos's and Aetheria's eyes met, they smiled at each other. Aetheria made an exaggerated curtsy to the other woman, smirking the whole while.

"Congratulations, my queen." Aetheria teased the Monarch.

"Yeah, congrats and stuff. What's up with all the chains? If you two are into some kinky stuff, you didn't have to make it a part of your ascension, you know?" Arkaziel joked with the Nephilim, seeing how close to the line he could go.

Kallos coughed a few times as if getting used to a new throat.

"Thank you." A chain extended from her wings to wrap around Aetheria's wrist and give her a tug into the Nephilim's waiting arms. Aetheria went with the tug gladly, and the two embraced powerfully.

"I didn't realize becoming royalty created such changes in a person." Aetheria's tone held full approval. "I like it. You've got that hint of ancient secrets and forces best left alone, a dash of Queen of Blades sexiness, and Anima was always the best summon in FFX, and I totally don't have a chain fetish, but I might in the future. We could add a bunch of bindings like my Void form uses and match; why are you smiling at me like that?"

"You are babbling, darling." Kallos's voice remained the same, by and large. She remained everything she had been before, only more. The beauty of her soul still stunned Aetheria, to say nothing of her physical gorgeousness, and their connection's depth hung on the precipice of evolution itself. Perhaps when Aetheria reached the sixth tier, a new element to their soul-bond would emerge.

"First time I've been on the receiving end of someone else transforming significantly, right before my eyes." Aetheria laughed nervously.

"I'm right here, you know. Hello? Void StarMane? Because I hide the tentacles, eyes, and extra tails, it doesn't mean they don't exist!" Arkaziel took offense to being both ignored and forgotten. Neither woman acknowledged his complaints.

"I suppose so, a taste of your own medicine. How do you like my new appearance?"

"I love it, and you. We can be gothy edgelords together for eternity." Then Aetheria's three eyes swiveled to Arkaziel, who had altered his shape to have six eyes on each side, spiked tendrils rising above his shoulders, and three extra tails. "For Pete's sake, Arkaziel. Read the room. We're having a moment here. Yes, I love you too; you're my favorite StarMane, and you are brilliant and fantastic, too. Okay!?" Aetheria's Minnesotan accent came through heavily.

"Was that so hard?" Arkaziel acknowledged at last and returned to his most diminutive cat form before he jumped up and sat on Aetheria's head.

"Still, learn to read the situation better." Aetheria huffed a little. She kissed Kallos on the cheek and surveyed the ruined grove. "We did a number on this place. Where to next; back to Uruk? We haven't gone north yet either, and I suppose there's probably some stuff to do in the fae forest still?"

An ominous presence joined them.

"That won't be necessary. You retain a skip token from the Tower of Aetherius, yes? Give it to me, and I shall open the way to a city. When you return, new scenarios will be waiting for you."

Moros appeared as an empty suit of armor that Aetheria would best describe as Dark Lord–like, with glowing red embers where eyes should be in the empty helmet. The charred and blackened armor had a dark, blood-colored cloak that fluttered on winds that didn't exist.

"Okay, sure." Aetheria manifested the token from her vault and tossed it into the armor. It surprised her. Moros let the coin go through the helmet, then rattle around inside the empty suit of armor.

"Enjoy the shopping trip, and try not to murder any more gods. You've created an uproar with the final death of Inanna." Before he vanished, the incarnation of Doom looked directly at Kallos. Seconds ticked away, but he did not speak. A doorway to a city opened, and still, Moros stared until the armor fell to the ground and turned to metallic dust.

"Your stepbrother is creepy, Ria." Arkaziel hit her in the face with his tail to emphasize his point.

"Agreed." Kallos frowned at the pile of metallic dust, but she nodded her acknowledgment toward Arkaziel.

Aetheria made a skit of sputtering fur made of dark ice from her mouth, but no one laughed. Not even a pity laugh from Kallos.

"Well, yeah. He's Doom, what'd you expect? Kittens and puppies? He's all about leading people to their inevitable fate, which, when you think about how the truth of this existence works and what happens to the people under his watch, well, that's a pretty shit job. Now, shall we find out what city we get to visit?" The tug of new horizons to witness, of new shops to dig through, and new sights to see activated the wanderlust in Aetheria, and the other two smiled at her contagious energy.

"Hopefully, it's a high-tier city with really good food," Arkaziel said, dreaming of food in his head and drooling on his tongue.

"This might be less conspicuous," Kallos murmured to herself. The Nephilim turned her golden gaze upon her new wings. While Aetheria thought they were extraordinarily beautiful, they would draw attention. Under the witch's gaze, the wings morphed into an armored mantle that trailed a cloak made of woven chains. The strange metal still caught the eye, as did the glimpses of tattoos on Kallos's skin, but as a sixth tier Cultivator, attention would come no matter what.

"Let's go!" Arkaziel whined, and Aetheria grabbed Kallos's hand and stepped through the portal.

All three appeared in a gondola that floated on a sea of colors. The entire sea shone with an inner light that could not, or would not, be contained to a mere one or two colors. The entire rainbow blossomed everywhere there was the sea. On the approaching horizon lay a city surrounded by rainbows and colorful auras, and a perpetual aurora of lights blossomed above in the sky. The autopilot gondola left a multihued wake behind them as it propelled toward the city at a quick clip for a vessel with no visible propulsion.

"This is Iridia, the Arcadian realm of Lugh." Arkaziel grimaced at all the colors. The closer they got to the city, the more Aetheria could see how it was laid out. A full half of the city extended over the sea and floated, while the other half had been created on land with a mysterious forest, rocky hills, and gorgeous cliffs that set off the colorful sea. All in all, it reminded her of pictures of Ireland. The visible architecture seemed to her a mixture of gothic fantasy and elven spires. There were curved walls and large domes everywhere she looked, and every building seemed to have been created with an impeccable eye for detail.

"It is said Lugh possessed skill in all arts and made a city to produce wonders. I can appreciate the beauty of his creation, but I do not know how deserving to be called the master of all arts he was." Kallos thumbed her chin while she took in the city and reached the same conclusion Aetheria had. She didn't know enough to tell if this was as impressive as it looked.

A bubble rose from the sea and burst, and a masculine voice escaped the bubble.

"There are mercenaries and god-hunters in my beautiful city. Defend yourselves as you see fit, but I shall hold you accountable to repair anything you break. They, too, have been warned."

Aetheria giggled, then laughed fully at the look Arkaziel and Kallos gave her.

"He sounds very Irish. Which doesn't mean anything to you, but does to me. More mercenaries aren't very surprising, in any case. Let's take care of them quickly so we can enjoy ourselves."

"Do not forget, those who have completed a tower can possess transversal tokens. If we allow any mercenaries or spies to slip out of the city, we could find ourselves face-to-face with genuine threats."

"Way to jinx it, Chains," Arkaziel hissed at the Soul Witch, even as the boat stopped against a wooden dock.

CHAPTER 34

Iridia

The entire southern side of Iridia faced the rainbow sea, and over eighty percent of it had piers, docks, and moorings for boats. Unlike most inter-tower trade cities Aetheria had visited, this one didn't shuffle you through an incoming gate or customs. *Does that mean Lugh keeps a closer eye on his city than some of the other gods, or that the cities that use customs are just making a show of it, and Lugh has already made a show of the whole city?*

Aetheria and Kallos hopped onto the dock from the gondola. Arkaziel still rode atop Aetheria's head, lazily glaring at the colorful city of Iridia as if it offended him on a deep, fundamental level.

"If you claw me, you're going to be walking," Aetheria warned the StarMane in the lull before the storm. The sky spun like a kaleidoscope; rainbows formed in the air and multiplied to bring more joy across the city, colorful yellow flowers with a scent like coconut drifted on the wind, and the atmosphere of the city shifted from a chilly summer day to the first day of spring, celebratory and enlivening. At the intersection at the end of the dock, a crier stepped out of a tavern and yelled for all to hear that free drinks were on the menu, courtesy of Lugh.

"Nothing says peaceful quite like a city about to be as drunk as Wisconsin, and the last thing the bounty hunters need is liquid courage to be even more stupid than they already were to accept a job involving us." Aetheria laughed. At the same time, Arkaziel just agreed with her, clearly forgetting the last time he drank some of the booze from Chronos. *It was peaceful when he passed out.*

No pillars of light illuminated Aetheria, but the yellow flowers on the wind seemed to drift toward her. Astute individuals would no doubt pick up on that or have their ways to track her, so Aetheria didn't bother to conceal her presence. She gestured upward, and a glyph of Ice formed roughly a hundred meters above her. A second, third, and fourth glyph appeared and orbited the first. In order, they read: Nemesis, Cryo, Ethereal, Void. Nemesis and Cryo were transparent ice, while Ethereal gleamed with the red of the Origin, and Void radiated lines of eldritch darkness that threatened to reach down and pluck the sanity of any who stared too long at it.

With a halfhearted glance, kilometers of the rainbow sea froze, and Aetheria hopped off the dock onto the solid ice. She casually skated across the ice while Kallos walked on air after her. The glyphs in the sky followed Aetheria and constantly remained above her.

"I am the challenger Aetheria. Come on down, anyone who's here and wants the bounty from Oizys. You've got an hour, in which I'll take all comers. All at once, one on one, whatever. After that time, anyone who attacks me in the city of Iridia shall be cursed, such that they will inevitably be betrayed by anyone they love or who loves them. Forever." The declaration echoed across Iridia, carried not by magic but by authority. The clarity of the message reached all ears, and even those who couldn't speak the language understood it clearly, as well as the declaration of the curse imbued by authority over not just love but inevitability itself.

"Come at me," Aetheria finished and then waited.

"How dramatic." Kallos laughed as she drew a delicate crystal wand into her hand.

Arkaziel hopped off Aetheria's head and landed on the ice, taking on a miniature version of his draconic form. He stretched out his wings and claws and eyed the shadows across the ice.

"Oh, come on, Ark! That's not fair. Are you looking into the future through the shadows of time to pick out who you will eat?" Aetheria waggled her finger at Arkaziel while they waited.

"No, no. I'm not doing that." The future shadows stopped skimming across the ice with his denial. "I'd never do that, not me." The deadpan response, accompanied by licking his lips, really helped sell the denial. Still, since Aetheria could detect lies, it was pointless for him to do anything but embrace mockery.

The first pair of opponents to step onto the frozen sea were human men. Both were nearly a head shorter than Aetheria. One wore a strange metal body armor that contoured perfectly to his body like a second skin, and as he walked, a halberd appeared in his hands. The other wore black robes adorned with stars and trailed dozens of loose threads of fabric that left afterimages of stars.

"I am Wen Bo, the Starlit Veil. Jin Tao and I shall collect the bounty upon you, but your companions may flee now," the robed man arrogantly declared to Aetheria and her party, even as starlight gathered around the Cultivator. Both men were somewhere in the sixth tier of power, but Aetheria didn't even bat an eye at the idea of taking them on alone.

"I'll handle these two alone." Aetheria smiled brightly at Kallos and stepped forward to beckon the two men toward her. "Come at me."

Wen Bo scowled at Aetheria as if she had dishonored him, while Jin Tao took the forward position. With each step, his pace subtly grew faster, and in a strange blur of motion, the Cultivator suddenly was upon her, swinging his halberd to attack her. She casually blocked the blade of the halberd with the meshed gloves of the Astrum Nexus, and his blade created a shower of sparks that the shape of her hands pushed into his face. A sparkling veil of lights appeared around Jin Tao even as a third arm manifested from Aetheria's midsection and delivered an open-palmed strike to the man's stomach. He flew backward, tumbling end over end and skidded for twenty meters, but the shimmering barrier didn't break, even if his brains were scrambled.

"Hah, fool! The Starlit Veil is unbreakable by man or god!" A square of Wen Bo's Starlit Veil appeared over Aetheria, then descended as if it were a mountain. Aetheria casually waved a hand, and rainbow-colored Frostfire flared up to consume the veil; nothing of the cube made it through the burst of chaotic fire.

"But, but . . ."

Aetheria appeared behind Wen Bo, and a single diamond-black talon pierced his chest. Wen Bo's inner world crumbled into a cloud of dust that tasted like chocolate cookies, his core fragmented into pieces that tasted like sour apple, and then his body wilted into dust and blew away across the rainbow ice, with nothing to sustain it.

"Wen Bo!" Jin Tao cried in despair at the demise of his partner and made a mad dash to strike revenge upon the woman who killed him. Hundreds of spears, daggers, swords, and other metal blades appeared in the sky to plunge at Aetheria. She danced between them with minimal movement. Not a single one managed to touch her before Jin Tao reached her and unleashed blisteringly fast attacks. Well, for most people they would be blisteringly fast; for Aetheria it was no more difficult than dodging the rain, thanks to her beyond-superhuman speed.

"Why can I not control your gloves?" Jin Tao screamed in frustration after his flurry of combination attacks never came close to touching his opponent.

"They're soulsteel. You have more chance of controlling the moon than my soul." Jin Tao's body fell to the ground in pieces, courtesy of the impossibly sharp black-diamond talons her left hand had become. Streams of dust flew from the diced Cultivator into her palm until nothing of value remained, and the few bits of carbon were carried off on the wind.

"Oh, I should try that. Trisecting people is classy as hell," Arkaziel gushed, in praise for Aetheria.

The crowd that had gathered along the shore cried loudly. Some cheered, some booed. Some readied their equipment to give this a try themselves. Still, those ready-ing for combat looked grim after witnessing a single fifth tier Cultivator demolish two sixth tier Cultivators with reputations as climbers and mercenaries, especially when a sixth tier Cultivator and a Beast Emperor stood in reserves on Aetheria's side.

"I did say you could all come at once," Aetheria shouted and waved at the crowd.

Aetheria's casual stance invited attackers to commit, and when three mercenaries in stealth appeared to plunge their weapons into her simultaneously, she simply stood there and took it. Of the three, only two of them managed to actually pierce her skin with their blades, and the black blood that coated their weapons made the metal sizzle and disintegrate. Above Aetheria, the glyphs in the sky glowed, and a volley of meter-long icicles impaled all three before they could react to their weapons melting. Aetheria finished each with a quick plunge of a taloned fingertip into their chests, her wounds already healed.

The floodgates had opened, though, and like berserk idiots, over forty adventurers ran across the ice to attack her.

"Make a spectacle of it, why don't you?" Aetheria asked Kallos and Arkaziel. Overwhelming power had failed to reach the minds of those employed by Oizys. Perhaps overwhelming power from someone other than herself would pierce the influence of Misery. Her stomach swam slightly at the idea of all these people being indiscriminately slaughtered to prove a point, but they had brought themselves to this point by accepting a deal with Oizys. *I don't like this. What's the better way?*

Arkaziel didn't have any moral compunctions about slaughter. The dragon-cat stared at the rush of attackers before their own shadows suddenly started to grapple with Cultivators and pull them down into the darkness. The screams of shocked horror and desperate panic as they struggled against the shadows that had followed them their whole lives tugged at Aetheria's heart.

Wisps of stardust shot into the field, and each one drew the souls right out of their enemy's bodies. The fifth tier Cultivators couldn't resist the overwhelming power Kallos had over their souls, and the few unlucky fourth-tiers who had been carried into this fight lost their souls before the wisps even got within ten meters of them.

"A gift you don't deserve, but I won't have guilt fester in my love's heart," Kallos spoke to the coalesced souls. "In the next cycle of your soul, be blessed with insights to guide you home."

Kallos raised a hand in benediction, and sacred light shone down upon the gathered souls, illuminating them and then transporting them on to the next birth in the cycle, blessed with insights granted by a miracle, touched by a rare manifestation of the infinite, warm light of Ein Sof.

No enemies remained on the ice. Their bodies had been consumed by darkness, and their souls were sent on to a new adventure in the Great Cycle. Onlookers stared open-mouthed at the trio. Those who had not been corrupted directly by the dictates of Oizys were protected by the ability to say no, unlike their party members who hadn't been able to fight the compulsions of the goddess.

"Anyone else?" Aetheria demanded.

No one else wanted to join the fallen.

"Let's go to the mall," Aetheria attempted and failed to sound enthusiastic.

"Think they'll have any fried phoenix in the market?" Arkaziel asked hungrily, disappointed that he hadn't gotten to eat more enemies. Wisely, he refrained from rebuffing Kallos for stealing his meals. The cat, too, could feel the displeasure within Aetheria over the situation and didn't want to add to it.

"Ascyn told me a tale of a leprechaun trading him a most fabulous meal in exchange for a few gold bars in Iridia once. Perhaps we should seek out a leprechaun? There's certainly enough rainbows to have no shortage of the small folk here."

"Leprechauns? Let's go, but if they say something is magically delicious, there's a good chance I might choke on my tongue laughing."

CHAPTER 35

Let's Go to the Mall

The natives of Iridia were all friendly enough with the party, despite the slaughter of so many Cultivators in broad daylight. Aetheria's guilt ebbed slightly at how pleased so many of the locals were. It seemed that most of the mercenaries had not treated the natives of the city kindly during their stay. With the perceptive abilities of Void Gaze at her hands, she could discern that the smiles were honest, not a front to placate the murderous Asura who had come amongst them. *It's the small things in life, like not being looked at like a genocidal monster, that matter.*

You have spent too much of your life under the delusions of mortality. Death is not the terminus of existence, it is no shroud to mark the cessation of existence. Your education has passed beyond the quaint notions of a final silence to the horrid symphony of life. Death is the transformative process by which your souls rejoin the sea of consciousness and dive back into the ocean of thought, forever part of the unfathomable whole.

"*In time even the divine form of Ein Sof changes. It was once Ayin, but now it is Yesh. Nothing lasts forever.*" Reverie disagreed with Fred. That they could somehow hear the other, but still could not address one another bothered her. Why would that be the case? *Or does Reverie mean that Nothing, as in Ayin, lasts forever, and everything else is transitory?*

Aetheria cast off the thoughts of existence, death, and attempts to rationalize her own actions. She had done what she had, and that was now in the past. Still, a small part of her wondered what had ever happened to her naive insistence she had been reincarnated as a heroine. *Oh right, I found out I was a weapons project produced by Khaos, Nyx, Aetherius, and Chronos.*

"That frown does not suit you at all, darling." Kallos grasped Aetheria's hand, and together they walked down the streets of Iridia. The colors seemed more vibrant, the scents more enjoyable, and warmth flooded her heart with their hands joined together. It wasn't that without her touch the good things were gone, but love awoke something magical in reality, a quality that made the suffering of the physical realms more tolerable.

"Do the paths to gnosis through denial of love and passions stem from the idea that if you make it miserable enough, you'll work extra hard to escape the cage?" Aetheria inquired of the Soul Witch.

"It's one school of thought. The paths to gnosis are many, but some are more difficult than others. The physical worlds are a place of corruption and endless trials, but that does not mean there is not good in lower worlds, nor that there is an absence of corruption in the higher realms. Existence is ineffable, yet we crave to understand it, despite an intentional limitation built within us to do so." Kallos shrugged.

"My, that smells good," Kallos murmured of the scent of a vendor with meat skewers.

"Oh man, I'll take ten." Arkaziel's head roused from Aetheria's left shoulder. He had chosen to sleep on the left shoulder since Kallos walked on Aetheria's right.

"We'll take twelve skewers, if that's not too many?" Aetheria asked the gnome who ran the meat skewer stand.

"No problem! What types ya want? I've got manticore tail tips—properly cleansed of toxins, chimera chops, vampire bat, spiced sphinx, and for the discerning customers such as you fine ladies, I've even got a little supply of Gorgon Tongue Twirls! It is said to give those who eat it the most skilled of silver-tongues."

"Let's go with two of the Twirls, and three of each of the others?" Aetheria conjured some coin for the man, once he gave her a total.

"What, why don't I get any gorgon?" Arkaziel whined while Aetheria passed the other skewers up to him, and kept the gorgon for herself and Kallos.

"The last thing this market needs is a silver-tongued Arkaziel running around buying everyone out of stock. It's for our own good." Aetheria declared the law for the StarMane.

"A most wise decision," Kallos agreed.

The first bite of the skewers were warm and juicy, and slightly mysterious. Aetheria thought it compared to beef tongue, but with more earthy notes like hints of salt and minerals. Gorgons were known for their lairs, after all, so it didn't seem unsurprising there would be a connection between them and their lair that even came into play with the flavor. The spices were simple salt and pepper, and something close to garlic. The aftertaste lingered in her mouth, pleasant, but it faded and left a brief hint of lightness and mystery, or perhaps numbness?

"I don't feel any sudden skill as an orator coming on. You?" Aetheria asked with disappointment.

"My tongue feels strange, certainly, but no. I do not feel any more skilled in the arts of persuasion."

"Not that kind of skilled tongue." Arkaziel laughed uproariously as the two's faces showed a faint blush, and they both had a light-bulb-above-their-head moment.

"Ohhh," Kallos and Aetheria echoed one another.

"Oh, dearies, why don't you look at my wares here?" A hideous hag disguised as an elderly grandma invited them to view her wares, most of which were hazy collections of essences, emotions, and other esoteric items that Aetheria had absolutely no use for.

Kallos, on the other hand, immediately noticed a locket with a glimmering aquamarine inside of it.

"I'll trade you a minor miracle for the pendant," Kallos said simply.

The hag's face brightened. "Deal."

With a snap of Kallos's fingers, the hag suddenly appeared to be in her twenties.

"Enjoy it while it lasts," Kallos said, and pocketed the amulet. From what Aetheria could tell, a soul lay trapped inside of it. Would Kallos use the soul for something, or free it? Aetheria suspected her love would free it, but she lacked the same affinity to discern knowledge of souls that the witch possessed. Perhaps the soul deserved to be trapped in there. As unlikely as that seemed, there was always a small chance that whoever bound the soul had been justified in doing so.

Colorful weapons alloyed with mithril and a blue metal Aetheria had no familiarity with littered every other stand, and every merchant had a seemingly endless supply of trinkets. Each trinket seemed to be more spectacular than the last, if you listened to the merchants, but their claims rang empty to Void Gaze, less truthful than the time Arkaziel claimed he had not ate a canary. Most of the items didn't even shine with true magic, as far as Aetheria could tell. After the fifth stall, she finally asked her companions.

~ Why can't I sense any magic on these items? Are they all just rip-offs?~

+Oh yeah, three-fourths are total bullshit, or hokey pseudo magic.+

-It is more complex than that, Arkaziel. The types of magic employed with most of these rely on sympathies and relationships that cannot be called proper magic. They function more as a derivative of chaos and concepts only those of the fae understand. Compare them to the quantum mechanics your old world had, Aetheria. They do not operate under their own power, like most magical equipment. Lacking the innate connection to chaos and the esoteric magic of the fae renders comprehension for us nonfae next to impossible.-

~So, even magic has types of hokey bullshit? That makes me feel slightly better about not understanding it. Wait, I have the Flame of Khaos in the Astrum Nexus. Why can't I discern fae magic through that?~

-You most likely could, but look at the way it twists the minds of those who use it. Do you desire to see the world the way fae do?- Kallos made absolutely no effort to conceal her disdain for the worldview of the fae, with their transactional view on everything.

"Oh, what's that?" Aetheria stopped before a stand that showed a mirror.

"A glimpse of things to come. I am called Ilysera, and this is the Mirror of Twilight Visions. For a small donation, I can show you a glimpse of the future, of a person or thing that will be quite meaningful to you. Interested?" The fae woman who spoke had ephemeral blue skin the color of sapphires, brilliant aquamarine hair that nearly matched the shades of Aetheria's own aqua hair, and a once-elegant white dress that looked a touch threadbare and ancient. Her iridescent silver eyes, which lacked any whites, contrasted beautifully with her skin.

Aetheria plucked an elaborate white hat from her repository. She couldn't quite recall whom it had belonged to, but she vaguely recalled it belonged to one of the fae they had slaughtered in the Twilight Verdure. The style matched the woman's dress, and even the nature of its wear seemed to be a perfect fit. Giddily, Ilysera took it and immediately put the hat on before she admired herself in her magical mirror, which showed her reflection as if it were a normal mirror. Only after the fae admired herself from multiple angles did she turn back to face Aetheria.

"Pay attention. You shall get only one glimpse!" Ilysera warned Aetheria, before the fae turned back to the mirror and started to run her fingertips along the beautiful gilded frame around the mirror, and chanted a spell in three languages at once. Aetheria could only understand one of the three, Primeval Sylvan.

"Mirror of futures not yet woven,
Show the face of fate's unspun thread,
Give us a glimpse of love unmet."

The enchanted glass of the mirror flared with powerful intensity as flashes of blue, red, black, and gold swept across the mirror in churning clouds. Intense magic built up in the mirror, a power of such potency to cause the seer to have tears form at the corner of her eyes, and even Aetheria had to wonder what insane power might breach the mirror. A fleeting image appeared, even as Ilysera's tears changed from water to blood.

A young woman, seemingly in her teenage years, appeared in the mirror. She had strawberry-blonde hair with the faintest traces of prismatic blue highlights. Her almond-shaped eyes were piercing, and the pink of her iris stood out greatly, to the point it felt impossible to look away from the depths of cherry blossoms and peonies held there. The woman's oval face and high cheekbones combined to give her an undeniable elegance, despite her youth. Full, pink lips and a well-defined nose complemented her face, and if one managed to look away from her commanding eyes, it felt impossible to not notice her luminous fair skin, and all-around radiant beauty. The glamorous teen bore a beyond-striking resemblance to Kallos.

The painful breathing and tortured sounds of the seer grew by the moment.

Aetheria and the image of the young woman locked eyes for the briefest of seconds. The teen laughed and waved, before the mirror turned back to clouds, then to the reflection of Aetheria. The cries of the seeress drew Aetheria's attention away from the mirror.

Kallos tsked softly, and laid a hand on the shoulder of Ilysera. Blood streamed down her face and stained her beautiful dress, until in a flash of power, the wounds were undone and the stains removed. The worn dress and hat looked like new, the threadbare and ancient appearance gone with the reinvigorating magics she cast.

"I can see again? I'm not even going to ask who that was, or who you people are. Thank you," Ilysera sincerely thanked Kallos, before the mirror vanished in a puff of magic and the blue woman fled in a pace just shy of a full run. Her retreat from them and the pain she had just endured created a knot of guilt in Aetheria's gut.

"Well then, this place is weird. Let's go back to the tower."

"Only after we buy more food," Arkaziel demanded, his gaze caught by a whole roasted griffin on a large, turning spit.

CHAPTER 36

Terribly Tiresome Tediousness

Now then, the three of you will be competing for this series of challenges." When the trio left Iridia, Aetheria hadn't known what to expect from the Tower of Moros. They had appeared in the throne room of a castle, filled with black flags adorned with a sun and moon.

"Competing for what?" Arkaziel inquired immediately about the most important part of the words the magical suit of armor spoke.

"In addition to the sense of satisfaction of being the victor, the winner shall receive a significant boost toward their next ascension, and the Atlas of Lost Realms." Moros's dry delivery about satisfaction no doubt created a desert somewhere, but with the mention of the atlas, an illusion of an ancient book floated behind him.

"The atlas is real? I always thought it was a legend." Arkaziel sounded interested.

"Yes, the Atlas of Lost Realms is a genuine artifact. Within its forgotten pages are guides through every tower, and the locations of lost dimensions of long-gone gods and ancient civilizations. Treasure beyond reckoning lies within its pages," Moros crowed about the fantastic nature of the item.

"Such relics always contain the seeds of tragedy," Kallos warned, in an attempt to diminish Arkaziel's greed.

"And what is the challenge?" Aetheria asked suspiciously, as she looked at the elaborate throne room around them.

"You shall each administer a kingdom for one hundred years. No simple delegation of rule to a regent and retreating to a cultivation cave. You must participate in the day-to-day rule of your kingdom. Each of you has been given equivalent starting kingdoms. You shall be judged out of ten on economy, military, quality of life, and population when the challenge ends." With those words Moros turned to dust, and Aetheria appeared in a different, but quite similar, throne room.

~Is anybody out there?~

Moros had disabled their telepathic links for this trial, unless both Arkaziel and Kallos were giving her the silent treatment over a chance to win. While that was possible with Arkaziel, Kallos would never ignore her, so it had to be Moros's doing.

The throne she had appeared on did not provide adequate support to her lower back, and hurt her butt a little. Impressive feats, given that her body transcended human weakness and her resilience and endurance made most gods look like kittens next to a tiger. Someone had created the throne with the intent for it to be uncomfortable, and for its occupant to feel the responsibility of their people.

"Worst tower yet. Hope you're having a barrel of laughs, Khaos." A soft curse under her breath, and the throne room around her experienced a popping sound, similar to when you change elevations. Only, in this case it had nothing to do with audible sensations, but the temporal flow of this test reality kicking into gear. She wasn't alone any longer; instead she shared the room with a dozen knights and a mustached and immaculately dressed man with a clipboard.

Aetheria quickly ended the audience, and on wings of ice took to the sky to surveil her kingdom. The flows of power through the land were what she could only call average, and almost no civilians stood out as sources of power to her senses. Only three of her citizens had attained the third tier, sixty had reached the second tier, and all the rest fell into the first tier or completely uninitiated tiers. The distribution felt like a real letdown, as it meant any true talents would need to be discovered and nurtured. She estimated the size of her kingdom to match the size of Rhode Island, give or take, and although she didn't leave her land's borders, it seemed the entirety of the realms were a rough circle with each country shaped like a pie piece, of which there seemed to be six.

Despite the lack of powerful citizens, Aetheria spotted four large cities and at least ten minor ones scattered between them, including a coastal town with a large fishery. She had the westernmost piece of the pie, and she could sense through her soul-bond that Kallos lay to the east somewhere.

It felt like a very basic grand strategy fantasy map, and it seemed like Moros had slotted three other nations into the contest with the three of them. Which meant she couldn't just expect there not to be attacks or military action over the course of the trial. Sure, Arkaziel was an asshole, but he probably wouldn't send an army after her, but the other three kingdoms had no doubt been included to act as spoilers to peaceful, diplomatic rule, or at least challenges to it.

Day 3

The introductory period to the Sovereignty of Aetheria had not even come close to an end. There were so many names to learn—her chamberlain, royal secretary, top general, butler, maids, courtiers, and so on—that she'd been forced to resort to addressing people indirectly for now. Not that learning people's names was her top priority. A strange species of sea monster had moved in and limited the output of the fishers, which required dispatching of additional troops. In the meantime, Aetheria supplemented the food stocks of her people by paying a wandering earth Cultivator to help increase crop output and incentivizing a first-tier farmer to push to the second tier with an investment from the treasury of both hard coin and cultivation resources.

It turned out the sovereignty had no major cultivation factions to oppose her, what with Aetheria's governance starting out being exceptionally authoritarian. Apparently, she was not only their queen but also their goddess. She had a hundred years to guide them to something more enlightened, but the absolute authority would allow her to act in any manner she wanted without concern for pushback, for now.

There were some rules that Moros had not informed them about to start. None of them were able to pull resources from their inventories or inner worlds to give to the kingdom. Aetheria's vast personal wealth didn't matter in the slightest. She couldn't so much as generate a copper coin, let alone bags of gold, to lubricate the bureaucratic machine. She could only draw wealth from the sovereignty's treasury. It struck her odd that Moros forbade access to their belongings but didn't care at all about their other powers.

On the first day, Aetheria had decided to test out her ability to alter inevitability in this scenario, and she did so five times. The first effort was to declare that a survey team would find valuable iron veins in the mountains to the west. Her second declaration was that nature would provide, and the rangers ought to search out new game. Thirdly, she declared that a powerful young priestess would make herself known in the city of Etheridge to stem the tide of a burgeoning plague. Fourth, she said a miracle phenomenon of mana would spur awakenings of many citizens in Pearl, one of the coastal cities. Finally, she declared it would be a bountiful year of prosperity for the sovereignty.

Two days later, Aetheria now had results on some of the fates she had tried to alter. The survey team did in fact find a vast vein of iron and mithril, but also unearthed a cursed undead lord. Aetheria had killed the mummy in a single blow, and broke the curse on the team members who survived, but a third of them had died before she interceded. The rangers had found evidence of a new herd of animals from the kingdom to the south, but they were a species known for making people ill if their meat was not fully cooked. No powerful young priestess had emerged in Etheridge, but Aetheria would give it one more day before she handled the scenario herself. The miraculous mana surges in Pearl did awaken nearly forty people straight to the second tier, but the city reported a vast increase in the size of aquatic menaces. The final declaration would take much longer to test.

Like genie wishes, it appeared Aetheria needed to be very specific in her declarations, or else Moros interpreted things maliciously. Despite the give and take that had been dealt so far, she had still come out massively ahead, but it felt like a very dangerous game. Sooner or later, the cost might be much worse than a minor undead lord, like something that could decimate entire cities before she could react. Her authority over other areas did not seem to come with equivalent repercussions.

Day 4
The powerful young priestess Aetheria prophesized had emerged in Etheridge. Not only had she stopped the plague in its tracks, she slew the demon that had apparently

been spreading the plague. Unfortunately, in the aftermath, one of her childhood friends stabbed the priestess to death. The attacker had been part of an underground cult that had summoned the demon in the first place.

This made Aetheria question a lot of different possibilities. Would the priestess have arisen there no matter what? If she hadn't forced it, would the woman have come into her power down the line, and not been an unnecessary sacrifice? If Aetheria had let a natural flow of events occur, would someone have investigated the cult and stopped the priestess from being stabbed? This scenario put an obnoxious craw into her mouth, because when she searched the answer through the Sefirot, the best she could discern was that it was up to Moros. In his own tower, Moros held dominion over not just impending doom, but fate in general. Unlike the Moirai, he couldn't touch those things outside of the tower, but here he was master over everything except her.

Day 9

Aetheria visited Pearl like a benevolent goddess. She descended into the city only after she committed genocide against the sea leviathans that were disrupting the fishery. The large sea serpents proved to be a fantastic solution to the food shortage. Not only did the sea serpents taste delicious, but their scales were immensely useful in creating a type of scale mail that would increase the defense and mobility of the army of the sovereignty by at least twofold.

The manager of the fishery assured her the sea serpents' organs could be used to lure lucrative prey into their coastal waters, and so Aetheria gave him permission to use the organs. What use would water-breathing potions be instead? She could always just pull some out of her repository; after all, she had hundreds of them. She didn't recall that the repository was off limits until well after she made the decision. Had it been the right one? When she found out that the manager tried to draw in whales, she felt like she definitely hadn't made the right one morally.

Even though he wasn't with her, she could imagine Arkaziel staring at her and asking why it would be okay to eat sea serpents but not whales. They weren't endangered in this place, it turned out; they just didn't often come to the waters off Pearl due to a lack of their favored meals. It amused her, the way Earth sometimes still clouded her thoughts and prejudice.

Day 14

The northern country of Assur declared war on the sovereignty. They sent a force of ten thousand men, thousands of tamed wolves, and wyvern riders. Aetheria met them herself and wiped out the enemy general and most of his leadership in the form of an Ethereal ice dragon. She ransomed some of the nobles back, and recruited anyone who wanted to join her willingly and made a vow of loyalty. Only a thousand of the men defected, but the four wyvern riders and their wyverns were a massive gain.

Day 23

Aetheria received a diplomat from Assur. The king decried her recruitment of his military and demanded his wyverns back. She refused the demands and warned she would invade their lands in seven days if they did not cease hostilities and make reparations for a mere mortal to provoke her, a goddess. She did offer to sell their army's weapons and armor back to them, if the reparations were an appropriate tithe to her divinity.

Not that Aetheria had fallen for the being divine thing. Assur had a large, thriving slave market and made a habit of stealing other countries' citizens and selling them, so they were on the chopping block for expansion of the sovereignty.

Death to slavers made for a great rallying cry, it turned out.

CHAPTER 37

War, It's Great!

Day 24

It turned out her advisors knew the names of all six kingdoms that had a piece of the pie for the large island. There was the Sovereignty of Aetheria, the Theocracy of Light ruled by Kallos, the monarchy of Assur, the democracy of Polterra, a militant isolationist monarchy called Eldergarde, and the Murdercat Tyranny. Clearly, Moros had ideas about StarManes. Ideas that weren't necessarily wrong, but it seemed a bit too on the nose for Aetheria. On the twenty-fourth day of their contest, the monarchy of Assur ceased to exist, as it was overrun by wave after wave of ice constructs that were followed by the admittedly lacking military of the sovereignty.

In strategy games, there were systems for managing territories you took from other kingdoms. There were no bars to show her how close to revolt the newly annexed lands of the sovereignty were, but the people were clearly displeased at a foreign ruler coming in, killing all of their royal family, taking control of the government, and in general upending the lives of every person of what formerly was Assur. Ice constructs couldn't win the hearts and minds of people.

Freeing them from slavery helped win the majority, but the wealthy minority were not fans of having to pay for labor. The rule of law couldn't allow newly freed slaves to seek vendettas. As much as Aetheria empathized with their desire to pull the wealthy from their homes and hang them in the night, murder wasn't the solution. Luckily, her advisors understood this, and approached the occupation of Assur with what felt like a fairly enlightened mindset for the ruling class of a sovereignty.

Day 36

The flames of revolution burned a quarter of the former capital city of Assur to the ground. Massive conflict had erupted overnight in all the annexed cities of Assur, and in the cold light of dawn the citizens had achieved their bloody revenge upon the former upper caste. On a personal level, Aetheria had to give a silent cheer for the people who had cast down their tyrants and claimed their world for themselves. On the other hand, they'd killed an awful lot of people who had skills and talents that would have come in useful for building a functional kingdom.

There was no upside to be found in the bloodletting. The few Tier Three Cultivators in Assur had died in their sleep, as well as all of the Tier Twos. Only the uninitiated or barely trained remained, and few of them could read. Her secretary, Alara, suggested she perform the Rite of Unification. Aetheria had no clue what that was until she summoned the knowledge of Binah. In the context of the Tower of Moros and the religion of Aetheria, it was a simple ritual that would bring unity and love to all under Aetheria's rule.

On paper, it sounded wonderful. In practice, Aetheria worried it sounded like mind control or denial of free will. She still did it, and the changes in the new citizens of the sovereignty were immediate. The flames of revolution were forgotten, and even when new leaders from the south moved into the new cities to help rebuild, they were welcomed with open arms as brothers. *I didn't take authority over war and love to mind-control people.*

Day 42
The northernmost border of the sovereignty, once part of Assur, had a massive demarcated border with the Murdercat Tyranny. A colossal wall of dark stone separated the kingdoms, with only a single point of trade. Diplomacy with the Murdercat Tyranny started on the forty-second day of Aetheria's trial. Arkaziel's diplomat brought an incredibly elaborate scroll that directly addressed Aetheria.

In return for a nonaggression pact, Arkaziel offered a trade of foods. While fair, Aetheria couldn't help but notice all he offered her were staples, while he wanted spices and delicacies. The exchange of timber for rock and metal actually favored her, but he refused to open the gates of the tyranny to travelers. Trade would occur only at the border, and no one, not even diplomats, was allowed to enter the Murdercat Tyranny.

Overall the deals were fair, so Aetheria accepted them. She had an unpleasant feeling that she really didn't want to know what her cat was doing with his country.

Day 93
Aetheria rued that she hadn't found a God of Education to devour. Authority over learning would have been very useful in building a kingdom. Authority over love allowed her to enforce unity, which helped foster nationalism and dedication to purpose, but it also took something away from the citizens of the sovereignty when she did it. Schools were being built in all cities, but people to run them were in short supply. New humans took almost a decade and a half to really be of any use to the nation, and until that time, they were massive resource drains.

Day 125
Magic could do a lot of things, but the people of the sovereignty made do largely without. While Aetheria could supplement the manual labor and industries of agriculture

and mining with magic, she refrained. For expertise to truly develop, she couldn't just send constructs out to do the work for everyone. In the short term it would have boosted productivity by ridiculous levels, but she didn't have the infrastructure to deal with that level of resource production, anyway. The food would have rotted in silos, and the metal would have sat in storehouses.

All levels of the government bent to encourage childbirth amongst its citizens, and incredible bonuses awaited those who would secure the future of the sovereignty. The discovery of a gold vein kilometers from the iron and mithril veins countered the steep cost of the population increase and education campaigns.

Aetheria missed talking to Arkaziel and Kallos. Reverie spoke rarely and with severity, and Fred was a barrel of laughs without a bottom. Her royal secretary seemed like a decent enough person, but they had nothing in common, and everyone in the sovereignty treated her as a goddess. This did not make for enjoyable conversations.

Day 315

Pregnancies were increasing. The population increase for the next year would be dramatic. The democracy of Polterra on the border to their south went to war with the Theocracy of Light over the absurd amount of missionaries that entered Polterra. An anti-religious populist had swept into power in Polterra, and with a choice between the peaceful Theocracy of Light and the Sovereignty of Aetheria, which had annihilated and annexed Assur in days, they chose to target Kallos's kingdom instead.

Their invading forces into the Theocracy vanished.

Day 343

An emissary from the Theocracy of Light brought a request for a nonaggression pact and resource agreements. The war in Polterra still raged, but the Theocracy of Light now had troops in the invader's country. Kallos had her troops move with delibera-tion, only annexing a new county after she had consolidated the previous.

Assimilation of Assur into the sovereignty seemed to be done. The Rite of Unification had done most of the work, but public reforms and quality of life increases sealed the deal. Within a generation it seemed unlikely that the people would even remember the name Assur.

The new gold vein allowed plentiful pressing of gold coins, but Aetheria kept a tight lid on any disbursement of newly minted coins. Gold in the coffers would not raise inflation, but if spent too rapidly the economy could be disrupted. Trade with Arkaziel increased. The waters on the northeast of the island seemed to lack in fish, and the Murdercat Tyranny were rabid for the delicacies of sea serpents and other large fish found off the coast of the sovereignty. When schools of tuna were discovered off what was formerly Assur, Arkaziel traded the immensely valuable orichalcum for high quality tuna.

Year 1.2

Birthrates were doing well. Death rates were close to normal for a civilization at this point in its advancement, but to Aetheria the mortality rates were far too high. She personally constructed holy fountains of blessed healing water in each city. The empowered fountains drew off local Aether flows to sustain themselves, and were slightly less effective than a minor healing potion. But buckets of water could be pulled from the fountains and retain their healing potency for up to two days. This lowered the mortality rates across the board.

Casual exposure to the divine water also seemed to have a side effect of increasing the awakening of the uninitiated onto the paths of the Winding Way. The five declarations of fate had, overall, worked out in a positive way so far. Aetheria decided she would try to refrain from declaring inevitabilities without a dire need rather than risk Moros's twists upon her alterations of fate.

Year 1.7

The sovereignty lacked skilled labor. With the massive surge in population, the number of women in the labor pool dropped significantly, and the demand for wet nurses soared. Aetheria turned to the knowledge of Binah to find alternatives that could work in this low-tech kingdom. With the advent of the healing fountains, alchemists were able to focus on mixtures other than healing potions as their primary product. This allowed for an alchemical nutritional supplement to be created that, as far as their tests showed, was as good as mothers' milk. Some of the alchemists suggested they could improve the population of the sovereignty by exposing the young children to mystical affinities at such a young age, but Aetheria did not allow that experimentation.

The sovereignty already had a goddess. They didn't need super soldiers. Especially not super soldiers who had no capability to give consent.

Year 2.1

Population increases continued to cause issues throughout the sovereignty. There were not enough trained people in any career to begin with, and removing large numbers of women from the pool only crippled it even more. Regardless, Aetheria directed her people to continue. The clergy worked extensively to train and educate those who could be taught to become educators, civil servants, and to learn skills that would better them all. While ice constructs could provide temporary relief to manual labor shortages, Aetheria emphasized repeatedly that those roles would be necessary in the future.

The Theocracy of Light finally concluded its war with Polterra, and the former ceased to exist in an official capacity. Kallos, now with a shared border, could meet with Aetheria in person at their shared border. Unfortunately, they were unable to get alone time due to the demands of rulership and expectations of their faithful. Being close, but unable to be able to speak intimately, felt worse than being separated. Even in the same room, their bond had been blocked by Moros.

Year 2.7

More and more of the former citizens of Assur moved into the original lands of the sovereignty. This helped with the unemployment in the cities they immigrated to, but the cities to the north were rapidly entering worse and worse states, with crumbling infrastructure and diminished services. Aetheria didn't have a solution to this besides shifting the economy of the northern part of her territory to agriculture. Low population density, high plant density.

Arkaziel requested certain crops and offered a subsidy for those. This helped lure a few citizens into the farming profession, but most were more interested in the chance to become land owners after five years of homesteading a farm. A new green-rush occurred in the former Assur territory. Aetheria distrusted Arkaziel's desire to import kale, though. It seemed highly unlike the cat.

CHAPTER 38

Down with El Presidente!

Year 4

High birthrates did nothing to counter the brutal workforce shortages that faced the Sovereignty. The current number of youth entering the workforce did not even put a dent in the losses caused by parenthood. Aetheria's advisors repeatedly suggested necromancy as a means to shore up the labor force, but she stood in firm opposition to that, and instead created hordes of ice constructs. As a fifth-tier practitioner of whatever the hell you called her path, Aetheria could easily control more if the necessity arose, but her subordinates opposed her doing more on the basis that a goddess shouldn't do everything for her people.

Despite the consternation this caused Aetheria, her people had food, housing, safety, access to education, and dreams of a better life.

Year 5

The bicentennial bloom of the great Wyrmwood Orchard occurred. While the trees themselves were hideous, and their branches looked like scaled snakes ready to devour you, the beautiful blooms could be used to create potent potions of both healing and poison. According to a quick search of Binah, the extract was beloved by all reptilian and draconic races. Aetheria stored a great amount of it to bribe Arkaziel with, and used a quarter of the harvest to bribe the gray stone dragons in the mountains near the coast to join the workforce.

Despite only being twenty or thirty meters long, which was tiny compared to the nearing two-hundred-meter-long draconic forms of Aetheria and Arkaziel, the stone dragons proved excellent builders. If you wanted something built in stone, there was no better engineer and geomancer to be found than a stone dragon. Despite the prevalence of magic, Aetheria constructed aqueducts and other large-scale public works projects, including impeccable stone roads between all of the cities, and even the small towns.

Year 6

The Night of Falling Stars occurred in the warmth of July. Thousands of shooting stars spread across the sky for an entire night, and the people of the sovereignty claimed their goddess had a higher chance than usual of granting their wishes on this night. For hours, Aetheria's head ached with the intrusive burden of prayers, which she refused to accept, which in turn gave her an even worse headache. Authority did not a god make, and she refused to assume the burdens associated with being a deity. This, in turn, resulted in a migraine of epic proportions that no amount of caffeine alleviated.

Four months later, the people spoke glumly about a darkness lingering over the land. Soothsayers, or more accurately, doomsday cultists, showed up out of the woodwork. Initially Aetheria suspected Arkaziel lay at the heart of the rumors, but as winter approached and rumors of demon lords flew on the streets, her inquisitors cornered a ringleader from the realm of Eldergarde. In a twist of fate, the Preachers of Light from Kallos's country had managed to bring faith to Eldergarde, and some of the new fanatical converts disliked the idea of a goddess ruling a country and took action to humble Aetheria. When Aetheria informed Kallos of the knock-on effects, her lover was most apologetic, but both agreed she hadn't done anything wrong.

Moros was just a dick.

Year 7

Aetheria had looked forward to the auspiciously lucky year. Instead, some of the fanatics from Eldergarde managed to summon a demon lord in one of the former Assur cities. The largest remaining city of the territory was reduced to rubble, and thousands of acres of cultivated farmland burned before Aetheria showed up and destroyed the demon lord, despite the fact that she slew him almost immediately. The demon was a fifth-tier demon and provided her with excellent crafting materials.

The left horn of the demon became the Infernal Horn of Spiced Mead, which, true to its name, generated continuous cups of warm, spiced mead of the fifth tier. Aetheria did most of the crafting on it herself since no one else in her region could even hold the thing until she purified it and made it safe. Mead, she decided, was good.

Meanwhile, Aetheria crafted the right horn into a war horn. The Ashen Winds Hellcaller had a few different effects, but its most potent was the Ashen Winds. When blown, the horn would summon hot, dry winds that carried the whispers of ancient demons, and enemies who succumbed to the whispers were driven into depraved acts of one of the seven major sins. The winds also afflicted enemies with dehydration and a weakness to fire. Alternatively, you could bolster allies with the Rally of Fire. Rally of Fire bolstered the strength and morale of allies and imbued their weapons with a temporary fiery attack effect.

Seven didn't seem to be Aetheria's lucky number.

Year 9

Arkaziel remained within his borders in the Murdercat Tyranny. The isolationists of Eldergarde fell to a revolution inspired by pilgrims and spies from the Theocracy of Light, which gave Kallos half of the landmass of the competition. Of the three of them, Aetheria had been certain Arkaziel would be the one to make land grabs and acquire his neighbors as soon as possible. Still, instead, he'd raised tall walls and taken an extreme isolationist stance other than trade for exotic food goods.

While Kallos and Aetheria's love and cooperation were without question, their followers did not understand the relationship between their two rulers. Each nation repeatedly ran into hiccups of dissent caused by the followers of the other, and with each passing month, the incidents seemed to occur more frequently.

Aetheria executed the High Priestess of the Sovereignty for this failure, and her replacement vowed there would be a stop to these actions that ran contrary to her decrees. Kallos committed to a similar path of action, including setting up an office of inquest to end the misguided.

Year 13

All of Aetheria's gains and progress went up in flames. Punishing those who sought to agitate against the Theocracy of Light led to a massive theocratic revolt based on the premise that the true goddess Aetheria would never kill her own to make peace with a foreign power. When the smoke cleared, a full quarter of the population of the sovereignty had perished in the religious strife. Kallos did not indicate the full extent of her nation's revolts but said the situation was unfortunate. It had been so long since Aetheria had been an ordinary human, and Kallos never had, so both women took the stark lesson on the impressive agency of mortal provocateurs to heart.

Sovereignty renewed a focus on public well-being, and Aetheria tried to move the path of the government more toward a communal-minded dictatorship. Still, the people were reluctant to abandon seeing her as a goddess. So much of the workforce still lay empty, with her constructs being the ones who performed so much of the menial labor, and her power had no comparison beyond the leader of the Theocracy of Light.

Year 21

Invaders came by sea. Eight years of peace between the three countries must have bored Moros into action. The invaders came in longships, abandoned them on any part of the coast they landed on, and then turned to guerrilla raid tactics. The raiders didn't seem to have a clear goal and fought to the death. Even the use of stun attacks and capture resulted in the raiders either going into a berserker rage when they awoke or committing suicide. *What a bunch of cheating bullshit, just sending waves of mindless barbarians at us. What is this, a game of civ?*

Shore defenses had to be quickly erected, and Aetheria turned to a pack of intelligent sea drakes to help safeguard the coast of the sovereignty. In response, Moros just sent more barbarian raiders and strengthened them.

Year 23

Moros finally grew bored with sending barbarians after their countries. One day, the longboats ceased their appearance. Two weeks later, a subterranean species of rat people almost succeeded in dropping the capital of the sovereignty into the underworld. Aetheria beat the subterranean invaders violently, destroying her main temple. Afterward, rat-man hide leather became a popular adventuring armor material, especially when they discovered caches of gems, crystals, and other loot within the subterranean holdings of the rat-people.

Aetheria repeatedly tried to make peace with the underworld-dwelling people, but even when she managed to arrange a parley, all the rat-men would tell her was that her humans were a disgrace to the great Mother Earth, and that they must be wiped out for the greater good.

The Murdercat Tyranny paid lucratively for rat-man carcasses. Even if there hadn't been a plethora of treasures to encourage the adventurous and militant of the sovereignty to exterminate the subterranean people, the equivalent of an open bounty by the Murdercat Tyranny ensured the genocide of the rat-men.

Year 28

Moros sent hurricanes full of aquatic life across the island: eels, sharks, squid, whales, and many terrifically venomous jellyfish. Aetheria spent days straight controlling the weather, unable to focus on anything more productive than preventing her nation from being tormented by the equivalent of a truly awful B-movie. When it finally ended, her people initially cheered for all the free seafood. But while the country grappled with the unpleasant smell of rotting fish, people grew tired of seafood, further exacerbating the public health emergency of all the rotting squid and jellyfish.

It took months for the scent of fish to leave the landlocked capital. Needless to say, the fishnado decreased sales from the fishery of Pearl for a full year before the citizens of the sovereignty regained their taste for seafood.

Year 31

The first generation of civil employees were nearly all retiring. Aetheria opted to replace as many as possible with second tier or above Cultivators, who had much longer lifespans and could, or should, live until the end of the challenge. While this would reduce needing to train replacements down the road, it meant having to deal with the hiccups of training people with no backgrounds associated with the new jobs, or in some cases, dealing with much more bombastic personalities than those previously in place. Cowing low tier Cultivators proved no challenge at all for Aetheria, but keeping the new officials from becoming little tyrants themselves proved to be a full-time job, and required instilling a sense that she could always be watching over their actions.

Toward the end of the thirty-first year, Aetheria realized she could use her authority over love to instill a nationalistic love of the common good of the

Sovereignty amongst her new recruits. Surely, this wouldn't backfire in any possible way?

Year 35

Fanatic nationalism, when not guided carefully, indeed became dangerous. Three of her midlevel officials had concocted a program to re-educate any citizens who were not properly dedicated to the grand future of the sovereignty. Aetheria caught wind of their plans before they did anything more than harass a dozen lower level officials, but it showed the dangers of using authority on others. It also left her wondering if authority was a danger to oneself. Could idle thoughts on matters she held authority on affect her? As someone with autopotency, had she inadvertently changed things about herself without intention?

The line of questioning led Aetheria down a rabbit hole of self-doubt and uncertainty that ended only after considerable research through the libraries of Binah reassured her that at her current power levels she couldn't rewrite her own existence or history unknowingly.

CHAPTER 39

Moros Makes Madness

Year 39

Inexplicably, a quarter of the crop fields of the sovereignty produced sweet corn. Prior to this occurrence, there had been no versions of corn that grew in the domain Aetheria controlled. What initially seemed to be a pleasant and tasty surprise, quickly turned into a salty, slippery mess. The planned crop rotations were messed up, and more devastatingly, nutritional balance for a large portion of the sovereignty suffered. Quick-growing vitamin-rich vegetables were prioritized to maintain a healthy population.

Aetheria herself enjoyed the sweet corn immensely, but she drew sustenance from her connection to the Origin and the Void, not food.

Year 42

What manner of horror does a bored god of impending Doom unleash on a year that Aetheria associated with towels, whales, aliens, hyperspace bypasses, and depressed robots? For each of the original countries in the trial, a floating city drifted in to invade territory. Each city had a powerful sixth tier Cultivator ruling them, and large cadres of psychokinetic soldiers. The overwhelming power of the invaders reduced half of Pearl to rubble before Aetheria neutralized the ground forces and took the fight to the floating city. The psychic leader made for an annoying opponent, even for someone who could see through illusions and whose mind had the protection of the Unutterable Black Flame of the Void.

Both flying cities fell to Aetheria, and despite the temptation to fortify or refurbish them for use in the sovereignty, instead she kept them both in her repository. There was something about flying cities that just screamed out to her to collect. It wasn't as if the sovereignty had a lack of land or overpopulation issues. With the way Moros constantly initiated problems that killed her citizens, even with incentives for high birthrates, the sovereignty barely made ground.

Year 50

Moros celebrated the halfway mark of the trial by creating an entire year of winter. No matter what magics, rituals, authority, miracles, or powers Aetheria or Kallos employed, they couldn't rebuff the winter for more than a day at a time. Moros didn't seem to believe in half measures, either. Snow drifts taller than Aetheria were the smallest to be found. She had to send hundreds of ice constructs out to clear the roads and help free people from their homes when snow buried them. The cold seemed to constantly dance the line between killing everyone and being just bad enough to make life next to impossible.

The cold didn't bother Aetheria herself, and many of her devotees were also cold and ice practitioners, so there was a slight advantage to this scenario for her people. Apparently in Kallos's territory things were a bit more dicey, with her love being forced to burn miracles daily to improve the infrastructure of her country.

Year 58

Tedium. Eight long years of nothing happening. No invasions, no climate disasters, no earthquakes, no revolts, just everyday normal existence. After the hectic back and forth of disaster after disaster, somehow the boring mundanity of it all wore on the soul in a way that external events couldn't. It reminded Aetheria of being a teenager, staring out at a particularly large snowfall, and sitting inside declaring how bored she was. The similarities were many: she didn't have a cell phone, no video game consoles, no computer, no friends to play with. Arkaziel and Kallos were forcefully separated from her, their telepathic bond suppressed.

Aetheria even tried to make friends with some of her subordinates, but that didn't work. To them she was a goddess who could obliterate their world with a stray look. Which, while true, she didn't make a habit of destroying people unnecessarily.

The nation prospered greatly in these years, but the tedium gave Aetheria her first glimpses of the ennui that awaited all immortals who allowed themselves to be chained in place by responsibilities. She yearned to walk new lands, see new sights, beat the stuffing out of people who she felt were morally repugnant, and share new sunsets with Kallos. Yet, she couldn't do almost any of that for the duration of this trial. At first, she'd thought a single one-hundred-year trial seemed light to make up the equivalent of fifteen floors in the Tower of Aetherius, but now she was of the opinion that fifteen floors was too few.

Year 69

Moros sent locusts and an affliction of the soul throughout the people of the large island. None of the three leaders could protect their people from it, but they themselves were immune. Food stockpiles allowed the sovereignty to pass through the year without starvation killing anyone, but the affliction of the soul seemed to be incurable. After eight months, when Aetheria and Kallos had a meeting over tea, the duo realized the affliction resonated with themselves. When they were chatting, smiling, flirting, and laughing the natives of the island all grew healthier.

After a bit of testing, they concluded it had to be genuine improvement of their mental states to improve the natives' health around them. Aetheria's attempts at faking it did nothing. Luckily, like with most things, Aetheria knew how to cheat, in harmonizing with the divine emanation of Tiferet. Through synching herself to the Sefirot, she balanced her emotions, and the people of the sovereignty improved in health, and the swarms of locusts vanished. It didn't make her happy, but it kept her just content enough.

Year 77

An earthquake split the island into three pieces. The Murdercat Tyranny, Sovereignty of Aetheria, and the Theocracy of Light were separated by roughly fifty kilometers of sea. The overall lack of shipyards would have been a far larger issue for the sovereignty if Aetheria weren't able to make large ice ships, and arcing bridges of permanent ice across the sea. The impact did prevent Aetheria and Kallos from being able to have even their occasional meetings on the borders, though. Thanks to her continued harmonization with Tiferet, this didn't send her into a spiraling depression of ennui. While annoying, Aetheria framed it as another mild challenge to easily overcome. With the proper mindset, no challenge was too great to deal with.

The constant harmonization with the Sefirot also gave Aetheria a closer link to Ein Sof. The increase in affinity seemed marginal, but every month she grew a little more cognizant of the immense power within the Third-Eye of Ein Sof. She still couldn't grasp it and smite people with it yet, but she liked to think that she would get there soon.

Year 89

Moros seemed content to end the trial with a whimper, or perhaps Kallos or Arkaziel hadn't handled the tedium of rulership well. Aetheria had shifted her resonance to Da'at, where all the Sefirot manifested as her mystical antidepressant and general cure-all. She could now manifest Ein Sof as an insubstantial light that chilled the souls of any who witnessed it, but she still couldn't make it do anything. Manifestation alone was impressive, given the entirety of the Ethereal and the Void were weakened components of Ein Sof, and almost everything else in existence (and inexistence) were derived from the Ethereal and the Void.

In Aetheria's mind Ein Sof represented Everything, the Void represented the weakened version of Nothing, the hollow echo of Ayin. Ein Sof then weakened into the Ethereal, the energy that powered physical reality, which then itself broke down into Aether and Nether, which in turn broke down into mana and its thousands of variants. It seemed unnecessarily obtuse, but then she probably just lacked the perspective to see it from the proper angle. Few beings gained access to Aether or Nether, let alone the Ethereal, and here she was, able to access every power in and out of existence. The more she considered the creation of her amalgamation of a soul, the more Aetheria came to the conclusion that Nyx and Aetherius had been duped by Khaos and higher players than they understood.

Nyx, as Callie, had been the cunning strategist for group PvP and dominated the social game on their server of *Eldest Fantasy Wars Online*. As a Primordial Goddess of Night, Cold, Fate, and who knew what else, she had sired children with herself, Erebus, Aetherius, and who knew how many other powers. Most were malevolent, or at the least, selfish. Her time as Overgod ensured Nyx had an awareness of the higher existences such as the Aeons, the eldritch Outer Gods, and the dazzling light of Ein Sof. At one point, Aetheria had been certain Nyx had a plan with an amazing endgame goal, but now she found herself doubting that. The Primordials she had met so far seemed to lack ambition outside of their natures as manifestations and representations of their natures.

Who then, pulled the real strings behind the formation of Aetheria's situation? Chronos seemed unlikely. Khaos seemed possible, but she was unpredictable, and even attempting to rationalize Khaos left Aetheria with a dull headache. Even the use of the Sefirot and the Flame of Khaos bound within the Astrum Nexus didn't help in working out the motivations of the transcendent goddess.

Fred and Reverie talked big games, but both seemed fairly unable to take direct actions other than manipulation. That left three possibilities in her mind: Aeons, or the Monad, or the Will behind Ein Sof; Outer Gods; or Khaos. Yet based on the powers she'd had access to from Khaos's Flame, did she have enough power?

Could a Flame be faked? What if the Flame of Khaos in the Astrum Nexus, and the one previously inside of her that the Black Flame devoured had been partial aspects to the greater whole? Why couldn't that work? It's not like Khaos had ever given her Flame to another person before, so she had no records to check. Even the library of Binah, which she treated increasingly as her own private Akashic records domain, didn't have much information on Khaos.

Year 99

Aetheria named the final year of the trial the Year of Kaiju. Every day some new giant monster lumbered out of the ocean and attacked her nation. Every day, she had to battle the massive monsters, which she then would throw into her repository to use for crafting reagents or foodstuffs down the road. By the end of the year, her stockpile of tier-six monster parts formed a pile nearly the size of her inner world. Why would Moros throw this endless horde at her? The amount of power he wasted seemed immense, but then she hadn't understood Moros's goals from the get-go. Maybe he didn't have one? Or maybe he'd just decided to fuck with his stepsister.

Regardless, the day after she killed something that looked an awful lot like the king of monsters, the trial ended, and Arkaziel, Kallos, and Aetheria all appeared at a table with tea and snacks set out, and the animated suit of armor that represented Moros at the head of the table.

"Wasn't that fun?" Moros inquired, but Aetheria couldn't tell if he was mocking them or being sincere.

CHAPTER 40

Winner Winner Chicken Dinner

The burning red embers behind the eyes of the armored helmet were all that could be seen inside the armor. Aetheria wondered if Moros preferred Al or Ed, or if he remained ignorant of Earth anime. Before she could get distracted by a prolonged daydream about Moros watching anime, Arkaziel hopped onto Aetheria's shoulder and hissed at the suit of armor.

"Let's get this over with already. Who won?" Arkaziel demanded.

"As previously mentioned, the trial will be judged on economy, military, quality of life, and population. I'll go by category, and I'll be brief. I'm sure you're all eager to move on to a city and reacquaint yourself with one another." Moros seemed amused at the idea of wanting to spend time with others, but his flamey orbs seemed to be focused on Arkaziel when he said it.

"Economy. Kallos, you get a seven out of ten. Aetheria, you get a seven out of ten, while Arkaziel gets a ten out of ten. You two ladies traded with each other and Arkaziel, but only minimally. Large amounts of untapped resources went unexplored in your kingdoms, and neither of you tried to find foreign markets. Arkaziel, on the other hand, focused on establishing relationships with the subterranean people, and sent large trade vessels to the northern continent, turning his country into the trade superpower of that world."

"Oh, you little sneak! You just pretended to be an isolationist to the two of us, didn't you?" Aetheria's accent thickened with her accusation, and Kallos and Arkaziel burst into laughter at her indignation.

"Well, yeah, duh. I thought you two were doing the same thing?" Arkaziel's feigned innocence warred with his confusion that they hadn't tried to pull anything.

"Arkaziel gets three points, Aetheria and Kallos each gain one. The winner will be the one with the most overall points at the end," Moros explained.

"Now, onto the military. The sovereignty had the strongest force if we factored in constructs. At the same time, Arkaziel made pacts with numerous dragon species to improve his elite ranks, and Kallos had the largest citizen army, with powerful support magic users empowering them. Kallos gets three points, Arkaziel gets two, Aetheria gets one."

"Wait a minute, why don't my constructs count? They won the war against Assur and took out most of your situations, too." Aetheria huffed at the unfairness.

"They were an extension of you; if I count your strength directly into the tally, then I must count the other two direct strengths as well. Moving on." Moros didn't bother arguing. His decrees were final.

"Quality of life for your subjects. Aetheria's people had the most freedom, and felt secure, but they were embroiled in turmoil over worshipping a goddess who made such overt friendly gestures with the leader of the Theocracy of Light, which followed a very different god. Two points. Arkaziel's people were kept unaware of the greater world through stringent measures, but were entertained by the arenas, recreational drugs, and high quality of food diversity. Three points. Kallos, your people were highly encouraged to live the life of a dedicated monk, and focus on the achievement of gnosis and freedom from this level of reality. Zero points."

Kallos laughed lightly, but she didn't object. Aetheria thought she looked amused. Moros disapproved of her methods, or perhaps she had expected it. They hadn't gotten to travel together within the tower enough to discern how Kallos handled trials and challenges truly. The last one hundred years suggested that she would do what she wanted, not necessarily what the trial demanded.

"Finally, population. Aetheria, your focus on an expanding population worked well, but losses to invaders and other events cost you. You and Kallos achieved the same overall population density in the end. You both get two points. Arkaziel, your total population exceeded the other two countries combined. Three points."

"What? How!?" Aetheria sputtered.

"Did you cheat, cat?" Kallos sounded suspicious.

"No, I used trade. I bought every slave and person I could from the northern continent, encouraged breeding, allowed polyamory, and promoted people with good genetic stock. I believe you would call it a breeding program? Oh, and I maybe used some of the aspected crops I cultivated to spread life aspects among the humans, thus ensuring a fast and fit breeding stock, then purified them with Aether every couple of years. Oh, and I took on other forms and impregnated a lot of women with DNA of their race."

"You had kids?" Aetheria blinked repeatedly.

"Isn't that cheating?" Kallos inquired.

"Well, no? I took on their race's genetic sequence, so the children got nothing of my essence or genetically superior stock. I shapeshifted into a genetically perfect version of a male of their race and produced some kids that would carry some of those superior genetic traits. Am I their father? No, a fictional super-version of a random male of their race is their father." Arkaziel yawned, indicating he was bored with the conversation and explaining his point of view.

"You created weak-souled abominations with superior physical bodies for the sake of a contest?" Kallos's disapproval bordered on contempt for the cat's decisions.

"Oh, hell yeah, I did, and I won." Arkaziel showed no remorse. "And not only did I win? I had those poor schmucks grow me a century's worth of cultivation supplies that I used to fuel my cultivation and stored a ton of it to sell, too. You two wasted a hundred years treating it like a real world when Doomsy here will delete it the moment we're gone."

"That's ten points for Arkaziel, six points for Aetheria, and six points for Kallos. Congratulations on the success of the Murdercat Tyranny, Arkaziel." Moros gestured with those words, and an orb of powerful energy appeared before the StarMane, who immediately ate it, not even bragging. The two women remained quiet as if Arkaziel had slapped them.

Moros's armor fell to the ground, and a doorway to the next trade city formed where he had previously been.

"I can't believe we just wasted a hundred years of our lives on that," Aetheria said. Her disbelief almost bordered on tearful hysterics, but she kept her emotions together and held Kallos's hand. Their bond functioned once more, and the emotional and physical embrace warmed her soul and relieved some of the pent-up frustrations she'd harbored for a century.

"I see why people avoid this tower. Eat your snack, and let's go, Ark." Aetheria's growing discontent with the trial only simmered into a more potent form as she thought about the wasted years condensed into a barely thought-out grading system that Moros could have put together on the fly. A hundred years of experience had been rendered into a few points, which felt gravely insulting. Had the entire thing been a test to see if they would actually endure such a ridiculous trial?

~I never really thought about it before, but with the whole no-fighting-each-other rules, only using intermediaries, and being in total control of worlds and towers both, these gods have never experienced real pushback before, have they? There's the Overgod, but it doesn't sound like they do a whole lot,~ Aetheria telepathically queried the opinions of Arkaziel and Kallos.

+If they got smacked around more, maybe they wouldn't be such jerks,+ Arkaziel opined.

-They are imperfect fragments of a reflection they can never match, nor can they comprehend the greater whole from which that reflection is cast. They are but motes of divinity in a reality they didn't create, doomed never to ascend. At worst, they will be cast into the Void and know the peace of oblivion; at best, they will be dispersed and lose what they were to become part of something greater than themselves.- Kallos took a more cosmic view on the matter than Arkaziel.

~Isn't that basically the same answer you'd give for a human, on a different level of scale?~

-Yes. Everything originates from the infinite light of Ein Sof, which once was the black flame of nothing. It is easier to judge them, perhaps, because they have greater power, but they struggle through existence, too, yearning for something they cannot find while retaining their identity, uncertain of what comes after their dissolution, much like humanity.-

+Sounds like a bunch of crap to me. StarManes were made by Chronos; that makes Chronos the best god. Everything else is just a step on my lunch buffet tour of existence.+

-You know full well the existence of the Overgod and his Archons, Arkaziel. Denial does not alter factual reality.- Kallos tsked at the cat.

+Factual reality is malleable. Existence is changeable. Time itself can be altered, and even fate can be rewritten. Look at Ria. What can't she change? And no using the word ineffable*!+*

The chains that hung from Kallos's cloak clinked and brushed against one another in agitation.

-Aetheria is no fluke. We lack the needed perspective to discern the truth behind her nature. That is our failing, not a failing of the powers that forged her. Speculation will only lead to disappointment. Gaze into the Third-Eye of Ein Sof, sense the growing Will within and how it resonates with her own. Coupled with her familiars, Reverie and Fred, we could wildly speculate that she could ascend to many different levels of existence.-

~Hang on a second, we could argue that? How come no one argues that with me?~ Aetheria squirmed under the attention of her companions, uncomfortable at being the subject of the conversation and the direction in which it moved.

-We could argue everything. I'm the daughter of Belial, and he's a draconic cat that wants to devour the universe one planet at a time. We're both quite skilled in being obstinate and imposing our worldviews upon others.-

"Let's see what's waiting for us," Aetheria demanded as she waved her hand in the air and pointed at the doorway.

This is how they ended up in a city with an overcast sky, spiderweb streets, inventive architecture, and overall a very spidery theme. It was the city of Fableton, created by the trickster god Anansi. Aetheria took one look at the place, and while it was cute, whimsical, and fantastic, she immediately noped out of it. Kallos did not argue with her judgment on immediately leaving the city, and Arkaziel only whined slightly about it. The StarMane honestly had eaten too large of a meal from Moros to get too invested in arguments about it and fell asleep on Aetheria's shoulder.

"We'll just count his snore as a confirmation vote to leave this place. Seems fair to me," Aetheria muttered.

"Entirely fair, more than fair. Even without his vote our majority carries the day. Very considerate of him to make it unanimous and vote with us, however."

When the trio vanished from Fableton, they did so without ever noticing the tiny spider that had prepared to welcome them with a lavish feast, heart-wrenching tales, and copious amounts of alcohol. It is said that StarManes know when they miss out, however, and Arkaziel assumed his lingering unpleasant mood when they awoke him at the new trial was due to these missed opportunities.

CHAPTER 41

Platform Hell

Arkaziel appeared on a small floating platform. A tiny ghostly image of Aetheria and Kallos floated above each of his front shoulders. An endless obstacle course stretched out before him, comprised of platforms at varying vertical and horizontal distances. It immediately made Aetheria think of old platform games, and part of her felt shocked Moros hadn't given Arkaziel a hat or mustache for the occasion.

"What the hell is this crap?" Arkaziel scoffed at the floating platforms.

"Looks like a jump puzzle. Seems like a useless challenge for a flying cat." Aetheria wondered idly if Moros had lost his mind. Arkaziel's angry hiss indicated Moros had sealed some of the StarMane's powers.

"I'm sure you're eager to get started, given how quickly you returned." A projection of Moros appeared next to Arkaziel on the platform. The spectral armored figure still had glowing red dots of flames in his helmet for eyes. "Didn't like Anansi's place? He was very disappointed you left before he could even greet you. He wanted to regale you with stories, share his favorite food and liquor, and taste the cooking of the second-best StarMane chef."

Arkaziel hissed at the projection and then at the spectral forms of Aetheria and Kallos. The cat's pride had missed an opportunity to be fluffed, and there was almost nothing Arkaziel hated more than missing out on having all of his worst traits praised by strangers.

"Wait a gods damned minute, did you just say second-best StarMane chef? Who the hell do you think is better than I am?" Arkaziel turned his righteous indignation on Moros.

"You've yet to prove yourself the equal to Bobbi Slay, let alone be her superior," Moros taunted.

"I have sealed the majority of your powers for this challenge. Arkaziel can use his feline grace to jump great distances, move objects with shadow claws, and fire blasts of light. Kallos may use her chains to attack enemies and the environment, grapple, and pull herself to distant places via chain hooks. Aetheria is the brawler, with potent punches against enemies and walls and defensive ice shields at the cost of speed." In

Aetheria's mind, Moros had an obnoxious smirk as he detailed the limitations he'd placed on them.

"And only one of us gets to be active at a time? No teamwork?" Aetheria had played puzzlers like this before.

"Correct." Moros turned to dust and blew away after his final answer.

"How do we switch?" Kallos asked the other two, earning a shrug in response from Aetheria.

"I control it. So, whoever's 'active' gets to swap out. Let's test out how quick it is." Arkaziel's words barely passed his mouth when suddenly the cat turned into the chain-winged Kallos, and the spectral kitty sat on the Nephilim's shoulder opposite Aetheria's tiny spectral form. Kallos's form blurred as she swapped to Aetheria, who flexed her hands and punched the air and swapped back to Arkaziel.

"Almost instant, so there's that. A little disorienting. Get your jump on, kitty cat." Aetheria teased Arkaziel, who stood on the platform's edge looking across at the series of platforms that were the path forward.

"I can't believe I'm being reduced to jumping around an obstacle course like an everyday feline. This indignity is almost as grave as being called the second-best StarMane chef. The nerve! And Bobbi Slay doesn't even come from the legendary line of gourmands I do. This is an insult to all StarManes descended from the incredible gourmand who—"

Arkaziel was interrupted as both women talked over him. "Quit delaying!"

Arkaziel hadn't yet experienced a true unified condemnation by the ladies, and his ears lay flat and his tail twitched.

"It's a grave injustice. We get it, Ark. Now let's blast this trial into the past and move on, right? Aren't you eager to get to the next trade city and be done with this? I am. I'll even buy you some extra delicious food besides what I owe you. Heck, I'll toss you a bunch of fruits from Cryostrialis. With what Moros gave you before, you've got to be close to the sixth tier, right?"

"Yeah, I'm real close. I'll be the first StarMane to hit the sixth tier this young in the last twenty thousand years. Some of those big, juicy fruits might put me even closer. Fine, fine. Behold the ultimate grace of a StarMane. Not even Moros can dampen my aerial acrobatic prowess." Arkaziel swallowed the next sentence as the intangible stares of Kallos and Aetheria bored into his head.

The cat moved to the far end of the platform, ran, and leaped through the air, and then skidded to a stop with a flex of his claws on the next platform. Arkaziel had almost overdone it but stopped himself just before he went off the edge of the new platform.

"Not flying is stupid," Arkaziel pouted before he repeated the process. With each jump, his leaps grew more accurate, his landing more precise. The spectral ladies avoided unleashing panicked screams with each jump, but their fists were clenched in white-knuckled grips. As spirits, they had nothing to latch on to and no way to release the terror of the speed of the reckless cat.

"I could've made a fortune off putting videos of you on streaming sites," Aetheria told Arkaziel. The cat puffed up his chest, and his next few jumps seemed extra on point, a clear indication that he failed to understand she wasn't complimenting him.

After dozens of platforms, the following section replaced the floating bricks with thin rails frequently surrounded by aerial enemies, so Arkaziel switched places with Kallos. The chains extending from her tattooed wrists were almost like grappling hooks, able to bind themselves to distant objects from which she could swing like Tarzan. The chain lengths that extended from Kallos's wings made perfect projectiles that elongated and bashed the horse-sized flying hornets to death. Once the Nephilim realized she could shatter their wings instead of bludgeon their bodies, it only took her two hits per hornet to send them flying to their deaths.

"Hanging from magical chains isn't at all disquieting; I expected it to be weird for some reason. Maybe it's the metal your chains are made out of that puts me on edge, and that effect doesn't work when I'm in spectral form?" Arkaziel talked a lot, but Aetheria rarely heard the cat babble nervously. *I suppose it's pretty rare that he has to trust anyone besides me to succeed. Maybe this will be a growing experience for him.*

Eventually, the railings and tiny ledges suitable only for Kallos's chains gave way to what appeared to be an endless brick wall. Once Kallos dropped onto a ledge, she swapped places with Aetheria.

"Aetheria, punch!" The Astrum Nexus glittered brightly when she demolished the brick wall to reveal a long stretch of tunnel filled with skeletons. The first two she saw had different weapons; the nearer had a sword, and the farther had a bow. Usually, she'd flash down the hall like a bullet and demolish both without a second thought, but she had none of her average speed. Her full-out run seemed to be roughly what a regular human jog would be, which felt very disappointing to someone used to breaking the sound barrier on a daily basis.

A large shield of ice appeared if Aetheria raised an arm and clenched her fist. When it was out, she moved at a walk. Relative to the slowness she already hated, this wasn't that big of a difference in inconvenience.

"Wow, look at her face. I don't think I've seen her look that annoyed since she realized I could talk." Arkaziel laughed at his bonded companion from the safety of his spectral form.

A fifth arrow bounced off the ice shield, and then Aetheria punched the sword-wielding skeleton in the face. Its upper skull turned into powdered dust, and its other bones clattered to the floor.

Suddenly, Arkaziel swapped out with her, and the cat quickly shot bursts of lasers at the bow-wielding skeleton.

"What the hell, Ria?" Ark whined but quickly ran down the hallway until he got to the next wall, and then he swapped back out with Aetheria.

"It is really difficult to be slow. Even though Moros took my speed, he didn't take my perception speed. So, everything is unbelievably slow, and I just want to punch reality; I'm so bored." The wall exploded into debris and dust as she explained her issue caused by the sealing of abilities.

"Besides, it's like a video game, right? You get a few really easy basic things to learn what you're doing, then you have to progress through increasingly challenging mixed trials to beat the levels. In this case, it's all about us switching quickly and appropriately. Kallos is the grappling midrange character who can get up and down and around any obstacles. You're the speedy nightblade that shoots lasers and runs fast with big jumps, and I'm the slow tank that smashes stuff. It isn't quite the paradigm of a game I played in the past, but it's sort of close." Aetheria swapped back and forth with Arkaziel as they traversed the tunnels, fighting skeletons and crushing walls.

Through walls and tunnels the trio emerged into subterranean caves, where Kallos navigated them through open areas and tall mushrooms, Arkaziel darted between spiderwebs and small platforms balancing on stalagmites, and Aetheria punched things. Aetheria definitely felt a little underutilized, but once worms spit acid at them, her ice shields necessitated her subbing in with great frequency.

After the caves, the final area took the shape of a tropical jungle. Kallos dominated the area, with her ability to swing between large branches while simultaneously killing treebound snakes, evil monkeys, and strangely swift sloths.

Eventually, the party made it to a large clearing. Just beyond the edge of the clearing there were glimpses of a village, but at the center of the clearing sat a large chest. Unwilling to risk being eaten by a mimic, Kallos and Arkaziel sent Aetheria to deal with it. Anticlimactically, when she pushed the lid open a shower of silver sparks shot into the air, and one particularly big blob of silver light arced up and came down. When it hit the ground, it transformed into a silver doorway to the next floor. Arkaziel and Kallos regained their normal forms.

Restored, they left the weird jungle behind them.

CHAPTER 42

Aetheria's Got a Gun

The unbearable heat of a high-noon sun burned Aetheria's pale skin. Or it would have if she were still a human with natural skin and a susceptibility to sunburn. A wide-brimmed white leather hat kept the sun out of her eyes and rested uncomfortably close to her Third-Eye of Ein Sof to boot. Her trench coat had gone from its usual black to white leather. She found herself in an unpleasant stance. Both flaps of her coat had been tucked back and around, presumably so that her hands could quickly access the pistols on her belt.

Now, Aetheria didn't know much about guns, but years of watching Westerns with her dad had taught her what a Peacemaker looked like. Two quintessential Old West guns were secured in holsters on her belt, one on each hip. In classic movie style, her feet were well spread, and a hundred paces from her stood another person in a similar stance. The other gunslinger was shorter, had only one gun, and his eyes sparkled with the promise of death.

To the left of the street from Aetheria stood a church, while on the right there was a saloon. Down the street to the left stood a general store, and on the right a bank. Between the church and the general store in a mostly empty lot marked off by a white fence sat wooden tables where the children at school sat at. Onlooking children were not the only ones who were caught staring, transfixed, at the spectacle on the street. Men and women lined both sides of the street. Aetheria couldn't help but notice Kallos, dressed in a gorgeous black and purple, two-toned rococo dress. The only person who stood out more than the Soul Witch was Arkaziel.

The StarMane had been forced into his human form. Which was to say, a one-hundred-and-eighty-eight-centimeter-tall black male, with short black hair, dressed in an attention-grabbing blue suit with sparkly lapels and immaculately cut black leather boots. The whiskey bottle and a rag in his hand somehow managed to convey the fact Arkaziel was the saloon owner or bartender, or maybe that was the flow of knowledge from Binah?

In contrast to the flashy style of Arkaziel and Kallos, the other people of Dry Gulch seemed a lot more mundane. The young woman in a schoolmarm dress in front of the general store seemed like an empty reflection of a person. She wasn't insubstantial by any means, and to all of Aetheria's senses, she was actually there. But she and all of the spectators, except for the enemy gunslinger, Arkaziel, and Kallos, felt the same way. Empty. Misty.

"*They are unfated. Moros has woven this scene and imbued only the gunslinger with a future.*" Reverie's usually bountiful patience had the tinge of castigation to it.

Time reasserted itself from the frozen-still image of a duel. A bell in the church tower rang. With each clang of sound, each copper peel of notes, the crowd grew agitated. Whispers and bets were made.

+*You got this, Blue?*+ Arkaziel inquired at the fifth peel of the bells.

-*What ridiculous scenario even is this? I rather like my dress, though, and there's something to be said for how ruggedly sexy you look in those leathers.*- Kallos hadn't heard the tales of the Old West.

~*I'm sure I'll figure it out.*~ Aetheria didn't want to oversell herself in a brand-new situation. As much as she wanted to play gunslinger in a Western, she'd be a lot happier if she'd had a tutorial, and knew what restrictions Moros had placed on her, and other vital knowledge.

The seventh peal of the bell drew Aetheria's attention to her opponent. His fingers danced near his thighs, ready to dart in at the last chime of the noon bell. He appeared to be more anchored in reality than even Aetheria, Arkaziel, and Kallos themselves were; an oddity for the tower.

"Last chance to back down, Sheriff. No law-person's going to bring down Chad Hellfire Hawkins." With the declaration of his name, literal hellfire exploded in the eyes of a demon. The human skin burned off as fire burned across his skin and gear. The flames left splotchy red skin exposed to the noon sun, a pair of horns on his head, and cloven hooves at the ends of his legs instead of feet.

The tenth clang of the bell drowned out the gasps of the crowd, the eleventh made everyone take a deep breath, and then the final bell of noon echoed down the main street of Dry Gulch.

No one cried *go*, but both Aetheria and her opponent drew their weapons. Aetheria aimed her Peacemakers, and pulled the triggers. Before the bullets spiraled out of their respective barrels, a blast of hellfire struck her in the face. Pain blossomed for a brief second, then vanished.

Aetheria felt the scorching heat of the hot noon sun. She was back at the ready position, and time stood frozen once again. What was the criteria for getting out of this? Did she have to win the duel? Do something else? Were her companions looping with her, or were they caught only to experience it once—the final loop?

Son of a gun, I hate time loops. The world unfroze exactly the way it had the first time. The noon bell tolled, and Aetheria's stomach churned anxiously.

+*You got this, Blue?*+ Arkaziel inquired at the fifth peal of the bells.

-*What ridiculous scenario even is this? I rather like my dress, though, and there's something to be said for how ruggedly sexy you look in those leathers.-* Kallos hadn't heard the tales of the Old West.

That answered one of her questions, and knowing that lifted some of the anxiety off her shoulders.

~I'll figure it out eventually, I'm sure.~ After how many loops? Well, that Aetheria didn't know.

"Last chance to back down, Sheriff. No law-person's going to bring down Chad Hellfire Hawkins." With the declaration of his name, literal hellfire exploded in the eyes of a demon. The human skin burned off as fire burned across his skin and gear. The flames left splotchy red skin exposed to the noon sun, a pair of horns on his head, and cloven hooves at the ends of his legs instead of feet.

The final noon bell rang mournfully, a dolorous sound that made all who heard it shiver.

Aetheria didn't draw her guns, and instead created a series of ice-walls between her and Hellfire Hawkins. The outlaw's hellfire inferno blasted right through all of the layers of ice and hit her in the face.

The noon sun burned at her flesh. Time had reversed and stood frozen once more. Aetheria pushed her mind into the uncomfortable realms of fate. Hawkins was fated to win his duel, and his opponent was fated to lose. It was as close to inevitable as anyone without the power of Ananke could get to inevitable, and there was something else, too. A rigidness to the fate. When she opened herself to the Flame of Chronos, she found that the flow of time had been rendered rigid and fixed. There was no wiggle room that she had noticed when using the powers of Chronos in the past.

+You got this, Blue?+ Arkaziel inquired at the fifth peal of the bells.

-What ridiculous scenario even is this? I rather like my dress, though, and there's something to be said for how ruggedly sexy you look in those leathers.- Kallos hadn't heard the tales of the Old West.

~ We're in a time loop until I don't lose, ~ Aetheria sent to the others, along with the experiences she'd endured so far.

+Cheat?+ Arkaziel suggested.

-You'll need to overwrite fate then, and unfix time.- Kallos's instructions were swift and completely without details. Unfix time how? Overwrite fate with what?

"Last chance to back down, Sheriff. No law-person's going to bring down Chad Hellfire Hawkins." With the declaration of his name, literal hellfire exploded in the eyes of a demon. The human skin burned off as fire burned across his skin and gear. The flames left splotchy red skin exposed to the noon sun, a pair of horns on his head, and cloven hooves at the ends of his legs instead of feet.

The final noon-bell pealed.

Aetheria teleported behind Hellfire Hawkins. A blast of hellfire hit her the moment she appeared behind him; the gunslinger had somehow moved fast enough to spin and fire the blast in the same amount of time it took Aetheria to teleport behind him.

The noon sun burned at her flesh as she returned to the start of the loop. Aetheria called on the power of the Flame of Chronos and created an immense temporal lever, which she used to free the flow of time into chaotic warbles instead of the fixed straight line it had been forced to flow in, and with the Flame of Khaos and the soul resonance of Ananke, she declared her immediate victory inevitable.

+*You got this, Blue? You seem annoyed,*+ Arkaziel inquired at the fifth peal of the bells, but he picked up on her emotions in their bond this time.

-*There is something to be said for how ruggedly sexy you look in those leathers, dear, but why are you so worked up? See how cute my dress is?*- Kallos, too, changed her reaction to the anxiety and annoyance pouring out of Aetheria.

~*Time loop, think I've got it.*~

"Last chance to back down, Sheriff. No law-person's going to bring down Chad Hellfire Hawkins." With the declaration of his name, literal hellfire exploded in the eyes of a demon. The human skin burned off as fire burned across his skin and gear. The flames left splotchy red skin exposed to the noon sun, a pair of horns on his head, and cloven hooves at the ends of his legs instead of feet.

I will win, I will win, I have to win. Aetheria chanted the mantra, imagining the results she required.

The bell rang loudly for the twelfth time.

Two Aether-filled blasts of cold struck Chad Hellfire Hawkins in the head, even as the hellfire blast hit her.

The hot noon sun warmed Aetheria's pale skin in a way she found slightly pleasant. Perhaps she was trauma bonding with the desert climate. Time hung frozen, and with the Flame of Khaos and the resonance of Ananke, she changed things. The outlaw Chad Hellfire Hawkins was destined to be killed by the Sheriff slash Schoolmarm Miss Kelly, while her deputy, Aetheria, watched from the sidelines with the beautiful banker Kallos. In a flicker of rainbow flames Aetheria appeared next to Kallos, the schoolmarm appeared in Aetheria's place, and then time flowed.

+*What the hell, why isn't it one of us in a duel?*+ Arkaziel complained when time reasserted itself.

-*While this does appear to be stupid, at least we're together.*- Kallos happily squeezed Aetheria's hand, her genuine pleasure evident as her smile shone brighter than the high noon sun.

~*Happy stories are the best ones,*~ Aetheria agreed, even as she bit her lower lip. The twelfth bell chimed. Sheriff Kelly shot the hellfire blast out of the air, then put a second bullet between Hellfire Hawkins's flaming eyes, courtesy of her amazing Demonkiller Holy Shot. Aetheria laughed happily.

But then the fragments of the hellfire blast re-formed and struck Sheriff Kelly dead.

"For Pete's sake!" Aetheria cursed under her breath.

Time froze, and Moros appeared.

"You sacrificed someone for your advancement? I thought you were the heroine?" Moros chided oh so gleefully.

"That only happened because in this place you have more authority than me. Outside in the real world, you wouldn't, and she would've survived." Aetheria stood resolutely behind her decision, even though she felt sick in the stomach.

"So even if I offer to let you keep trying, you acknowledge I would win?" There was no visible indication that Moros smiled, but deep in Aetheria's soul, she knew there was a massive douchebaggy smile on his lips. If he had lips in any form, or even had an actual form, anyway.

"I acknowledge you would win." Aetheria smiled sweetly with the words, even though inwardly she wanted to punch Moros until his armor was crumpled into a modern art piece. But it seemed very clear Moros wanted to hear those words spoken, without caveats. When Moros got it, he seemed perplexed momentarily, then moved on.

Of course, what Aetheria had actually meant was Moros couldn't win. Under the rules of the hellfire hitting her causing a time loop, Moros would win every time. But it wouldn't matter if the hellfire did hit her, because it couldn't hurt Aetheria. Arbitrary rules vexed Aetheria, and no doubt Moros knew that. *So why is he intentionally trying to piss me off?*

"To the next challenge, stepsister," Moros opened the dimensional door, and Arkaziel and Kallos were liberated from the flow of frozen time.

I hope Moros hasn't spent too much time on Earth's internet.

CHAPTER 43

The Infinite Room

Aetheria, Arkaziel, and Kallos appeared inside of a large room. The floors were beige, the north wall black, the east wall red, the south wall blue, and the west wall green. The ceiling was a mustard-yellow color that earned an "ugh" from Aetheria and an "eww" from Kallos.

"It's just an empty box with nothing to eat. Unless . . ." Arkaziel ran one of his razor-sharp claws against the beige floor. A show of sparks erupted, and a terrible sound akin to nails on a chalkboard echoed across the square room, giving each of them extra exposure to the repeated screech. Not even a scratch remained on the floor when Arkaziel stopped.

"My poor ears," Aetheria whined as she examined the floor. A stomp of her foot did nothing but give her a sore foot, which instantly healed.

Kallos squinted at the floor, and one after another of the chains on her wings smashed into the floor with the clang of metal against concrete, and showers of sparks. After a rapid burst of thirty chains, spiderweb cracks ran through the beige floor before they melded back together, leaving no signs any damage had been done at all.

"Show-off," Arkaziel muttered, his wounded pride injured and on full display after the witch damaged the floor and he failed, never mind that even her damage had immediately healed itself.

"Well, it's basically indestructible." Aetheria shrugged and walked toward the black wall to the north. Even at a jog, the wall never seemed to get closer, and when she broke the sound barrier at a light run, it still stayed the same distance away. Aetheria had to run back to her friends, which seemed to shift the other walls farther away, too.

"That's totally not disorienting to watch. Seems like we're in some kind of infinite room puzzle? Or am I seeing things differently from you two?"

"Nope, the walls moved farther away when you moved toward them," Arkaziel agreed.

"Our goal must be to escape from an infinite room. No doubt a paradox or a law is in place that we can use to aid our escape." Kallos tucked her legs underneath her and closed her golden eyes. Most people would fall on the floor doing that, but Kallos levitated in the air while she meditated.

Arkaziel, on the other hand, had summoned a whole buffet table of food and went to work on the arduous task of eating it all. Literally eating it all, even the bones and cartilage of his meal got devoured, which created the terrible sounds of organic matter being crushed, shattered, and broken by his impossibly strong jaws and teeth. There was a saying that greater dragons' claws and fangs could cut anything, and while that might be an exaggeration, it did seem close to the truth. Or perhaps outside the tower it was truth, and inside the gods suppressed it?

"Guess I'll just investigate the physical stuff first?" Aetheria said to herself.

What was the first thing she tried out? Walking backward. The wall still stayed beyond her ability to reach, even walking backward. When that didn't work, she tried moving in zig-zags toward a corner, but the walls still stayed beyond her reach. Teleportation simply didn't work, no matter what method she tried.

+*Can you freeze it?*+ Arkaziel inquired telepathically, his real mouth full of a whole boar.

"That's not the worst idea ever." Aetheria focused her senses on the walls, and attempted to freeze the concepts of the walls—layer after layer of ice formed around the walls while she froze the concept of the wall.

The walls still moved away when she tried to approach the icy walls.

"Nope, that's not going to work either. There must be a rule in play that supersedes being frozen and counteracts teleporting. Can you use shadows or light to get closer?"

+*No. I already tried to step through the shadows, but I failed. I tried to snare the walls, but I couldn't pierce them, either. I even tried to manifest sticky light in the corners while you were running, but it didn't even slow the movement.*+ Arkaziel candidly admitted to his failures after watching Aetheria also fail.

"Guess I'll see what else I can do." Aetheria mimicked Kallos, but she created an ice pedestal to sit on rather than levitate.

None of her divine authorities seemed likely to get her out of this situation. War, love, sex, and beauty were great authorities, but other than using war to amplify their attacks, the other three seemed useless concerning their particular problem.

None of the essences in her soul stood out as the solution to the problem. Not one of the five gods still mixed into Aetheria's soul, Ananke, Izanami, Quetzalcoatl, Ouranos, and Phanes, were space authorities. Although, Phanes's authority on creation might allow Aetheria to manipulate the room in some manner. Harmonizing with the essence of Phanes sent power coursing through her cores, and wings made of red Ethereal lightning formed behind her.

Augmented with the power of Phanes, Aetheria attempted to freeze and draw the walls back in. This failed utterly; for all her infinite strength, it felt comparable to a puppy trying to drag a dump truck by biting a tire and pulling. When that failed, Aetheria tried to create stationary doorways out of the room, but reality refused to allow doors to form inside the space. Despite numerous other attempts with Phanes's power of creation, she couldn't construct anything that would negate the rules of the room.

If Aetheria focused on creating things unrelated to the room or getting out, they would manifest just fine. This is how a small floating island appeared in the sky.

Next, Aetheria tried the temporal powers of Chronos through the Astrum Nexus. Regressing or accelerating the flow of time did not affect the distance of the walls. Aetheria had hoped, at the least, that they would come closer again if she rewound time, but the walls appeared to be out of sync with time.

Aetheria's final attempt with the Astrum Nexus was to use the Flame of Khaos from the right ring. Yet try as she might, she couldn't get the walls to move or a door to appear by altering the state of reality within the room. This wasn't unexpected. The Flames within the Astrum Nexus were static at Tier Four. No matter how much energy she pushed into them, they wouldn't grow or expand to higher tiers.

"I think I have figured it out," Kallos said with a hint of optimism while she stretched.

Arkaziel's mouth was full of a bass.

"What are we dealing with, oh wise and sexy witch?"

"Well, darling, from what I can tell, the power and laws binding this box are all outside the box. We must slip through the cracks to manipulate those laws. To do so, I believe a joint attack by all three of us may be enough to create a large enough crack to touch the outside laws. If we are quick enough, we should be able to create a doorway out and be done with this obnoxious trial through brute force. If not, we must complete the act which will spawn the doorway out."

+*What act?*+ Arkaziel had swallowed the bass and now worked on a meter-long sandwich.

"The trigger appears to be your ascension to the sixth tier, Arkaziel. How close are you?" Kallos squinted at the cat, clearly trying to discern the answer for herself by investigating his soul.

Arkaziel didn't answer until he finished eating the meter-long sandwich, which only took him about ten seconds. Despite the speed, or maybe even because of it, watching Arkaziel eat made Aetheria feel slightly sick to her stomach. A tiny cat just shouldn't be able to eat that much, and the dragon had terrible table manners, but that wasn't even the worst part. Somehow, it always seemed to sound like he was eating drywall screws, even when he chewed on something soft like bread and lettuce.

"Close-ish. I'm still processing Moros's orb; I'll have fully absorbed the power in two or three days. That should put me close, but it won't get me all the way there. One more powerful enemy, and I should be there, or lots of fruit from Blue's ice tree."

"Eat up," Aetheria said while she gestured, and large, Ethereal-power-infused fruit from Cryostrialis rolled across the beige floor toward Arkaziel.

"What, we're going to take the slow path? That's not like us." Arkaziel eyed the duo suspiciously, even as Aetheria conjured a cabin out of her repository.

"No? Are we just dimwitted brutes who can only solve things through murder?" Aetheria wasn't sure if she should be offended or not.

"Besides, we can enjoy our time together while you process your evolution. It's a win for everyone, yes?" Kallos grinned.

"Well, we do solve most of our problems with murder and then eating whatever we murdered," Arkaziel answered Aetheria.

"That's mostly just you. Sometimes me, but definitely you. Kallos for sure doesn't eat our enemies." Aetheria wagged her finger and pointed at Arkaziel.

"Even if I wanted to eat our enemies, you two gluttons leave nothing behind you. I have no interest in such acts, but I feel compelled to point out that even the choice is usually denied me." Kallos verbally poked the other two, before she wandered into the cabin.

"Oh, right." A sign appeared in Aetheria's hand, and she hung it next to the cabin's door. The sign had been made from multicolored ice, and it read "No Beast Emperors allowed, Beast Sovereigns only."

"What the hell? I don't get to come in? At least give me a bed!" Arkaziel complained loudly.

After consideration, Aetheria manifested a giant cat bed for Arkaziel, and tossed it near the cabin's chimney. The chimney radiated ambient heat, which she knew Arkaziel liked.

"Don't screw around too much, but you don't need to push too hard either, okay?"

Arkaziel responded positively to her tone and smile, some of the bitterness fading from his tone and emotional connection to her.

"I'll give you and your lady a few days, but at least soundproof the cabin?"

"You dirty-minded cat! And don't worry; I already did." With a wink, Aetheria skipped inside the cabin, leaving Arkaziel with the giant cat bed, dozens of fruits the size of the cabin, and an infinite box.

"I should've asked for something more valuable than fruit. Where is all the light coming from in here, anyway?" Arkaziel wondered while he stared up at the strange mustard-yellow ceiling. The idea of trying out the authorities that he'd stolen from the manifestations of Nergal and Ereshkigal against the puzzle crossed his mind. Still, the time and food to reach the sixth tier were impossible to pass up, even if they wouldn't remain to stare in wonder and praise each incremental step toward his evolution as was proper and just.

Inside the cabin, the two women drank tea and watched Arkaziel's reaction to being left alone.

"He took that better than I thought he would. He's more offended than lonely." Aetheria noted what she picked up from their bond.

"StarManes may be slightly more complicated creatures than I have previously given them credit for. He is closer to the sixth tier than he realizes, though."

"Won't he have to confirm a Law or anything?"

"No, Arkaziel must undergo a trial to become a Beast Sovereign. Part of the energy he metabolizes will be used to call out and shift his soul to a primordial plane, where he will take on a series of challenges. The nature of the challenges is said to vary depending upon the race of the beast. I have never spoken with a StarMane Beast Sovereign, but given his heritage, it seems likely he knows what to expect better than either of us do."

"Yes, I suppose so. It shall also give us a chance to see what effect possession of authority has upon his evolution and a glimpse of what to expect when you ascend."

CHAPTER 44

Birth of a Beast Sovereign

Beast Cultivators were, in many ways, superior to humanoid Cultivators. Arkaziel didn't need to meditate on the fundamentals of the universe, or cycle energy. He just had to devour enemies, consume their power, and metabolize it into his own. The downside, of course, was that humanoid Cultivators loved to kill beast Cultivators and use their high-spec bodies as crafting materials. In addition to the humanoids, there were always other beasts who wanted to eat you and make you their gain before you ate them to make them your gain. Trust, in this environment, was short-lived, even inside of clans. Given his diet since hatching, he had fed more quickly than almost any other StarMane he had knowledge of within his genetic memories.

Yet here Arkaziel was, struggling to maintain pace with Aetheria. The victory in the last trial had provided him with substantial advancement, and even so he felt barely ahead of his companion, despite hunkering down to advance even now. Arkaziel had stolen kills, swiped cores in combat, siphoned power from Aetheria's infinite supply of the Ethereal and Void, and he only eked out ahead of her because of a trial reward. Yet there was no cause to celebrate beating her; if a situation required Aetheria to break through to win, she would. Rules didn't apply to her. She broke restrictions as if they were suggestions, and even the will of the gods in their own towers barely constrained her.

Arkaziel's bond-partner was ridiculous. He'd sensed that immediately, and his parents had agreed to send a newly hatched kitten into a tower with an adventurer they'd just met, because all three of them had sensed that deep down Aetheria was special. She had played at being human at first, or so Arkaziel had thought, until he realized she thought she was one of those monkey-people. The greatness of her soul and aura, the immaculate control of her soul, and the raw power of her soulsteel proved the extent of her existence being beyond humanity. Not even a sixth tier Cultivator should be able to forge soulsteel that would shatter the strongest of god-forged adamantine.

Initially, the link to the Soul Witch seemed like probable cause for some of the abnormalities around his partner. The Nephilim daughter of Belial had made a legendary name for herself for crushing the Tower of Aetherius, and some of the witch's powers bled through her connection to Aetheria, but it had not been the powers of Kallos that made Aetheria's soul so powerful.

Aetheria herself credited it to Nyx, Khaos, Chronos, Aetherius, and whatever they had done to her. Arkaziel had his doubts about this. When they had been exposed to the Void, that should have been it for both of them by any standards Arkaziel knew. Elder god corruption should have consumed them and transformed them into an existence that had little to no similarities to what they were before. Yet, somehow, Aetheria resisted the corruption and even created a form that transcended the Void. Whatever lay under the seals, chains, and locks of her Voidform, Arkaziel really didn't want to know. No, that wasn't true, he really wanted to know, but knew he shouldn't, but he was a cat and needed to know, damn it.

Somehow, their connection had provided him with enough resistance to the corruption of the elder gods that he not only fought it off, but maintained his sanity and identity. If that weren't enough, his bond-partner then turned around and bound tenets into his essence that gave him full control of the Void. Even if Aetheria credited one of her imaginary friends with the knowledge, it went beyond anything Arkaziel could fathom. Yet once she'd done that, things had started to make more and more sense for Arkaziel.

Once Aetheria developed her third eye and started accessing divine realms as if that was something people did, things started to click into place for Arkaziel. He wasn't sure how, why, or when, but clearly, Nyx imbuing Aetheria with the Black Flame had not been an accident. It may have been an accident in the plans of Nyx and the others. Still, some force greater than Primordials and elder gods had to be involved, which meant powers from a higher existence or possibly even from the highest of existences. The Infinite Light that Aetheria and Kallos talked about was a phenomenon unknown to Arkaziel, and as a general rule, StarManes hated it when they didn't know things.

What was the point of being a super fabulous, genetic memory-sharing, dragon-feline hybrid species bred to eat gods if you weren't more unique and powerful than everyone else? Still, Arkaziel had grown in power beyond his wildest dreams. He'd consumed and integrated his twin, incorporated the Void, and wielded almost limitless Ethereal power, thanks to his connection to Aetheria. Power storage was one of the few limitations StarManes suffered under. Thanks to the soul connection to Aetheria and her infinite supply from the Origin, Arkaziel could rampage for days without feeling a fraction of exhaustion.

The infinite room around Arkaziel and the cabin suddenly vanished in a spiral, and Arkaziel appeared upon a moon orbiting a blue star. An immense figure towered in space, looking down at the kitten. A blue dragon peered down at him, its body so large it went past the blue star and across the entire solar system.

"Small for a Sovereign candidate, aren't you?" The dragon's voice shook the universe, or at least the moon that Arkaziel sat on.

At this point, Arkaziel would usually grow to his proper size. But the leviathan before him was so ridiculously immense that growing even to his full size wouldn't impress the dragon. What were four or five hundred meters compared to a being that light itself couldn't completely cross in a second? Like the tides, a wash of color flared slowly across the immense dragon as her scales changed colors with the light. Blue became red.

This could only be one particular legendary dragon.

"All of us are small compared to you, Tiamat. Few exist to match the stature of the first dragon." Arkaziel bowed his head to the color-shifting figure.

"Yes, yes, I'm fantastic. You know it, I know it, everyone knows it. Kiss my ass later if you survive the trials to join the ranks and earn the right to be one of those blessed by fate to rule." Tiamat squinted, and eyes the size of planets blinked at the tiny cat.

"What's this, then? Have you already acquired authority? Death, undeath, underworld, destruction, and pestilence. Few are the candidates that come with a portfolio of their own, although some of these do not fit you. Would you like to trade them, little one?"

"Trade them for what?" Arkaziel asked with a gleam in his eye.

"I'll trade you shadow for undeath and underworld. Unless you wish to make your lair in an underworld?" Tiamat laughed at the idea.

"That's an acceptable trade," Arkaziel agreed and manifested two orbs of dark power. Both were actually made out of Ethereal power, despite the fact that they looked and acted as if they were primarily Nether. The orbs shone with unpleasant colors that hindered the appetite and brought unpleasant tastes to the tongue just by looking at it. Tiamat traded him an orb of the darkest of grays in exchange.

"Death, destruction, pestilence, and shadow. Much more fitting for our little apocalypse dragon, wouldn't you say?" Tiamat seemed proud, but Arkaziel was the one to puff his chest up some. Gaining authority over shadow, for him, was like Aetheria gaining authority over cold. It was one of his central powers.

"The trial of ferocity tests strength and physical might, and awards a candidate their first authority. You have passed by holding possession of death. The trial of wisdom tests your mind with puzzles and conundrums. You pass with possession of destruction. The trial of determination tests your leadership and willingness to sacrifice to achieve your goals. With possession of pestilence, you pass. Only one trial remains. Partake of my blood and survive it coursing through your veins."

Arkaziel hissed at that. The Blood of Tiamat was a corrupting thing, but then, could it do any more damage to him than what the Void did? All beasts had a figure like Tiamat, a leviathan of power and age. Did all dragons get Tiamat, or did he get unlucky and draw her instead of Bahamut?

Tiamat raised both forelegs and ran one of her claws across the impossibly dense, color-shifting scales until a drop of blood the size of a city fell toward the moon the kitten stood on. Arkaziel jumped into the air, growing in size to swallow the blood orb in one go.

If the flesh and blood of Nidhogg had a terrible taste and smell, then the blood of Tiamat could only be described as concentrated toxic waste that had been condensed for all of history. The fumes from the blood alone could melt the skin off a human at two hundred yards. Even the flesh of Arkaziel burned under the corrosive power of Tiamat's crimson gift. The few drops that hit his scales, which had diverted adamantine weapons, caused them to melt like wax before the flame.

It had been a long time since something as vile as Tiamat's blood had hurt him. Not that there were many fluids as potent as the blood of the first dragon, whose color constantly changed. Arkaziel literally dissolved into a pool of liquid, skeleton and all. The liquid formed a giant orb, and then pulsed with power aligned to the four authorities that Arkaziel possessed.

Death manifested as a cold mist that left trails of frost across the surface of the moon, with skulls and scythes forming and unforming in the mist that clung like a lover to the re-forming Arkaziel. The air was rent by claws that were the first thing to emerge from the ooze sphere that Arkaziel had become, and his claws left reality-crumbling flames where they passed. When his front paws hit the moon, it was like an earthquake went off. The ground shattered from the immense pressure, and waves of force and fire cracked a huge segment of the moon as destruction asserted itself. Pestilence manifested as a neon-green haze that rose from the shattered ground of the moon and coiled around the emerging form of the StarMane as if he were Nidhogg, the toxic rot dragon. The sphere exploded with darkness and shadows, and the clinging powers of authority all seemed to merge into a terrible mist bestowed with the power of the Void and all four authorities.

Arkaziel grew, and grew, until Tiamat laughed.

"A grower, not a shower?"

"I've never had any complaints," Arkaziel hissed through a new throat. His form had become more draconic than he usually veered, with evil-looking spikes and tentacle appendages at joints. Arkaziel's size had surpassed that of most cities, and he now measured in kilometers rather than meters. At a quick guess, he placed himself at around thirty-two kilometers long. The black Void mists curled around him in currents a kilometer thick, and black lightning crackled from Arkaziel's golden eyes.

"So what happens now?" Arkaziel asked Tiamat as he looked himself over. Physical changes, even for a shapeshifter, could be disorienting.

"Now you grow bigger. You've reached the smallest of peaks of what a beast can attain, but you have a long way to go to ascend to the heights of Sovereignty. It's been ages since a Void dragon survived evolution. Your kind drew hunting parties once tales of your madness spread. You don't seem to be corrupted, though. How are you hiding it, whelp?"

Arkaziel smiled in a show of fangs, and a flash of light filled his golden eyes.

Tiamat laughed, and the moon Arkaziel stood upon crumbled from the force of her laughter, and then the StarMane fell through the cosmos back into the stupid infinite room. His chance to ask Tiamat any further questions was lost in his show of pride.

CHAPTER 45

Rematch of the Dueling Spices

The trio appeared in the amphitheater of a large, gorgeous park. Bustling all around the area was some kind of fair or festival, and the venue seats were rapidly filling. Aetheria and Kallos found themselves with front-row seats, while Arkaziel appeared in human form on the stage. Two sets of identical magical cooking tools had been prepared, and a big banner that hung across the stage said Defeat Bobbi Slay.

The pixie from their previous encounter with Bobbi Slay couldn't be found anywhere. Instead, the man in charge of festivities seemed to be a human, somewhere in his sixties, with silver hair, and if not for an impressive mustache he would have reminded Aetheria of the host of *Endangerment*, the general-knowledge quiz show back on Earth.

"Well, folks, here at the Cultural Festival of Zestopolis, we're in for a treat. The rematch between the trickster Arkaziel, eater of his own dish, and the Sultana of Spice is about to get underway. I'm your host, Rex Tebek, and this is *Can You Beat Bobbi Slay?*"

The silver-haired charismatic man turned to a dark-skinned woman with piercing yellow feline eyes like Arkaziel's, purple hair done in hundreds of elaborate braids, and her lips shone with metallic purple lipstick. She had a pair of cat ears and a tail that whipped back and forth behind her like a serpent ready to strike. Aetheria was slightly surprised Slay remained a fifth tier Cultivator, the same as last time they had seen her. Slay wore a chef's apron over a provocative gold dress.

"Tell me, Bobbi. Are you looking forward to defeating your self-described rival? Do you have any fears of keeping up with a sixth-tier?" Rex held the microphone for Bobbi to say something.

"Oh, Rex. He may be a sixth-tier Beast Sovereign, but he's still a second-rate chef without a chance of competing with me. You might have climbed a tower, you mangy scrub, but you aren't on my level. He'll never earn the title of Supreme Flavor Master, and certainly not the Star Anise of Destiny anyone who beats me gets."

"Brutal words from the Queen of the Kitchen. What do you have to say for yourself, Arkaziel?" Rex moved the microphone over to Arkaziel, who also had a humanoid form similar to Bobbi's, albeit male.

"I've tasted the blood of Tiamat, Rex, and let me tell you from experience, the only thing worse is Bobbi's over-spiced dishes."

Arkaziel and Bobbi's yellow eyes locked in a staring contest. Literal sparks ignited in the air between them, close to Rex. Rex, being not suicidal, quickly got away from both of them.

"The contest today is a three-part challenge: an appetizer, main course, and dessert. Ready, set, *cook*!" With Rex's excited proclamation, the still-growing crowd cheered while Arkaziel and Bobbi moved into their respective kitchen areas of the stage.

"What'll you be cooking for the appetizer?" Rex asked Arkaziel, who had pulled out large mushrooms and was in the process of preparing them.

"Well, Rex, if I can call you Rex? I'm preparing a little dish I like to call Magic Mushroom Bruschetta. The mushrooms I've chosen bring out a wide variety of subtle flavors, and in addition to providing a euphoric sensation through magic, there's also a bit of taste magic involved, too. You see the Flavorshade Shroom here can mimic anything it's cooked with, while the Zephyr Sporecaps will bring a light and airy quality to the whole meal. On top of a slight tang, the Zephyr Sporecaps reinvigorate the taste buds, preparing you for a fantastic culinary journey. Best of all they'll clean all the spices from the judge's palate."

Arkaziel's smile bordered on vicious, as he taunted Bobbi.

"And what are you making for appetizers, Bobbi?"

"I'm making something that'll take you back to your youth, Rex. Spicy Flame Salamander Soup will pick you up, dust you off, and send you to Flavorland, which isn't very far since we're already in Zestopia."

"That's an old classic, Bobbi. I assume you're adding your twist to it?" Rex's dubiousness that Bobbi would make a simple old classic got cheers from the crowd.

"You know it! I'm adding a dash of Winter Essence to the noodles, to provide an immediate contrast to the heat generated by the salamander chunks. To make up for the loss of heat, I'm also adding a garnish of fireflash parsley."

"That sounds amazing, Bobbi! You're the Queen of the Kitchen for a reason."

Ten minutes later, the StarMane duo gave the sole judge their plates. The judge was a race Aetheria had never seen and looked like an elephant man with pink-purple skin. The undulation of his trunk, the glee in his eyes as he sniffed the dishes, and the happiness visibly gushed from the man with each bite of both dishes.

"For those who aren't familiar with Benedict Crispin, he is from the noble Household de Flavoré, who are one of the most outstanding gastronomical cultivating sects in the realm of Savoria. Not only does Sir Benedict possess a Mystic Palate, but his Aura of Gastronomy maintains the freshness and temperature of any dish that enters his personal space. If all of that weren't enough, the Elderwood Dinnerware Sir Benedict dines with allows him to not just perceive but taste the chef's emotions and intentions during the cooking process. Let's have a hand for our venerable judge." Rex Tebek hurried the pacing of his words once he noticed that the judge wasn't waiting for his narration, but jumped straight into eating.

"So, what are the results of the apps, Sir Benedict?"

The elephant man hmphed. "It's a tie, Rex. While Bobbi's dish embodies the pure essence of spice rendered beautifully in the crisp salamander chunks and the refreshing nature of the Winter Essence, Arkaziel's euphoric journey through psychedelic gastronomy and pure unadulterated desire to win elevated the dish to parity with Bobbi's."

"Boo!" The crowd jeered the judge, but the chefs each smiled darkly at the judge before they returned to the cooking stations and started to prep their main dishes.

"Well, that has to be a poor way to start the contest. It's been ages since you've lost an appetizer challenge. What are you going to make for the main course, Bobbi?" Rex teased the annoyed StarMane.

"I didn't lose, I tied. And he won't get even with me again now that I'm fully in the game, Rex. I'm whipping out Bobbi's Inferno Curry."

"The Inferno Curry!?" the entire crowd stammered together.

"That's right, Rex, the dish so spicy that even the God of Heat, the Divine Alchemist of Spice, Lord Zestaron himself, had to drink from the fabled milk of Audumla to salvage his tastebuds."

"And do you have any of that tonic on hand for Sir Benedict?" Rex inquired not so casually.

"Oh yes, I've fashioned a coconut milk drink to go with the Inferno Curry. As long as Sir Benedict eats and drinks in less than a four to one ratio, he'll be perfectly fine." A dangerous edge undercut Bobbi Slay's tone that left Aetheria wondering if Rex shouldn't be far more concerned for his own safety than the judge's.

"Well, for my own safety, I'll be standing over in the kitchen with Arkaziel. So, how do you feel about the tie, Arkaziel?" Rex beat feet to escape the nearly eye-scorching fumes of spices the female StarMane cooked with.

"It's a joke, Rex. Sir Benedict just wanted to spare Slay's feelings. Just watch, I'll dominate her in this and the next round. Not a living soul has tried my Mystic Mermaid Stew and not fallen in love with it. Now, I know what you're thinking: oh my gosh, he couldn't be cooking with an ingredient as inhumane as a mermaid. You're right, Rex. What I use in my stew is actually a mix of deep-sea delicacies hit with the Essence of Mermaid to go give it a spark of wonder. Every bite of my stew is subtly different from the last, and it builds to a climactic finish that no man and few women can resist."

"I'm noticing a trend of euphoria and wonder in your cooking today. Is this common with your cooking style?"

"No, not at all. I usually cook for my companion, who not only is completely immune to any effects like this but would deliver retribution if I quote, unquote *poisoned her* with drugged food." Arkaziel rolled his yellow eyes with the words, shocked at the lack of consideration Aetheria gave him.

"Remind me to spritz him with a waterfall later," Aetheria hissed through clenched teeth to Kallos.

"For obvious reasons, I'll be eating the Mermaid Stew first," Sir Benedict informed Rex when the dishes were presented to him. The noble gourmand eagerly ate the entire bowl of stew, then started in on the Inferno Curry. Despite the makeup melting off Rex's face from mere proximity, Benedict ate almost half of the Inferno Curry before he had to tap out.

"For the main dishes, the winner is Arkaziel. The esoteric wonder and joy spread from the humble stew is an epiphany that any cultured palate would yearn to experience. Bravo! Bobbi, it's just too hot. You balanced it as best you could, but hotter isn't always better."

"You aren't beating me, twerp." Bobbi flashed the claws at the ends of her fingertips menacingly at Arkaziel, who smirked back at her happily.

"Even if you win desserts, you only eke out a tie, Slay."

"That's where you are wrong. In the case of a tie, the judge and Rex have to choose a winner, sudden death, based on an improvisational challenge. You are out of your league, kid, but if you think you can win, how about we make a little wager?"

"A wager?" Arkaziel's ears perked up above his head, and his tail swished in a show of avid curiosity.

"I win, and you pass the bond to your human to me. You win, and I'll accept a bond with the most miserable person you know."

"Oh, that's a risky proposition. I know so many miserable people who would be perfect to curse with you. It's the gift that keeps on giving misery," Arkaziel taunted again, undeterred.

"It's a deal, then," they both said. The two shook hands to cement and solidify the bet, before they rushed back to their stations to make the final round, dessert.

Rex, seeing the literal sparks of magic around Bobbi, didn't go near her side of the kitchen yet. Instead, he went to Arkaziel's side.

"That might be the biggest bet in the history of *Can You Beat Bobbi Slay*. You must be awfully confident to bet the bond with your partner?" Rex Tebek prodded verbally.

"There's no danger; I've got this in the bag, Rex. There's not a thing in this universe that can derail the bond between a StarMane and their chosen person. Bobbi's about to learn the lesson so many people in history have. If you don't want to get lost in the darkness, don't stand in your own or someone else's shadow."

"And never bet against Aetheria and her good boy, Arkaziel."

Rex decided it would be safer to question Bobbi, after he saw the madness in the StarMane's eyes. Madness, darkness, the depths of the Void that echoed inside the cat. Inside, where the chaotic blood of Tiamat still evolved and grew with the apocalypse dragon.

"You forgot to ask what I'm making!" Arkaziel called after the fleeing Rex, who dutifully came back.

"And what is it you're making?"

"A Starlight Panna Cotta, of course! It is topped with crystalized flakes of the Ethereal, and soft echoes of the Void are laced throughout its starlight-lit gelatin."

After the briefest exposure to the Void-imbued gelatin, Rex foamed at the mouth while he chanted Nyarlathotep's cursed name. Each muttered syllable spit foam into the air. The chanting and foaming at the mouth continued from the ground, where Rex flailed until Aetheria and Kallos intervened to heal the man.

"Oh my, I'd better prepare my antacids," Sir Benedict predicted.

CHAPTER 46

Bring Flavor to Life

Two immaculate plates rested before the elephant-man food critic, Sir Benedict Crispin de Flavoré. The wide-eyed judge beheld the splendor of the dishes before him with more than a little bit of awe, and unusual for a judge, existential dread. If having two StarManes staring him down were not bad enough, the dishes themselves radiated powerful magics, essences, and imbuements by the sixth- and fifth-tier chefs, Arkaziel and Bobbi Slay. Poor Sir Benedict had not felt put on the spot so much since the first time he had presented his own cooking to Lord Zestaron.

The first bowl held simple, elegant sorbet with some fresh herbs. The pieces of crystalized ginger were not the only nonsorbet ingredient, though, as small pieces of crystalized magic sent off sparks of intangible fireworks into the air and against the plate. While perfectly harmless, Bobbi Slay was known for her mastery (and some might say overuse) of spice, and her flavor profiles, like her magic, were fiery and explosive.

"The Sizzling Ginger Sorbet is a classic dish, but it's a proven winner. Enjoy." Bobbi smiled daggers at Arkaziel and slid her glass bowl forward to Sir Benedict.

Even from the front row, the strong scent of ginger and sweets reached Aetheria, and if she didn't have absolute control of her body, her stomach would have rumbled.

"Really, who makes you watch a cooking contest and doesn't feed you?" Aetheria complained to Kallos, who nodded in agreement.

The elephant man ate the entire bowl of sorbet, and looked sad when the bowl contained no more.

"Now, I present you with my Starlight Panna Cotta. I've imbued the gelatin with the wonders and essence of the cosmos itself; note the delicate interplay between light and darkness across the work. While imbued with the shallowest echoes of the Void, the crystalized fragments of the Ethereal will buoy the soul and dispel the psychosis and corrupting effect of the Void. Poor Rex just needed some of the crunchy nuggets of crystalized power, but alas, the host isn't allowed to snack." Arkaziel presented his ultimate triumph.

Unlike a normal panna cotta, the creamy gelatin dessert was mostly transparent and showed stars, planets, black holes, and other cosmic visions within its jiggly, enthralling mass. If one stared too long at it, tendrils of the Void reached out to try to pluck their sanity.

"Should this be my final meal, I leave all my worldly possessions to my daughter," Sir Benedict murmured with some suspicion, but he wielded his spoon bravely and vanquished the entirety of the panna cotta.

"I say, I've never tasted the crystallized Ethereal power before. It's enlivening, elevating, and brings your mind to the edge of an epiphany. The story of creation has never been rendered so finely in flavor. I dub you the Supreme Flavor Master! Present this chef with the Star Anise of Destiny!"

Sir Benedict Crispin de Flavoré exploded, and Bobbi Slay hissed.

"What a bunch of bullshit! All of your dishes were rife with drugs, psychedelic magic effects, soul-altering magics, and don't think I didn't notice the subliminal influence you were using in the light!" Slay rounded on Arkaziel, the still falling chunks of Sir de Flavoré already forgotten.

"I certainly don't know what you mean, but if I did, it's all within the rules of your competition, so why are you acting like I cheated? Besides, you sealed your fate as a loser the moment you brought my bond to Aetheria into this." Arkaziel tilted his head to the side, the earnestness of his confusion on display for anyone to see, but his last words came with a hard edge.

"Explain," Bobbi demanded.

"As an unbound you have no idea of the importance of a bonded companion. We share emotions, thoughts, advancement, and a friendship that has triumphed over the Void itself. Combine that with a judge who can taste the emotions a chef imparts into their dishes, and even my cooking will triumph over your superior culinary skills every single time. You never had a chance in this contest, Slay, simply because of the judge and your life devoid of anyone of meaning."

"My agent and I are great friends, I'll have you know. We get coffee once a year; it's very fulfilling. Oh. Oh." Bobbi Slay seemed to have heard what she just said, and the epiphany of shallowness hit her full in the face. That and a large chunk of Sir Benedict's large ears finally arced back down from a great height, and it did hit her, literally, in the face.

Bobbi took a few bites out of the ear, nodded approvingly, and stored the chunk into a storage ring.

"Fine. A bet's a bet. Who are you going to leash me to? It'd better not be a gnome. I hate gnomes."

Arkaziel smiled widely, and gestured for Aetheria and Kallos to come over.

"Oh, I told you this was a bad bet to make. May I introduce you to Aetheria, my bonded companion. She's the stepchild of Aetherius and Nyx, holds the Unutterable Black Flame of the Void, the Red Flame of the Origin, and hers is the path of the Pleroma. She's amazing, and wonderful, and the best friend a dragon could ever have. She doesn't even get mad at me when I eat people, as long as they're our enemies."

Aetheria couldn't help but blush, hearing Arkaziel praise her so.

"And next to her, with the edgiest look this side of being a vampire, is Kallos Metanoia. Her, uh, what's the phrase? Wife? Girlfriend? Spouse? Life partner? Whatever, they are a couple, but you've probably heard of her by a different name. She used to be called Aoibhe, the Soul Witch, daughter of Belial."

Bobbi Slay studied the tall, blonde Kallos. The words Arkaziel talked about slowly registered in her mind, and a look of dread crossed her features.

"You're going to give me to the Soul Witch? The one who thinks gnosis is fun? Will she even eat my cooking? I thought she was all about ascension, whether you wanted it or not?"

Arkaziel laughed, Aetheria looked confused and baffled by this turn of reputation for Kallos, and Kallos narrowed her eyes at the two StarManes.

"Oh please, those stories are all based on challenges in the tower. You can't blame someone for following the dictates of a trial in a tower. They are pass or fail, you know. I've never forced gnosis upon anyone, for what it's worth, nor would I try. It defeats the purpose to send someone unprepared and unwilling to the higher realms. I also love food, and I still enjoy the physical world. For all that this existence is a torturous cage to be escaped, there are some good things to be found within it." Kallos was attempting to clear the air, but both StarManes looked skeptical, and Aetheria didn't seem to know what to say, and remained quiet. She did grasp Kallos's hand and provide support, though.

"Am I the only one who's not okay with Bobbi blowing up the judge?" Aetheria asked her companions. "We don't just blow up people who minorly annoy us."

"Blame Moros. That's the deal when I do shows in his tower. The judge is always fated for impending Doom. Which is me. I'm the impending Doom. BOOM. Or *fwooosh*." Bobbi made, or attempted to make, the sound of burning, but Aetheria thought it sounded like wind.

"That's the deal, or that's the expectation? It seems to me you could've just left him alive?" Aetheria pushed at Bobbi's reasoning.

"Well, I suppose you could say it is the expectation or the implication. But you know how Moros is. If I don't do it, he'll just meet a bitter end some other way, at the hands of someone who won't enjoy it nearly as much or will perform the execution with far less style." Bobbi shrugged, not that concerned.

"If you're going to join us, I want you to understand that life isn't just a cheap thing to be casually disregarded. Even the natives of the towers are real, genuine souls between reincarnations." Aetheria stared at the cat woman with all three of her eyes.

Arkaziel and Bobbi giggled, and even Kallos had to stifle a snicker.

"Why are you laughing?"

"Look, Blue, it looks like you are shooting a laser pointer out of the Third-Eye of Ein Sof when you get mad," Arkaziel explained between laughs that he had a hard time stifling.

"Point remains!" Aetheria reiterated.

"That doesn't make much sense, though. If this existence is just a cage we're stuck in as your girlfriend believes, doesn't me blowing people up help them get the motivation to escape it faster?" Bobbi arched a delicate brow, thinking she'd won. "Besides, these natives are genuine souls, which is big news to me. Where'd you learn it from?"

"It's long been theorized, and I had come to the same conclusion myself during my stay in Solace," Kallos murmured, using her reputation as the Soul Witch to back up Aetheria.

"Let's see. I learned it from Nyx, but others have confirmed it, including Kallos." Aetheria shrugged. "Are you familiar with the Sefirot? I can project into all of the emanations at my leisure, but the emanation of Binah functions as my library these days."

"Alright, I won't just randomly obliterate people, then. So that's your choice, twerp? You're sticking me with the Soul Witch?" Bobbi didn't seem to consider breaking her bet to be an option. Aetheria decided that to try to understand StarManes seemed pointless, and their species rules seemed to be mostly made up and then propagated to descendants via genetic memory.

"Oh, you know it." Arkaziel smirked, vicious glee apparent in all of his mannerisms.

"Well, what do you say, Soul Witch? You want to partner up? I'm Bobbi Slay, or Zephariel'Realmara'Etheriassa'Flemme—" Bobbi stopped when Aetheria and Kallos held up a hand.

"We love your StarMane names, but we are on the clock and have a tower to climb. You and Arkaziel can talk about your real names all you want." Aetheria tried to broker the peace of an angry dragon being interrupted while introducing themselves. Bobbi was, however, shockingly chill about it.

"No, I get you. Why do you think I go by Bobbi Slay? Not all StarMane traditions are good ones. Some were just leftovers of powerful assholes who left a shitty legacy behind, and no one has bothered to remove them because we all remember being that asshole, and part of us thinks, well, you know, maybe that isn't the worst idea ever."

"Yo, Moros. Bobbi's on team Aetheria now. We good?" Aetheria called out to the air.

"Of course, Aetheria-nee." Moros's disembodied voice filled the room. Bobbi's face looked shocked that the god answered just like that.

"Nope, no, no. I don't need to know you're a weeb, and I'm pretending I never heard that."

"Oh, the Star Anise of Destiny." Bobbi chucked a seed pod at Arkaziel that glimmered with fortuitous energies, and the scent of licorice filled the air so strongly all four were eager to move toward the silver door, but Arkaziel coughed.

"Bobbi's got to make the bond with Kallos, then we can go. No cheating." Arkaziel waggled his finger obnoxiously in an attempt to gloat over Slay.

"Don't I get a say in this?" Kallos asked.

"If you don't want me, I'll stick to my show . . ." Bobbi grinned.

"Do you turn into a cute kitten like Arkaziel does?" Kallos asked the most important question.

"Oh yeah. I love napping in that form. It's the best."

"Very well, you may be my companion. Do try to have better manners than Arkaziel. The bar is so low you shouldn't have a problem."

CHAPTER 47

Uranus Brings the Gas

The now-four-member party appeared in a meadow of tall grass. Strong winds brushed the grass in irregular gusts, which created a gorgeous wave effect throughout the various grasses. Ahead of them a series of white marble platforms floated in the air, climbing ever higher into the sky and the clouds. Yet, as Aetheria took in the beauty of the meadow, her smile vanished at the sensations on the wind. Bitterness, mysteriousness, and cold aloofness resonated inside of Aetheria's soul in a way that left her no doubt who lay waiting for them at the end of the platforms.

"Can you feel it? There's a fragment of Ouranos here, the real deal." Aetheria narrowed her eyes at the platforms. Inanna could have conceivably been a coincidence, but either Moros had conspired with Khaos and Nyx, or Moros had collected the fragments of the dead and nearly dying gods in her soul on his own, or perhaps he collected all the nearly dead gods? Either way, her suspicions about Moros's involvement in her future were at an all-time high now.

"I can feel it through you." Kallos nodded.

"Those winds aren't for flying," Arkaziel pointed out. To demonstrate, he jumped into the air with wings, and fell back down to the ground. He even shapeshifted into a lighter form and attempted to glide on the wind, and that, too, failed.

"We have to jump up all these platforms? That's so lame." Bobbi scowled and cracked her neck before she then cracked her knuckles. "Leave it to me, I'll create a volcano and we'll just walk up some magma ste—" Before Bobbi could finish her sentence, Aetheria just tapped a boot gently to the ground, and stairs of ice formed, connecting all the platforms.

"The meadow is pretty; let's not ruin it with a volcano? Next time." Aetheria tried to assuage Bobbi's explosive personality, but it seemed like the chef barely heard it, her eyes still widened in shock. Aetheria was the first to step onto the stairs, and was halfway to the first platform before Bobbi snapped out of it and walked up the stairs with Kallos.

"The ice isn't cold or slippery, at all. I didn't know a human could master an element to this degree in the fifth tier." Bobbi seemed to be fishing for information.

"Aetheria's been able to alter all of her elements since she awoke as a Cultivator, and it is perhaps best to think of her as human adjacent. Since fire is your element, let's try a little experiment. Ria, would you please toss Bobbi a sphere of your frost flame, darling?"

A snowball-sized orb of mixed aqua and red flames formed immediately in Aetheria's hand, and she tossed it lazily back to the lagging pair.

"Consume it, if you can," Kallos instructed Bobbi, but the StarMane studied the orb first, before finally just taking bites out of it as if it were an apple.

"Holy cow, that's tasty. There's a lot of sweet Ethereal power, a tinge of something darker, and a sense of inevitability," Bobbi gushed between bites.

"Do all StarManes gain the ability to consume Ethereal power, or are you like Arkaziel?" Kallos inquired.

"My wish for completing the Tower of Hestia was to become an Ethereal Cultivator. Prior to that I could only consume mana and Aether. That little twerp was an Ethereal Cultivator by birth? What a lucky little shit." Bobbi grumbled, but fell quiet since she and Kallos caught up to Aetheria and Arkaziel. Unlike Bobbi's humanoid form, Arkaziel lazed on Aetheria's shoulder in the form of a kitten.

"From what I can pick up, there's only one trial, immediately before the temple," Aetheria informed the others. "Every platform will show us glimpses of Ouranos's existence, to prepare a vessel for his resurrection. Make sure to remember who you are, and don't let him implant himself in your head. Nearly insensate and essentially dead doesn't make him guileless or weak; this is still the Primordial sky we're talking about, one of the few children of Nyx and Phanes."

"It sure comes back to Nyx a lot," Arkaziel complained.

"Give me one moment, and I will strengthen everyone's soul against intrusion." Kallos held up a hand, and spectral chains flowed from her wrists like serpents, binding each of the other three in chains that then sank into them.

"New trick? That's a lot more flashy than casting a spell. What can't your chains do?" Aetheria asked with a grin.

"It's faster, as well," Kallos noted cheerfully.

When the four stepped onto the white marble platform, they were able to note the beautiful, ornate inlays worked into the top of the platform. The wind came with strong gusts, but it didn't try to push them off the platform. Instead, it carried memories to them.

A city half floated, half rested on an impressive peak. In one of the grand halls of the city, five people stood around a table. Aetheria could identify each by their aura and having seen these forms at least once before, except Ouranos, who she knew from his own memories. Nyx sat at the head of the table, and next to her sat Aetherius on one side, Khaos on the other. Gaia also lounged in a chair, unconcerned.

"And we have no idea who actually killed Phanes?" Nyx queried the other four. A new scepter lay on the table before her, similar in appearance to the torch that Aetheria had kept in her repository for so long now.

"Something out of the darkness." Khaos shrugged in a gesture of indifference.

"Did Erebos act, then? He claims to have played no part in the death of the Overgod, and yet, who else would have gained from the death of Phanes?" Gaia sounded bored, even more indifferent than Khaos.

"You have far more to gain than Erebos, Mother." Ouranos spoke boldly to Nyx, such that the others all grimaced at his disrespect.

"If I had killed Phanes, I would not have been so careless as to lose the Scepter of Rule," Nyx hissed at her son.

"The new one is nearly as powerful as the original. What does it matter?" Khaos seemed unperturbed by the familial spat.

"As best we know. Phanes showed little of the genuine article's capabilities, even to me." Nyx did not have the same faith in the recreation that Khaos did, given the scornful look Lady Night gave to the torch-looking scepter.

"Phanes was an immigrant from another universe like myself and Chronos. He did not bring the scepter with him—it was given to him by Bythos. Why not simply ask the Aeon for another one?" Khaos asked with exasperation.

"I have already sought audience with Bythos and Sige; they denied me and banished me from the Pleroma." Nyx's anger blazed at being denied by anyone, despite being Queen of all Creation on top of being Lady Night.

"Erebos remains the primary suspect, then?" Aetherius looked unconvinced, but also uninterested in discussions of the scepter.

"He claimed there is a darkness outside of reality, beyond the safety of the Dreamland, where dwell impossible leviathans of powers that are antithetical to our own. Despite the newness of our realms, he claims them to be ancient, and forever. As if such things could possibly exist." Gaia's laugh mocked the ridiculousness of Erebos's claims, and the others joined in.

"Could Ayin have returned?" Ouranos asked quietly.

"She vanished when nothing became light. Perhaps she moved on to a new existence with the formation of the Monad, the way Chronos, Phanes, Khaos, and Ananke did into ours? Why would she return? We don't even know if she's real, or just a scare tactic employed by the Aeons." Aetherius dismissed the possibilities.

The vision faded.

Aetheria touched Kallos's hand and squeezed it hard, and opened her thoughts to the other woman.

~Khaos lied in that meeting. She isn't from another universe like Phanes or Chronos at all. Why would she lie about that, and how did the others not sense the lie if I could?~ The telepathic conversation included only Aetheria and Kallos, not the two StarManes.

-You're certain? Of course, you are. You see through the Void and the Ethereal, and Khaos had no cause to be on the defense against any sort of Void sensitivities at that point in time, it would seem? Or perhaps that is the truth as Ouranos thought it? That makes no sense, though.-

~No, it doesn't make sense. Also, I have the scepter that they were talking about. When we have real privacy I might need to test it out, now that I hold authority over love, and that was the clue Phanes left to use it.~

"Hey, what's Dreamland?" Bobbi Slay asked confusedly, but Arkaziel and Kallos shrugged the question off.

". . . the realm where the gods lived, before they constructed the towers," Aetheria answered with a small delay. "Let's see what else we've got to learn here, and we'll sort it out before the temple."

The next platform drew them into another memory.

Nyx sat upon a throne, the duplicate scepter in one hand, a glass of ambrosia in the other. Ouranos stood behind her throne, a stalwart, silent guardian.

"You claim to have reached a solution to avoid any more deaths of the gods? Speak then, fallen Aeon." Nyx spoke imperiously toward the figure before her, yet the black-haired, white-skinned human male with black wings treated her no better than a peer.

"The weak and the feeble among you fear for their lives, as the mortals you shepherd do. The answer is not to bind Death, as so many demand. Such imbalance would require the Monad to intervene, and then there would be death and destruction beyond all reason, for my brothers and sisters are not tawdry shapers of the material as your kin. With the construction of towers, the balance of Life and Death and the Infinite Cycle would remain. Your precious babes would be protected once they erected their own tower, and surely those who fail were destined to die anyway?" Belial's sales pitch had so many holes in it that Aetheria wanted to drive a bus through it, just to see if she could.

"Why would we trust a corrupted messenger of Bythos?" Nyx didn't hammer at Belial; they just stuck to the point. She did seem strangely docile for Nyx.

"I have the plans here. Look them over yourself. They will work, and no one will lose."

"You are the Dark Angel, the liberator of souls from the cage of the material world. Why would you endeavor to help keep those you have vowed to free bound for all eternity?"

"Freedom is not a thing so easily won, Nyx. I am the Dark Angel, but the journey to the Pleroma can only be reached by those who undergo gnosis. If they cannot even reach gnosis despite the setback of the tower, they are unfit to revel in the divine splendor of Ein Sof."

"I will inspect these plans," Nyx answered noncommittally.

"Even I could tell that wasn't my father," Kallos cried as the vision faded.

"How did Nyx, and the people around her, fail to notice that wasn't Belial? The corruption on him was so thick it made my skin crawl. That was the Messenger of the Sleeping Idiot, He of the Nine-Hundred-and-Ninety-Nine Avatars, plain as day. The illusions around him were weak." Aetheria scratched at her chin in confusion.

"Uhm, yeah, no. I looked; he looked just like Belial?" Bobbi said.

"There was a touch of the Void, but I couldn't see through it," Arkaziel admitted. "Your detection abilities are just too strong lately, Blue."

"So, Nyx made a deal with an elder god without realizing it, and they set up Belial to take the fall. Why, specifically, Belial? Was he the only Aeon in physical reality at the time?" Aetheria tried to figure it out.

"Belial's purpose is gnosis, and the towers not affecting gnosis was a colossal lie." Kallos's voice held an edge of anger and wrath Aetheria hadn't experienced yet. There was no doubt in Aetheria's mind that Kallos would hold someone accountable.

CHAPTER 48

Why Did Mars Turn Red?
It Saw Uranus.

Did you notice how far we're up already?" Arkaziel asked as Aetheria took the first step off the platform they left onto the ice bridge she had constructed, linking them all together.

A glance backward and down at the ground showed they were already close to the clouds, despite only having experienced memories on two platforms.

"It seems we're being teleported while experiencing the memories. Good catch, Ark." Aetheria praised the black kitten and ruffled the fur on his head.

"Aww, it's not like it takes a lot of skill to look and see things, Ria. You're just focusing on the job, that's all." The little kitten purred and nuzzled at her neck for warmth at the compliments.

"Gag. Are these two always this saccharine?" Bobbi, still in humanoid form and still walking under her power, asked Kallos.

"Sometimes? It is a bit much, but my darling is a sweetheart, and then there's Arkaziel, who loves nothing more than being praised, regardless of the sincerity involved." Kallos's harsh characterization of Arkaziel's character earned her a dark glare from the kitten.

"Quit dawdling, you two, we're at the next platform already!" Aetheria called back to urge the other two on.

Ouranos stood behind and to the left of the throne of Dreamland, as was his lot in life under the rulership of his mother, Nyx. Heir to Phanes or not, she still ruled with scepter and throne. His time would come, sooner or later, though. Gaia, his consort of choice, sat with him.

"There are no other challengers?" The cold voice of darkness itself, Erebus, flowed from the shadow-clad figure to the right of the throne of the gods.

Silence reigned in the hall of the gods, while the corpse of a god rapidly rotted into swarms of flies that flew to Erebus to be devoured. The Mirage Dove, Sirelios,

God of False Hope, had been snuffed out like a candle before the power of the Primordial Erebus.

"With no other opposition, the plan will move forward. Dreamland will be left behind, and we will raise our towers in full, physical reality. No more will the youngest of you know the yoke of death, so long as you succeed in creation of your own tower. Aetherius has bravely volunteered to construct his first, and in doing so, create a training ground for all who would make their own to test themselves against before creating their own tower."

"Go, prepare. Whatever is left in Dreamland will be lost to us. We will not return here. The Overgod has spoken. Now go!" Nyx commanded with authority that had nothing to do with Night.

Slowly, gods trickled from the grand hall, whispering and plotting. Soon, only Aetherius, Gaia, Ouranos, Nyx, Khaos, and Erebus remained.

"I'd better get started unless there's anything else, Nyx?"

"No, go begin." A gate from the Dreamland to material reality manifested for Aetherius, who departed with a nod toward the others.

"Do you think he'll succeed?" Khaos asked boredly. The light in her eyes seemed dull, and tedium and ennui wasted away any lingering interest or concern that might have once been held in them.

"Aetherius is the Primordial of Divinity; if he fails, what chance does any Primordial, let alone god, have? He will succeed, and in doing so, the power of his tower shall propel the weakest to succeed by the power of victory." Nyx's coldness was a match to Khaos's indifference.

"The burden of granting so much power will strain even Aetherius, surely?" Erebus asked.

"Perhaps, perhaps not," Ouranos chimed in. "He is Aether, and the distant light of the higher realms spills ever infinitely down to us. He stands greater than almost any other Primordial; that is why he is the first. Should he be weakened, his power will regenerate with time. For the sky shall support the highest heavens."

"All of us here shall support Aetherius as best we can, right Erebus?" Gaia teased the dark counterpart of Aetherius, manifestation of Darkness and Nether, who had acted annoyed ever since they decided Aetherius would be the one to build the first tower. Any elevation of divinity over dark divinity bothered Erebus, but Nyx held the Scepter of the Overgod. For now.

"Gather the treasures from the reliquary; the dimension ship will be leaving in an hour. Anyone not on board will be sealed in the Dreamlands for eternity," Nyx commanded before Erebus could respond to Gaia.

"What of Chronos?" Khaos asked halfheartedly, her voice so soft the others almost missed it.

"He has already gone into the Material Plane. He intends to refine Ananke's essence until he can create her a new body, regardless of her desires. No one expected her to discorporate so utterly over Phanes's death, let alone to refuse the idea of the towers so vehemently." Gaia shook her head.

"The Moirai have taken over much of her duty, but they are Fate, not Necessity. Even in the factions without an equivalent to her, only the authority of fate has been appearing. It seems even disincorporated; there can be only one Ananke." The shadows around Erebos writhed, disquieted by the loss of one of the few powers that dwarfed his own.

"Go, now. When I move the throne and the Elsyium Font, it will release powers that will annihilate anyone who remains. I will be along to the vessel shortly." Nyx's voice hardened, allowing no argument, as she stared at the throne with no small amount of dread.

"Good luck, Mother." Ouranos departed with Gaia.

"What the hell was all of that? The Tower of Aetherius was meant to be a cheat to power-level noob gods? What a bunch of bullshit!" Aetheria growled as the vision faded, and there was only a single platform left between the temple and platform the party appeared on.

"It just me or were all the Primordials pretty dumb not to pick up on the fact that the one who could see the inevitable basically killing herself represented a really big problem for their future?" Bobbi asked with a voice dripping sarcasm.

"The thought crossed my mind. Did you notice the difference between Khaos between the visions? What happened there, do you think?" Aetheria asked while ordering her thoughts.

"Do you think their vessel is still out there, somewhere? I could use a vessel." Arkaziel focused on the most important matter, as he saw it.

"Focus. Do you know what challenge the final platform will hold, darling?" Kallos inquired.

"It's a sixth-tier wind elemental, but I can't discern whether there's more to it or not." Aetheria shrugged unworriedly. "I'll just hop over and devour it. Maybe it'll boost my air affinity."

Before anyone could object to Aetheria's plan, she jumped to the next platform instead of using the ice stairs. A massive figure formed before the platform, a creature that looked like a miniature tornado, with two even smaller vortexes of wind for arms. As it formed, Aetheria lifted a hand, and tentacles made of condensed void energies assaulted the creature, and in seconds nothing remained of the elemental.

"That sort of felt like killing a boss during its opening cinematic," Aetheria murmured to herself.

"That's exactly what it looked like," Moros's disembodied voice agreed with Aetheria out of nowhere. "I went through all the effort to set up a fight for your darling new companion. Air versus Fire, the greatest of ancient enemies. I even set up a few minion waves for Bobbi to show off her explosive magic, and you just steal the spotlight from her debut fight to acquire a little extra air affinity. How utterly shameless of you, stepsister."

Aetheria couldn't discern a source for the voice, despite turning all of her senses to the task of doing so. It was pointless, though, because the tower was Moros. He didn't need to manifest to interact.

When the other three caught up to her, Aetheria offered an apologetic smile to the group.

"Ope, my bad. I apologize, I got a little carried away with the idea of shoring up my wind affinity before I eat Ouranos, as if that won't fix up my wind affinity all by itself. That would've been a great welcome-to-the-team boss smash for you to show off with, Bobbi." Aetheria apologized, in case Moros's thoughts matched her companion's.

"No biggie. I'm awesome, so if you see it now or later, what's the difference? I do have a real question, though . . . how the hell did I gain strength from you eating them?"

"You did?" Kallos tilted her head curiously, her golden eyes flashing different colors as she invoked different senses. "I'll be. Do you see it, darling?"

"Yep." Aetheria changed her sight to see the Cosmic Strands. Immense ties bound Aetheria and Kallos together, while a slightly smaller strand bound Arkaziel and Aetheria. The bond between Kallos and Bobbi was much smaller, but would grow in time. Small bonds went from Aetheria to Bobbi, as well, slightly thinner than those between her and Kallos. A few thin bindings even went between Arkaziel and Bobbi.

"That could become a mess if we're not careful. The bonds between me and Kallos and me and Arkaziel have bled into everything else, it seems. You're also connected to me, Bobbi. The deeper your connection to Kallos, the more you'll probably connect to me, too. When I devour things, the strength is shared with everyone who's got soul-connections with me. Welcome to the team."

"Try to use Aetheria's powers," Arkaziel demanded of the other StarMane.

"What do you . . . oh, I see. I can't touch the speed; it's like moving through water to get to that, but damn, girl, how much Ethereal power do you have? And what's with all the Void?" Bobbi's body shone with Ethereal power she drew from Aetheria's limitless supply.

"I'm directly connected to the Void and the Origin, so I'm pretty much an infinite power supply. Feel free to draw through me if you need to, but I wouldn't recommend touching the Void unless you want to go through the whole Void-Cat transition Arkaziel did."

"For such a grand entry, this is a very simple temple." Kallos seemed disappointed that the temple wasn't immense. Instead, it was a large square with white marble columns and a triangular roof, with the center open to the sky. Light shone through the open roof to bathe a statue of Ouranos, which held a fragment of the Primordial soul of the sky.

"Are we doing the same thing we did to Inanna?" Kallos seemed eager.

"I bet this one will draw all sorts of fun while you summon his essence." Arkaziel licked his chops, and nose.

"Summon? Inanna? What are you talking about?" Bobbi demanded clarification.

"The last temple we ran into held a piece of Inanna's essence. We used it to summon all of her essence that remained, and I ate what I wanted and sent the rest on in the Great Cycle. Ouranos is also one of the essences I hold, so if we summon and eat him, I can purge him from my soul, take his authority, and send him into the cycle, all at once."

". . . and all three of us gain some, too? Alright, I'm not regretting losing to the twerp so much anymore." Bobbi rubbed her hands together eagerly, a dark hungry gleam shining in her eyes.

"That's right, Slay. Air's on the menu." Arkaziel cackled, until Aetheria dropped a ball of water onto him.

"I hate when you make us sound like the bad guys," Aetheria chided Arkaziel.

CHAPTER 49

Starry Ouranos

You take that side, I'll take this side." Arkaziel gestured, and a demarcated line burned across the floor of the temple.

"Seems reasonable. What if we get overwhelmed?" Bobbi inquired, and Arkaziel actually laughed at that question. "What? I know you're a twerp with more power than sense, but you don't even make fallback plans? Are you an idiot?"

"He is," Kallos answered from before the statue. "This should do the trick."

Kallos waved a gauntleted hand, and orbs of glimmering starlight formed in the air. Three, then three, then a final three more, for a total of nine orbs of celestial-touched Ethereal power.

"I want to play!" Aetheria glanced around, and from the ceiling, icy stalactites hung down, and formed into ice-spear throwing turrets.

"Hey, that's enough now. Quit trying to steal all of our kills, you two," Arkaziel whined.

"Who cares who kills them, if we all share power anyway?" Bobbi asked a shockingly common sense question that left Kallos and Aetheria both wondering if their understanding of StarMane arrogance had been a bit too particular to Arkaziel's brand of megalomania.

Maybe they aren't all murder cats after all? Aetheria mused to herself while she constructed a zodiac wheel on the ground out of ice.

"The more important question is how we split the loot." Aetheria could almost see the dollar signs forming in Bobbi's eyes.

"Whoever needs it, I suppose? Loot has never really been a thing for us, although I call dibs on all sky cities. Collecting those is sort of my thing," Aetheria answered, a little confused.

"What kind of loot? Do you mean food? We just store it, then eat it when we want to."

"These two *special* cases don't use equipment, Bobbi. If anything catches your eye, you most likely can keep it. Arkaziel just eats things. I use soul-manifested equipment. What little equipment Aetheria uses is soul-forged by herself or, like her gloves, Vulcan." Kallos pat the StarMane on the shoulder with the words.

"Wait, so you guys don't even have a flaming sword, gauntlets of godly strength, indomitable shields; you just bulldoze everything with brute strength?" Bobbi laughed, and her incredulous voice turned to glee. "I've never not had to hold back before when working with others."

Aetheria recognized the reckless glee that shone from Bobbi's eyes, and grinned at the newest member of the party. "Welcome to the team, Bobbi. The only reason to hold back with our group is so we don't cause collateral damage or friendly fire."

"My preparations are ready." Kallos smoothly drew attention back to the matter at hand.

"Here we go!" Arkaziel giddily clicked his claws together.

"Ouranos, Sky so ancient and vast,
Dismembered and scattered by Cronus,
In your temple, we call you now,
Pass through the Gate, to be one at last."

Aetheria's voice was smooth while she chanted the incantation, but torrential tides of power flowed from her into the zodiac wheel she had constructed of sacred ice. Without the built-in power of a font like at the temple of Inanna, Aetheria had to provide the power this time. With the addition of the Flame of the Origin, the seal burned with red energy, and the inner part of the wheel turned pitch-black as the celestial doorway opened.

"The celestial door is open, the hour of judgment at hand; appear before us, oh shat-
tered soul of Ouranos, and know finality."

"These two really aren't encouraging him to come, are they? It's just, 'come die.' I so wouldn't come if I was him." Bobbi couldn't contain her commentary.

"Ria's probably using the soul of Ananke to make it a compulsion, so choice doesn't matter. If I were a god known for sexual assault, these are the last two people I'd want summoning me." Arkaziel shook his head, and gestured to the edges of the temple, where eddies of power formed, and streams of air elementals formed to assault the temple. Three twilight replicas of Arkaziel appeared and aggressively leaped out to exterminate the first wave.

Wisps of energy emerged from the celestial gate to coalesce into an orb in two of Aetheria's hands. The essence of Ouranos varied from deepest sky-blue to almost black, and the potency dwarfed that of the so-called Queen of Heaven, Inanna.

"Not much personality left here, lots of power. Ohhh. He had more than one authority, which I guess makes sense. Wonder if he had more before Cronus dismembered him?" Aetheria babbled as she wove her fingers in and out of the thickening essence of Ouranos, deftly using the red and black flames to purge Ouranos from existence and steal his power.

"Oh? The sky and what?" Kallos held a thin rod of platinum soulsteel that shone with purple light. It served as the focus of the spell that drew Ouranos's essence from across the universe to them.

"Uhh. Seems like astronomy? Whew, I was afraid for a minute when you said to use a zodiac wheel that it'd be something like astrology, then I'd be all nope, no way, I don't believe in that crap. Nice." Aetheria's voice was punctuated by explosions, lasers, and what sounded like a good time on the outer edges of the temple, but she had to keep her primary focus on Ouranos. *I wouldn't put it past a crafty Primordial to play dead and seize on distraction.*

A cold north wind swept through the temple, and a Titan stood where none had moments before. This particular Titan stood twice as tall as Aetheria, and had white hair shot with blonde streaks; simple, if well-tailored, robes of blue; and a sash around his shoulder that glittered with the stars and constellations. His eyes focused upon the wisps of the essence that passed through the gate to join Aetheria's orb. For all that the orb grew slightly with each mote of Ouranos, it shrank slightly with each working of Aetheria's fingers through it.

"What business do you have here, Titan?" Kallos challenged his presence.

"I am Koios, and I am only here to observe the final passage of Ouranos. You do a far more thorough job than my brothers and I were able to do to him." The Titan didn't appear to have any goodwill toward Ouranos, so Kallos did not object to his witnessing the demise of an ancient enemy.

"And we've got him; cease the call," Aetheria murmured to Kallos, and bent her will entirely upon the orb. Long seconds passed slowly, the sounds of battle faded, and Aetheria laughed as the last of the essence of Ouranos returned to the Great Cycle to be respun into a new tale, or perhaps to reach a lower, or higher, realm.

"What about you, Titan? Sure you don't want to throw down? I don't have authority over any kind of intellect or wisdom yet."

"I'll be returning to Tartarus, unless you object? I have no desire to fight a losing battle. You obscure it well, but after ages in the pit, you learn to sniff the Void. Your particular scent is somehow better, and worse, than the foul stink of the elder gods. Whatever you are, I have no desire to find out." Koios turned into a breeze and vanished back the way he had appeared, as wind.

"What the hell? You can't say I smell bad then run away!" Aetheria shook her fist at the sky, and Koios bounced off an invisible barrier, back into a solid form. The dumbfounded Titan stared at the invisible wall.

"You took possession of sky quickly." The Titan rubbed his nose and stood. "I apologize for insinuating you smell of the Void and comparing you to the elder gods."

"That's better. Go back to your pit. If any of your siblings want to throw down, I'm always game."

Koios laughed. "How absolutely befitting of someone with authority over war."

The Titan vanished for real, at the new mistress of the sky's mercy.

Once the Titan was well and truly gone, Kallos looked at Aetheria, and when no answer immediately came, she asked a pressing question.

"What's your wind affinity like now?"

"Like this." Aetheria gestured, and a flurry of snowflakes danced around her in complicated movements, and with another slight gesture, dozens of wind blades demolished the statue of Ouranos at the center of the temple. "I can finally control wind awesomely, just in time to not care because I'm on the edge of grasping Ein Sof." Aetheria couldn't stop from laughing, even as the doorway to the next floor appeared.

"Onward and upward?" Arkaziel asked as he and Bobbi joined Aetheria and Kallos.

"That was a nice starting exercise, but those elementals were weaker than I'm used to." Bobbi grinned, but it did nothing to hide the minor flush to her cheeks of a combat lover who wasn't quite satisfied.

"That's because you're drawing from Ria, and of course fights are easy when you have unlimited power to dump onto them. You'll get used to it. Boss fights are the best," Arkaziel commented with a bit of condescension.

"No shit, Sherlock!" Bobbi rolled her eyes at Arkaziel. "Obviously fights are easier with infinite energy, but it's more than that. My attacks were elevated, my explosions hit harder, and just having more energy to draw from wouldn't change that."

"That would be Arkaziel and Aetheria affecting you through the bond. Arkaziel has authority over destruction, amongst other things, while Aetheria has authority over war."

"So just because of the convoluted mess that is soul-bindings in this party, I've grown in destructive power? Nice. Your lack of reliance on equipment makes more sense now. Anything else I need to know about?" Bobbi asked with a sarcastic edge.

Aetheria considered, then grinned.

"Well, I also have authority over beauty, sex, love, sky, astronomy, and Arkaziel also has death, pestilence, and shadow. So, be careful with flirting, murder, getting or giving sicknesses, and I don't even know what kind of implications shadow has." Aetheria shrugged.

"If I were someone less amazing than I am, you'd all be enough to give me a complex. As it is, it's still pretty close."

"How's it feel to have one less god in the mix of your soul, Ria?" Arkaziel asked, with an unexpectedly caring question.

"Nicer. Like getting rid of Inanna and Ouranos pushed me further away from the Tree of Death, maybe? If it's even real, and not just a fairy tale to mess with my mind. Fred is kind of a dick."

When void chained quartet of divinity fades to naught,
In the Void's heart a silent war will be fought,
In their demise, the Stars shall weep in sorrow,
The tapestry of reality shall fray,

In its stead, a new hierarchy ordained . . .
Or perhaps, the realm will be undone.

Oh screw you, Fred!

Aetheria relayed the prophecy, or poetry, to her friends.

"Nice, let's eat them all superfast. Sounds like a good time. Especially if some of their friends are dumber than that Titan, like Ereshkigal and Nergal were. Kallos and Bobbi could use some appropriate authorities themselves, after all." Arkaziel made a show of thinking of others, even as all three ladies stared at him with narrowed eyes.

"Maybe if you're going to pretend to be in the sharing mood, don't drool while you say it. It really ruins the idea that you'll actually share. Or are you the first Beast Sovereign to be so young he's going through puberty, and you can't handle being near an adult female?" Bobbi piled scorn on Arkaziel, who stared back at her indignantly.

"That's enough, you two. If we're all done, let's go. I'm sure our host is bored of watching you bicker," Kallos chided them with the dim hope that being spied on by Moros would keep the StarMane duo in line at least slightly.

"I just realized, there's always a dramatic wind blowing my scarf and hair now, unless I focus on stopping it. *Awesome*." Aetheria cackled like a madwoman.

CHAPTER 50

Slay Slaughters Swiftly

Oh joy, another arena." Aetheria dropped her sarcasm before the other three had even fully come out of the teleport, thanks to the edge she possessed in speed.

Unlike the usual arena challenges, the gang appeared in a front-row viewing booth. A dramatic apparition of Moros with a long, tattered bloodred cape blowing on no real wind stood before them. Aetheria couldn't help but feel he was copying the way air constantly played around her scarf, coat, and hair for dramatic effect now.

"Welcome to the Arena of Hubris, where no doubt one of you will make a terrible mistake and be felled by your pride, or so this challenge usually goes. There are one thousand enemies for this challenge, most of which are average dross. Two hundred of them are powerful, twenty are floor-boss level, four are what you would fight at the quarter mark in other towers, and one is on par with the boss of lesser towers. I have drawn your lots. You will pick how many monsters you will fight, but the distribution of enemies is random. Questions?"

All four either shrugged or shook their heads.

"Bobbi, Arkaziel, Kallos, Aetheria. Choose your numbers. Oh, I forgot to mention, if your group does defeat more than five hundred of the monsters, you all get a prize. For every hundred more, the quality of the prize increases."

Only Kallos appeared unswayed by the power of loot.

"Four hundred!" Bobbi declared with dollar signs in her eyes and violence in her heart.

"Five hundred!" Arkaziel refused to be one-upped.

"Fifty," Kallos said while giving Aetheria's hand a squeeze.

"Can I have more than are left?" Aetheria wondered, but a headshake from Moros answered that in the negative. "Fifty, then."

The StarMane duo didn't even have the decency to look apologetic when Aetheria sullenly said fifty, and then slouched into a loveseat with Kallos to nurse her disappointment.

With a gesture from Moros, Bobbi appeared in the center of the earthen-floored arena.

"A new wave will be released every twenty seconds, regardless of whether you have defeated the prior wave. Begin!" Moros's final words echoed like thunder, and suddenly, the arena was filled with the projections of spectators as the first set of gates opened.

Who the heck are the people who pay to watch this and the "shows" like Bobbi's cooking spot? I should ask her later.

"It is a mixture of gods, ancient Cultivators looking to vicariously relive their glory days through up-and-coming Cultivators, sect recruiters, the extremely wealthy, information brokers looking to sell weakness data to others, and the unoriginal who hope to copy the moves of the elite."

Do you watch it?

"I watch everything."

Creepy. You don't watch me and Kallos in the bedroom, do you?

Reverie didn't answer that, but Fred's laughter echoed in her mind ominously.

In the arena, Bobbi had grown a pair of batlike succubus wings, and taken to the air. With a wave of a clawed hand, a giant ball of fire appeared underneath her at the center of the ring, and concentric rings of fire flowed outward from it in repetitive waves.

The first batch of twenty were-badger enemies had no choice but to rush toward the center of the ring. Two particularly large badger-men tanked the waves of fire to protect those behind them. When they almost reached the center, the first two collapsed into burning heaps, and the subsequent were-badgers futilely tried to jump up toward the levitating Slay. A cruel smile played on Bobbi's lips as she watched the grounded badgers burn to death. The first gate shut, and the second gate opened. Ten salamanders rushed out but stopped to bask in the heat of the fire. They chittered and danced happily, momentarily forgetting their purpose.

Only two were-badgers remained, so Bobbi dropped to the floor of the arena to dispatch them with her claws. The flurry of motion drew the ire of the salamanders, and they all rushed toward Bobbi, but she lifted a hand. A surge of Ethereal power formed a glyph on the lead salamander, who exploded two seconds later. The explosion caused bits of lizard to fly everywhere, but also passed the glyph to its comrades, who also detonated two seconds later.

"Why does Bobbi fight as a person, and you fight mostly as a beast, Ark?" Aetheria wondered.

"I'm going to go with it's because she's sick in the head. Most StarManes have their favorite forms, for whatever reason. Pure dragon is really popular; our glorious true forms are dangerous, after all. And then there are so many types of humanoids. Seriously, why are there so many types of humanoids? Opposable thumbs are convenient, especially if you don't have telekinesis or shadow hands. Since Bobbi specializes in fire and explosions, I'm going to go with she likes opposable thumbs." Arkaziel's speculation struck Aetheria as a mixture of superficial and accurately in-depth such that she felt like he'd purposely phrased things that way.

The third gate opened, and a single enemy emerged. A human woman in a kimono, a wakizashi and katana on her hip, long flowing white hair, and a porcelain mask covering her face casually strode into the arena. The first wave of fire to approach her split in half, and the sound of a sword being sheathed dimly followed. The ball in the center of the arena also split in half and sputtered out, and the warmth from the arena diminished.

"Oh, a challenge!" Bobbi formed an explosive glyph over the swordswoman, but it simply split in half, and Bobbi had to deflect the invisible-to-the-naked-eye ranged qi attack from the swordswoman with her claws.

"What type of extra senses does Bobbi have?" Aetheria wondered.

"Heat Sight, Ethereal Sight, possibly more," Arkaziel opined.

"She gained Soul Sight from bonding with me," Kallos offered.

Bobbi dropped to the arena floor, and chef-knife blades appeared in each hand, even as she got rid of her wings. In a flash of movement, both women met in showers of sparks as blow after blow went back and forth between the two. Despite only using the katana, the swordswoman managed to parry every attack by Bobbi, but Aetheria could already tell the StarMane's strength and speed were too much for the swordswoman. When the next gate opened, Slay's tail darted around, and a barbed spike delivered a fatal blow to the swordswoman's neck while she was overextended blocking Bobbi's knives.

"I'll treat your weapons well," Bobbi told the corpse, which she quickly looted before a flock of forty pink flamingos swarmed into the arena.

"Oh, the smell. That's vile." Bobbi screeched between coughs as a fireball scorched half of the flamingos to death. Her chef knives vanished, and Bobbi instead used the katana and wakizashi combination to dispatch the remaining birds. Wherever she cut, lines of flame hung in the air for a few seconds like an afterimage, and butchered and cooked flamingo hunks fell to the ground.

"That's cool as hell, but who wants to eat floor food?" Aetheria criticized.

"Five-second rule," Arkaziel mumbled, licking his chops. "As I said, Slay really needs a power like my Shadowhand. I'm sure she has Flame Devour, but that doesn't let her store things; she can only consume them, like my Devouring Darkness."

The next gate opened to reveal a light-blue dragon that reminded Aetheria of the Chinese dragons. The long-bodied serpent shot out of the gate like a bullet, and vortexes of wind formed as it circled the outside of the arena once. Bobbi launched blasts of fire against the dragon, but they dispersed in the winds around the dragon, and explosive spells were redirected harmlessly into the air by its scales and wind.

"Tough one. A wind dragon that's feasted on some antimagic metal enough to have gained magic-reflecting scales. Great defense, but the downside is it also lowers the dragon's overall magical abilities. Totally not worth it, if you ask me. A strong offense is its own defense." Arkaziel elaborated on the dragon's nature for Aetheria, who pet his head for being a good boy.

"So how is Bobbi going to counter? All of her attacks are failing to reach, but the wind dragon doesn't seem to be able to launch anything meaningful, either; Bobbi's easily evading all of its wind attacks, and the next gate is . . . there."

A pack of thirty slavering, barking dogs charged out of the gate and right into the inferno of fire and wind. None came through the other side.

"Did you miss when the temperature quit going up in the booth? Moros had to shield the audience. Bobbi's raising the temperature in there gradually, but she's immune to heat. She's going to bake the dragon, while its area of effect attacks and the general overheating demolish any opponents who come out of the rest of the gates. Clever lady. Once she gets the arena to be like a sun, nothing but the quarter bosses or the super boss are going to last long enough to actually exit the gate." Arkaziel praising anyone but himself felt weird enough that both Kallos and Aetheria were eying him.

Arkaziel's summary of the situation proved to be exceptionally accurate. The next gate to open resulted in the birth of an inferno as the creatures immediately combusted. The dragon itself kept igniting and going out, but its antimagic scales had taken a significant toll. When the following gate opened, another immense burst of flames and heat were generated by more combustible material and beings entering the ridiculously hot arena. The dragon fell to the ground, and didn't get back up. Slay wandered over to dump its corpse into her storage, but didn't relent on increasing the baking temperatures of the arena. In fact, without the dragon to distract her, she raised both arms into the air to create massive vortexes of fire to fuel the temperature rise even more.

Gate after gate opened to explosions of flame and death, until the counter for Bobbi's enemies clicked up to 399.

When the final gate opened, it was like a vacuum had appeared. The heat and fire just vanished, and a humanoid form with a scaled face, six tentacled arms, and three legs emerged. It wasn't a replica abomination, either. Moros had allowed an honest-to-goodness eldritch abomination of the Void into his tower.

"You dick," Aetheria cursed Moros.

"I am fortifying her soul through our bond as much as I can. Hopefully she can dispatch that *thing* quickly, or we might be in for a repeat of birthing a new Void kitten." Kallos seemed on the fence about whether this was a good thing or a bad thing.

"Is that what we are, Team Void?" Arkaziel asked wonderingly.

"Just because we can all tap the Void doesn't mean Bobbi needs to." Aetheria shook her head.

The vast expanse of the cosmos is but a shallow replica of the Void. In the depths of the abyss, on the edge of descent into the bosom of true Nothing, the blackest of Flames dance. Transcend the worthless shackles of physicality, be burned in my Flames, and emerge knowing the death of galaxies, the secrets of the Void, and cast aside the ancient tapestries of fate that bind lesser beings.

Aetheria didn't swear at Fred. The shocked expressions on Bobbi's face, mixed with the look on Kallos's and Arkaziel's faces, told her that she wasn't the only one who heard it. Fred had never spoken to one of her companions before.

"No deal, I'm already fucking awesome." Bobbi rejected Fred's offer without a second thought.

"I thought he couldn't talk to other people?" Arkaziel asked as Kallos started to ask the same thing.

"Guess our bonds have progressed to the point he can, but it felt like he had to expend a lot of effort to do it, and he doesn't seem able to not include me, so there's that at least?"

Neither Arkaziel nor Kallos looked amused at the so-called bright side.

CHAPTER 51

Defiant to the End

The heat and flames Bobbi had used to obliterate every other opponent, even a magic-resistant wind dragon, vanished in mere moments when the eldritch abomination appeared. Bobbi didn't seem to underestimate the nihilistic opponent as it trundled through the gate into the arena. Footprints that swam with corruption marked where the corrupt thing stepped, and even the air around it warped and skewed in defiance of the laws of reality.

"I hate reality warpers!" Bobbi cried, and with a wave of her hand, the whole arena filled with hundreds of miniature explosions of different sizes, and the cascade grew into a powerful wave. Each tiny explosion blossomed into ten more fireworks-sized explosions, which then propagated into ten more. To Aetheria's Ethereal Sight and Void Sight, the explosions were very interesting because each one emitted slightly different frequencies of oscillating power that rapidly built into some kind of wave.

"Failure is all that mortal flesh can achieve. Succumb to nothing." The eldritch horror spoke through a mouth of fangs and, with a gesture, sent corrupt arcs of power at Bobbi. The fireworks-like explosions somehow nullified the abomination's control enough that she easily dodged what should have been a hit.

Bobbi emerged from her evasive maneuvers not as a humanoid but as a ten-meter-long feline dragon. Her scales were a light red that bordered on pink, and a layer of ephemeral, spectral crimson fur partially concealed the lighter scales from viewers. Unlike Arkaziel, who wore only the collar from Chronos, Bobbi's draconic form had a collar, two pierced ears, ornamentation on her most prominent horn, and a wristlet on each of her four limbs. All of the equipment radiated powerful enchantments to Aetheria's gaze.

The dragon breathed in, and the abomination laughed.

"Dragon fire is nothing compared to the eternal dark of the Void. Your reality anchor shall not hold much longer." More arcs of power flared from the abomination, but Bobbi dodged them easily this time. She left a trail of flames behind when she accelerated across the arena, and when the projectiles finally vanished into the explosive network of fireworks, she stopped and unleashed her breath.

"It's pretty clever, the way she can stabilize reality with that explosive field." Aetheria hadn't considered such a thing would be possible. Could she do something similar with ice to counteract reality warpers?

"It's impressive, sure, but it's a StarMane technique. All gods have some degree of reality warping, so if you want to eat one, you need to be able to stop them from fleeing or turning the tables on you." Arkaziel seemed far less impressed than Aetheria with the tactic.

"I've never seen you do the equivalent," Kallos noted.

"Reality doesn't bend very often around Aetheria," Arkaziel said with a tinge of disappointment at his inability to show off.

The blast of flame from Bobbi's Flamebreath was a multihued cascade of flames that Aetheria had never seen before. Well, some she'd never seen before. She'd seen the silver astral flames and the blue frost fire before, but what were the purple, indigo, yellow, and green fires? For all the bravado of the abomination, the flames burned its terrible oily skin, burnt numerous tentacles to ash, and took it to the brink of death. Even Bobbi looked shocked at the attack's effectiveness, but she quickly capitalized on it.

In a flash, the dragon closed the gap, and Bobbi's form flowed into humanoid. A glowing white longsword appeared in each of her hands, and she unleashed a devastating combo attack. Each time one of the white swords pierced the abomination, an immense explosion of order erupted within the abomination. It was the first time Aetheria had truly seen anything work effectively against the Void, especially an item, so she assumed they were both exceptionally powerful and priceless.

When the fireworks field and ordered white explosions died down, Bobbi stood above the oozing remains of an eldritch abomination.

The counter clicked to four hundred.

"See? I'm awesome." Bobbi reappeared in the booth midsentence, and Arkaziel vanished into the ring.

"Good job, Bobbi! You kicked some major ass. I didn't know there were effective counters to the Void like that." Aetheria praised the StarMane.

Your Order is but a fleeting illusion, a transient dream in the eternal slumber of the cosmos. It is a candle flame that shines only briefly against the encroaching darkness, snuffed out by the merest breath of my will.

The Void is no mere absence, it is the foundation and canvas upon which reality balances. It is the silent pause between notes of the Cosmic Song, the cold darkness between the stars, and the immense gaps in your understanding. Arm yourself with laws and rules, but the Void embraces all, consumes all, and inevitably all semblance of Order will burn in the black flames of my embrace. There is only one final fate, and it is for all to become dust on the cosmic wind, fleeting and insignificant, in the restoration of Ayin.

Fred's megalomania wasn't new, of course, but the Black Flame rarely got so worked up about Aetheria giving even minor praise to something.

"Thanks. What'd you think, boss?" Bobbi asked Kallos.

"You did very well. I'm glad to have you as a partner. Good job." Kallos smiled one of those encouraging smiles, and even though it wasn't directed at her, Aetheria felt her mood lighten and soar.

"Thanks, mind if I take a cat nap on your lap? I'm exhausted after that!" Before Kallos even had a chance to answer, Bobbi became a pink and purple version of a tabby and jumped onto her lap, where she curled up and dozed immediately.

"Oh my gosh. She's so cute. If you don't want to hold her, I will." Aetheria pleaded.

"No, she wanted to rest in my lap. Besides, you've got to cheer Arkaziel on, right?" Kallos seemed to quickly understand the benefits of a StarMane companion, judging from the way she petted Bobbi, or how quickly she'd warmed up to letting even Arkaziel cuddle her since joining them in the tower.

Cheering Arkaziel on didn't need to happen. The Beast Sovereign grew to half the arena's size and unleashed nine orbs of twilight shrouded in black lightning. That was it; that was all the StarMane did. The orbs shifted between gates and destroyed everything. The only other ability or magic he employed was Devouring Darkness. Shadows claimed the remains of whatever monsters he fought. When the counter went to five hundred out of five hundred, not a single enemy had passed the gate into the arena.

The sheer absurdity of Arkaziel's tactics left the crowd murmuring in confused disappointment. They seemed uncertain who to be more displeased at, though. Were they supposed to blame Arkaziel, who didn't break any rules, but also acted without any sportsmanship, or should they blame Moros for allowing the dragon to deprive them of their entertainment, or both? Before Kallos appeared to take Arkaziel's spot, the crowd largely seemed to have decided upon neither.

After all, Moros was Doom, and Arkaziel had already killed Ereshkigal and deprived Nergal of half of his authority. Beings who rarely knew fear were uncomfortable at the display of power Arkaziel had shown off, especially once they were reminded of who and what he was.

When Arkaziel appeared in the booth and Kallos vanished, his excellent mood dimmed at the sight of Aetheria having moved the displaced kitten that was Bobbi onto her lap.

"What the hell?" Arkaziel whined pitifully, with large saucer eyes and a sad boy voice.

"I've got room for both of you!" Aetheria proclaimed, but instead, Arkaziel hopped onto her head and batted her in the face with his tail, his go-to move to show his displeasure with her.

In the arena, Kallos lifted a hand, and concentric rings of black and purple power flowed outward from her to cover the entirety of the arena. The first beasts to emerge from the gates and step onto the rings, a pack of toxic ostriches, were immediately bound in chains like her tattoos. Once the chains wrapped around the creatures, they discolored to a washed-out gray, then dispersed to dust on the wind, all life force and essence drained from them.

The air filled with the sounds of dangling and clinking chains, the dirge of thousands of souls seeking escape from the horrors of existence. The disquieting song evoked damnation but also a light at the end of the tunnel. A light that stood just beyond reach.

A four-headed ogre that Aetheria assumed was a quarter boss emerged, and even it couldn't escape the immediate binding chains. It chanted spells from each head, but the chains of Kallos's wings flowed and intercepted each spell. For each effect of fire, acid, lightning, and cold, a chain imbued with the effects of that spell shot out of the concentric rings with a blade at the end. Four ogre heads looked shocked as the chains plunged through their mouths and out the back of their throats, deployed the spell effects into their mouths, and then dragged them to the ground where their life force and essence joined the belongings of the Soul Witch.

Aetheria would have been cheering, but she had two sleeping kittens, so she opted to send warm emotions through their bond. All too quickly, though, Kallos had killed her fifty, and Arkaziel and Bobbi fell into an empty chair.

"Since I usurped Ouranos, I'll show you all something new!" Aetheria spoke softly, but the words carried across the entire arena. Aetheria tapped the tip of her right boot against the earthen floor, and ice covered the entire arena, the walls, and even formed a transparent dome beneath the protective field Moros raised to keep the effects in the arena. Then with a wink, she puffed a small breath out, and gusts of terrible wind filled the space, creating a vortex that flowed everywhere.

"I don't really have a name for this one yet, maybe something like Frostwind Annihilation? Do people even name their abilities anymore?" Aetheria meant the latter as a joke, or at least as a rhetorical question. She didn't expect anyone to answer it.

"Only those who cannot obtain immortality on their own seek a legacy achieved through naming things. Well, also the narcissistic and the egomaniacal. So, a lot of people." Moros seemed unable to resist answering her, but Aetheria had difficulty telling whether he was making fun of other people or her.

The counter ticked up while Aetheria stood in the center of the arena, tapping her foot impatiently. Nothing ever managed to enter the terrible destructive force of the winds and nearly absolute zero temperatures to face her. When it hit fifty, Aetheria restored the arena to normal.

"So what happened to the super boss? I really wanted to see one." Aetheria appeared in the booth while she asked the air, and a projection of Moros appeared.

"Arkaziel obliterated it at the edge of the gates." Moros's impressive echoing voice sounded less regal when he pouted.

"Where's our shinies?" Bobbi asked the crucial question, not caring about the trial's disappointing engagement.

With a dramatic wave of a black gauntlet, four items appeared to float before each of the victors.

Bobbi received a bow made from what looked like simple black wood. When she reached out and touched it, runes came to life along its entire length, and an ominous aura exuded from it when she drew the string.

"Is this Doom's Warbow of Ruin?" Bobbi asked excitedly.

"Yes, it was my bow in ages long past," Moros answered, with a hint of longing.

Arkaziel received a ring, which annoyed the StarMane until he realized he could do what Bobbi did and make it into an earring, and even as he thought that, it remolded itself into an earring.

"You aren't even going to ask what it is or does?" Moros found the StarMane's actions arrogant, even for their race.

"Pft. I know what it does! It's the Earring of Final Doom. You use it to mark a person's fate to end in a fixed way. Very stylish."

Aetheria stared at Arkaziel and Moros, uncertain if the tacky gold earring was stylish, if Moros was provoking Arkaziel, or what the subtext was. She couldn't figure it out, even with Void Gaze.

Kallos received a golden mask, which she identified immediately.

"You are giving up the Mask of Myriad Fates?" Kallos stored the mask, but she seemed to be curious about the number of personal items Moros doled out to them.

"Your companions are all shapeshifters, and while a witch of your talent could do the same, I thought it would be a fitting gift. Consider it my welcome to the family gift, Kallos-nee."

"Stop it with that!" Aetheria hissed at Moros, not wanting to hear the weeb jargon.

"Thank you," Kallos murmured, even though she'd earned the prize herself.

"What's this?" Aetheria turned over a slender black tiara.

"Doom's Obscurity. It will enshroud you with concealment; even the most powerful will have difficulty piercing through the cloak of fate or will misidentify you. Wear it only when you wish to be unknown and unseen," Moros informed her, before he summoned the door out of the arena.

"Enjoy Tezcallián." Moros laughed and vanished.

"He ran away before I could ask why giant armor-wearing Moros has a tiara, let alone one covered in black roses." Aetheria couldn't hold back a smile, and it was infectious to the point all four were smiling when they stepped into the City of the Smoking Mirror.

CHAPTER 52

Tezcallián

The quartet appeared in a forested valley. Majestic cloud-kissed mountains rose sharply on either side, and long Mesoamerican dragons flew across the skies. The party rode in an open-roofed carriage pulled through the air by a pterosaur. The creature flew with a grace that Aetheria envied, and its scales shone with an eye-catching iridescence. Dinosaurs were, of course, the coolest thing ever. The sun had already begun its descent for the day, and the final hours of dusk added an ethereal beauty to the valley.

A large black disc floated fifty meters above the valley floor, with rivers of liquid crystals spilling off the sides of the city in mesmerizing waterfalls. Roads of luminescent stones ran across the city, creating a kaleidoscope of colors that reflected against the shining black obsidian structures. At the center of Tezcallián, an immense palace of obsidian and gold rose into the sky. Immaculate gardens surrounded it, and in this brief transition between day and night the flowers sung while the trees whispered ancient tales to the few sages gathered to hear their stories.

Fountains of liquid crystal flowed from the palace across the city, the "waters" imbued with powerful healing, rejuvenating, and sustaining energies, according to Aetheria's Ethereal Sight and Void Gaze. The streets were full of all sorts of peoples, humans, animal kin, serpent people, wandering spirits, and even the demons and other races rife in all of the tower cities. Their carriage took them to the grand palace at the center of the city, to the central spire made of extremely reflective obsidian, and landed upon a platform that had not been there while they approached.

The city didn't ring when Aetheria stepped onto the platform, which she thought was nice, although Arkaziel looked disappointed.

A spirit slumped against the wall addressed them.

"Tezcatlipoca awaits you within. The champion's welcome will commence when your meeting with him is done."

A door newly formed in the reflective obsidian spire, and the party made their way into not a grand hall but a comfortable sitting room. Already seated on one of the couches was a man with pure black skin, an easy smile, and pearlescent eyes that shimmered dozens of colors at once and constantly changed. As far as men went, he was handsome in a very striking way, and he exuded an aura of power. His clothes were in the style of the Aztecs, and Aetheria thought he looked somewhat elegant and warriorlike at the same time, but she was confident he would exude that sense even naked. The loincloth could not be called elegant, but the half cape, half apron that Binah informed her was called a tilmahtli certainly seemed elegant in comparison.

Perhaps some of that elegance was due to Tezcatlipoca's strong, muscular body on display, or maybe it was a facet of his nature as a trickster. The only thing marring his physical perfection was the prosthetic left foot made of an obsidian mirror that constantly emitted faint lines of smoke, filling the air with the scent of incense and further elevating the notion of mystery and awe around him. Aetheria found it odd to associate a god with the smells of a head shop, but that's the way it was.

"Welcome to Tezcallián, *sister*, Kallos, and cousins." Tezcatlipoca winked at Bobbi and Arkaziel.

"Got any grub?" Arkaziel asked, and one of the tables filled with a glorious feast. Arkaziel immediately went to the table to help himself, and Bobbi joined him after a moment of hesitation and a nod from Kallos.

"Sister, hm? I assume you're talking about the fragment of Quetzalcoatl I possess?" Aetheria helped herself to a seat on the couch opposite the god, and Kallos joined her.

"Indeed, I, too, possess a fragment of his essence. My understanding is that with a second fragment, you can call the rest and provide a final rest to my pitiful brother?"

"I could, yes. Why should I help you?" Aetheria had planned on doing it anyway, if only to purge her soul of the gods mixed in.

"When the last challenge to be the Overgod took place, Quetzalcoatl thought his chances were decent. As a child of our pantheon's Demiurge, he thought he could stand equal to or above any other god. He did not count on Ialdabaoth entering the contest. Ialdabaoth's power was such that he accepted the challenges of Quetzalcoatl and other comers one after another. Quetzalcoatl was toyed with, made a mockery before the gathered gods, and reduced to fragments as a testament to the might of Ialdabaoth. Even the other Demiurges who gathered to claim the title of Overgod fared no better. Izanami, another Demiurge, was destroyed even more barbarically than Quetzalcoatl. After the unleashed barbarity, no others were willing to challenge him, and he ascended to the role of Overgod."

"Izanami too?" Aetheria murmured softly, and a stir of anger and darkness emanated from the fragment of the goddess's essence inside of her, along with the essence of Quetzalcoatl.

"Yes, and her defeat more than Quetzalcoatl's or any others sealed the ascension of Ialdabaoth. Izanami was a powerful opponent, and most of the other Demiurges have had their turn at Overgod in the past and saw it as a boring, hollow thing. Control of the Archons is hardly worth the hassle."

"He should have been reborn according to the cycle as your destined rival, no?" Kallos sounded confused.

"The Overgod declared there would be no revival of the gods who challenged him, so there has been no revival. In place of revival, final death is all that can occur, which in turn could let a new Quetzalcoatl be born. This is the cycle that our existence follows anyway, but it was corrupted by the creation of the towers and our unchanging re-formations."

"I'll give him his final death. Please bring me the fragment." Aetheria decided to make this quick, since the city outside seemed like one she was eager to explore.

"No negotiation?" Tezcatlipoca held a large essence fragment bound to a large feather from a white dragon serpent that Aetheria suspected had belonged to the deceased Quetzalcoatl. Although the feather's base color was white, it had a robust aqua-metallic blush.

"What's there to negotiate? Unless you want to give up one of your authorities to me? I'll be taking Quetzalcoatl's. Whoever empowers a new god can make up for my fee." Aetheria smiled, proud of herself for sticking up to take the authorities. While she did not necessarily need them, having them seemed better than not.

"Hah, no. I'll be keeping my powers, thank you very much. Ōmeteōtl can bear the burden of birthing a new, white Tezcatlipoca." The god's smile bordered on sinister, ruining his mysterious and unknowable aura.

"Pity, I quite fancy acquiring authority over night at some point." Aetheria feigned a tsk, before she stood. "Are we doing this here?"

"Yes, none may enter here without my leave. I will prevent any outsiders from peering into affairs not their own." Tezcatlipoca gestured, and the walls shone with a powerful barrier.

"Not fighting anyone is a pleasant change to this. Very well, then. Kallos, if you would assist me. Arkaziel, Bobbi, if you two watch our lovely host and ensure he doesn't do anything untoward while I care for Quetzalcoatl? If he acts up, kindly incapacitate him. Not that you're going to be a bad boy, right?"

"Is this the thanks I get for brokering the deal of your rebirth? So little trust." Tezcatlipoca laughed, but he didn't seem offended. In fact, the god seemed pleased, as if he would have been offended if they hadn't mistrusted him or taken precautions against him. Aetheria wondered how much of that came from the god dismissing the StarManes as a true threat, despite Arkaziel having already tasted the true flesh of gods twice now, and their false avatars so many times Aetheria had lost count.

Aetheria folded her legs up underneath her, and a circle outlined by the faces of the feathered serpent filled the magic circle, each rendered in immaculate celestial ice tinged with the flavor of Quetzalcoatl's essence.

"Quetzalcoatl, the Resplendent One, Feathered Serpent of the Heavens, embrace the legendary wisdom and grace and appear before me. Bridge the celestial door, and rejoin this essence of yourself so that you may know peace. I summon you, Lord of the Stars of the Dawn!"

The words, combined with Aetheria's overwhelming Ethereal power flowing into the circle, produced the celestial door immediately. At that point, Kallos laid a hand on Aetheria and the existing orb to increase the strength of the pull of the ritual. The other three in the room watched in rapt attention as miniature spectral serpents flew from the gate into the glowing essence bound in the feather.

Tezcatlipoca's expression showed open wonderment at the magic displayed before him, but he quickly schooled his features back to one of passivity.

It took the duo almost twenty minutes to draw the last fragment into the room, before the celestial door sealed shut behind it.

"Someone did not want to let you go, little one," Aetheria murmured to it, before she set to work on the essence of the god. She removed the authorities, absorbed most of its power, and then sent the last of it on to the Great Cycle, where who knew what would happen to it. Oblivion? Rebirth?

"What do you think, Kallos?" Aetheria held two orbs.

"Why didn't you absorb all the authorities?" Tezcatlipoca asked confused.

"I suggest you give wind to Bobbi, and if you don't mind, I'll take the other?" Kallos said after a moment.

"That's good with me. Eat up, Bobbi." Aetheria handed wind to Bobbi, who looked confused for a few moments but then ate while Kallos absorbed the other orb.

"How benevolent of you to share with your friends. Why give up law, wind, and air so freely, though? Oh, I see. You have sky already, the ultimate authority over wind, air, and weather." Tezcatlipoca nodded, then lowered the barriers around the palace.

"The city of Tezcallián is open to you, Challenger. When you descend, the Welcoming will begin. I have shooed any mercenaries who might seek you out of my city, so enjoy yourself for as long as you wish before you return to that dullard, Moros."

CHAPTER 53

The Vilja Experience

The days spent in Tezcallián ran by in a blur. Kallos quickly adjusted to her authority over law and air, while Bobbi spent hours a day trying to prank Arkaziel with her new command of wind. Aetheria had a bit rougher time, with the addition of creation, life, knowledge, learning, renewal, agriculture, and fertility. She had initially refused to take on the fertility aspects of Inanna, but having a second chance to take them made her reconsider. Even if she didn't see an obvious use to them initially, the importance of fertility and hearth gods and goddesses in every pantheon couldn't be understated. The addition of creation to her already long list of authorities made her ice creations easier and more powerful than ever, but came with the caveat that she had to control her idle thoughts lest she create things.

Aetheria found that maintaining a connection to Da'at allowed her to more fully control her authorities and not have them run wild. Even the iron-willed Kallos had to restrain the newly acquired authority of air, as it did not align with her existing powers and archetype the way law aligned. Maybe someday she'd find another law or similar authority and pass it onto Arkaziel to see what kind of hijinks might ensue due to the mismatch.

The days of leisure ended when each had minimalized the flare-ups of their new authorities, at which point they took the portal back to the Tower of Moros, whereupon they found themselves in a room of richly upholstered recliners, and the large armored figure of Moros reclining in the equivalent of a recliner throne.

"Welcome back, stepsister-nee," Moros greeted Aetheria warmly, while the other three merely got a nod.

"I told you to stop that; it's weird." Aetheria grumbled and claimed the sole loveseat to sit with Kallos, but the two ended up with kittens on their laps.

"My, what a happy little family. Your next challenge will count for the entirety of the sixty-first to eighty-ninth floors. Finish, and you will be at the final trade city, and within sprinting distance of the heights of my tower."

The silence to his proclamation seemed to visibly satiate Moros, as if he'd been fishing for reactions. Stunned silence was a rare reaction for this particular party, and it didn't last long before it was replaced with suspicion and disbelief.

"This is a trial I call the Vilja Experience. Each of you will live the life of Vilja, a young human woman on another planet. The starting will be identical for each of you, and none of your abilities will work in the simulation. Your job is to make sure Vilja reaches the age of twenty-one. Why would you want to be the winner? I'll give the winner a suitable authority. Fire for Slay, light for Arkaziel, spirit for Kallos, and night for Aetheria. If, inexplicably, you all get Vilja to twenty-one years old, you'll each get the prize."

"So we can all win? I see," Kallos murmured, while the StarManes had a dazed look in their eyes. No doubt Bobbi imagined what she could do with the authority of fire, her primary element, while Arkaziel would gain the counterpart to his shadow authority, and Aetheria definitely liked the idea of getting night. She could beat Nyx at her own game!

"Survive to twenty-one. How hard could that be?" Arkaziel laughed madly.

"Don't jinx it, Ark!" Aetheria and Bobbi chided the black cat simultaneously, while Kallos settled on staring daggers at him.

"Is this a one try and done, kind of thing?" Aetheria wondered. If they had a couple of lives it'd be easier.

"You'll be run through a quick tutorial, but then yes, you get one try. No redos, no falling back on save points, no rewinding time. Just one shot, like the original Vilja got. Enjoy." A sound like a guillotine falling echoed through the room, and all four members of the party convulsed, their eyes shutting and their bodies going limp in the love seats.

Aetheria Vilja stood in the trampled grass in the courtyard of the Oak Palace. At a whole eight years old, she was a slender, weak girl, with piercing eyes and an uncanny talent for asking adults questions they didn't want to answer. Aada, her twin sister, stood opposite her with a wooden stick held in a perfect mimicry of the soldiers who served their family.

"You hold it like this, Vil," Aada repeated. Despite being twins, Aada had already grown slightly taller than Vilja, had broader shoulders, and possessed an uncanny strength. She also had black hair, compared to Vilja's blonde. Since they were born, the people of Taivaslinna had celebrated the birth of their count's twin daughters, for the Norn Stones had revealed their natures the day they had been born. Strong, dependable, personable Aada had the boon of the Warden. Even as an eight-year-old girl, young Aada could swing around a broadsword one-handed if the call to arms came.

Vilja, quiet and aloof, had the boon of Growth. With a wave of one of her slender hands, and the expenditure of energy, she could call a seed to full adult growth and bloom in seconds. She could singlehandedly sustain a city's population with harvested goods on a permanent basis without resorting to energy restoration potions, or power transfers. The last person to have the boon of Bounty had lived nearly two hundred years ago, and from the scattered documentation and accounts, it seemed the boon of Bounty had been a lesser version of Growth. The citizens of Taivaslinna called the eight-year-old the Lady of Plenty, for none knew the empty stomached pain of hunger as long as they themselves contributed to the society of the city.

But being the Lady of Plenty didn't increase Vilja's strength, speed, or even endurance. Her physical stamina and energy restored significantly swifter than almost anyone else's, but the only way to increase her baseline was the old-fashioned way—working out. Which meant her warden would follow her, outdo her, and not understand why her presence was such a thorn under her skin.

Time around their impromptu training ground seemed to slow down. Clearly, a choice had to be made in this moment. Aetheria could feel in herself, her resonance to Vilja, that the easiest thing to do would be to blow up, run away, or go train with someone else. Instead, she looked Aada in the eyes. The young girl clearly loved Vilja, and desperately yearned to be loved by her.

"Okay," Vilja said without emotion, altering the grip on her stick to match Aada's. Her twin's eyes widened briefly in surprise, then a soft smile appeared on Aada's face in stark contrast to the expressionless one on Vilja.

Okay. So I don't have full control of her body, and indirect control over her actions. It's like a visual novel, maybe?

Vilja and Aada went back and forth between taking stances and practicing swings. Aada even noticed Vilja couldn't quite do the bigger, more dramatic style.

"Let's ask Dad about getting you a rapier! I bet that would be perfect for you. Rapiers are all about precision and skill, far more so than longswords, broadswords, or axes. Maybe you could use a wand in your left hand?" Aada, driven by a breakthrough in their sisterly relationship, came on a little strong, but for the first time she could feel the smile form on Vilja's face. Barely. It was the smallest smile imaginable, but when Aada saw it she looked as happy as someone who won the lottery.

"That's a good idea, Aada. Let's go find Father before it is time for afternoon studies."

"Yeah!" Aada grabbed Vilja's hand and pulled her twin after her into the Oak Palace.

The city officials, soldiers, and house staff all looked askance at the two young girls running wild through the center of their home as if it were any other house in the city, and not the Oak Palace. Disapproving stares or not, the two navigated the vast expanse of the palace and found their way to Count Aho's study. After a brief wait, the castellan on duty let them in to see their father.

"Aada, Vilja, you don't come to see me during your free hour very often. Were you both sparring?" Aho had the height of a bear, but Aetheria wondered if it wasn't because she was forced to see the world through the eyes of an eight-year-old. The tall man had black hair with only a few streaks of silver in the bangs and temples, and despite the black military uniform and cape, the air of command. In the city-state of Taivaslinna, being able to defend yourself and others was not the assigned role of men or women, but all citizens.

"Vilja practiced with me today, Dad! She even smiled!"

Vilja watched her sister and father with what Aetheria would term *resting bitch face*. The girl's eyes were anywhere but on other people, even family, and her hands were held behind her back so neither could see her clench her hands nervously.

"Oh, you practiced with Aada? I thought you swore you'd never practice with someone with a soldier blessing after that incident with Astrid?"

Vilja just shrugged her shoulders.

"I think we should get her a rapier, Dad! Vil is so fast and precise, and she learns stances and blows the first time, every time! With a rapier and a dueling wand, she might even beat me!" Aada's enthusiasm captured Count Aho fully, so much so that he didn't notice the sudden wariness on Vilja's face.

She's worried about stepping on Aada's toes, even though she's not a soldier? Why? Does she have a photographic memory, or something?

"Well, what do you say Vilja? Would you like a practice rapier and dueling wand?" The count smiled, doting father that he was, but only indirect eye contact and a miserable-looking daughter looked back at him. Aetheria could see the ache in him, at his inability to connect to his daughter.

"Of course she does! You said you did, right Vil?" Aada pressed her silent sister for confirmation, and Count Aho looked back and forth between the two. Clearly these scenarios had happened before, and obviously Vilja backed out in the past. Time seemed to slow, but Aetheria had already mentally pushed Vilja to proceed.

"Yes, Father. I would like that, please."

"Yay!" Aada jumped and clapped her hands, and it seemed the smile on the count's face could light the entirety of the Oak Palace.

"I'll see to it you have a set by tomorrow. Would you like to learn with Aada at first, or should I send an instructor down?" Aho tried to look into his daughter's eyes, but her blue eyes switched away before he could get a clear look into them.

"I will practice with Aada. When I won't embarrass the House of Oak I will call on an instructor, I promise."

"That's decided, then. I'm very proud of both of you. Now you'd better get to your afternoon lessons, or Kaisa will have both of your ears for being late two days in a row. Try to pay attention. The dignitary from Bergen should arrive in less than a month. There are few enough free cities left, and we need to maintain good relations with them."

"Yes, Father," Vilja agreed, while Aada just grumbled under her breath about stupid diplomats.

The two girls ran off, and from behind a screen their mother laughed.

"You'd never know those two were twins. Aada's dark hair against Vilja's blonde, their stature, their personalities . . ." Count Aho shook his head ruefully.

Countess Kaarina patted her husband on the shoulder.

"The boons manifest in mysterious ways, and Vilja's is a newly seen boon. The engineers were uncertain whether the translation from the Norn Stones was Growth or something else entirely, if you recall."

CHAPTER 54

How to Cut with Silence

Stop! How did you parry that, Vil?" Aada panted, shocked that Vilja had so deftly used her training rapier to parry and disarm her.

Aetheria knew the basics of fencing. Footwork, attacks, defensive techniques. For weeks Aada and an older military man called Captain Liefson had drilled footwork and parry with Vilja. At first the young girl had clumsiness issues, but she overcame those far sooner than Aetheria felt an eight-year-old should have. Each day the girl seemed to come into her own body, and while she only grew marginally stronger or faster, she seemed to learn efficiency with a fanaticism that bordered on scary. The slightest of changes in stance and balance combined with a surprisingly robust understanding of momentum for an eight-year-old in a fantasy world created the illusion of far more proficiency than Vilja possessed.

"You were overextended slightly on your right leg after my feint, so I was able to use a circle parry to push you off-balance. Your strength can't save you from bad footwork, Aada." Vilja sounded harsh in her critique of Aada, but her face remained expressionless, and for those brief words Vilja made eye contact with Aada.

"She's right, you know. Just because a rapier isn't your weapon of choice, Aada, doesn't mean you can treat it like a longsword. Perhaps you should go back to your longsword? Vilja will encounter far more longswords, broadswords, and axe wielders amongst the demons and other city-states than she will of warriors using the same weapon." Captain Liefson grunted from his seat atop a barrel.

"Yes, Captain," Aada agreed in a sing-song voice with the exact amount of eye roll. She peeked at Vilja out of the corner of her eye, but her sister didn't laugh or crack so much as a smile at the groan her response elicited from the captain.

"Run parry drills until the next bell, then run the footwork course. Don't be late for your afternoon classes." The captain waved and heaved his old bones off the barrel. "The Bergen ambassador will be arriving today. The scouts reported their party is two hours from the switchbacks. They should arrive just before dusk. I reckon the countess will be searching for the two of you before long."

That evening, dressed in proper dresses as befitted being the count's daughters, the girls were forced to sit at the head table with their father, mother, the Bergen diplomat, and one of the merchant lords of Bergen, who supposedly happened to be traveling with the diplomat out of convenience for the armed escort, despite the merchant's brother being one of the Council of Bergen.

"The city-state of Alarai is no more. The demon lord burned it to the ground," the diplomat said, concluding his tale of woe and treachery. "Only one independent nation remains on the coast, at which point Lamentosa will have conquered all of the ports. It's only a matter of time before he makes inroads toward the center of the continent, Count Aho."

"Why is it only a matter of time? He controls the heart of trade, he can squeeze us all out over generations, and he's immortal. There's no need for him to rush. He will consolidate his holdings for the next decade, according to my spies. We have ten years to build a coalition that will withstand the combined might of the demons and the fallen humans." The count disagreed, and the diplomat gave the merchant an annoyed look, as if the count shouldn't have known that intelligence yet.

"That is what our spies say, as well. But we cannot delay to prepare. The Council of Bergen wishes for a gesture from the Oak Palace to cement our alliance in the hearts and minds of all people." Sweat beaded upon the diplomat's forehead, while the merchant's eyes narrowed greedily at the young girls.

"And just what is it that the Council of Bergen would ask for?" the countess asked with a dangerous tone. Countess Kaarina of House Oak was known across the city-states for her cool pragmatism, ruthless logic, and being not only immune to poison, but a mistress of poison. To dine in her presence was to put one's life in her hands, even though she had never, as far as could be proven, poisoned anyone in formal settings.

"Ah yes, well. Lord Bryant wishes for the Lady of Plenty to be married to his nephew . . ." The diplomat trailed off at the cold glare of the countess.

"My daughters are people, not possessions, Ambassador Allard," Count Aho said. "It is the way of Taivaslinna that no man or woman shall ever be forced to marry another against their will, nor can one own another person. Even if those were not core tenets of our people, not a person of Taivaslinna would agree to Lady Vilja's removal from the city. There would be riots in the streets, and our alliance would unfortunately have to be ended." Aho's voice grew hard, and his eyes shifted to the merchant, the very brother of Lord Bryant, and father of the nephew they wished to marry Vilja to.

"Oh, they are just peasants, Aho," the merchant said. "Cut their rations, flog a few, and the matter will be settled in days. If you want to maintain the alliance with Bergen, you have no choice but to marry your daughter to my son."

Vilja, of course, burned with anger and rage at being talked about in this manner when she was sitting right at the table. Aetheria didn't blame the girl. The pompous asshole stared at the young girl as if she were a prize for him, not his son, and Aetheria wanted nothing more than a body with which to punch the asshole. Unfortunately, she couldn't take direct actions and couldn't use her abilities, but Aetheria had found she could influence the world with the authorities she possessed.

The flow of time in the room slowed, and Aetheria could sense different options coming, divergences of fate. Vilja could defend herself. Kaarina could defend her, Aho could defend her, Aetheria could strike with one of her authorities. But Vilja wasn't looking to any of those people. She was looking toward Aada out of the corner of her eye, barely perceptible.

Come on, Aada. Be the Warden your sister needs. Love came in many forms beyond romantic love. Familial love, sisterly love, was a powerful force, and one she could empower.

Aada's chair screeched back so hard the legs splintered, and the young girl dramatically stood and drew her dagger with the symbol of the House of Oak on it, proof of her heritage.

"I challenge you to a duel for the honor of the House of Oak, Aodren Bryant. You have acquitted yourself in a manner befitting a villain, and then dare to suggest my father take leave of his oaths and obligations as the Protector of the Gates to Heaven to fulfill your petty, boorish desires toward my sister?"

"Preposterous! Silence this uppity child, Aho, or I shall have my bodyguard slay her on the spot." Aodren scowled and looked toward his bodyguard near the wall. The House of Oak guards already held a blade against his neck.

"As Ambassador Allard will tell you, Bryant, a duel called for the honor of a house, especially the ruling house, can not have champion duelists or proxies. You must either risk your life and duel Aada yourself, seek restitution for your offense, or be exiled from Taivaslinna. As a member of the family of the House of Bryant, your family would, of course, also be exiled from Taivaslinna, and your merchants would no longer be allowed to peddle in our lands." Aho smiled a cruel smile, and while the ambassador and merchant sweated, he winked to Aada.

Good job, Aada!

"You can't expect me to duel a child! I know you fools live up here in the clouds, but have you all become daft with elevation sickness?" Bryant appealed how dishonorable it would be for an adult to be forced to face a child.

"I will give him a handicap, Father," Aada offered with a smile, and for the first time in ages, the House of Oak heard a giggle escape from Vilja. Her face remained expressionless, so they were all forced to question whether it had actually happened, but a new fire burned in Aada's eyes.

"Well, make your choice, Aodren. Duel Aada with a handicap granted to you, pay whatever price she may extract from you, or be exiled." Aho spoke more forcefully this time.

"Count, surely . . ." Ambassador Allard stopped at the raised hand from Countess Kaarina.

"Actions have consequences, Ambassador. None are above the law here, not Aho, not I, and certainly not visitors who have scorned our hospitality."

"She's a bloody Warden! She could rip the limb off an ogre and beat a dozen orcs to death with it, and you'll give me a damned handicap? This is ridiculous; you're simply posturing to put me into a terrible position with no way out. Well, I won't give you the satisfaction. Name your price, girl." Aodren pulled a magic bag from his pocket, clearly expecting to be told an amount of money.

"You will give your first son to Taivaslinna, to be raised as a warrior to fight for all humanity. In this place, he will have the opportunity to be educated without your egregious disposition, and will find examples of honor and nobility to remedy the profound deficit in both empathy and decorum that your odious presence has no doubt imbued him with." Aada stumbled over the words slightly, as she strained to hear the whispers of her twin, who didn't seem to open her mouth at all.

Oh man, these girls are awesome. Aetheria cheered them both on, uncaring that her manipulation of love and war had helped cement the sisterly bond between the twins.

Red-faced, Aodren Bryant put his purse away. Only after he swallowed an entire glass of mead did the merchant speak.

"Fine. Aatos will be sent here when we return to Bergen." The dark gleam in Bryant's eye said there would be repercussions from this move.

"Why, Aodren, why so dour? Your son will be right where he is capable of attempting to woo the Rose of Taivaslinna. You should, of course, warn him that Vilja has far more thorns than any normal rose. That concludes tonight's dinner. Ambassador, Aodren, please join me in the parlor. I have another visitor we must speak and negotiate with." Count Aho gestured toward another room.

"Come on, girls, let's get you to bed. Tell your father good night." Countess Kaarina moved to round up the girls.

"Good night, Father!" the two echoed, while staring at the masked figure in dark robes waiting at the door to the sitting room with one of the top spies of Taivaslinna. Aetheria almost fell flat on her face, despite not having a body at the moment. She recognized the man, even behind the mask. The single good eye of the robed figure of the man winked at her, able to see her despite her not being truly there.

What the shit is Odin doing here? If he can see me, maybe I can influence things through him? No, come back, girls!

Despite her intentions, Aetheria was pulled after the twins toward bed, her inability to leave their proximity thwarting her chance to speak to Odin.

CHAPTER 55

Botany Meets Magic

The more Aetheria observed young Vilja and Aada, the more it became apparent that Vilja stood out from others due to her neurodivergent behaviors. What surprised Aetheria the most, though, was that the people of Taivaslinna didn't treat her unkindly. For a low-technology world, the people seemed to be exceptionally enlightened regarding other people. This, of course, had a reason, which Aetheria found out in the next lesson with Kaisa.

"How many generations has it been since the continent of Vexendun first reappeared in our world?" Kaisa, a dark-skinned woman with a multitude of braids and a schoolmarm dress, handled the twins' lessons.

"Nineteen generations?" Aada guessed.

"It's been twenty-one generations, or five hundred and seventy-six years since Vexendun reappeared, and five hundred and seventy-one years since humanity fled the other continents to seek refuge here. It's been nineteen generations since our ancestors found Taivaslinna, the House of Oak, and the Norn Stones." Vilja answered in a near monotone, but she added the last bit on to show that Aada had been on the right track.

"That's right, Vilja. Why did our ancestors have to flee the continents of Thaloria and Auristara?"

"Because of Shadowfang, the Wolf Demon Lord!" Aada cried out, eager to prove her knowledge.

"And?" Kaisa grinned at the exuberant answer, but urged a further answer.

"Plagues, demons, and Ragnarok's approach. Odin warned us that the only way to survive was to flee to Vexendun. The haughty elves and dwarves refused to acknowledge Odin's warnings and stayed to defend their homes, so now there's almost none left."

"Good answer, Aada. What happened then?"

"When everyone departed from Skidbladnir and Hringhorni, Odin sent Hringhorni into the ocean with only Baldr's body, and lit it ablaze. The funeral of Baldr set the stage for humanity's next saga here in Vexendun. The elvish mage,

Juvaryn Flamecloak, lit Skidbladnir aflame and declared we could never go back to the lands ruled by Shadowfang. Freyr smote him dead for daring to burn his ship." Vilja's dispassionate retelling lacked the drama usually imposed on the story when it was told with actors, puppets, or even just read aloud.

Aetheria, on the other hand, was starting to put the pieces together. Ethnically, it seemed like Taivaslinna was exceptionally diverse, but the truth was none of them were originally from this continent. Their identity as a people had been built out of disparate refugees of multiple origins into a homogenous whole. Or at least, after five hundred some years, it seemed to have blended together in harmony.

"Aada, make sure you reread the history book before Brigadier. Now go along, it's time for your lessons with the warlord. I heard one of the squadrons managed to capture a Mantis Reaver, and he might let you join the rookie squad fighting it."

"A Reaver! Bye, Vil!" Aada fled the room as if she'd been offered candy, while Kaisa moved to the wall to pull down a small plant. It had thorns, a single white flower similar to a rose, and a sweet, melancholy scent.

"It bloomed?" Despite the lack of expression or tone, Aetheria could tell the young girl was actually shocked. The longer she spent with the girl, the more she felt what the young woman felt. For such a monotone and firmly controlled person, her emotions were constantly overwhelming to Aetheria, to the point she wondered how the girl wasn't constantly screaming at people.

"Yes, it did. Do you remember what this flower is called?"

"Frigg's Tears. The first one grew when Odin left her to wander the world. They became more common after the death of Baldr, the Shadowfang diaspora, and Father said one blooms every time a human is killed by the forces of the demons, and whole fields appear when a free city falls." Vilja recited the history of the plant.

"That's right, and do you know what properties the flowers have?"

"The nectar heals wounds, as well as awaken those who have fallen into comas, and the more unscrupulous alchemists claim it can be used in love philters."

"What can you do with this one?"

"Let's see." Vilja smiled, and Aetheria witnessed Vilja's magic for the first time.

The young girl tapped a finger against the stem of the flower, and its flesh thickened, and like a time-lapse video the plant grew about six inches taller, with multiple gorgeous flowers forming. The beautiful golden stamens of each flower looked like drops of amber, and shone with potent mana.

Wait a minute. Where is the Aether? There's no Nether, either.

"*This is what you would term a lower existence,*" Reverie answered, speaking for the first time since this trial had started. "*Aether and Nether are limitless only in the two highest physical realms. After that, they become rarer and rarer, until only mana exists. Go low enough and even mana becomes scarce.*"

Thanks for the info, Rev. Aetheria mulled that over. She had assumed that Aether and Nether were a constant, everywhere, but that wasn't the case. Had her Earth been in a lower existence, or just a place where people hadn't awoken their potential, or had it been sealed to act as a nursery for her powers to stay controlled?

While Aetheria had been distracted, Vilja had turned one plant into five.

"Your energy stores are growing, Vilja. Ask the count to test yourself with the Norn Stones again. Maybe you gained a level? You gain a new ability at eleven!" Kaisa looked at the young girl excitedly.

"Maybe." Vilja nodded. "Things have felt different lately."

"Different how?" Kaisa asked worriedly, but Vilja only shrugged and didn't elaborate.

Can she sense me?

"I'll collect the seeds from these, and we'll continue to grow more once I verify with Old Halvard about their ability to process them. Have you managed to further your control of how the plants grow at all?" Kaisa put the plants back near the window to bask in the sunlight.

"I grew a yew into a shaped hedge," Vilja offered tentatively.

"Really? That's amazing! How big was it?"

"The size of my sandbox," Vilja said slightly evasively.

"I'll just go down and look myself, then, I presume your sandbox is underneath it?"

"Yes." Vilja nodded. "Can you tell me about the Gibborim again?"

"Sure, but then we'll go back to lessons. The Gibborim were the first ancient peoples to rule our world, before any other races. They created the Norn Stones to codify and identify magic, and they ruled the whole world. Then a meteor came. Dust clouds, disease, and corrupted animals tore the empire to pieces, but the Gibborim came here to Vexendun, where the meteor impacted. After struggles against the weather, monsters, and plagues, the mightiest of all Gibborim, Azarel and Valdor, made it to the meteor. They fought a monster larger than a mountain, sealed the evil, and sunk Vexendun in the gaps between worlds to protect the rest of existence from an evil so great even they couldn't defeat it."

"How do we know Azarel and Valdor succeeded?" Vilja wanted to know.

"The Gibborim sage Kazdor recorded it with the message he left for those who would come after." Kaisa didn't like the turn the questions were taking. Some things had to be taken on faith, but these were things they'd found evidence of since coming to Vexendun.

"What happened to the rest of the Gibborim?" Vilja asked.

"Maybe they left?" Kaisa shrugged uncomfortably.

"They probably died." Vilja didn't sugarcoat her thoughts.

"It is possible, but they left many great artifacts behind for us. From the Norn Stones, Encyclopedia Alchemia, the Book of Magic, to Taivaslinna itself. What other wonders are behind the Gates of Heaven, or hidden in the forbidden ruins?"

"Father says the corpse of the great monster is behind the gates, and that's why the monsters inside the center of the continent are so much stronger than the ones outside. Time's up." Unlike children Kaisa had previously taught, Vilja declared time was up somewhat forlornly, but maybe that was just something she imagined in the monotone delivery.

"Practice with your dueling wand. We will dedicate tomorrow to Force Bolt."

"Yes ma'am." Vilja nodded before she scuttered out of the room, dragging a very curious Aetheria with her. Vilja took them to the count's office, where after a few minutes of waiting, she was allowed in.

"Your visits are growing more common, Vilja. I like it." Count Aho gave his daughter a warm smile, even though all that Vilja returned was the same neutral, slightly bitchy-looking, expression she almost always had.

"Kaisa thinks I may have leveled up. May I use a Norn Stone?"

"Of course." Aho set a black and blue sphere on the corner of the desk. It was covered in glyphs and runes that Aetheria could sense magic from.

"Scan," Vilja commanded when she picked up the sphere in both hands. Despite being the size of her head, she didn't seem to struggle with its weight at all. Motes of light emerged from the stone to spin around her in a spiral, before the lights returned to the stone.

"Display," Vilja commanded when the motes had returned, and beams of light emitted from the sphere as if it were an LED projector to generate the image of text on a section of the wall that had been blackened out specifically to show the results better.

Name: Vilja of the House of Oak
Race: Human
Age: 8
Boon: Growth
Level: 11
Abilities: Quick Growth, Modify

What the hell? She gets a system but I don't? What a bunch of bullshit.

Aetheria raged at the injustice of it all for a few brief seconds. Count Aho, Vilja, and Countess Kaarina, who emerged from behind the screen she usually sat behind, all stared at the projection in confusion.

"Modify? Is that even in the Book of Magic?" Kaarina asked with consternation.

Aho pulled a thick replica of the aforementioned text from his desk, and flipped through the pages.

"Not exactly. Modify is listed as a sub-skill to elemental control abilities. The exact example the Book of Magic gives is for Boon of the Firelord, Ability Control Fire [Modify], which allows for precision alterations to fire's properties." Aho frowned at the book, then looked back up at the projection.

Nothing had changed, though.

Aetheria felt bad for Vilja, and willed with all of her heart for the girl to gain more of an intuitive understanding of her power. Even if she remembered she had authority over knowledge, learning, and so many other areas, she would have tried to give more to the girl who struggled so hard to make sense of powers not contained in the Book of Magic.

"I think it means I can modify my plants," Vilja said with a touch of confidence, just a touch, in a near whisper. Aetheria winced at the feeling of pain, of nails digging into her hand, as Vilja controlled herself through pain.

"I'll practice with you tonight, Vilja." Kaarina smiled reassuringly, and her hand squeezed her daughter's shoulder. Aetheria saw the pain in the mother's eyes that confirmed for her that Vilja's methods for controlling her emotions had not gone unnoticed with the countess. Count Aho seemed blissfully unaware, and Kaarina did nothing to draw his attention.

"What kind of practice?" Aho asked, curious.

"My Detect Poison ability will allow us to experiment to see if Vilja can modify the potency and concentrations of poison in plants she grows, if she can remove it, and of course, if she can make a plum sweeter."

Vilja and Aho seemed to fully grasp the implications of how powerful Modify might be, while Kaarina had already realized this and moved on to dreams of a sweet, delicious, juicy plum fresh from a tree.

"Why don't the two of you head down to the garden and test out plums first? Your mother isn't going to be able to think straight until she gets a fresh plum, Vilja." Aho rolled his eyes at his wife.

"Let's go, Mommy." Vilja's small hand wrapped around Kaarina's larger one, and the ladies made for the garden.

CHAPTER 56

Black Plums

Lines of black plum trees rose along the once-cleared edges that led from the gates of Taivaslinna down the steep cliffs to the plains below. It had been a full two years since Vilja and Countess Kaarina had perfected the ultimate black plum, and the trees now filled the boulevards of Taivaslinna and the switchback trail that led to the city. When one made the trek up the long trail in spring, it was whispered the fragrant aroma of the plum blossoms gave strength to the weary to make it all the way to the top, and the guards who manned the watchtowers were fine with travelers taking a plum or two, so long as they were consumed on the trek and the refuse wasn't left on the trail. More than one guard helped themselves during their patrols and watches in the towers.

Aatos, the twelve-year-old son and previous heir of the House of Bryant had arrived a year ago, after the family could no longer afford to delay the political promise that had been made without offending both Count Aho and the people of Taivaslinna. Thus, Vilja, Aada, Count Aho, Countess Kaarina, and the girls' instructor, Kaisa, sat around the informal dining table with Aatos, with a plum pudding cake in the middle of the table that had been completely demolished. A relaxed and content smile dwelt on every face, except for Vilja's.

"When will the refugees from Montagren start arriving?" Aatos asked the question that all of the younger children in the room wondered.

"It's hard to say, lad. Rumors say that the Duchy of Dolce also was under siege. If that's true and the route through Dolce is closed, refugees would have to travel by back paths or route to Bergen before coming to us. That's a long route, but given Bergen's reception to past refugees it's in their best interests to come to us. If Dolce manages to resist, or people made it through before the roads closed, two more months. If they have to take the Bergen path, three months. Either way, we've increased construction of more housing." Count Aho didn't talk down to the children about the severity of the situation humanity found itself in. They would live through the conflict to come, hopefully.

"The last peddler claimed life under the demons isn't that bad," Aatos remarked.

"He was a useful idiot, Aatos. I already told you that. The demons sell him their wares cheaply through trade houses they own, buy them more expensively in other cities they own, and then give him a commission to sell more wares in unconquered territory, so he can blather on and on about how much coin he rakes in, how fantastic the demons are for trade, the safety of their roads and order, all while thinking he's responsible for the profit he makes. If he had even a shred of analytic capability he would have noticed all of his deals favor him outrageously, and wonder why that was. Instead he pats himself on the back, and tells everyone how great he is and how easy it is to succeed under the demons." Vilja hissed the words out, while everyone else looked at her slightly shocked. It was rare for the girl to speak a full sentence, let alone go on a rant.

"Yeah . . ." Aatos trailed off.

Aetheria felt inclined to stop those sorts of harsh diatribes from Vilja, but the girl had to grow up on her own, not just be constantly stifled by the invisible ghost that dwelled within her.

"None of that. We're celebrating Aatos's being with us for a year now." Kaarina put an end to the glum mood simply with a smile. The only person who didn't put a smile on their face to match the countess was Vilja, whom Kaarina allowed to sulk.

"Dad, did you see the new golems Aatos got working?" Aada turned the subject around.

"Oh, did you get one of the ancient Grigori golems to work?" Count Aho sounded surprised.

"Well, sort of, sir. Grimnir and I managed to get it operational. If I directly pilot it, it moves and operates for up to a half hour at a time before it drains me of magic. We're pretty sure there's some kind of central device that empowered the golems in the ruins, or gave them remote control, since most of the models we've looked at don't even have direct pilot capabilities. Grimnir suggested I do some archeology in the ruins, if you'll allow it."

The "ruins" beneath Taivaslinna were nearly another city the size of the one aboveground, but everything down there had been made out of traditional building materials of clay bricks or shaped stone, unlike the unbreakable gray-scaled material that made up all of the buildings that had been in Taivaslinna when it had first been found. Newer structures always stood out, since they were built with regular stone, bricks, or wood, in the upper city.

"I suppose. You girls wanted to search the ruins, too, so take Grimnir and young Astrid with you."

"Astrid is kind of creepy, Dad." Aada tried to argue her inclusion, but Aho shook his head.

"Astrid's father is one of my most loyal retainers, and she's one of the most promising prospects for the elite forces of your generation. You don't have to worry about her stealing your thunder, Aada." Aho completely misunderstood Aada's reasoning, but the young girl dropped it. Aatos and Vilja said nothing, while Aetheria all but jumped up and down clapping her hands. Grimnir was Odin, the only person in this scenario who could see or talk to her.

Two days later, the procession of Grimnir, Astrid, Aatos, Vilja, Aada, and three other adult guards made their way down through the guarded entrance in the House of Oak to the ruins concealed in the mountain. There was no light in the spiral staircase that led from the secret exit down two hundred and forty steps. Vilja counted each step, and murmured the number she was at on increments of twenty.

The ruins were largely just rubble. Without the unknown material of the upper city, the regular materials of the under city had crumbled over the ages. Yet, treasure troves had been unearthed repeatedly in the ruins. The Norn Stones had been found in the ruins, as well as a few ancient weapons. Not all of which matched Grigori designs, but variance was expected given the difference in materials and styles of what did get found.

"The south sector has been gone over the least, if that pleases you ladies?" Grimnir feigned deference to the count's children. Vilja shrugged, uncaring.

"That sounds like an excellent idea, Grimnir. Astrid and I shall take the lead, with you two, while Lord Grimnir will bring up the rear with Vilja and Aatos." Aada leaned into the role of future commander, barking orders that were quickly obeyed. Vilja and Astrid stared wordlessly at one another until Aada coughed, and both moved to follow orders. Astrid matched her gait to Aada's, and then popped on some black goggles that let her see as if she were in broad daylight.

"You've earned Night Goggles already?" Aada asked, impressed.

"Oh yeah, I got these last week. The Knight Captain was very impressed when I managed to permanently blind an Orkoraptor and lead it into a trap. We killed it!" Astrid's pride left her words echoing out into the dark ruins, and she got shushed by Grimnir.

Only Aetheria, Grimnir, and Astrid really saw the embarrassment Astrid's words triggered from Aada, who hadn't been allowed on an Orkoraptor hunt yet.

"Is there anything even alive down here?" Aetheria asked Odin. She spoke, but no one but the god could hear her anyway.

"*Aye, lass. There's many of the Grigori's creations, and more still of the dwarves', down here. Mix in mana flows that power the city above, and some ancient machines still running down here, and monsters are born on the regular.*" Odin's response came telepathically.

"What killed the Grigori, anyway?" Aetheria wished she could poke at the debris. Her Ethereal Sight pierced through all illusions, hidings, and rubble. There was so much more to this place than the humans who lived above it realized.

"*Eldra'Vexus. The Grigori chased it to this planet from the stars. Like all obsessed people on crusades, they didn't much care about the native races of the planet. They were here to exterminate what they considered evil, and they did their best to do it.*"

"Wait, what do you mean did their best?" Aetheria didn't like that phrasing.

"The Eldra'Vexus killed so many of them they couldn't even kill it, so they sealed it. Maybe they always meant to seal it, but they gnashed their teeth that they couldn't kill it."

"What is it? Why didn't you help them?"

"Help them? That damned thing killed and ate the pantheons of Zeus, Izanagi, the elves, dwarves, and many of my own people. Truthfully, only Loki, myself, and Frigg remain, and Loki is so damaged he cannot incorporate for at least another millennium."

"Damn. What . . . was/is it?" Aetheria couldn't imagine a creature so able to utterly annihilate so many gods, and then thrash a spacefaring race advanced enough to chase it across the cosmos to boot.

"A cursed swarm of scales." Odin didn't seem eager to relive the memories.

"Could it beat the demon lord?" Aetheria wondered.

"The cure would be worse than the disease," Odin answered and went silent. *"The forces of good, or even the forces in favor of humanity's survival weren't the ones that raised this continent. It gave humanity a way to escape ages ago, but why didn't those grave dangers ever follow the humans here? Because they wanted humanity on this cursed continent."* Grimnir almost sounded paranoid, but if he had lost his children, the Aesir, Vanir, and Jotun, and who knew what else, then there was no telling how stable the old god might be.

"We've got some lights over here. It seems like they're being exposed to some kind of energy flow and powering up?!" Astrid sounded amazed, and then Aatos rushed up to look. Aetheria, who could see the flows and eddies of power, watched as an orb drew strength from her proximity.

"That looks a lot like the orb in the staff of the Grigori in the stories, it does. Look, it's waking up! Oh wow, every step closer Vilja takes it glows even more!" Astrid practically jumped up and down, while Aada readied her shield in case she had to step between the orb and Vilja.

Grimnir, of course, knew it wasn't reacting to Vilja, but to Aetheria. Still, he grunted and eyed it.

"Give it to the Lady of Plenty. Have it worked into a wand or rapier, and you'll have one mighty weapon there, Vilja." Grimnir took no precautions when he picked the orb up and passed it to Vilja, which agitated Aada greatly, but his callous disregard for it being dangerous calmed the others.

"Two shadows are coming. Can you handle the rear one, Grimnir?" Astrid asked a little worriedly.

"I've got it." The tall, masked man stepped back, his gleaming spear readied. Astrid herself unsheathed two long-bladed daggers, and then concentrated. An orb of energy appeared between her daggers, shimmering between yellow like the sun, an evil black, and light blue like Aetheria didn't know what. The colors shifted quickly, about fifteen times, until it landed on the evil black.

"Aww, poop, it'll work though." Astrid dipped both her blades into the orb of energy, and the orb vanished, but now each of her daggers had an evil black aura. When a humanoid mass of shadows came straight toward the party, Astrid met it head-on, parrying its nonsensical attacks to drive the creature toward Aada. Aada slammed her large, sparkling white shield, into the shadow's face. Despite being insubstantial, the shield still stunned the creature, and Astrid quickly killed it from behind.

The shadow to the rear never even made it in range of anyone; Grimnir's spear killed it in a single blow.

"There's something glowing that way, but I'm pretty sure that's where the shadows came from, too." Astrid looked to Grimnir after they'd waited a twenty count and no more shadows swept in at the group.

"I see it, aye. Lead the way, Lady Astrid." Grimnir gave his consent to the young ladie's plan.

"Something over there is important," Vilja said quietly, while caressing the sphere she held.

Aetheria looked at the orb, at Vilja, then toward the awakening console awaiting them.

Destiny is so cool! I bet Arkaziel never even comes down to this place. He's probably just got Vilja learning how to cook or something inane.

CHAPTER 57

The Console

Shadows flitted into and out of existence in the thick rubble around equipment that powered up for the first time in, Aetheria didn't know how long. The merest trickle of the Ethereal her ghostly presence brought with her, or maybe even the trickle of Ein Sof, was enough for the Grigori's magical or technological marvels to regain function after staying dormant for so long. Four more shadows had to be dispatched before the group made it to the console, with Grimnir finishing off two, Aada and Astrid sharing a kill, and Aatos using a mechanical Raven golem for the fourth kill.

"Did you make the Raven for him, or did the Grigori actually leave constructs of your sacred birds behind?" Aetheria couldn't refrain from asking.

Odin didn't answer her. He pulled silent treatments whenever she said something he didn't like.

"Why was this gathering so many shadows? Look, there's a thinness to reality there!" Astrid exclaimed, practically jumping up and down. Aetheria could see it because she had Void Gaze and Ethereal Sight, even here. Astrid presumably saw it via either the goggles she wore or a power from her boon. No one else could visually see it, although Aetheria was sure Grimnir could, but he just pretended not to.

"It's the Grigori script. It says . . ." Vilja coughed, after wiping dust off the screen to more clearly read the ancient language. "It says, Grigori Magi-something Matrix. Subject: El-dra Vex-us Contain prow-tuh-kaal. Temporal Estimate: Seal failure in twenty cycles; life-force termination in seventeen years." Vilja, the most proficient with Ancient Grigori read the words to the rest, although she struggled with some of the rare phrases of Grigori terminology.

Grimnir looked like a man who'd seen a ghost, then seen the ghost sent to hell forever while he laughed.

"Message: Dear Esteemed Guardian of the Ethereal Realm, Critical anomalies have been detected in the containment field surrounding the Eldra'Vexus. The Ethereal seals, which have held for eons, are degrading faster than anticipated. Projections indicate total seal collapse in approximately two decades. However, the life essence of the Eldra'Vexus is expected to extinguish three years prior to the seal failure in the event of no resurgence in Eldra'Vexus energies.

"In summary.

"Seal integrity failure: weakening seals must be reinforced to prevent a possible resurgence and revival of the Eldra'Vexus hive intelligence should the shields fail earlier, or the Eldra'Vexus ingest extra life essence or sustain itself at an even lower level than previously documented.

"Life Force Monitoring: Constant monitoring of the Eldra'Vexus life essence is critical to ensure its demise as projected." Vilja paused to clear her thoughts and sip from a canteen.

"Is anyone wri—thank you, Aada. The count will have to be informed of every word of this. Not a word about the Eldra'Vexus outside of the count or countess, you all understand?" Grimnir's voice turned authoritarian, flexing his position in the military in a way he previously hadn't bothered.

"There's more. Urgent Actions required: Initiate seal reinforcement. Engagement of Ethereal amplifiers may fortify and prolong containment seals. Enhance life-force surveillance to observe fluctuations of Eldra'Vexus vitality, and initiate countermeasures to cease positive life-essence gain by Eldra'Vexus. Prepare contingency measures in the event of unforeseen resurgence of the Eldra'Vexus (see document: Soulrend Sacrificium)." Vilja had to sound out the name of the document twice before she was even slightly confident in its pronunciation.

"Note: The balance of your material realm rests upon the stability of the Eldra'Vexus containment. You must act swiftly and decisively, or your world may be found by those less benevolent than the Grigori. Transmission End." Vilja coughed again, and studied the faces of those around her.

"The screen changed. What's that statue?" Astrid asked, unreasonably close to Vilja, who just now noticed it wasn't Aada behind her and bit her lower lip, and dug nails into her palm to prevent herself from screeching. Aetheria hated to see the reactions, but she couldn't actually talk to Vilja, which made mentoring the girl difficult.

"Presumably that's the Eldra'Vexus." Vilja's voice gave no indicator she still drove her fingernails painfully into her palm to control herself. She sounded just as flat and monotone as ever.

"I'd wager you're right there, lass. Look at the thick jungle, and when it switches to the sky view, there, you can see some of the fliers that live in the heart of the continent." Grimnir praised the young girl, while he stared in much more understanding of what was on the screen than any of the youths had.

Aetheria, from multiple points of view, pieced together the Eldra'Vexus had petrified, or had a petrified exoskeleton or hide. Yet what the console showed undoubtedly looked like a three-headed winged hydra with physique more of a Komodo dragon than a fire-breathing sort. It looked fast, agile, tough as hell, and if she understood the perspectives, at least thirty stories tall. Even through the screens, the sealed monster emanated a hungry aura that made Arkaziel at his hangriest still look like a cute, cuddly kitten in comparison.

"What's this map and text say now? How'd you get so good at Grigori, Vil? Could you tutor me? It'd help my control and repair on the Grigori constructs so much." Aatos gushed with a little jealousy at the ease with which Vilja used the console. Praise made Vilja uncomfortable, though, but in this case the discomfort of praise distracted from the still too-close Astrid.

"It's descriptions of the Soulrend Sacrificium. It shows a sketch, and says that it pulses with Ethereal energy. When activated, it emits a spectral light, the air around it vibrates with terrible power, and it will kill almost any sapient intelligence using the life force of its wielder. It bypasses physical defenses and immunities, and directly attacks the soul. The damage it inflicts is an abomination against creation from which no creature has ever regenerated or resurrected. It has served as a deterrent in Grigori history to disincline purported immortals to test out the true extent of their immortality." Vilja read on, struggling here and there with a few words, but with every sentence the young girl spoke Grigori slightly more fluently.

I might have overdone the learning blessing. Aetheria hoped no one else noticed. Odin stared enraptured at the console, so much so she was sure he didn't notice.

"The weapon is not without drawbacks. The death of the user is assured and unavoidable. It is a physical weapon which requires proximity to the target before activation. Unpredictable effects have occurred when used on hive intelligences in the past. Additionally, the chance of success against the Eldra'Vexus is estimated to be less than seventy percent. The Eldra'Vexus, as a hive-avatar, is one of the most formidable entities in the known universe, possessing immense power and unknown ancient knowledge. The unpredictability of the weapon itself only increases the risk to both user and the world." Vilja trailed off.

"What's the map?" Grimnir emerged from his thoughts to ask.

"A map of the continent, it looks like. If that's Taivaslinna, then the mark is . . . Bergen." Aatos spoke up, seeing why Vilja had looked so gloomy once she interpreted the map.

"We've never found Grigori ruins in the city." Aatos shook his head.

"Maybe you just haven't looked in the right places," Astrid chimed in. "I bet Vilja could find it in no time."

"That's enough, Astrid." Aada put a hand on the rogue's shoulder and gently pulled her away from Vilja. "Father would never approve of Vilja or I leaving for Bergen, especially with the uncertainty of the refugee situation looming strong. Any noble from Taivaslinna would be at great risk of becoming a political hostage in any territory not our own."

"It's a last resort; it kills the user. I would surmise that not just anyone could use it, either. We should study this artifact and the console for further documents, but if we can use any Grigori technology left in the ruins, our options might improve beyond those listed. People have been down here for so many generations and no one's used this console before, so there has to be even more systems, tools, and other Grigori technology that could secure the Eldra'Vexus or be useful in defending Taivaslinna from the demon lord."

Vilja spoke with certainty that Aetheria envied. She'd never been that put together when she was eleven, but she also hadn't grown up in a society with magical powers as the daughter of the ruler of a city-state, and on Earth you were barely treated as an adult into your twenties, let alone at sixteen like they did in this world's culture.

"Can we copy that map?" Grimnir asked Vilja.

"Yes. It says we need a piece of carbon. I don't know what that is." Vilja shrugged.

"Look about for some black rocks, Astrid." Grimnir sent the thief to scrounge the dilapidated ruins around them. "Graphite, charcoal, coal, sometimes diamonds. The Grigori usually stored a source of carbon near their devices."

"Found it," Aada chimed in, as she sifted through a stone frame with thin diamond sheets inside, which Aada handed to Vilja. Vilja messed with the console, held up the diamond sheet, and then blasts of light embedded the map onto the sheet in a very detailed copy.

"Isn't this what Bergen looks like now? Why isn't it a map of when the Grigori lived?" Vilja asked Grimnir, who frowned and shrugged at the question he couldn't answer without violating his attempts to pass as a human.

"Did the Grigori leave satellites in this place? Or is it a magical grid of some sort?" Aetheria asked Odin.

"*I can't tell from down here. I haven't taken Sleipnir into orbit for ages, but the last time I did I saw no traces of Grigori technology. Their technology trumped our divine powers. It is possible that they cloaked them from us, or that there is a surveillance grid in place.*" Odin deflated in that moment, looking like a fragment of the Odin she had met in his beloved city of Nidhogg's Bane. They were definitely not one and the same—this shadow seemed closer to the humans here than to the divine figures Aetheria had encountered.

"Alright, Aada will carry the maps. I 'printed' two. We should report to Father immediately, this is—EEEE!" Vilja cut off and screamed when she turned around and saw a very large specter push through the disturbance in the dimensions. A large spectral scythe swung right for Grimnir's head, but he parried it with the gleaming spear.

"Quick, Aada, how do you harm a Greater Poltergeist?" Grimnir called to the young girl even as her shoulder shimmered and emitted a white glow.

"With silver, objects imbued with spiritual or holy energy, and of course, holy water." To unparalleled perceptions of Aetheria, it looked like Aada charged exceptionally fast toward the specter and slammed it with her shield. To the view of Vilja and Aatos, Aada seemed to blur and suddenly was in front of the specter, hitting it with her shield. Aetheria squealed a little at how cool the Shield Charge looked, since it was a move straight out of every type of roleplaying game and video game that involved shields, ever.

The specter did seem to solidify after being struck by the shield. Once again, Aatos's raven swooped in and pelted the enemy with sacred energy, while Astrid, who'd still been rifling through fractured storage containers, came at the back with daggers glowing blue-white. For all that the young kids' attacks dealt damage to the specter, they didn't do enough. Even when Grimnir's spear struck it, the specter seemed to remain powerful.

"Oh come on, Vilja. You're life, you're made to take death on," Aetheria cried to the young girl, who seemed to come out of shock at seeing the ghost. She threw seeds that looked familiar into the ground, and two large versions of Frigg's Tears grew where the seeds landed. Vilja quickly ran to the first, cupped her hands to receive some of the nectar from the flower, and threw it into the face of the specter from behind the melee combatants.

The water sizzled and burned the specter more terribly than any attack yet.

"Holy water?" Grimnir shouted in surprise, but stabbed his gleaming spear into the areas fully made vulnerable by the still burning water.

Next to Grimnir, Aada commanded the specter's attacks, either blocking them with her holy shield or creating sparks of light when she parried its claws with a silver longsword. Even when Vilja repeated the attack with the nectar from the second flower, it just wasn't enough, though. Vilja seemed to freeze up, uncertain of what she or any of them could do.

"It's not nice to summon a specter that could kill these kids, old man," Aetheria hissed angrily at Odin, even as he failed to pull his weight in the fight.

"*I wish, lass. This is what the Eldra'Vexus called a Hero Unit. This specter is the undead version of Hel, after the queen ate her.*" Odin seemed both sincere, and terrified of the creature. He was really not living up to her image of Odin.

CHAPTER 58

Go to Hel

Not only did these humans get a system with levels and powers, but they were in a world where they had phrases like Hero Unit. Or Odin talked about them, at least, even if none of the humans knew the least bit about them. Aetheria had to contain her jealousy a little bit, because it seemed like the kids and Odin were in a bad situation.

"Die!" the Specter of Hel commanded, as one shadowy claw lifted dramatically. Four more greater undead rose from the surrounding rubble. A Death Knight, two skeleton mages, and what Aetheria really hoped was a centaur's skeleton wielding a bone spear.

"You will not harm my companions! I am the Warden, and this is my vow." Aada, all of eleven years old, slammed the bottom of her shield down hard onto the skeletal, bony feet of one of the mages as she shouted those words. A burst of radiance spilled out from her shield in a nova of power. The undead who were hit by it caught on fire, white flames that burned at the essence of the unholy necromancy that propelled them. The allies the white energy hit were instead bolstered in speed, power, and their weapons imbued with temporary holy aspects.

Vilja already bunkered down with the two soldiers immediately behind her, so that there could be no surprises. Count Aho's orders were crystal clear; Vilja was to be protected no matter the cost.

Astrid, her weapons now double augmented, ran between the two mages, unleashing an impressive-looking combo against both mages before she slid across the ground to somersault into the safety behind Aada's shield, where she tapped her weapons together and said the magic word, *boom*. Each attack she had made with the ability active-charged her enemies into living bombs, and when she activated it, the energies detonated. Unfortunately, even the undead mages were so much more powerful than the children that only small cracks and fissures were created in the skeletal bodies, but their spells were interrupted.

Odin dueled the Death Knight, his spear emitting a holy light to match Aada's, but the skilled knight countered him repeatedly; only the incredible cutting power of

Gungnir allowed Odin to hold a small advantage. The strange centaur creature had tried to flank the party and engaged the two men guarding Vilja. Small nicks against undead like these could be lethal, but Aada's holy blessing countered the deadly powers of undeath at first. But the amount of damage the humans were dealing versus what was being dealt to them was not in their favor.

Aetheria had already blessed Vilja repeatedly, with knowledge and learning, and agriculture wouldn't help her in this combat situation. Encouraging the use of life as a weapon seemed, to some extent, wrong, but it was the best shot this group had. Aetheria touched the strand of Vilja's being, and with authority over life and renewal, gave the girl something new. It was almost like a question mark went above Vilja's head, and she tossed seeds. Impossibly quickly, five long, bushy stalks of dill pushed up from the soil of the ruins, three of which entangled the specter of Hel, one the centaur, and the last overextended to entangle both mages.

Vilja strained. Whatever she attempted to do exceeded the abilities of her internal energy, but the act of modifying and then growing the abnormal dill stalks drained her of power. Aetheria focused her will and employed purification, the Great Cycle, light, and life authorities directly through Vilja. Something about the authorities she used tickled the back of her mind, but she couldn't put her finger on what. The young woman lit up like an LED headlight, searing the retinas of everyone. When the light dissipated, the skeleton mages were being constricted to death, vastly weakened, and the centaur creature had disintegrated. Odin took the opportunity to kill the Death Knight with a flare of divine power, and the cursed shadow of Hel had changed.

"*You restored Hel?*" Odin asked in shock.

Indeed, the figure before the group was not even a specter anymore. On the right side of her body, she was a beautiful living woman, with dark hair, gray eyes, and attractive features. *I always did like the goth look*, Aetheria mused. Of course, the other half of her body was that of a corpse, or draugr. Withered, desiccated skin, thin hair, long yellowed fingernails. Not at all attractive, unless someone had very particular ideas about beauty. What Hel lacked in attractiveness she made up for with a grim, solemn aura of authority. Underworlds were typically bleak, awful domains, and their nature was reflected in the aura of their masters.

Aetheria did her best to hide her presence from the reborn god, who looked to Odin and the humans, and seemed to relive some kind of memories. Clearly, she spoke telepathically with Odin while the silence stretched out and the soldiers, children, and even Odin shifted uncomfortably. Finally, after minutes of everyone wondering if they had been saved only to die at the hands of a goddess, Hel spoke.

"You have my blessing, child." Hel reached out her skeletal hand, and a dark bolt of power shot to the orb Vilja still held, imbuing it with additional power besides what it had absorbed from Aetheria's direct actions earlier.

Then the bones of her fallen soldiers formed a doorway, and she stepped through it to Hel. The bones collapsed into dust behind her.

"Wow." Astrid gaped at the departing figure.

"That must be a mighty powerful orb you hold there, lass. Surely it was a relic left behind by Azarel or Valdor themselves." Grimnir shifted the focus toward the orb, rather than Vilja, but he was the only one present who knew what really happened.

"It would make sense, and the Grigori heroes were said to be masters of life and death." The orb now swirled and churned with the powers of life, death, and decay and had attuned completely to Vilja, whom the orb seemed to register as the source of Aetheria's intervention.

"We'd best get back to the palace. No one is in shape for another fight." Aada took charge of the group, with Grimnir giving her a nod, approving of her wise choice.

"Oh man, I can't wait to tell people about how amazing this was!" Astrid practically jumped up and down.

"I can't believe we lived." Aatos seemed shocked they all survived an encounter with such powerful undead, and with the Goddess of Death herself.

"State secrets, Lady Solarshadowblade. Unless the count gives his permission, this won't be going beyond the count and countess themselves," Grimnir warned everyone.

"Fall in," Aada commanded. "Astrid, you're in the lead with me. Aatos, Grimnir, please guard the rear, and you two guard Vilja." Aada got the whole group moving toward the surface once more. They still had to get back to the stairs, and then climb all two hundred of the despicable steps that were slightly larger than those built by humans, to get to the surface.

Eventually, the party made it back to the Oak Palace. The debriefing room near the secret stairs was a room that prioritized function over form. The chairs were basic hard wood. The tables, plain. The only refreshment was a pitcher of water. The objects in the debriefing room had been destroyed many times in the past by objects brought up from the ruins, so nothing of value was kept in the room. There were also guards outside the door, in case anyone inside the room suddenly acted out of character. Possession had rarely occurred, but it was always a problem when it did. Vilja, like Aada and Grimnir, knew the water in the pitcher was laced with holy water. It was why each of the three already drank, and encouraged the others to do so as well.

One of the bodyguards assigned to Vilja passed out violently when he drank, and they had to hold him down and force more into his mouth, until he stopped convulsing and spewed dark ichor from his mouth.

"Why couldn't I see his possession?" Astrid asked Grimnir, as she tapped the goggles she wore.

"Possession is hard to see, lass. No doubt the spirit snuck in while we fought, and embedded itself deep in his flesh to avoid being found. Those goggles aren't all powerful, or absolute. They merely give you a better chance at seeing these things." Grimnir's warning of over-reliance seemed to go right over Astrid's head, but before he could belabor the point the door opened, and Aho and Kaarina stepped in.

"Alive still?" Kaarina asked immediately upon seeing the soldier on the ground, and the traces of dark ichor left upon his lips.

"Yes. He'll recover, only a second application of holy water was needed to destroy the spirit, a weak spirit, all things considered," Grimnir said.

"Are you girls alright? What happened down there?" Aho demanded, as he dropped to his knees to hug Vilja and Aada to him.

"We found some very important information, Father, and Vilja found a relic we think belonged to Azarel or Valdor themselves."

"Orb," Vilja said the single word, as she held up the apple-sized sphere. It held the appearance of a crystal ball, nearly, with faceted reliefs inside its structure, and the churning power it had absorbed from Aetheria and Hel giving it the aura of a grand and mysterious artifact. The way the powers within flowed and ebbed toward Vilja couldn't be ignored, as the orb had obviously bound to the girl.

"Well, what do you want to do with it?" Aho asked.

"I suggested a rapier or wand, since Lady Vilja has become adept at both," Grimnir interjected.

"The quartermaster told me about a style of sword similar to the rapier. A Schiavona, he called it. But it could thrust and cut, and sacrificed only a little extra weight. I would like that." Vilja had her own opinion of what she wanted, now that her strength and height were not as limited as when she had been an eight-year-old.

"We'll have the blacksmith work up a few prototypes. Once the orb is merged into a weapon it cannot be undone. So we will find a weapon you like first, and make it with the future in mind," Kaarina declared. "What is this important information you found?"

"We encountered a console in the ruins that activated upon our approach. Shadows and specters were coming through a breach, too. A terrible specter summoned a Death Knight and skeletons, and we held them off until Vilja's orb glowed super bright and vaporized them, and then there was Hel, who thanked us and left through a doorway of bones." Astrid leaped into the retelling, but her desire to talk made her speak quickly and summarize everything to almost uselessness.

"It seems the realm of the dead's master has returned." Grimnir spoke in the lull of silence after Astrid's outburst. "But far more troubling was the information upon the console. The ancient enemy of the Grigori is still alive, and the seals on it weaken. There also is a Grigori ruin below Bergen they aren't aware of. I'll have my spies begin searching immediately, if you wish."

The count looked to his wife before he nodded.

"Find it. If we can get there first and pluck whatever weapons the Grigori stored to fend off the Eldra'Vexus we might live long enough to worry about the demon lord." Aho's voice held a bitter, cynical tone that was rare for the usually upbeat man. Aetheria felt bad for him, but he seemed to handle the news well, that the demon lord conquering the continent wasn't even the biggest existential threat facing his city.

Or, perhaps, the House of Oak had already known the Eldra'Vexus would be a threat again someday? What had the other consoles they'd found previously said?

"Now, I want each of you young heroes to use the Norn Stones to see if you made any new gains." Kaarina set two of the Norn Stones upon the table.

CHAPTER 59

Heaven's Requiem

All day long, the twins had been forced to suffer through the pageantry and press of the celebrations of their sixteenth birthday. The press of the nobility and powerful of Taivaslinna had taken up their morning, which Vilja had been found to be the most offensive. Riding through the streets of Taivaslinna in a carriage with her family, stopping every block to speak with and hand out treats to any who approached, had been a much more enjoyable experience, but it had taken up the afternoon. Now, the girls had only a scant two hours before the banquet would start, and the girls both lay on Vilja's bed half asleep when the count and countess entered the room.

"Kaisa said you two were trying to catch a nap. Now isn't the time, I'm afraid. We've got your presents!" Aho's enthusiasm stirred the girls from the bed, and both twins' eyes went wide at what their parents held.

Kaarina held a sword with a basket hilt, thicker and stronger than a rapier, with an incredibly gorgeous blade that seemed to eddy between bright and dark. Aetheria thought it rather looked like Damascus steel, but the similarity was superficial at best. The elaborate handguard made the entire sword a thing of beauty, and Vilja threw herself toward her mother to grasp it.

"Wow, it's beautiful." When Vilja touched the hilt, the whole sword emitted a dim glow in acknowledgment of its chosen wielder.

"Master Forgeheart forged it himself, and said the blade told him its name is Heaven's Requiem." Kaarina seemed reluctant to be parted from the beautiful weapon, and displayed a mixture of pride and envy of her daughter for acquiring such a seemingly legendary weapon.

"May I?" Vilja asked Kaarina, and when she got permission, Vilja swung the sword through the air and made a few practice thrusts with it. The powerful magic of the blade seemed to cut the air itself in a way no sword she'd previously held did. Vilja, unlike Aetheria, couldn't see that the blade provided mild boosts to strength and agility, giving the girl a tiny taste of what those with soldier boons always felt.

"Absolutely beautiful. That's awesome, Vil!" Aada squealed and hugged Vilja from behind.

Aho coughed, drawing attention back to him and the kite shield he held.

"Master Forgeheart made an accompanying piece. Allow me to present the holy shield Eir's Mercy." Aho grinned as Aada's eyes lit up. The family crest of the House of Oak filled the front of the kite shield in golden heraldry. A solitary oak leaf floated on an unseen breeze, while the rest of the shield was a beautiful white.

"Oh wow. It's so sturdy!" Aada's happiness surged when she took the shield from her father, who struggled to contend with its weight while Aada herself moved it around as if it weighed no more than a twig.

"Master Forgeheart said it should never break, so no more blaming this shield for any mistakes, right?" Aho grinned and ruffled Aada's dark hair.

"And now that you're properly equipped, you'll be accompanying us to the ruins in a few days' time. I wish to see the new discoveries your squad has found. Grimnir brags your retainers up a lot, you know."

"You're making Astrid our retainer?" Aada's query struck Aho as slightly panicked, but neither of his girls showed any outward signs of disagreement with the idea.

"Yes, Astrid, Aatos, and the scout and warrior Grimnir moved from the first expeditionary squad. Valterri and Otso. All four are officially being assigned as your retainers as of today. They've been petitioning for it for weeks, years in some cases, and your mother and I are tired of denying them. You've inspired their loyalty to such an extent that it is only proper to reward it. Unrewarded loyalty can turn to disloyalty all too swiftly."

"Besides," Kaarina interjected, "you are both adults now. It's only fitting you have retainers."

"I don't feel like an adult," Vilja said under a cough, but Kaarina didn't chide her as Vilja expected. Instead, her mother smiled at her. It was a strange expression that neither Aetheria nor Vilja quite understood.

The next day, messengers brought word of two important notes. Grimnir's spies, with the in-depth knowledge of Bergen provided by Aatos, had finally found the ruins of the Grigori beneath the city. The bad news was that all of the traps and defenses of the ruins seemed to be intact, and it would take a significant investment of forces, or a skilled strike force, to make it into the ruins and obtain the lost Grigorian technology needed as a fail-safe against the Eldra'Vexus. Grimnir assembled a team of his best men and sent them to deal with the ruins.

The other messenger brought news of the inevitable but final fall of Montagren. The city-state had held out far longer than expected, thanks to their evacuation of most of the civilians to other lands. The soldiers held the siege for years until finally their provisions ran out, and the demon lord's army marched into Montagren uncontested.

Then, a few days after their parents had informed them of it, they were summoned to the secret entrance to the ruins, along with their retainers, Grimnir, their parents, and three other soldiers who were Aho and Kaarina's personal bodyguards. The sun had barely crossed into the sky on this particular Odinsdagr before the procession made it down all two hundred stairs to the ruins beneath. The last expedition the twins had made down there had uncovered a partial building with three consoles inside, but they had not fully powered up before the scheduled time to return had passed. The count hoped to be able to activate them today.

Bioluminescent plants grew along makeshift paths. Not only did the plants provide lighting and paths to follow if you knew the color-coordinated routes Vilja had laid out, they also provided a source of food for a snack while walking. The count and countess were above picking berries in ruins, but Astrid, Aatos, Valterri, and Otso seemed to have no compunctions about eating from the plants Vilja grew.

"The ruins have come a long way since you first came down here. I'm proud of you girls." Aho praised them, fully sincere. No more were the ruins around the entry dark, creepy, and unlit. They were relatively bright, they had been sorted, and with the steady elimination of threats, more squads and researchers had been dispatched to further the search for Grigori technology and knowledge.

"Thank you, Father." Aada beamed with pride, while Vilja's resting bitch face scared the low-level spirits away from the party as they walked along paths edged in light-producing flowers.

After nearly a half hour of walking, they were on a path lined with glowing red plants, and the partial structure finally appeared. Once it might have had two stories, but now it only had one, and a lot of rubble. The consoles inside had a dim glow that increased in intensity as the party moved closer.

"Astrid, sweep the area. Valterri, take the overhead canopy position and deal with any strays that come our way. Otso, you're on door watch, sorry." Aada snapped commands, and their squad jumped to it. Only Astrid seemed annoyed, once she finished sweeping the building and had to sweep the exterior.

"We've never encountered these particular types of consoles before. Any ideas, darling?" Kaarina studied the Grigori technology with caution and curiosity.

"Hmm. I have an idea. We'll have to see what it offers us access to. The first Count of Oak described something similar, but the location was lost during the rule of the fifth count, and never reclaimed. What sort of enemies were in this area?" Aho asked while the screens grew brighter. In moments they would switch on in truth.

"Ants," Vilja said with distaste. Insects, while useful, were not her favorite.

"Ants?" Kaarina asked, her face scrunched up as she imagined regular-sized ants.

"Very large ones, the size of horses, Mother," Aada clarified.

"Was there an ant leader?" Aho wanted to know, while he impatiently waited for the consoles to turn on.

Aetheria wondered why no one questioned why the systems activated due to Vilja's proximity, but maybe they did, and she just couldn't eavesdrop on those conversations because she was tied strictly to Vilja?

"Yes, but it didn't leave a carcass when we exterminated it." Aada shrugged.

"It was bound to this area by a curse. Killing it broke the curse, and the link to what sustained it. I believe it was one of the apex predators captured by the Eldra'Vexus in legends," Vilja quietly added.

"Lady Vilja's blade seems to sever the connection between the lost minions and the Eldra'Vexus. Her participation in reclaiming the ruins has been beyond helpful, with many of the enemies we clear out not returning a week, month, or year later as the case had previously been." Grimnir shrugged.

Aetheria, however, wondered if it was just Vilja's presence and weapon, or if the return of Hel to her throne had something to do with the equation. Did Hel now vacuum up the souls of the dead, monsters included, and it just hadn't been being done before? What happened when all the Gods of Death died?

"Is it Vilja or Hel?" Aetheria asked Odin.

No answer came.

"The screen is on, Vil." Astrid pointed out when she walked back into the building. "Area's all clear, boss," she told Aada.

"Hmm." Vilja cleared her throat, coughed, and drank some water. "System Alerts. Azazel's Vigil has been successfully repaired, and is now fully operational. Tamiel's Redoubt remains offline and requires service. Please conduct maintenance as soon as possible. Until Tamiel's Redoubt is online, successful defense against Eldra'Vexus invasion remains less than one percent probable."

Once Vilja cleared the alerts, each of the three consoles displayed different information. The first screen, with a red exterior glow, contained information about Azazel's Vigil.

"Azazel's Vigil seems to be long-ranged weaponry deployed from the city's four cardinal towers. No wonder we've never been able to get inside of them. The first count initiated a repair sequence, and the system never came back online in his lifetime." Aho studied the data, but none of them had any clue what they were actually reading about. Aetheria, on the other hand, recognized missile launchers, chain guns, and turrets when she saw them. If the unbreakable walls of Taivaslinna had that kind of weaponry, the city might be able to hold out against enemies for nearly ever.

"Here's a list of the materials required to repair Tamiel's Redoubt. Nothing too exotic: stone, gemstones, and gold. We might have all of this, or be able to get it in less than a year," Vilja estimated, although Countess Kaarina laughed.

"A hundred pounds of raw gold? That's a lot. We'd have to melt some currency."

"We do have an awful lot of old currency of fallen free cities in the treasury. Grigori technology is surely worth more than coins being reminted," Aho disagreed.

"Is that the Eldra'Vexus?" A familiar feed ran on the third console.

"Yes." Vilja nodded. "The Eldra'Vexus somehow extended its life again. It is now slated to expire after the seal fails." This was not news to Vilja or Aada, or the count and countess, nor probably to Grimnir. The others, however, had not been kept abreast on the continued information gained from the first console the group had discovered years ago.

"What does this diagram show, darling?" Kaarina asked Vilja, peering over her daughter's shoulder.

"Proximity detection of strong inhabitants of the heart of the continent. These red dots are creatures at level sixty, and the orange are in the fifties." Silence ruled after Vilja spoke.

"Over level sixty? But the maximum is level thirty-three?!" Astrid practically bit her tongue off.

"For humans. The Eldra'Vexus is this blue here. Level ninety-nine."

No one spoke for a time after that bombshell.

CHAPTER 60

Don't Split the Party!

Vilja and Aada celebrated their twentieth birthday quietly, with their parents and tutor, Kaisa, who was essentially treated as a member of the House of Oak at this point. With their squadron of elite soldiers they had not only managed to repair Tamiel's Redoubt, but also discovered a cache of high quality materials with which to create new equipment for the elite forces of Taivaslinna. Grimnir's secret agents had managed to clear the first level of the ruins under Bergen, and were aghast to learn that there were greater depths to go.

Vilja broke the comfortable silence in the room after Kaisa had retired. "How do you plan to handle the Bergen ruins, Father?"

"Do you have a proposal?" Kaarina asked in a delighted tone.

"Yes. Send Aatos, Valterri, and Astrid. Reinforce them with one or two of Grimnir's best soldiers. Those three can handle any surprises that might arise, especially now that Aatos reforged the Thunder Palace orbs. If they cannot acquire the tool beneath Bergen, we should consider it a lost cause."

"Won't that slow your progress in the ruins?" Aho countered.

"No. Aada and Otso have learned to work together very well. With the addition of me, we are more than capable of finishing the exploration of the ruins. A traditional scout and a priest would be more helpful to the last area than the others would be."

"Both Astrid and Valterri are incredibly skilled scouts, Vilja." Aho held up a hand.

"They are. But the scout is the least important of our team at this juncture. Very little of the ruins remain unexplored. One of the expeditionary forces would be adequate." Vilja shrugged. "Additionally, Astrid is an offensive powerhouse; her addition to the Bergen team will let them take down strong foes much more quickly than any other addition, unless you are willing to let me go to Bergen? No? I thought not. Then it must be Astrid, and Valterri is the best complement to her, and Aatos stands in the middle, able to control a battlefield while alternating between offense and defense."

"The Council of Bergen suspect their city is being infiltrated by the demon lord. We are uncertain if this is a misidentification by our agents in the city, or if Lucien is finally on the move again. If we don't send a team who can succeed, especially before the fall of Bergen, we may be the last free humans in this world." Aho's tone held defeat.

"So it's settled, then?" Aada asked.

"Yes. Grimnir will brief them, and they shall be dispatched swiftly. Without this Grigori weapon we may never defeat the Eldra'Vexus. The watchers have informed me the seal is now expected to fail in five years, while the creature's vitality has continued to increase."

"And have you found a working method to defeat or bypass the tyrant lizards of the forbidden lands?" Kaarina smiled at her rhetorical question. Aetheria had learned over the years that the girls' mother loved rhetorical questions when she knew the answers and Aho did not. It was a guilty pleasure for the blonde assassin, one she savored.

"Yes. Vilja tested the new poison from her tenth-generation castor bean plants. When she stays within range and cultivates them, something about Heaven's Requiem makes the poison even more potent. Initial tests showed a single application was powerful enough to take down a stegosaurus. When the poison left her proximity, or was stored for some time, it was enough to make the lizards sick and drive them away, but not kill them," Aada reported almost verbatim from the report she had written for her mother.

"It is the blessing of Hel upon Heaven's Requiem. Magics channeled through it by me seem capable of ignoring the vast difference in strength between me and my opponents, but that effect does not seem to linger outside of my personage. Sorry, Father." Vilja did not sound sorry to Aetheria, but her complicated emotions defied Aetheria's attempts to unknot the tangled web in Vilja's heart.

"You're both very special girls. Maybe you were sent to us by Odin, to save us from the demon lord and the Eldra'Vexus. Fate certainly seems to be conspiring to make it that way. I will curse the Fates for setting up such tribulations, but I will not stand in your way from doing what you must. I will try to ensure you will succeed when the time comes, though." Aho's words, and the look in his eyes, said he hated that the children would end up dealing with this, when it was his duty as a parent and count to do so. He had failed at his job as the leader of the House of Oak.

"Thank you, Father," Aada and Vilja echoed each other, with a sincerity that partially soothed the heart of their father.

Aetheria had grown fairly complacent in her participation in Vilja's life. The girl had, for the most part, learned to stand on her own two feet. Rarely did she get into a situation that required Aetheria to intervene, and instead she had just settled back and enjoyed the relationships between the House of Oak members. In that time, she had started to understand a little of what the mysterious smiles of Countess Kaarina meant, as she started to view the twins as little nieces. Maybe her lax involvement in the trial was a bad thing. Maybe her growing connection to the twins and their retainers was a bad thing, but Aetheria didn't really give a damn.

There was no reason for them, or all the people of their city, to suffer. So Aetheria nudged things here and there. The crops, already maintained by Vilja's growth powers, were a little better than even what the Lady of Plenty normally provided. The weather remained mild and pleasant, which people falsely attributed to Count Aho's control of the Oak Throne. The blessing of purification upon Oak Palace extended to the main gates, revealing demons and the possessed before they could even enter the city. She wouldn't admit to sending out a few curses empowered with her authority of war to slow down the marauding armies of the demon lord, but she had done so. The more powerful Vilja grew, the more Aetheria could alter her world.

So she did, or at least she tried to. Without a name, faction, thing, or idea to tie a curse or blessing to, she needed visual lines to affect reality. So, despite a desire to help all of the humans of this awful shithole of a world, she was largely limited to Taivaslinna, since Vilja only left the city once every few months on a short excursion with the expeditionary forces into the forbidden lands behind the Gate of Heaven. Those excursions were something of a fun experience for Aetheria, since the forbidden lands were full of dinosaurs. The ability to see them in something approximate to their natural habitats was amazing. It took a turn from being a great check on her list of things to do in life when she saw how dangerous the dinosaurs were, and how vastly outpowered the humans were against the higher level dinosaurs.

Cute and big and awesome turned scary quickly. If Aetheria had her body she could have tamed the dinosaurs, or forced them into submission through brute strength, but she could only impart minor miracles and blessings, or decree fate if she focused very hard, but she tried to avoid that since Moros always exacted a terrible price in every other trial when she did it. Maybe she had already intervened too much, but she wanted these people to come out of things well.

"Oh, I unlocked my ultimate skill today." Vilja drew all eyes toward her with that admission. Even Aada looked surprised that Vilja had achieved something and not told her. But the admission, Aetheria knew, stemmed from Vilja's panic at the awkward silence that had hung in the air after their father's strained admissions.

"You're already level thirty-one?" Kaarina gaped at Vilja.

"How'd you get a whole level ahead of me? No fair," Aada pouted, but in a fake way before she broke into smiles at Vilja. "Well, don't keep me waiting, what'd you get, with your super mysterious boon even the Grigori knew nothing about."

"Good job," Aho said before he pulled Vilja into a hug, and she had to struggle out of his arms before she could tell them what she had unlocked.

"It is called Verdant Union. I can connect to the earth and ecosystem and merge our strengths, and use localized power to supplement my own for a few effects. I am certain it makes me look like a dryad or nymph." The last sentence marked one of the rare occasions where Vilja smiled unintentionally. The thought of being a dryad or magical creature struck a childish wonder within Vilja, who had never quite felt like she belonged with other humans anyway. The emotion, and reason for it, made Aetheria want to hug the girl, but she couldn't.

"I believe this power will be very useful to aid in reaching the heart of the continent, if our team can acquire the Grigori artifact."

The next morning the retainers Aatos, Astrid, and Valterri were shipped off to Bergen with merchants. In the best of times it would take a month for merchants to get to Bergen, if they stopped at each of the villages along the way, but the plan was to only stop when they needed to have safe harbor at night. Time was not on their side with the seals and the awakening of the Eldra'Vexus, nor with the emergence of the demon lord's spies and troops.

Aatos dyed his hair and would wear makeup to hide his identity from his biological family while he was in Bergen, and the other two were masters of stealth. Vilja and Aada each blew a kiss after the departing group for good luck, which seemed to unnaturally raise the spirit of the departing crew. Once they had vanished from the primary gates of Taivaslinna, the two ladies set about to work with the crafters, expedition forces, and to train themselves. Aada had a fire lit under herself to catch up to Vilja, but Aada's gains had come slower than Vilja's for a while now.

Vilja continued to refine the poisons of the castor plant, day after day, in attempts to create a poison that would be usable by the soldiers of Taivaslinna to thwart monsters, demons, and maybe even the Eldra'Vexus. Aetheria was legitimately amazed at the process Vilja used. She would quick-grow seeds. Modify the plant, then mature it into producing seeds, and repeat. And she would do that, again and again, until she ran out of energy, then start all over again when she recovered. The absolute dedication to her projects astounded Aetheria, and it wasn't just the poison.

Vilja also bred vines with thorns. Between Grow, Modify, Control, and her ultimate ability to form a symbiosis with the environment, Vilja could accomplish some impressive feats with the plants she bred, and she kept working on them. Despite all factors indicating the break points for returns had been exceeded after the thirtieth try, she kept going. It made Aetheria feel somewhat guilty, in fact. The much, much younger Vilja had far more dedication and detailed control over her abilities than Aetheria herself did, but Vilja also had much more simple and ingrained abilities.

Or so that's what Aetheria told herself. The truth was, Aetheria had overwhelming power to such an extent she had never needed to learn the tiny details of her abilities. Every third or fourth tier Cultivator should know how to perform the esoteric basics of their path, so Aetheria's ability to create conceptual ice or frost fire didn't make for any great accomplishment. So, Aetheria vowed to learn a little from Vilja and rededicate herself to mastery of her own abilities. In pursuit of this new goal, she experimented with authority and increased Vilja's blessing count with renewal, so that she could experiment more.

Strangely, Vilja seemed extra moody that night, despite all of the extra time she got to spend iterating upon plants. *Does she hate doing the boring stuff, too? Oh gosh, I hope I didn't screw up.*

CHAPTER 61

Blackjack!

Despite Aetheria's concerns, Vilja adapted to the extra productivity with renewed vigor, although some days even the young woman stopped when she would have previously, seemingly satisfied with a day's work. No matter how much Aetheria tried to poke through Vilja's head, the girl's emotions remained difficult to read. Only a few days after linking to Bobbi, Aetheria had been able to adequately identify the StarMane's emotions and easily make use of telepathic and empathic bonds. With Kallos, the two approached unity when they touched.

Perhaps Aetheria just expected too much out of the scenario, or maybe Moros punished her approach to this entire trial? Doubtless, Bobbi and Arkaziel, at the least, took direct control of Vilja, and maybe Kallos, too. The Nephilim put the higher good above smaller morality problems, and since she was only half human herself, maybe that let Kallos distance herself from any disturbing questions that arose from controlling another's body? At the end of the day, Moros set the challenge, and they had to do it.

The days ticked by, and Aada's diligence to training was every bit as profoundly over-the-top as Vilja's. When, two months before their twenty-first birthdays a missive arrived from Bergen, the twins both transformed into training demons. The group had found the artifact. It wasn't quite what the Grigori left, but they were en route. Aatos had been lost within the tower. Aada and Vilja had moped for days in Vilja's room, until Kaarina swept into the room.

Aetheria expected Kaarina to be mad, to tell the girls off, or put them in their place for mourning the young boy that Aada's bravery had saved from a terrible life with an abusive father, but instead Kaarina cried with the girls and held them until they were done crying. Then she talked to the girls about Aatos, and they remembered the fond times, and how he'd always tried to sneak his extra desserts to Aada, once he learned Vilja didn't really care about extra dessert and rarely even ate all of hers.

"How did a messenger beat them back?" Vilja asked when her voice no longer quavered.

"The raven Eidolon returned to Grimnir. Apparently Aatos gave minor access to Valterri, who relayed the message and sent it to Grimnir." Kaarina grimaced.

"So, this happened today, then?" Aada sniffed and rubbed at her eyes to ensure no moisture remained.

"Recently. Grimnir couldn't get confirmation of which day it happened from the Eidolon. Whatever Aatos did, or whatever enemy they ran into in the ruins, it caused some memory issues with the raven."

"That means they won't be here for at least a month more, possibly two." Vilja looked out the window of her room, into the darkness beyond.

"Yes. Are you still going to demand to be the team that passes through the Gates of Heaven with this Grigori weapon?" Kaarina asked, but she didn't seem to savor asking her daughters rhetorical questions without their father present, for she had no smile on her face this time.

"We will, or Aatos's death will have been in vain. Aada and I are the strongest fighters in Taivaslinna, and for whatever reason, the Grigori technology seems to work best for me." Vilja nodded, no question or hesitation in her answer.

"If we can't do it, the demon king won't matter. It'll turn into an apocalypse between the demon king and the Eldra'Vexus, and if anyone survives that, they'll be ruled or assimilated by the winner. That's not a life worth living." Aada shook her head.

"I'm very proud of you two girls. I'll be joining your training sessions until your retainers arrive. You've learned to fight like soldiers, and adventurers. Now it's time to learn the art of a killer." Kaarina, the usually sarcastic, sassy, or humorous mother, looked terrifying when she turned her thoughts to murder.

Day after day, Kaarina pushed her daughters harder than either had ever been pushed by a trainer, but it matched the intensity with which the twins drove themselves, and so was not the shocking torture Kaarina may have made it out to be. For every trick and revelation Kaarina's training taught the girls, Kaarina learned more about the truth of her girls. How Vilja refused to make the same mistake twice. She would repeat every test until she could beat it, and when her solutions didn't work, she just tried again.

What Vilja possessed in versatility in combat, a dervish of the artifact-level sword in one hand and wand in the other, Aada made up for with a defense that couldn't be beat. Aada's shield was a shield, her sword was a shield, and her magic was a shield. The Warden boon gave Aada defenses and physical capabilities that exceeded even Kaarina's extremely rare Jormungand's Venom boon. Where the mother exceeded in speed, Aada exceeded in durability, endurance, and implacability. Even Kaarina's poison abilities, disregarding her ultimate power, which she wouldn't use on her daughter, couldn't pierce the protective qualities of Aada.

Aetheria would have likened Aada to a paladin. She had holy abilities of a few varieties, defenses against nearly everything, and glowed a lot. The flashy moves and holy auras screamed for enemies to look upon her, to be drawn in, and then never escape from her. Aada was inexorable and unyielding. Every day the two twins teamed up against their mother, and every day they grew slightly better. After a month they invited Otso to join them, and improve his coordination with the twins. Sometimes he worked with Kaarina, and sometimes he joined the girls against their mother.

Vilja didn't cease her obsession with overpreparation, either. She cultivated multiple types of magical plants that she then worked with alchemists to turn into potions. When her parents learned of this, Kaarina gave Vilja a duplicate of the ring she herself wore. It allowed for the storage of alchemical supplies, potions, vials, grenades, poisons, needles, all at the beck and call of a minute energy expenditure, with no chance of the items breaking while stored. Spatial magic was complicated, and those with the appropriate boons only came along once, maybe twice a generation across all of humanity, so any enchantments like this were worth a fortune, and would become treasured family heirlooms for even the richest of families.

That both rings were identical in appearance seemed beyond coincidental.

Three weeks after the raven came, Aho received communications from Bergen. The lords of Bergen had received a declaration of war from the demon lord, and had been given the option to surrender peacefully and become warrior slaves to be sent as chaff against Taivaslinna, fight and die, or be starved to death in a siege. They begged for a visit from the Lady of Plenty to shore up their food supplies and make a siege impossible, or for even more wagons of food than what Aho had already redirected to them for preparations of the siege. They also begged for any and all help.

"What can we do for them?" Aho asked his wife and daughters, but it was Grimnir who answered, which startled the count, who had forgotten he was present.

"Nothing," Grimnir said flatly. "All of the tools of the Grigori are unmovable and secured to the Holy Fortress itself. We have sent them all the food we could spare on trains for years. Perhaps they should have done as you suggested and conscripted more supply wagons before that damned Lamentosa made his move."

"We might be able to sneak them some of our recent alchemical munitions?" Vilja tried to offer something tangible to Aho's conscience.

"We offer them salvation. After we dispatch the Eldra'Vexus, we shall dispatch Lucien Lamentosa, as well," Aada said with the sincerity of a vow.

"Yes, the Eldra'Vexus is more pressing."

"Astrid and Valterri should be back soon. Can we not leak the knowledge of the ruins to the Council of Bergen that they might use the ruins as a shelter?"

"The raven Eidolon is still functional enough that I could deliver a message to the council with it, if that is your desire." Grimnir nodded at Vilja's suggestion, and the hopeful look in the count's eyes.

"Do it. I don't know what was all down there, but it might help them against Lamentosa." Count Aho gave the order, and Grimnir departed.

Two days before the girls' twenty-first birthday, a tamer from the furthest watchtower sent an eagle with a message that Astrid and Valterri had crossed into the territory of

Taivaslinna and were en route to the city. A collective sigh ran through Aetheria and Vilja at the safe return.

The evening before the girls' twenty-first birthday, with the duo expected to return to the city on the morrow, Aetheria found herself in another staff meeting with Odin.

"This is my last night here, Odin. On the morrow it'll be up to you to watch over these girls. I've done everything I can to help them reach their potential."

"*You've done more than I thought any spirit could. What are you, lass?*" Odin finally asked, rueful and displeased that he was forced to ask.

"Who knows? I'm from a higher dimension, close to the lowest heavens."

"*And all those authorities? You've more than any god I've seen in this blighted world.*"

"It doesn't matter. I'll be gone. It's all on you, Hel, and Frigg, from now on. If there's anything you want to ask me to do before the end, now's the time."

Odin looked thoughtful, or perhaps he sought inner wisdom, or maybe he looked to the future. Whatever he saw, he opted to make only one request.

"*Give the lass a protection if you can, a second life. Without such a blessing, she will reside in Valhalla soon.*"

"Done," Aetheria said as she plucked multiple authorities. Life, renewal, the Great Cycle, war, and death were all bent to bless Vilja with what Aetheria hoped was a get-out-of-jail-free card. In the back of her mind, Aetheria noticed the disconnect between using the Great Cycle even though she didn't possess it presently. Would she obtain time soon, or had she broken authority?

"*Travel well, lass. I had hoped you would be the secret weapon against the Eldra'Vexus.*" Odin waved. While they talked, the meeting had come to an end, and Vilja dragged Aetheria away from Grimnir and the others. Aetheria sat in the girls' room all night, trying to hug or support her.

"It's been an honor to watch you grow up, kiddo. I hope you do good." Aetheria said her goodbyes, and when the stars roughly aligned at midnight, Vilja hugged herself.

"I can almost hear you. Almost. Don't leave me?" Vilja begged the invisible presence. No answer came, and a raven cawed its welcome to the hour of midnight, and Aetheria was gone. Yet a multitude of blessings and boons warmed the cold left by Aetheria's absence within Vilja's heart. It was not the same, no, but it was something.

CHAPTER 62

Kami-no-Yasumi

The infinite flows of power combined with a physical form once more under her command were the dead giveaways that Aetheria once more had control of her body. Bobbi, Arkaziel, and Kallos seemed to be enjoying the return to their bodies as much she was. Each flexed their fingers, stretched their hands, and even tested out their magic to ensure everything was as it should be.

"I didn't expect all four of you to manage to keep Vilja alive to twenty-one years old. Certainly, I anticipated Arkaziel would, at the least, get her killed."

Arkaziel, happy to be a cat again, curled up on Aetheria's lap.

"Oh, it came close quite a few times. Humans are so frail. It was quite the hassle." Arkaziel laughed, and Bobbi agreed with him. Even Kallos nodded. Aetheria frowned at the other three.

"You all succeeded, though, and that's four timelines with Doom sown. Now, one of you did the unexpected. Aetheria didn't take direct control of Vilja, and instead only influenced the child the entire time. Why don't each of you give a brief summary of the situation in which you left your Vilja."

"So, taking from my idea with the country challenge, I focused on producing alchemical resources. When Astrid left for Bergen, I had produced enough alchemical weapons to commit a whole lot of war crimes. The whole demons-aren't-people spiel really landed when it came to using weapons of mass destruction. I'm a little sad I didn't get a chance to see any of the munitions go off." Arkaziel pouted.

"I realized she could give herself a fire affinity through growing the right kind of plants. By the time Vil and Aada were trying to tame a raptor matriarch, I had her trained up as a proper fire mage, and with all those delicious magical plants at hand, she could burn through the level difference between her and the dinosaurs. Still, what kind of asshole puts a bunch of level thirties up against level forties and fifties?" Bobbi shook her head.

"I attempted to follow the instincts of the girl and tempered her emotions with calmness. By training diligently she learned tactical skills with her sister, and employed a compounding hex to overcome the level differential between humans and their enemies. The demon lord died outside of Bergen; Aada finished him off when the compounding curse rendered the demon into little more than ground meat." Kallos smiled happily, quite proud of herself.

"Wait, you killed the demon lord? Overachiever!" Arkaziel seemed uncertain whether he should be jealous or if Kallos had simply wasted effort.

"I followed her around, and tried to help her achieve her goals on her own." Aetheria shrugged. "So, she became a badass duelist, got very talented with her plant control, and formed a healthier relationship with Aada, Kaarina, and Aho. I also maybe guilt-tripped Odin into giving that Aatos lad some lessons in Eidolon creation; I hope he survives the trip to Bergen with Astrid and Valterri."

"Who?" The other three looked at Aetheria as if she were crazy.

"Which who do you mean?" Aetheria asked defensively.

"Who the hell was Aatos?" Arkaziel looked lost.

"I don't remember a Valterri." Bobbi shrugged.

"Aatos? The kid Aada saved from the merchant lord, that they wanted to marry to Vilja?" Aetheria laughed nervously.

"Oh yeah. I totally killed that merchant guy. He had a kid?" Arkaziel shrugged.

"And Valterri was the young expeditionary forces scout with a crush on Aada. Practiced every day until he could hit almost any target. They called him the Unerring?" Aetheria looked for recognition in the others, and found none.

"I lost most of the expeditionary squads trying to find a weakness against the higher levels past the Gate of Heaven." Bobbi shrugged.

"Ditto." Arkaziel laughed.

"Valterri helped us defeat the demon lord, but he was no scout. He was a dual wielding skirmisher who fought next to Aada." Kallos smiled a little. "Their courtship was very cute."

"Yours actually made headway with Aada? Mine never got past the crush stage." Aetheria sulked a little, until Moros coughed.

"If you're quite done with sulking, your rewards as promised. Fire for Bobbi, light for Arkaziel, spirit for Kallos, and night for Aetheria." With a wave of his hand, four streams of power left his hand to target each of the party. Even more sparks of flames than usual flickered around Bobbi, while Arkaziel sparkled with light. Kallos glimmered with a disquieting purple aura, and night cloaked Aetheria as if she were Nyx. Kallos and Aetheria had the decency to not maintain the visual effects of their new authorities, but Bobbi and Arkaziel only amped up the sparkles in defiance of subtlety, and downright hostility toward the mere idea that less was more.

Aetheria had to admit, night felt fantastic as it settled into her essence. It was missing something, though, but she couldn't identify what. Perhaps she needed darkness, or maybe there was an authority over Void? Wouldn't that be ironic?

Only the most glorious of beings can be said to hold authority over the Void. She who made us, even unintentionally, was the greatest being in all existence. Woe that we cannot know her, nor she know us.

"Now, go bother Izanagi in his dreadfully boring city." With a wave, all four tumbled through the silver doorway to elsewhere.

Kami-no-Yasumi sat beneath a mountain that looked a lot like the pictures Aetheria recalled of Mount Fuji on Earth. Two rivers crossed through the gentle rolling hills of the city, which necessitated a large number of curving wooden bridges over the water at regular intervals across the city. The curved roofs, tranquil ponds, and lush gardens left the air filled with the sound of water and the scent of flowers. Sakura trees filled the avenues, and their blooms enriched the beauty of the city.

The riverways were filled with boats that paddled themselves, while the city streets were full of multihued spiritual horses with flaming hooves, glowing manes, and eyes that shone with the light of the cosmos. Small dragons of various elements pulled wagons and carriages, and more than a few enchanted palanquins that moved via magic alone were intermixed. A few people even rode iridescent insects. The party appeared in a chariot made of clouds, pulled by kirin formed of clouds. Much like in Tezcallián the vessel took them to the center of Kami-no-Yasumi, to the grand shrine and home of Izanagi.

The god waited for them, a spear slung over one shoulder of his Shinto garb.

"You are the Liberator of Souls?" Izanagi stared right at Aetheria, and she could feel a depth of anger rise in her soul that she had never felt before. The shame, the pain, of a loved one ignoring your wishes, seeing you at the absolute worst, and then fleeing . . . Before Aetheria knew what happened, Izanagi slammed into the wall of the temple, and her hand ached.

"Yes, I deserved that. Take this." Izanagi wiped blood from his mundane human features, then wiped it onto a cloth doll of Izanami, which he then tossed to Aetheria. "To the north of the city there is a clearing, and a cave with an entrance to Izanami's realm. Perform your ceremony there. Should you survive the wrath of Ialdabaoth and Izanami, return, and I shall show you my gratitude."

"Sorry about that, but not really. The memory just flowed through me, then *bammo*, right in the face. I'll put her to rest, I promise." It seemed silly to have gotten off the cloud chariot, only to then get back on the cloud chariot, but Izanagi was the one who set this all up, not Aetheria.

The aforementioned area to the north lay at the foot of the mountain, where a massive boulder blocked the entrance to Yomi, Izanami's realm of the dead.

Aetheria created an icy depiction of the blocked cavern across the open area, and settled into the middle with the doll.

"I do not like the way Izanagi casually referred to the wrath of Ialdabaoth," Kallos murmured as she set up next to Aetheria.

"I don't either. Do you think we'll have some Archon visitors this time around?"

"Why else would he specifically warn us?"

"A subtle way to discourage us from ending the cycle he has been caught in since his own birth? Even Primordials struggle with letting go, it seems." Aetheria shrugged, uncertain what kind of feelings a Primordial would keep throughout all of that time, especially when the two had been apart longer than they had been together. Yet for Izanami, when Aetheria touched her essence, the bitterness and hatred for her scornful lover had consumed much of her being.

"I've never eaten an Archon before, have you?" Arkaziel asked Bobbi.

"Nope, but I bet they taste better than any undead abominations that come out from behind that rock." Bobbi grimaced at the blocked entrance to Yomi, and the unpleasant scents that managed to sneak around the rock.

"Oh, you don't like undead? I'll focus on them, then. You take the Archons, but save at least one for me. I want to find out what they taste like. Can you cook their wings? Every other creature with wings, the wings are the delicacy, but Archons are all glowy and shit." Arkaziel mused about it so much that even Aetheria's mind was suddenly filled with mental images of dozens of variations of fried Archon wings.

"Focus, Arkaziel." Aetheria had to chide him for spazzing out about the chance to eat Archon wings, which had not looked nearly as appetizing to her as he was imagining.

"My bad. Start the ritual whenever. Bobbi and I will handle whatever comes." Arkaziel had already grown into a ten-meter-long draconic form, with a menacing aura of destruction around him, while Bobbi remained in a humanoid form and summoned orbs of flames.

"Izanami, Creator and Ruler of Death, I have opened the gate. Come to me, and know peace." Aetheria did not weave an elaborate ritual this time—with each addition of authority, her ability to command reality increased significantly. What would have once required elaborate phrasing and meticulous iconography, she now accomplished with two sentences and a wave of her hand, and the Celestial Gate formed and opened, at which point Kallos laid a hand on the doll and amplified Aetheria's summoning.

Aetheria wasn't prepared for the boost that Kallos's acquisition of authority over spirit would add to the ritual. Fragments of essence flew from the gate to Aetheria, the majority of them dark, awful-looking specters who whispered dirges of hate for Izanami and Amaterasu. Some still held vestiges of light and love for Izanagi.

Unlike Ouranos, who had been dismembered and reduced to a shadow of himself in ages long gone, Izanami had been a primordial deity at the height of her power when she had been shattered at the choosing of the last Overgod. The amount of essence and power that flowed through the gate was staggering, and the emotions of Izanami were so strong as more and more of her essence gathered that the emotions and memories of Izanami awoke in the essence inside of Aetheria.

In addition to the flow of power, emotion, and painful memories, the stone sealing Yomi shattered into thousands of pieces, as lesser gods and beings subservient to Izanami came in answer to her cries of hate. Yet it was not Arkaziel or Bobbi who struck down the first disgusting abomination that crossed into the clearing from the cavern, but a bolt of blue light that resolved into a spear piercing the abomination to the ground. The blue flame engulfed it and burned it to ashes.

"Undead are an abomination against our lord, and must be dispatched. Surrender the essence of the wretched Izanami, and you will only be judged for disobedience of the Overgod in regard to defiance of Quetzalcoatl's divine punishment." The voice of the first Archon sent unpleasant shivers down Aetheria's spine.

CHAPTER 63

Archons and Death

Yomotsu Ikusa emerged first from the shattered debris that once sealed Yomi. Their appearance was a direct homage to the horror that Izanagi witnessed when he first glimpsed Izanami by the firelight of his comb within Yomi. Bodies with flesh infested with maggots, terrific wounds, and armor from across all of the history of regions in which Izanami had control of the underworld. Just as many had no armor, as those who did pieces of Powered Magitech Armor, scarletite or orichalcum pieces, or plain old hide. Their weapons were all made of dark mottled metals that promised to leave weeping wounds should they touch living flesh.

A deep breath, and then a constant stream of light engulfed the initial tide of the Army of Yomi. Sacred Ethereal light streamed from Arkaziel's maw, with arcs of black lightning chasing along the beam of light that obliterated every undead it touched in seconds. Even the entrance to Yomi seemed to weaken ever so slightly before the barrage of power.

+*Tiamat must have known this would happen, and that's why she took underworld from me. I could've usurped Izanami's hell. It's all but undefended right now.*+ Aetheria felt amusement in Arkaziel's telepathic voice, rather than annoyance. For all that the cat wanted everything, he didn't seem too interested in ruling hell.

"Relinquish the essence of Izanami to us or be destroyed!" the lead Archon demanded one more time.

"Kaboom!" Bobbi gave an answer to the Archons, as a swirling vortex of fire appeared amongst them and exploded violently. Waves of heat reached even Aetheria and Kallos in the magic circle. Yet, when the flames died down, the three Archons stood without a single scorch mark on them. All three had lifted a hand and blocked the attack.

"To throw fire and explosive forces at the servants of Ialdabaoth is heresy. Your choice has been witnessed by designate Harmas." The lead Archon gestured, and a hail of blue lances formed in the air and shot after Bobbi. She dodged the first two, used a burst of flame acceleration to dodge the next, and then took a few in her back and one in her left calf.

"Oh shit, that hurts!" Despite Bobbi's cry, the weapons vanished as she consumed the energy within. "You dickbags aren't even real beings. You're just spiritual constructs bound with carbon."

Bobbi's counterattack held all of the authority from wind and fire she could muster, as a vortex of fire and spiritual wind engulfed the Archons. The flames scorched their carbon forms, while the winds cut gouges into them. Shields of energy and material appeared to shield them, but the shields quickly crumpled before the might of Bobbi's wrath. That she spent all of her energy every two seconds, and had to constantly draw from the limitless lake that was Aetheria, wasn't something the Archons could sense. All they knew was a mere fifth-tier with two authorities was crushing them.

"Mission failure likely," Harmas commented, and each Archon glowed with a celestial inner light, and Aetheria heard the ticking of a clock, even though there was no one around.

"Denied." Kallos gestured with her free hand, and the glass ball she held shot out of her palm like a bullet into the vortex of fire and wind Bobbi maintained. The ball ceased to exist, but whatever build-up of energies the Archons had initiated failed completely. A follow-up blast from Arkaziel with a stream of light and black lightning created an immense flash of energy inside the vortex, and then all of the magic inside fell apart into chaos.

Two hunks of charred carbon hit the ground, but the Archon Harmas still stood, and his counterattack came in the form of a massive nova of energy that Bobbi couldn't avoid. Well, she could avoid it, but doing so would leave Aetheria and Kallos in the blast range. Dutifully, her form rippled and morphed, and when the pulses of energy hit her, they hit her dragon scales first. Dozens of her scales broke or fragmented in the blast; she bled from multiple locations, but she wasn't out of the fight yet.

At the exit of Yomi, powerful undead hags worked joint magics to try to surpass the never-ending waves of destruction Arkaziel sent at them. Arkaziel's light, destruction, and death authorities had held the creatures back, but Arkaziel created a miniature sun in the gate of Yomi when that failed to deter them. He combined light, pestilence, and destruction into his new miniature sun, whose blazing rays obliterated all undead that it touched and spread the destruction to all nearby undead as if the burning Divine Light were a contagion. Unknown to Arkaziel, the rays also weakened the spiritual existence of the Archon.

Kallos cast a mild healing on Bobbi, her main focus still on amplifying Aetheria's gathering of the essence of Izanami, which was proceeding at a whiplash pace, with more and more fragments and motes flowing through the celestial door, until the power of Izanami engulfed Aetheria like a tsunami, and Kallos had to retreat from the potent corruption of the goddess.

"Reinforcements," Harmas demanded of the air, and a blue summoning circle centered on the corpses of his brethren formed on the ground.

Arkaziel breathed shadow and destruction on the circle, unweaving it and canceling the summons allowing only one more carbon entity to form, which died in the potent destruction before it could stabilize and protect itself.

"Why won't this asshole die?" Bobbi hissed, most of her wounds healed, as she sent burst after burst of conceptual fire at the Archon.

"It's a spiritual being with more power than most gods, Bobbi. For lesser Archons, standard attacks might suffice, but for a greater Archon, you must destroy the spirit. The hunk of carbon it uses as a body is merely a sign of its corruption and attachment to the physical world, and unrelated to its ability to exist." Kallos spoke calmly, yet in her palm an orb of purple and black energy grew, and grew.

"Stand down, abomination. Ialdabaoth suffers the continued existence of Belial; their agreement does not include you, half-breed." Harmas summoned a ball of blue flames and threw them at Bobbi and Kallos. The power in it would have been enough to vaporize a city the size of Las Vegas, but Bobbi reached out with a draconic, clawed paw and caught the ball, then slowly popped it into her mouth, and chewed.

"Did you forget I have authority over fire?" Bobbi laughed mockingly.

That's when the sphere of energies vanished from Kallos's hand, and appeared much larger around the Archon. The black energy lashed down at the Archon, while the purple energies reinforced the cage.

-That won't kill him, but it will keep him in place. Hit it with everything you can, if you're able to act independently of your sun, Arkaziel?- Kallos wasn't sure if Arkaziel had to concentrate on the sun, or how much action he could take and not lose control of the gateway to Yomi.

+You got it.+

=Yes, ma'am.=

Bobbi unleashed first. She didn't have time to unleash a multistage attack, so she went with her breath attack. A concentrated blast of fire with a vortex of powerful piercing winds around it, but for some reason her flames and even the air came out pitch-black.

Arkaziel, on the other hand, unleashed beams of light from his eyes, but like Bobbi, his attack also came out black. This wasn't that abnormal for a Beast Sovereign that used Void, shadows, and twilight magics regularly, but in this case it should have been pure divine radiance like the conjured sun blocking Yomi.

Kallos withheld the grimace and looked toward the immense pillar of darkness that roared where Aetheria stood, but nothing had changed there, and her concentration had to be maintained to prevent Harmas escaping.

The two attacks struck the Archon, and at first it seemed neither would have the punch required to kill the spiritual form of a greater Archon, until a fist of dark glimmers formed and squeezed the very life out of the ephemeral carbon body of the Archon. The hand of darkness radiated not quite evil, but a sense of decay and corruption that certainly bordered on evil. Even the Archon, a being of absolute order, could not resist the overwhelming corruption of the dark fist. The light of his being dimmed, and dimmed. The hand squeezed so tightly some of the carbon pressurized to diamond, and it continued to mercilessly tighten until the light of the Archon's essence vanished and the carbon vessel exploded like an overripe tomato squished in the hands of Hercules.

"Why did that look an awful lot like an attack Izanami would make?" Arkaziel asked dryly, his yellow eyes moving to the column of darkness that blazed around Aetheria.

~Because it is. I refuse to die without taking at least one of the Overgod's servants with me. You, too, would fight until the bitter end, Dragon of the Apocalypse, do not tell me otherwise. The Blood of Tiamat in your veins will never surrender to anything, perhaps not even you.~

"She's got you nailed, Arkaziel." Bobbi mocked the sputtering Arkaziel.

"How about it, Izanagi, want to go to the next universe together?" The voice sounded ragged, pained, hurt, but the vulnerability and loss of spite and anger made Izanami's tone very different from how she addressed Arkaziel.

Only one of those present had heard that voice without the anger, bitterness, and spite before. Izanagi stepped from behind a sakura tree, Ame-no-Nuboko, the Heavenly Jeweled Spear, rested upon his shoulder. How had Aetheria or the others missed the subtle nobility about the god earlier?

"You would forgive me, here at the very end? How like us. If only I had listened to you in Yomi."

"Yes, I forgive you. I loved and love you, which is what fueled my anger. The time for the past is gone. My time has ended. Will you follow me into the dark once more?" A spectral hand of darkness reached out from the immense clouds of power that still surrounded Aetheria.

"I will, and this time, I will stay with you." Izanagi stabbed his spear into the earth, and walked into the dark vortex. Each step he took into the unbridled essence of Izanami caused his body to disintegrate, but the god had a smile on his face as he stepped into the darkness, just as he had stepped from heaven down to land—hand in hand with Izanami, together.

The darkness was not of Izanami's making, but of Aetheria's, and the darkness devoured them both until not even a speck of their existences remained. With the death of Izanagi, the realm of Kami-no-Yasumi begun to quake, and a door to the Tower of Moros opened next to them.

"Great, you destroyed a Demiurge's tower? Did I say great, I meant *what in the name of Nyx were you thinking?* That's not going to go under the radar. Get through the door, now." Moros's orders were barked with an immediacy that left no one, not even the StarManes, dawdling. All four leaped through the doorway back to the Tower of Moros, as the Tower of Izanagi fell into the Void. Literally into the Void, since it had lost all of its sustenance when Aetheria consumed Izanagi. What played out now was the dissolution of the empty husk of Izanagi, the fading of an afterimage that no longer existed.

"What the hell, Ria, when did you grab the spear?" Arkaziel asked as they tumbled into a small office. Indeed, Aetheria had the jeweled spear, Ame-no-Nuboko, in her hand.

"Oh please, Ark, as if I'm going to let something this shiny fall into the Void. Or are you just mad I grabbed it before your shadows snatched it? That's right, I saw you play for it!" Aetheria's mood, despite the destruction of a god, was high. Even when Moros started coughing to draw the attention of the group to himself.

CHAPTER 64

To the Top

You killed a Demiurge, destroyed a tower, and did it publicly. At least Izanagi had the forethought to shift his dwellers, natives, and climbers to the Tower of Amaterasu before he died. None of the Archons escaped, and you destroyed the summoning circle and incoming reinforcements." Moros paced as he talked. "That delays word getting out unless Amaterasu talks. Most of the kami are not fans of Ialdaboath, so we have some little time, especially if I set the flow of time inside faster than out. Yes, it'll have to work. I can't just cheat and teleport you to the top, or it invalidates the tower and ruins everything."

"What are you even talking about?" Aetheria crossed her arms before her, and fixed the panicked suit of armor with a three-eyed stare that put even Moros in his place.

"You already adjusted to the consumption of two Demiurges? Good, good. I won't let you just pass to the top of my tower, but I do get to choose what tests will happen between here and the top of the tower. Go fast, go quick, and be prepared at the top. If you do not play to win, you won't." Moros mumbled the last as he turned to dust, and a gust of wind blew the dust into the wall where a stone tunnel now opened out into a floor.

"Oh, here." Aetheria passed a small orb to Kallos, Bobbi, and Arkaziel. "They both had creation, but I already have it, and I already have life too."

"How many of these is it safe to have, anyway?" Bobbi questioned as matter and energy converted back and forth around her.

"It very much depends on your soul, if you start to feel a strain when you absorb an authority, stop, and don't absorb any more. Soul vessels can break, and even I would be hard-pressed to restore it in a timely fashion if that occurred. I believe I could contain one or two more, while Aetheria here could likely hold all authorities," Kallos offered.

Creation went to Bobbi and Kallos, while life went to Arkaziel. While in the cloud of Izanami, Aetheria had gained quite a few new authorities. Death, decay, fatherhood, motherhood, purification, and because of either the combination of life and death, or from Izanami and Izanagi together, she gained the Great Cycle. Aetheria didn't rightly know how to feel about possessing both fatherhood and motherhood. On one hand, her entire life she'd thought of herself as a woman. On the other, she could turn herself into a glass bottle, become anyone of any race, real or imagined, and possessed powers beyond the ken of even the most powerful of gods. Worrying about what to call herself was a problem she wasn't ready to tackle.

Floor 91

The tunnel led to a fairly small wooden cabin with a fifty-piece puzzle on a rustic table. After giving each other a baffled look, Arkaziel solved it in half a minute. It was a picture of Phanes, entwined with a serpent and surrounded by an egg, which in turn was surrounded by a zodiac circle. The door to the next floor appeared.

Floor 92

The same cabin now had a giant bowl in the middle of the table, and four smaller bowls around it of different colors.

"Seriously?" Aetheria rolled her eyes in disbelief at how ridiculous these challenges were. Bobbi spent a minute moving the balls to the proper bowl, and again, a doorway appeared.

Floor 93

The same cabin, again, but there was a piece of paper on the page. When Kallos touched it, she vanished into a three-dimensional construct of the maze on the piece of paper. It had the difficulty level of the sort you would find on kids meals at breakfast restaurants.

"He really wasn't joking about making this fast," Kallos murmured when she popped back out of the paper next to Aetheria, and the door to the next floor appeared.

"Did we screw the pooch by letting Izanagi go with Izanami?" Aetheria looked at the other three in askance.

"No good deed goes unpunished, Blue," Arkaziel said with the wizened air of a miser.

Floor 94

"This is starting to feel a little insulting, don't you think? Surely we could've still gotten through something more challenging than what I would've encountered at a county fair for a floor challenge?" Aetheria lamented when they reappeared in the cabin. On the table ten pairs of cards were arranged for a memory test game. Only her Void Gaze saw right through the cards, so it wasn't even a chance for her to do trial and error.

The door opened once more.

Floor 95

A paper with the familiar crosses for tic-tac-toe lay on the rustic cabin table this time, along with a pen. Kallos picked it up, but when the invisible opponent intentionally lost, she gave an annoyed sigh.

"This is a bit disheartening, isn't it? Why is Moros so panicked? It's very unlike the embodiment of inevitable Doom." Kallos's disappointment and sulk got her a hug from Aetheria.

"Or very like him, if he can sense a new Doom." Arkaziel pointed out the unpleasant probability.

"We'll find out soon enough," Bobbi grumbled quietly.

"I can't sense any impending Doom yet," Aetheria murmured after harmonizing to Ananke.

Floor 96

"No, I am not doing that!" Arkaziel practically shouted his disdain for the puzzle that appeared on the table of the cabin. Before them were thirty wooden blocks of five different shapes, with a basket topped by a lid that the shapes fit through. It was a toy for the youngest of children, toddlers and babies, to increase their depth perception, shape identification, and muscle coordination.

"Me neither," Bobbi added indignantly.

"This seems to have crossed beyond being a little insulting to intentionally insulting." Kallos made no move to touch the puzzle. Her golden eyes strained to look anywhere but at the brightly colored blocks of wood.

"Oh come on, it's just a few blocks of wood. You'll fight Archons, but you're too good for a kids toy?" Aetheria put her hands on her hips to lecture the others.

"Then you do it," Arkaziel hissed.

"It'd be more beneficial for your character to overcome your hang-ups." Bobbi turned on Arkaziel.

"Agreed, clearly the trial is not the joke of sorting shapes, but overcoming the arrogant self-superiority that would keep you from completing the test." Kallos picked up on Bobbi's tactic and turned on Arkaziel as well.

"No, no, its fine. I'll do it. After all, Arkaziel doesn't have thumbs, how would he even do it?" Aetheria reached for the first block.

No one stopped her.

"I'm pretty sure you told me about Public Service Announcements from Earth against bullying and peer pressure." Arkaziel made no move to play with the blocks.

"Fine, I'll do it. This is ridiculous." Aetheria rolled her eyes and slammed the blocks into place. Even after her outburst, the other three just watched her, judging. *At least no one has a camera.*

Floor 97

A piece of paper lay on the table. The only thing on the paper, in large blocky text, were the words: find the pen.

"He's definitely trying to piss us off at this point." Bobbi hissed at the unseen Moros, as the sheet of paper burned to ash to reveal the pen previously hidden underneath the paper.

"He's losing what little goodwill I had," Kallos agreed.

Arkaziel didn't join in badmouthing Moros, an unusual choice that worried Aetheria, since normally the StarMane joyfully allowed his most basic emotions to rule him, except in times of trouble.

Floor 98

The cabin now had two doors, both with faces on them.

"Answer our riddles, and we'll give you clues, so that you can figure out how to leave this room, that's what you've got to do." The talking doors spoke at the same time in high-pitched sing-song voices. Aetheria noticed immediately that a large vertically hung painting was the real exit from the room thanks to Void Gaze seeing through all deception.

"Can we just burn the cabin down around us? I'd rather do that." Bobbi announced her desires with a large ball of flame dancing above her palm.

"Why do you get to kill the doors? I want to kill a door, too," Arkaziel whined.

"That's enough, you two. Are we really being reduced to this?" Kallos looked to Aetheria, and followed her gaze to the painting.

"Nope, I already found the real door. I'm not answering riddles for singing doors if I don't have to." Aetheria gestured, and the painting melted from reality as she mixed the authority of decay and the destructive properties of frost into something best described as creeping frost that disintegrated whatever it crawled across. "Divine wrath might be overkill for a painting, but I guess that's where we're at."

Floor 99

The penultimate floor of the Tower of Moros was straight out of an anime, and a Japanese love hotel. The city street they appeared on didn't go any other way but to the hotel. A sign swung above the door that read in Ath, Never Forget Love.

"Ugh. I knew all that stupid weeb shit he babbled about was going to lead to something awful. I am not going in there." Aetheria shook her head, and refused to step inside the door to the love hotel.

"Not even with me?" Kallos grinned seductively.

"No! It's all weird, and he'd be watching, and who knows what other gods are watching in these towers. Nope, not going to happen." Aetheria shook her head, emphatic and unmoved by even the gorgeous Kallos. That the Nephilim was (mostly) joking made it easier to refuse. *Thanks Void Gaze, for letting me see through to the truth.*

"Someone's got to go in there," Arkaziel pointed out, annoyed he'd been forced into humanoid form.

"Oh come on, twerp. I'm sure it's just an empty scare tactic by Moros and the door to the big boss fight is on the other side." Bobbi grabbed Arkaziel's hand and dragged him into the hotel. Kallos and Aetheria both stared after the two, curiosity spawning strange ideas in their heads.

Five minutes later, Arkaziel opened the door.

"Seriously, just come in. The door to the top of the tower is next to the front desk. Are you two just going to sit out here, or can we get this show on the road?"

"You lost your tie, Ark," Aetheria said with a smirk.

"You're awfully sweaty," Kallos noted with an arched brow.

"What? Oh yeah. Bobbi *tried* to kick my ass at a game called foosball. I showed her the true power of a Beast Sovereign. She's a terrible loser, though, and burned the table to ashes."

When the ladies followed Arkaziel inside, there was indeed a door to the top of the tower next to check-in, and to the side in the recreational room, Bobbi was paying the desk clerk for the pile of ashes she had reduced the foosball table to.

"This whole scenario was a lot funnier in my head," Aetheria lamented, just a little.

"What, you wanted me to hook up with Bobbi? She's got to get on my level if she wants a piece of this amazing man."

"That is *not* how that conversation went, you dolt. You aren't getting a piece of this amazing woman until you get on *my* level, and can beat me in a legitimate cook-off. Unless you want to admit I'm the best, and you're third or fourth best?"

Aetheria walked away from the argument to step through the portal to the last level.

Every sense Aetheria possessed for danger went into overdrive the moment she activated the doorway.

CHAPTER 65

DOOM

The final challenge of the Tower of Moros lay at a physical top of a very large tower of black obsidian. Over one hundred meters in diameter, sharp appendages rose from the edge of the tower and reached up into the sky like claws. Atop each of these black claws burned red flames. Sigils of hundreds of different languages covered the floor in layers, making it next to impossible to discern what the individual glyphs said unless you charged them with magic. In the center of it all a large black throne with red silk cushions the color of blood housed Moros. Clad in black armor, the Daemon of Impending Doom looked like he might have forged a few rings of power in the past.

"Do you believe yourselves to be the architects of your own destiny?" Moros's query hit the tower like thunder, an impact carried on gale-force winds and driven by malevolent intent. The force of impending Doom bore down on the two StarManes, the Nephilim, and the once-human in a way that other parties who climbed the tower experienced far more severely than this group had ever felt it.

"Nah," Aetheria answered softly, but it cut through the wind. "We didn't set the board. That was all Khaos, Nyx, Aetherius, Chronos, and you. But we are going to be the ones who decide how it finishes. You don't have to do this." Aetheria didn't plead, or beg. She simply offered Moros a chance to take a different direction than the one he seemed determined to force.

"The strength of others will not carry you through to the end. To change this disaster of existence will require the power to topple gods, undo the work of multiple Overgods, and reverse so many wrongs. Is it even worth it? Would it not be better to topple the table and start over?" Moros stood from his throne, and it transformed into a massive war hammer.

"Much easier to fall upon your sword and let someone stronger fix your legion of mistakes, yes?" Kallos taunted the daemon. In one hand, she held a white staff, in the other, a wand; her chain wings had emerged on full display, and even the black of the Heavenshadow Nebulite shone brightly against the dark clouds of the sky, but not nearly so bright as the radiant glow of the tattooed chains across her body.

"If you haven't noticed, she toppled two gods without fighting. What chance do you have against Aetheria, much less against all four of us? You're boned, Moros." Bobbi's expression was ferocious and wild, revealing all of the frustrations she had bottled up and waited eagerly to unleash in bursts of violence.

"If you want to die, I could just eat you? Chomp, chomp, no more problems for Moros." Arkaziel offered a benevolent, peaceful solution to the posturing of Moros.

Moros raised the head of his war hammer to the sky, and the red glow of all the red flames at the end of claws on the border of the tower intensified. In their flare, a red dome formed around the top of the tower, sealing the heavens. As the red glow spread, hundreds of runes lit across the floor. Aetheria and Kallos countered dozens of them, but there were simply far too many for even them. From glyphs spilled one of two things. Physical chains, made of a black metal Aetheria recognized as Ebonschism, seemed to be the primary creation of the glyphs. The dark metal was said to be quenched in the fears of the Fates, and could only be forged in the remains of a dying star.

Even the mass of chains of Kallos's Heavenshadow Nebulite managed to put only minor nicks and dents in the emerging chains of Doom. The mess of multitudes of chains sparking and impacting one another filled the air with the clash of metal, and Kallos held the front line against the chains, since she could meet each one with a chain from her wings or body.

"Your dream of the laws of heaven raining down upon the realms of the physical are as ridiculous as the delusion that Belial is anything but a villain," Moros called mockingly to Kallos as she desperately defended against the chains of impending Doom.

Aetheria, Arkaziel, and Bobbi were not idle. The glyphs that had not spawned chains had instead spawned weak forms of their fears. Some were of old fears, some were of new fears, but each was a fear born from the heart of one of the four made manifest. These manifestations didn't need to make contact, or shoot beams of psychic power, or even reach them to do damage. Just seeing the manifestation of their own fears caused a pain deep inside, both in the mind and heart, that couldn't be denied.

When the fear did damage, it vanished, but if it was hit by a spell from someone else, it would also vanish. Fighting off pain, the two StarManes lobbed large area of effect spells to destroy as many illusions as possible, and Aetheria tapped her toe against the ground to shoot a layer of creeping frost across the entire rooftop, temporarily disrupting the glyphs creating chains and illusions alike.

"We cannot be on the defensive against Moros. That's how he wins." Aetheria's quiet voice cut through the sound of battle, and she stepped forward to block the head of the giant war hammer when it swung at Kallos's head. Showers of sparks filled the air, and for once it was Aetheria who went tumbling across the tower like a baseball hit by a steroid-using super-athlete.

~For your information, that's the real deal guys. Not an avatar.~

Aetheria stood before Moros as if he'd never hit her, so quickly did she move back to protect Kallos, and the second blow of the combo she deflected in another show of sparks, but this time she didn't go flying. That Aetheria's skin turned black, she gained a meter of height, grew four more arms, and her hands turned to thirty-centimeter-long diamond talons spoke of the extent of Moros's prowess. Her Voidform was rarely needed for her to dominate a fight.

The black chains, belts, and bindings held by powerful seals glowed with a terrible light that hurt to look at, and her third eye shone with a black-purple version of the Divine Light of Ein Sof. Dark, chittering whispers pressed down from the red dome above the tower and nibbled at the sanity of anyone who tried to understand what they said.

"Already? I thought you'd fight me as a human, or a god, not . . . *this*." Moros scoffed at the Voidform Aetheria chose, and he stepped into a mess of red flames, and re-formed into a massive wolf made of black and red energies she could only describe as Doom-aspected Ethereal power.

"Oh hey, it's Fenrir," Arkaziel said, before unleashing a blast of twilight energy at the wolf. Arkaziel then slammed into the ground, caught in a tangle of Doom, and his body bashed like a club into the floor repeatedly, until he broke free with shapeshifting.

"Careful there!" Bobbi cried out as she made wings and took to the air. Not that the tendrils of Doom didn't reach into the sky—they did. They constantly formed across the top of the tower as if Moros had no limit to their creation, and when the wolf raised its head and howled, each of them felt a disruption to their nervous system that slowed them down. Arkaziel and Bobbi both got caught again, and Kallos only avoided it because her chains worked like dozens of grappling hooks, pulling her constantly in different directions to avoid the tendrils of Doom. If she kept it up she could even land a spell, but that's when the dark bolts of Doom flew from the wolf's maw like fireworks, each bolt locked on and tracking the party.

Or, they would have, if a flash of darkness didn't move through and slice them in half, destroying the entire barrage of Doom bolts. The flash stopped at one of the Doom Wolf's legs, and Aetheria slashed with all six arms, as thirty long black-diamond talons ripped the energized flesh of the wolf to pieces, reducing the wolf's mobility temporarily.

A loud roar shook the tower as Arkaziel transformed into his draconic form. Twilight surrounded Kallos, Bobbi, and even Aetheria, and the tendrils of Doom exploded while the roar echoed. It was the Doom Wolf that couldn't move fast enough this time, and Arkaziel's jaws clamped around the neck of the wolf, while Bobbi and Kallos wove spells and blasted it like artillery.

Aetheria joined Arkaziel's physical combat with the Doom Wolf, her claws biting deep into the energy sources powering the wolf, as well as the manifestation itself. Nothing had ever survived multiple assaults from her Void Talons, and that was before she had gained the authority of death, decay, the Great Cycle, and war. But all of those authorities in singular or combination did jack all against the true being of Moros.

Despite Arkaziel's jaw clamped around the Doom Wolf's throat, it still managed to open its mouth and unleash a brief howl to stun them all, followed by another massive barrage of Doom bolts. This time it aimed them all about Bobbi and Kallos, whose artillery had dispersed nearly a quarter of the figure of the wolf. In another flash, her Voidform appeared before the two ladies, and she turned into a whirlwind of motion as she sliced and destroyed each bolt before it could reach a target.

-You are fighting with the wrong weapons, darling. Moros himself tried to tell you that already.-

Before Aetheria could ask what Kallos meant, Arkaziel ripped the essence of Moros from the wolf and threw him so hard into the tower that the structure shook under their feet. Only the tower kept shaking, and when Moros stood, he had gained another ten meters of height. So had the clawlike appendages at the edge of the tower. Then beneath them the blocks of the floor churned, some went up, some went down. Demon figures of fear appeared, intermixed with run-of-the-mill monsters, and environmental effects like lava, poison gas, and toxic waste.

Each of the party had to split apart and fend for themselves. Arkaziel reduced his size and summoned his twilight clones to dispatch as many demons as he could, their bodies falling into maws of darkness and becoming his strength as he devoured them. He hunted for Moros, but the dark armored embodiment of Doom was nowhere he could see or smell.

Each minute that the environmental factors continued, the more mental damage the party took from the specters of their fears, a gasp of air taken at the wrong moment, a jump just a little too close to magma, to say nothing of the barrage of spells volleyed by monsters that crawled out of gaps in the constantly shifting blocks of the floor.

They had no way of knowing how long it would last, until Aetheria slammed a foot through one of the blocks, fracturing it into multiple pieces, and froze the entire top of the tower into place. The magma, the gasses, the spells, all of it froze in space-time, unable to escape her icy grasp.

Moros clapped, as he appeared in the form of a behemoth of a suit of armor even larger than the last. A torrent of blood flowed from his crimson cape to the ground, where it took the form of smaller, human-sized doppelgängers of the God of Doom.

"Prove to me you can craft destiny, Aetheria-nee." The true Moros beckoned Aetheria to him with an empty, black-gauntleted hand, which as he finished filled with the hilt of an axe, while his other hand still held the war hammer.

"At least you didn't pull out a katana and lick it, or something cringe." Aetheria's body shimmered from black Voidform to human flesh, and she ditched the extra limbs, too.

"Given up on the Void already?" Moros laughed.

"No, I just know how to beat you, and it isn't with darkness." Aetheria flashed a dazzling smile at Moros, and the clouds in the sky calmed and parted, rays of light shone down upon the top of the black Tower of Doom, and illuminated the once-human in a corona of light. "It's with love, bitch."

CHAPTER 66

DOOM Gets DOOMED, DOOMILY

After a proclamation like "I know how to beat you" and "It's with love, bitch," Aetheria's long history of loving anime, comics, books, and TV told her she should be able to one-shot Moros in the face. When she instead blasted him with winds infused with love, it didn't do shit, other than knock him off-balance, and it wasn't the attack that sent him off-balance; it was all the laughing he was doing.

The miniature Morosi all cast powerful magics that put the entire team onto the defensive. These weren't hollow sixth tier Cultivators, but seventh-tier fragments of a god in the heart of his own domain. Even the ridiculously overpowered group couldn't just brute force their way through this fight, and Kallos prepared a massive curse while the two StarManes protected her. Even with their combined defenses, their barriers and summons were destroyed in a single hit, and it seemed questionable whether they'd be able to maintain a defense long enough for Kallos to unleash a curse. Arkaziel maintained a slight edge over Bobbi, having already reached the rank of Beast Sovereign, but even he took damage with each hit, and the usual instant-healing slowed to bursts of focused self-healing.

Aetheria put that out of her mind, and punched the still-laughing Moros in the face so hard his helmet exploded, but as she moved to deliver a follow-up blow, the broadsword cut through her hips, and then the war hammer knocked her legs away. Or tried to, but strands of darkness pulled her back together. The Dark Lord–looking helmet had already reappeared, but Aetheria's next punch landed against the center of his armor, shattering the shell. Moros, who didn't seem the least bit inconvenienced, struck her so hard she flew through and killed three of the little Morosi before she slammed into one of the dark claws at the edge of the tower.

"Damn, where'd all that Aetheria-nee energy go?" Aetheria's body took no damage, but she still experienced the pain. If Moros was stronger than her, she just needed to be stronger than him. That was the core tenet of autopotency. In a flicker of movement she reappeared behind Moros, touched a palm against his armor, and froze him. A coating of ice formed, thickened, and then shattered, before Moros's war hammer struck where she had stood.

"You tricky son of a bitch," Aetheria hissed, reappearing behind him again.

"I am Inevitable Doom, the deliverer of comeuppance to everyone and everything. To fight me is to fight the laws of existence."

Only one truth is inevitable for existence, that it must end.

Usually the appropriate response to anything Fred said was to tell him to piss off, or ignore it. But Fred and Reverie represented the penultimate powers of existence, only the Divine Light of Ein Sof could trump either. One-hit-wonder or not, ignoring Fred outright would be a mistake.

Let me guess, you want me to use the Black Flame on him? You versus Moros?

I am a reflection of the true end, of the most glorious emptiness to ever not exist, whose return will seal the end of everything. Open yourself to my power, and be rid of Moros.

"*Moros touches the watered-down divinity of the lesser realms. Open yourself to the glory of Ein Sof, and you will not need the parlor tricks of Ayin's shadow.*" Reverie suggested his own alternative, which frankly, sounded a lot less troublesome. Except for the fact every time she grasped at the power of Ein Sof, she missed. It was like an illusive ocean, and when she ran her mental grasp to control the power, it never worked.

The StarManes and Kallos had managed to kill ten of the Morosi, but each had been forced to draw power from Aetheria, their personal reserves empty. Even her soul aperture could only allow so much energy to pass through simultaneously without being damaged, but her soul healed just as rapidly as the damage came. It did not reduce the pain she felt inside.

-Darling, we are losing this fight. How do we turn it around? I've only got enough energy left for one miracle, and Bobbi is nearing her breaking point, even with Arkaziel healing her.-

To wield the power of the boundless or the true void is to step beyond the restraints of flesh. Moros plans for you to evolve, but the egg is not ready to hatch. Desperation from the one who claims to control inevitability, how ironic.

"*To ascend to a higher being is no sacrifice, open yourself to the Light,*" Reverie urged calmly.

"Pay attention," Moros growled as his mighty fisty punched Aetheria in the nose, but this time the blow stopped, the armor touched her flesh, and momentum vanished, and all three of Aetheria's eyes leaked mixtures of aqua and red energy.

"I am, and I'm not going to play this the way any of you want me to. You, Khaos, Reverie, Fred, none of you get to choose what path I take. This is my life, and it's going to go the way I want."

Aetheria suddenly stood in a place of half light, half dark. Two insane figures of fragmented geometry looked at her from the heavenly plane. Nothing looked at her from the darkness.

"What is your Law?" Bythos asked.

Aetheria didn't know how to answer that. What was her Law? *I don't suppose he'd be happy with something like "Fuck you, I won't do what you tell me," so maybe something like . . . Oh crap, what's up with this pop quiz anyway?*

"There is no need to rush. We have frozen time. We have as long as it takes," Sige said.

Even though Aetheria had never heard the chiming voices of the Aeons before, it felt familiar, and their accent for speaking Ath was somehow reassuring. She let her mind wander, let the emanations of Da'at flow through her, flipped through the books of Binah and absorbed their knowledge.

"Every end plants the seeds for something. Even what seems to be the final ending isn't," Aetheria murmured after consideration.

"Clunky," deemed Bythos.

"Try again," Sige agreed.

"Each end sows seeds; no finality, a prelude to rebirth." Aetheria tried again, but she fumbled the words, and the Aeons didn't even need to tell her she needed to work on it more.

"Existence is a journey of Eternal Becoming," Aetheria said finally, staring at the two geometric patterns.

"What is existence?" Bythos inquired.

"Everything. The cycle of Nothing to Something, and Something to Nothing. Yesh me-Ayin, and Ayin me-Yesh. The cycle may differ, but even when only Ayin exists, everything exists in potential."

"Yes," the Aeons both agreed.

"Declare your name and Law," Bythos demanded.

Name? Metanoia obviously would be her surname. Aetheria had already agreed to that with Kallos. Yet what was her first name? She could maintain it as Aetheria, but she wasn't really the daughter of Aetherius, and the intense connection she'd felt to her little cleric of Aetherius in *Eldest Fantasy Wars Online* had been so long ago. It was not the name that her soul sang into the Cosmic Song. That name had been written in the library of Binah ages ago, and could be felt by any who experienced the cold finality of the light of Ein Sof she emitted.

"I am Telos Metanoia, and Existence is a journey of Eternal Becoming."

A bloodred and aqua-blue eye opened from the vast nothing below the three beings. It observed them momentarily, making even the Aeons uncomfortable, and then the eyes closed. Disorientation and wobbliness consumed the world, and then stability returned.

A giant fist still touched her nose. Telos grasped it with her right hand, twisted, and flipped the immense armored form of Moros onto his back. Internally, the Transformative Flame of Eternal Becoming gained substance, and absorbed the Unutterable Black Flame of the Void and the Red Flame of the Origin into itself.

Telos gestured, and a pillar of radiance illuminated the entire armored form of Moros. The light held brightness, but the faint blue tone gave hints to the frigid cold within it. The armor disintegrated, revealing a humanoid shape of a man forged from shadows and darkness. The demons had been born solely from Nyx, and thus were entirely entities of darkness. A fact of reality which none of them could ever overcome, no matter how they moderated their behavior or how powerful they became.

"So you chose Yesh." Moros laughed. "Everything ends, Aetheria-nee. It's inevitable." The light froze and burned the essence of Moros, yet the daemon showed no sign of pain.

"No, I didn't. I chose both, and it's not Aetheria anymore. It's Telos Metanoia." Inside the pillar of Ein Sof, Moros burned, and Telos walked into the light to touch a hand to his heart and commanded the authority of love and renewal and the Great Cycle with one hand, while her other turned into a dark taloned thing that devoured his authority.

"You can be a being of light, next time. Or just a human. You should try it, it's a good time." Aetheria offered advice to the dying Moros.

"You're not going to let him live?" Arkaziel asked from beyond the light, surprised.

"This is his wish, his inevitable unavoidable end declared by himself with every ounce of his authority, and then enforced by bribes with the Moirai. It's why he's tried to piss me off and annoy me at every step since we entered the tower, anything he could do to ensure this outcome. He's done, and I don't even know all of it. He could still fight me, but he isn't."

"I was Doom, but you are **the end**."

"*An end*. Beginnings follow all ends, eventually," Telos corrected Moros.

"An end for me, at least."

"Goodbye, Moros Olethros," Telos murmured, and the pillar of light intensified and fully disintegrated Moros. The light vanished, and already the tower started to crumble.

"The hell? We don't get our wishes?" Arkaziel hissed.

"Telos, huh?" Kallos grinned, a resting Bobbi kitten held in her arms.

"I've got them, but we need to go, now." A silver door appeared next to them. The other side showed the courtyard around the Tower of Moros back on Grief. A blue door appeared a few meters away, as Telos ushered them through the door to Grief. The silver door closed, and the blue door opened into a collapsing world, but they had no way to see what happened after that.

They stood in the courtyard of Inexoria, back on the world of Grief. Behind them the tower shook, shuddered, and imploded into a pile of rubble. Very little of the tower had existed physically on Grief, so it was a shockingly small pile of rubble compared to what one would have expected from a tower that had once reached into the upper atmosphere. With it fell the protective barriers around Inexoria, and any of the other special magics worked over ages through agreements with Moros.

The tax collector/guards stared dumbly at the group and the rubble behind them.

"Someone go get the High Climber!" the chief tax collector commanded the others. No one knew what to do. The tower was gone, and three Tier Sixes and a sleeping Tier Five had just appeared.

"Who made that blue door as we left, anyway?" Arkaziel asked, taking the form of a kitten and cuddling up on Telos's shoulder.

"A greater Archon." Kallos grimaced.

"Yes. The collapse of the tower won't kill it, either, but it'll take time for it to escape the Void and catch up with us."

"I think I preferred normal bounty hunters." Arkaziel yawned. "I'm so sleepy. And hungry."

"You'll have plenty to eat soon, little guy. We don't have time to waste on more towers, so we're just going to go kill Oizys to finish that promise off, and then it's off to see the wizard."

"What wizard?" Kallos asked in total confusion.

Winds drifted through the plaza, and dramatically lifted Telos's long aqua-blue scarf, and flourished her black trench coat. The multihued strands of her red, blue, and black hair were also lifted by the wind, unbound by the usual ponytail consumed in her evolution, the fight with Moros, or the teleportation. Her hair had grown to nearly mid-back length, but she could change that on a whim; who needed a stylist? The constant production of the light of Ein Sof from her cores had only grown more pronounced, leaving a trail of glitter and stars between her cleavage and forehead where the Third-Eye of Ein Sof absorbed the excess energies. Sunlight sparkled against all three of her eyes in a way that most people would find painful, but Telos just smiled up at the sun, looking directly into the bright retina-searing light.

"Khaos, and her little snake, Ouroboros." Telos laughed at the way Arkaziel licked his lips so hungrily, remembering how tasty the snake had tasted last time.

About the Author

Jamie Kojola is the author of the Odyssey of the Ethereal series, originally released on Royal Road. In her free time, she enjoys gardening, sewing, gaming, crafting, and playing D&D. Kojola lives in Minnesota with her two children, spouse, and three cats.